TAKING
FLIGHT

TAKING FLIGHT

Adrian R. Magnuson

PINK FISH PRESS
SEATTLE, WASHINGTON

Book design © Pink Fish Press
"Lost and Found" used with permission
Bird art ©Inkart Productions Roger Hall, Scientific Illustrations

Printed in the United States of America

ISBN-13: 978-0615659299
ISBN-10: 0615659292

Printed in the United States of America
First Edition

10 9 8 7 6 5 4 3 2 1

www.thepinkfishpress.com

PINK FISH PRESS
SEATTLE, WASHINGTON

For Vanessa, the bravest girl I know.

Lost and Found
David Hollies

The first few times
Being lost was frightening
Stark, pregnant
With the drama of change
Then, I didn't know
That everywhere is nowhere
Like the feeling when an ocean wave
Boils you in the sand
But as time goes by
Each occurrence of lostness is quieter
Falling from notice
Like the sound of trains
When you live near the tracks
Until one day
When a friend asks
"How often do you get lost?"
And I strain to recall a single instance
It was then that I realized
Being lost only has meaning
When contrasted with
Knowing where you are
A presumption that slipped out of my life
As quietly as smoke up a chimney
For now I live in a less anchored place
Where being lost is irrelevant
For now, only when there is a need
Do I discover where I am
No alarm, no fear
Just an unconscious check-in
Like glancing in the rear-view mirror.

Fledging

Barn Swallow
Hirundo rustica

JEREMY

Why don't parents ever listen? I stare out into the rain watching planes taxi back and forth, knowing one of them will soon take me where I don't want to go.

Dad and I argued all the way to the airport. He gave me the same dumb reasons why I have to spend my vacation with my mother that he's pounded into me for the past two weeks. I'm tired of hearing it.

This isn't going to work. Just like last summer, Dad flies off to save the world and Mom flips out as soon as I arrive. Bet it won't be a week till I'm in foster care, stuck watching TV with a bunch of losers I don't know, going nowhere and doing nothing. Begging doesn't help. Dad says he has to leave; the kids in Africa need him more. Mom promises things will be different this time, she'll stay on her medications, but that's what she always says.

"Look at me, Jeremy."

"Why? What's the point?" I say, still facing away from him.

"Come on, Jeremy."

"Come on, *Jackson.*"

"Don't call me that. I'm your father."

"Hmmph."

"Fine. Have it your way."

"Yeah, like that ever happens."

"Everything's going to be all right. You'll see. Rose promised."

"Mom never keeps her promises."

I'm still not looking at him, but I can hear Dad rifling through his briefcase.

"Look, I need to go. My plane leaves in twenty minutes. Sorry you have to hang out here all afternoon. You've got money and the credit card?"

I nod.

"I switched the ticket to coach. Still don't understand why you wanted that."

I shrug. Bad enough being a rich kid flying alone. People in first class always ask you questions. Maybe coach will be different. I'll just listen to music for six hours.

"Any chance I could get a hug?"

When I don't answer, he puts his hand on my shoulder for a moment then gets up and walks away. I can feel tears running down my cheeks.

ABBY

"Your car's gone," my friend said as we pulled into the driveway.

"Wait here while I check the house," I replied, already launching into a mental checklist of what to do next. Damn, where had Harry gone now? I took the front steps of our tiny ranch two at a time, then ran from room to room, hoping for a scribbled note. Nothing, just an empty coffee cup and half-eaten saucepan of congealed Kraft Macaroni & Cheese. His favorite, God help me. Panic began to set in as I flew through the kitchen door into our overstuffed garage.

"Stop it," I said out loud. "How far could one crippled old man go?"

Through the open garage door I could see my friend watching, her worried look a reflection of what I felt. She'd heard all my stories and more than once driven me along the maze of local roads leading to beach or trailhead, or to Sebo's, where we'd find Harry happily wandering from aisle to aisle searching for some exotic piece of hardware or odd gadget.

My expression must have shown defeat as I dragged back to her island car, an old Subaru Outback, its bald tires and moss-covered flanks long past worth washing.

Through the open window she said, "We'll find him," with a certainty born of past successes.

I smiled, but we both knew I didn't share her confidence. Each time Harry had been harder to find, harder to bring home. Ever since the accident he wandered farther afield. It was as if Harry sensed a not-so-distant future when he would no longer be free.

Three hours later, after my friend and I had driven every south-end road, paved, gravel, or dirt, we returned home, hoping against hope to find the car and Harry back from wherever in hell he had been. But no, the driveway remained as we had left it—devoid of one fire-engine-red sedan and one gray old man. I assured her I would phone the moment I heard anything, either from or about Harry, and put on what I hoped would seem a positive expression and attitude. I waved as she drove away then went directly to call Harry's son.

Come on, Oliver, answer your phone, don't let the machine pick up. But it did, as usual. "Hi. This is Oliver Herndon," burned brightly in my ear, and I could feel my blood pressure rise, half anger, half anxiety.

"I'm away from my desk right now but if you leave a message I'll get back to you as soon as possible."

Beep.

Beep, my ass. I know you're there. "Oliver, your father has gone AWOL again and we can't find him. I...I don't know what to do. I don't..." I paused, trying to think what degree of pathos in my voice would ring in just the right tone.

Before I could speak again, he answered. "Abby?"

"Oh, thank God," I said. "Just got home from shopping; the car was gone. No note and none of the neighbors saw a thing. Harry seemed just fine this morning, almost his old self. I went out shopping with a friend for an hour but then we stopped for lunch—"

"Damn it, Abby, you know you can't do that."

Screw you, Oliver. Those words fought to be spoken out loud, but I swallowed them whole, cursing myself for having to play this helpless female game.

"Don't be angry with me, Oliver. I'm doing the best I can. And I have to get out sometimes. He was with me at breakfast, really focused. We talked about you and the kids, about how well Nessa is doing in school and about Lainey's new boyfriend. He had all the facts straight."

"Sorry, Abby. I'm not angry; I'm just frustrated. This is, what, the third or fourth time he's done this? Why don't you take his license away?"

"Don't be ridiculous, Oliver. You don't honestly think that would stop your father from driving, do you?"

"No, but at least he'd get arrested when he got pulled over for driving too slow or stopping in the middle of the road when he forgets where he is. I suppose he still has a credit card too, right?"

"Oliver, you're not being fair. How can I take away his freedom? It's the only thing left he values."

"Alright, alright. I'm sorry. I just don't like to think of Dad lost someplace and not knowing where he is. He'll be terrified."

"He won't, you know."

"Won't what?"

"Won't be terrified if he's lost. The last time he remembered the whole episode, including every damn bird he saw along the way. He just didn't know where he was. And, of course, he didn't know how to get home."

There was a pause; Oliver must have been trying to absorb this new idea. What was he thinking? Was he beginning to realize what a mistake it was for us to have relocated all the way across country? I knew we shouldn't have. We should have stayed in New Hampshire where Harry knew the roads. But I wanted to be near my grandchildren in Seattle, and Oliver had promised to help later when Harry got worse.

What I really wanted was for Oliver to move back east. It was wrong for me to want this. But I did want it. I wanted Harry's life to be like it was before this damnable disease began stealing it from him, the way it was just five years ago. Why couldn't they fix this? Useless drug companies. He could take a pill to give him an erection, but not one to help him remember what to do with it.

HARRY

Over the hum of the plane engines, I hear a deep voice break into a squeak, "What happened to your foot?"

Damn, almost asleep. I open my eyes to a skinny, dark-haired urchin of a boy standing in the aisle and staring across the empty seat between us at my mismatched feet. I'd removed my shoes at the beginning of the flight. Suppose I could have kept the left one on to hide the prosthetic, but then the kid would probably have asked something different. I close my eyes again.

"It fell off."

Merciful silence from the urchin. Then he croaks, "Did not."

"Did too."

More silence but I can sense him shifting about.

When do children come to understand sarcasm? Apparently not at the 11 or 12 I take the kid to be. Still, he's got spunk. Maybe if I don't say anything he'll go away.

Peering between half-shut lids, I watch him fidget. Obviously the kid has to pee and if he doesn't get into the toilet soon he's going to leave me a puddle. Great. Just what I need for the rest of this six-hour flight, the stench of urine.

Sigh. I'm wide-awake now, might as well do something. I grab the cane that's hooked over the arm of my seat and rap it hard against the bulkhead, on the other side of which is the galley and our inattentive flight attendant.

She pops quickly around the corner. "Sir, please don't do that."

The airhostess school must provide a special etiquette class on how to be blunt, officious and polite at the same time. I glance at her nametag: Elizabeth.

"Look, Betsy, the kid has to pee. Either get him a cup or see if you can hurry along the old makeup queen who's been hogging the head for the past twenty minutes. I'm guessing junior here is your responsibility, right? I'm sure Mom or Dad or Aunt Tilly waiting at JFK would appreciate it if he didn't wet his pants."

She gives me a cool blank stare. The school must teach them this too. Then she bends down and engages the kid's attention. Good plan, maybe he'll forget he has to go for a moment.

"Sweetheart," she says in her smarmy southern accent, "Go on back to coach and try the bathrooms there."

"I did. They all say 'occupied.' And I really have to pee."

The kid's face is contorted in discomfort, so both Betsy and I can see he's telling the truth. Do 12-year-olds lie? I have no idea, but someplace I remember hearing that at the very least they don't lie convincingly the way teenagers do. But maybe I'm wrong.

"Alright, sweetheart, I'll see if the lady in this bathroom is almost done. You just try to hold on, okay?"

The kid pumps his head up and down and scrunches his face, then he crosses his legs and wraps his arms tightly, the last shreds of control apparent in his posture. I'm not hopeful. Betsy presses her ear to the head door and taps. "Ma'am, are you okay?"

There's a muffled response I can't hear but can imagine. The makeup queen has been sitting next to me for the past hour since we took off from Seattle, combing, preening, and checking her appearance in the tiny mirror that forms the lid to her makeup compact. Failing to see herself adequately no matter how many angles nor at what distance she's held the mirror to catch light from her seat's reading lamp, she has proceeded to sequester herself in the first class head to put on her face. Lost cause in my opinion, and, having noted the dots and dashes just forward of her ears and accompanying cartoon smile, I'd say the facelift hasn't worked either. She looks like an escapee from the latest Batman movie.

"Yes, ma'am, but I have a young man who really needs to use the toilet. Could you step out for a moment?"

More muffled words and a long minute later, the door opens, my seat partner exits carrying a hastily assembled armload of bottles and cases, and the squirmy urchin charges in. His groan of release is audible to all of first class. Meanwhile, the makeup queen retakes her seat and stows the accoutrements of her beauty regimen into a handbag that's more commodious than the one large carry-on I've stuffed into the overhead compartment. She slings the strap over her shoulder and waits, face knotted, one knee flung over the other, foot twitching, her body language screaming impatience louder than any words she might say.

When the kid pops out, she hustles in again. I close my eyes and pretend to be asleep, but it's useless. I know he's standing there. I can feel it. Leave me alone kid. Go back to the cheap seats where you belong.

"Thanks," he says.

"You're welcome," I respond without opening my eyes. "Just wanted to make sure you didn't piss on the floor in first class. Coach is fine, though."

"Okay, I'll remember that for next time."

Who knew? The kid does understand sarcasm. Must hear it at home. Then it occurs to me that his parents can't be with him. They would have made him to wait in coach. Probably divorced Mom put him onboard to go visit remarried Dad back east. Makes you grow up fast. Creates cynics given enough pain and time. I've been there. I know. Even at this kid's age, whatever it is.

"What really happened to your foot?"

Sorry, Kid. Not ready to launch into a lengthy discussion of my missing appendage. Betsy dutifully appears from wherever in the small cabin she's been hiding and attempts to defuse what she worries may devolve into a confrontation. Maybe she knows me better than I think. That etiquette class again.

"Time to go back to your seat now, sweetheart."

I agree but cannot bring myself to pass up the opportunity to throw a monkey wrench.

"Not so fast, Betsy."

"It's Elizabeth, sir."

"Hebrew. 'My God is a vow.' Really doesn't sound like you, Betsy, but I'll take your word for it. How about Liz then, because face it, Liz, you're no queen of England. And if you ever were an Elizabeth Bennet, the airline has beaten it out of you. Come to think of it, you're no Liz Taylor either. More like Liza Minelli, but I digress. So, Liza, why don't we wait till the makeup queen is done, in, oh, say, an hour or two. Till then the kid hangs out here in her empty seat. That way you can keep an eye on him while he entertains me. Deal?"

Her look shows disgust, but she caves. "Fine, sir," followed by a sigh, and a shrug, and an exit stage left. Oh, and one parting shot, "Buckle up."

"Your choice, kid. Hang with me, or head back to coach."

"It's Jeremy."

"Jeremiah. 'God will raise you up. God will set you free.' Hebrew. Also common."

"It's just Jeremy."

"Well, Just Jeremy, I think it suits you."

"Mom doesn't think so."

"Why's that?"

He shrugs. Interesting. Before I can ask further, he changes the subject by gently kicking my prosthetic foot.

"Ow," he says, sorry now that he did. Doesn't look like much, but it's sharp-edged and made mostly of dense carbon fiber. Makes one hell of a weapon.

"That'll teach you."

"Mom wouldn't agree with that either."

Intriguing, but then I'm easily intrigued. "Want to see?"

Jeremy nods. I roll up my pant leg to expose the entire expensive contraption. High-impact plastic and aluminum. The prosthetic ends in a form-fitted sleeve over what's left of my upper thigh. There's just barely enough actual leg to anchor the device. The foot is designed to produce a natural spring in the step and can be adjusted, though not by me.

"It's removable."

"Co-o-o-ol. Show me."

"Sorry, too hard to get it back on. Maybe some other time. But here's the really cool part, the knee actually works." The leg has a computer-controlled reticulating joint, which allows the wearer to take a normal stride instead of shuffling along stiff legged. I can even run a little, though slowly. Still getting used to the motion and not quite trusting it yet. Can't seem to get my head to believe it won't crumple under my weight and send me flying ass-over-teakettle.

Jeremy is engaged in close observation of the inner workings when I ask, "Want to see something creepy?"

That brings Betsy-Liz-Liza quickly from where she's been hiding out of sight but within earshot. Her worried expression pleases me. I love to push.

"Chill out, Liza. I'm no pervert."

This comment elicits from Jeremy a genuine chuckle.

I raise my eyebrows and look over the top of my eyeglasses. "Thought we agreed you'd be entertaining me, not the other way around."

He smiles broadly and chuckles again. I fish around in my valise for the prosthetic control, an HP iPAQ with specialized software to calibrate and adjust the prosthetic knee. With a tap on the screen, the knee does its self-calibration thing, whirring, lifting, and twisting before coming back to rest.

"That is so cool," he agrees. "Spooky."

"Even spookier when I take the leg off and make it do that from across the room. I like to put it under my bedcovers and freak out the cat. I can get it to just twitch a little or really kick."

Liza has been observing and flashes me a sympathetic grin. Not part of the plan to entertain her too, so I aim a quip in her direction, "Hey, if you think *that* levitation was impressive, you should see what my little blue pills can do."

Jeremy looks puzzled; the Viagra reference is lost on him, but not Betsy-Liz-Liza. She stalks off, my innuendo bridling.

"See Jeremy, that's the one true advantage at my age, you can say nearly anything you damn well please. Something to look forward to sixty years from now."

He still looks puzzled but shrugs it off.

Just then Ms. Facelift shows up. Her perfume precedes her, a sense-deadening overapplication that, for one ironic but fleeting moment takes me back to my 'days of wine and roses.' The kid's reaction is more instinctive and speaks for both of us. He reaches up to pinch his nose.

"Well?" she says, and I can't tell if her remark is a response to Jeremy's slight or an invitation for him to scamper off.

He looks from me to her and back, uncertain. "I better go," he says, nasal reply issuing from between thumb and forefinger, still squeezed tight.

"Thought you just did?"

He gets the joke and grins, but remains uncertain, waiting for my next move.

I ignore him, and ask Ms. Pungent in my mildest manner, "Don't suppose you'd care to take the empty seat across the aisle next to that nice gentleman? Has to be better than putting up with a crusty curmudgeon like me for the next four hours."

Liza, to her credit, is hiding in the galley. Wants to let this play out without getting involved. Smart girl. Well trained. Wish I could say the same for my ex-wife. She never knew when to shut up.

"Hmmph," Ms. Pungent says, turning. "Maybe this young fellow can teach you better manners."

"Quite possibly, though I think it's more likely I'll teach him some worse. It's my nature to corrupt."

JEREMY

After the plane lands, Elizabeth asks the lady whose seat I've been sitting in if she would walk me up to security. I complain that I'm thirteen, but Elizabeth doesn't believe it. Big deal, I tell myself. Don't argue.

I wait out on the jetway with Elizabeth until the lady gets her wheelie bag set up. In the meantime, the old guy I'd been sitting next to leaves the plane, lugging his bag over his shoulder. As he passes us, he says, "So long, Elizabeth," getting her name right for the first time. There's a hitch in the way he walks that makes him slow. We overtake him pretty quick and leave him in the dust. He nods. "Good luck," he says.

"Thanks. I'll need it." The woman gives me a funny look but doesn't say anything.

I walk alongside her, ignoring what she says, which is boring. I'm thinking about Harry. He's a funny old guy. Told me his name is Harry, not Harold. Made a big point of it.

"First wife called me Harold," he said. "Don't like being reminded of her. My students call me Professor Herndon. They love me but fear me. Or maybe they fear me but love me. There's a difference, wouldn't you agree?"

No idea what he meant. Sounded the same to me and I told him so.

"Ah, to be young and foolish again," he replied. "Growing up is overrated."

Harry looks like a bag of bones in an old suit worn through at the elbows. Must have been a bigger man once. Now he's stooped and shriveled, the way my grandfather was just before he died. But his eyes are quick and clear like a bird's. Couple of times he called me Oliver and once he called me Jay. Granddad mixed up names too.

Don't want to be called Oliver, whoever he is, but I like Jay, so I told Harry to call me that.

"Jay, huh?" he had asked. "What sort of Jay are you? Blue, Gray, Scrub, Steller's, or Pinyon?"

"Pinyon?"

"Desert Southwest. Beautiful pale-blue bird. Eats pine nuts."

As we walk along the concourse, dodging people who hurry by, the lady keeps chatting me up.

"Where are you coming from?"

"Seattle."

"I was just connecting...back home to New York. I hear the Puget Sound area is beautiful."

"In summer it is; the rest of the time it's raining."

"Do you miss it?"

"Of course, school's out. I should be hanging with my friends right now."

"Well, you'll love New York in the summer too. Where does your mom live?"

"Central Park West at 94th."

"Can you see the Harlem Meer?"

I nod. I don't bother explaining I have to stand on the windowsill and even then it's so far away I can barely see the water. You'd think she'd know that.

"What a beautiful place to walk around everyday, flowers blooming and all the water birds."

"It's a dirty duck pond you can't swim in. The Reservoir isn't much better."

She looks pissed, but at least she shuts up. I know I'm supposed to be thankful my mother is rich enough to own her apartment, but I'm not.

When we clear out of the security area, Mom is waiting; Harry is nowhere in sight. Mom gives me the hug the woman is waiting for, the kind that says I'm safe now, and she leaves us. But I'm not safe; I can see it in the way Mom stands, stiff as a boogie board, and I can hear it in her voice, "Jeremy, it's so good to see you." Not what a mother says after nearly a year apart. Even I know that.

"And I'm ever so happy to see you too, Rose."

"Why do you do that? Why do you always pick a fight? I'm here, aren't I? What more do you want?"

"If I have to explain, you wouldn't get it." Suppose it's dumb to piss her off, but I have to know where I stand. "Sorry," I say, "Can't we just go?"

"Ugh. This is your father's fault," she says and walks away toward baggage claim. I follow three paces behind. The noise she makes walking reminds me of piano lessons, my left hand playing base chords, right one melody, but out of sync. Her shoulder blades chop in and out to the tap-tap-tap-tap of her high heels. Her shiny suit material buzzes. Harmonious discord, my piano teacher calls it. I can never please her. Don't do much better with Mom either.

I trudge along behind. She ignores me. Not even a backward glance. And she thinks I have an attitude! She's the problem, not me.

HARRY

Up ahead, the kid and his mother are arguing. Their ongoing point-counterpoint and Mom's manic flailing slow the pace; I have no difficulty keeping up. The prosthetic knee action is smooth, and though I tap along with the cane for balance, it's more theatrical prop than true support.

Can't hear all of what's being said, but the body language speaks volumes. Then Mom stalks away and Jay follows in the desultory way of adolescents. I decide to watch. Call it morbid curiosity. Call it reminiscing. Reminds me of a time in my life I'd be better off forgetting but can never resist dredging up. War wounds, battle scars.

I keep them in sight for the most part, but since Jay told me he checked a bag, I also know where they're headed. Humanity streams by with purpose on either side. Jay and his mother make an odd pairing; mom's New York *haute couture* juxtaposed with the kid's black Metallica t-shirt and baggy jeans.

Mom is a lot younger looking than I would have expected had I thought about it in advance. Maybe mid-thirties. Could be older; not sure I'm much of a judge anymore. If this were the '50s, you'd call her a "looker." Today the kids just say, "hot." But I'm not really thinking about mom; it's the kid I'm concerned about. I'm curious too. Never wanted any of my own, or even a marriage long enough to make one, though I suppose time isn't much of a limiting factor in procreation. Parenthood, on the other hand, requires a commitment far exceeding that of marriage. You can't divorce your children, though some try. Jay's mom may fall into that category. But maybe I'm just projecting.

I ride the escalator with some trepidation. Silly, I know, but I'm always conscious of my metallic appendage, and it does come off, and not always when you want it to.

At the bottom of the two-story drop into the bowels of baggage claim, I see Jay hang a right. I take a left and skulk in the shadows along the far wall. I drop my bag next to me and watch to see what will happen. While they wait for his duffle to spit out of the conveyor, their argument continues. Mom's animated histrionics are matched in obverse by Jay's disinterested slouch. I recognize that posture. It's the one you use when preparing for the guillotine: all acceptance, no regret.

I wait for the denouement and it comes quickly. She throws her hands in the air and walks away with no backward glance. For his part, Jay watches motionless but for his eyes, which follow her all the way out of baggage claim.

JEREMY

I'm happy Mom left, but I'm pissed too. Shit. Knew she wouldn't take her meds. Finally my bag pops out, and I kick it over to a row of seats. Now what? I could fly back to Seattle but I doubt they'd let me change the ticket. Maybe I could buy a one-way back. I know where the spare house key is hidden. I pull out my wallet. The credit card and the $80 Dad gave me. Can a kid my age even buy a plane ticket? Maybe, but I probably don't look old enough. How about a bus, but where would I find a bus station? Maybe I could hitchhike. Mom would hate that. I can hear her now, going on about all the pervert pedophiles lurking around every corner. Yeah, right.

"Wait here! And think about the way you treat me," she had said as she walked away. "And call your father!"

"What about the way you treat me!" I called after her.

Suppose I could text him, but Dad is out of cell range by now. He's connecting through Washington D.C. on his way to Johannesburg then to whatever village in whatever country Doctors Without Borders is sending him this year. Dad kept going with the explanation but I wasn't listening.

"Why can't I have a nanny like when you go to conferences?" I had asked him.

"Because you need to spend time with your mother."

So lame, and I told him so.

"And because she needs to spend time with you."

Just as lame. "But she doesn't want to!"

That stopped him. He gave me his "sad dad" look. "I know your mother can be difficult, but that's why it's so important. It may not seem that way, but she needs you."

The whole conversation still pisses me off. I unzip my bag, turn it upside down, and empty the contents onto the nearest row of seats, then tear off my backpack and fling it to the floor. I stand staring for a minute, hands jammed deep in my pockets. I can't carry all this crap. Okay, Jeremy, stop and get your act together. You need to lighten the load. I wonder what I can fit in my backpack. Not much, my *Sibley* and *Audubon* bird books and binoculars take up half the space.

What the hell do I do now? Will she come back? Not sure I care.

ROSE

She stood in line at the first airport bar she found. The two women in front of Rose ordered, a grande latte for one, a mocha for the other. She tapped her foot impatiently, irritated by the inordinate amount of time it took to prepare their drinks. Go to Starbucks if you want coffee, she thought, glaring at the backs of their heads. The women chatted animatedly, oblivious to Rose's displeasure. In due course, the young man brought their steaming cups of coffee, then turned to Rose.

"Vodka soda."

He paused for a moment, as if weighing whether she was joking, but her stern expression and glance at her watch, as if to say 8:00 a. m. is a fine time for an eye-opener, convinced him. "Lime or lemon?" he asked.

"Surprise me," Rose answered, her tone leaving no doubt that a surprise was the last thing she wanted.

While the bartender turned and pulled a bottle off the mirrored shelf, Rose walked back to the end of the bar and sat on one of the stools. "Easy on the soda. No ice," she called out.

"Double?"

"At least."

With her drink in front of her, she appraised the young man. A boy, really. Hardly old enough for this job. Cute in an unsophisticated way. Not from New York, she decided, too polite. But where? What few words he had spared her, he spoke evenly, no obvious accent. Nor were there any clues to his ethnicity. His pale coloring and dark hair reminded her of her husband, though the boy was country white bread to Jackson's New York Jewish rye.

Thinking about Jackson snapped Rose's thoughts back to her son still waiting in baggage claim. Jeremy was such a little teenaged shit. She missed those younger years when he had been quiet and respectful of her. Now he wouldn't deign to walk beside her, always a few paces behind as if being led to the gallows. He had little patience. Their short conversations quickly devolved to sparring. There was nothing she could say without her intentions being misconstrued.

Rose glanced up from her empty glass. The bartender stood before her, smiling, his head tilted to one side and brows raised in question. She lifted her glass a fraction of an inch and said, "Again." His smile broadened and he nodded.

Rose followed him with her eyes as the boy refreshed her drink. He poured and checked to see if she was watching. She met his eyes and did not look away, even when he returned and set the glass in front of her.

The boy seemed unwilling or unable to leave, so Rose asked the first question that popped into her head, "Are you really old enough to tend bar?"

"Are you old enough to drink?" he shot back.

"Apparently. You didn't ask for ID."

"Maybe you better show me. You wouldn't want to get me fired, would you?" He smiled and raised an eyebrow.

Definitely cute. Rose fished her license from her purse and handed it to him. His hand shook as he grabbed it, expression shifting from amusement to surprise as he calculated her age, 41. When Rose laughed, the boy colored deeply, sputtered a few words, and left her to wait on another customer. But he kept stealing glances, and each time he did, Rose smiled and returned the look. She was still smiling when she strolled back to baggage claim.

HARRY

A small crowd of busybodies is beginning to form around Jay. Not good. Soon some well-meaning idiot will call security. Get the cops involved and your options go out the window. I speak from experience. Pisses me off when they drag my butt home after they figure out I don't know where home is.

I begin to shuffle along in his direction, my bionic leg whirring, but before I can cross the distance, one of the TSA uniforms spots him. I hang back while the big cop hovers above the kid. Can't hear what's being said but I can guess. Jay grabs his knapsack off the floor and starts digging. He tosses his binoculars and bird books onto the pile of clothes and gear beside him. The rent-a-cop must have asked to see Jay's boarding pass. Bet it says unaccompanied minor.

"Jay," I shout.

He looks up, startled, as I move in. Can't let the fuzz take control.

"Sorry I'm late, Jay. It's a long walk from the curb with this bum leg and I had to drag my duffle along. Didn't leave enough time. Thanks, Officer, for watching out for him. I'm very grateful. Jay here's my only grandson and his mother would skin me alive if she knew." Not far from the truth probably.

"We better get a move on if we're going to catch our flight, boy. And I'm not carrying your bag like last time." I give the uniform a wink.

The cop is still unconvinced. I can see it in his eyes. But Jay pipes right up, "Okay, Gramps. I'll carry yours this time."

That gets a laugh out of the big cop. His belly shakes like it's about to fall off.

"Have a good trip," he says and moves off.

Jay crams his stuff back in his bag and we head in the opposite direction. After 100 yards or so we stop at another set of bench seats, collapsing onto them.

"Looks like you got dumped," I say, and that's all it takes to drop the kid. One shot and the tears and pissed-off yammering commence. I'm no good at this. I just let him work it out. Anyone else would know what to do or say. Not me, that gene is missing. It is genetic, isn't it? Nature, not nurture? Hell, could be either. I sure didn't learn it from my parents, a father tied to his literary research and professorial responsibilities, a mother consumed by university intrigue and women's organizations. Children should be seen and not heard, and not seen all that often either.

While Jay rants, alternating between tearful outbursts and breathy epithets aimed at one parent or the other, I try to figure out what to do next. After a few minutes, I give Jay a nudge and ask if he's interested in breakfast. He rubs his eyes and runny snout on his sleeves and nods in affirmation. He stuffs his gear unceremoniously back into his bags then we leave baggage claim behind, following our noses to the food court on the upper level, its olfactory potpourri of spice and cooking oil both enticing and repelling.

JEREMY

I walk behind Harry, pissed at myself for breaking down in front of him. At least he didn't put his hand on my shoulder and say something stupid like, "There, there. Everything will be all right." Something Dad's girlfriend would say. She never thinks before she opens her mouth. Not her fault, I guess. She's closer to my age than Dad's. He treats her like it too. She's wrong; everything will not be all right. Not if they find me.

I hate it when I cry. Makes me think I'm just like Mom, sobbing into her pillow, door slammed behind her. She says she's emotional. Dad says she's mercurial. Google says she's bipolar, my search for 'lithium' returning the most common use for the bottle of pills she hides in her underwear drawer. Parents are so clueless. They forget you can look up anything online if you can just figure out what to search for. I'm probably better at it than either of them. 'Bipolar' makes a good search word too. Amazing what you can learn. So I know it's the meds she doesn't take that makes her the way she is, but it's hard not to think she's just a bitch.

HARRY

The food court is hopping when Jay and I arrive, but there are still empty tables. "So, what sounds good to you? McDonald's?"

He nods. Good guess on my part. Mom probably doesn't let him eat such unhealthy food.

"I like their Sausage McMuffins. All that grease goes right to lubricating my old bones."

Hint of a grin there but it quickly disappears.

"Noticed your *Sibley*'s. You a fan of our feathered friends?"

Another nod.

"I come back east every year on vacation and do some birding. Lots of great places to spot them up north."

"Nothing in the park but pigeons."

Ah, he speaks. Good sign I'm on the right track. "Actually, Central Park is full of birds, though all the warblers have continued their migration by now. Should still be finches, sparrows, wrens, chickadees, peewees, vireos, woodpeckers. And hummingbirds, lots of hummingbirds, attracted to the park flowers."

A shrug then more silence. Better stop selling the birds of New York City. Wait, one more try. "Forgot to mention the falcons. They catch pigeons mid-air then disassemble them back at their aeries, great thatched nests they build on the sides of skyscrapers. You can watch them rip apart the feathers and flesh if you know where to look. It's gross."

"Really?"

"Absolutely."

"Cool."

He's right. It is cool. So is the word, one of the most flexible in the English language, though clichéd and overused. Still, it is a word subject to gradations of nuance that lend it a spectrum of meaning from disdain to acceptability to par excellence then back to calm self-control. A truly cool word, despite its detractors.

Breakfast goes well. We compare birding life lists. All the usual suspects, from Red-winged Blackbird to Yellow Warbler, populate Jay's. It's an impressive list for a kid his age.

"I'm thirteen!" he blurts, after I insult him with my 11-year-old guess. But he excuses my *faux pas* with a self-deprecating admission, "I'm small. Nobody believes I'm almost fourteen."

He's proud of his 76 sightings. He asks how many I've accumulated and is stunned into silence by my answer: 298.

"You must have been all over the world," he says, seemingly downhearted.

"Nope, just the U.S."

"No way!"

"Yes, way. There are well over 900 North American bird species. And that's not including Mexico. I've seen less than a third of them."

"Really?"

"Scout's honor," I say, holding up the three middle fingers of my right hand. "There's more than ten thousand worldwide. The birder's holy grail is six hundred. There's even a club. Doubt I'll ever make it to those hallowed halls, virtual as they are. But I'll make it to three hundred. That's when they call you a serious birder."

"Seventy-six is pretty lame, huh?"

"Not at all, especially if you don't get to travel much. And lots of those nine hundred are accidental sightings, or birds that visit only rarely. I'd guess hitting six hundred is only really possible if you travel a lot and chase after those unusual ones. Besides, you're thirteen. Plenty of time ahead."

"I guess."

Well, got him to talk anyway. Foolish of his parents not to encourage this obvious interest and avocation. Then again, he couldn't have gotten to 76 without some help.

"I'm guessing mom isn't a birder. How about dad?"

"Mom thinks feathers belong on hats. Dad and I go birding when he can get away. Just up and down the coast. We've been as far south as San Francisco and as far north as Vancouver Island. How about you?"

"All over. West coast, east coast, Alaska, Texas, Florida, Desert Southwest, Northern Plains, Rocky Mountains, and Minnesota."

"What's in Minnesota?"

"Mississippi Flyway. Warbler wave starts in April. Over fifty species, though not every one flies the Mississippi. Great way to add to your life list."

"Cool."

There's that word again. But he's right, it is cool to watch the rapid flecks of color invade Minnesota's winter sticks just as they begin to bud out. Even a rank amateur will score a dozen or two. A good camera helps. Makes it easier to distinguish the subtle variations among species from inside the comfort of home rather than out in the cold, wet Minnesota spring.

"So, Jay. How about trying Mom? Maybe she's chilled out by now."

ROSE

She searched baggage claim then had Jeremy paged. No answer. Either he was still there and deliberately giving her a hard time, or he called his father and caught a plane back to Seattle. In either event, there was little Rose could do, so she waited right where she left him.

By 10:00 a. m. over two hours had passed. She tried paging a few times, and walked the baggage, food court, and ticketing areas from one end to the other. Her patience long since exhausted, she wanted to go home. She considered calling Jackson, but that would give the man another opportunity to find her incompetent. Besides, she was nearly certain now that Jeremy was on his way back to Seattle, and she couldn't face another argument with his father.

Again Rose asked herself, what do I feel? Anger? No, though she could still sense irritation at being made to play Jeremy's little game. No, it was relief. All her anxiety of the past week had drained out of her. She could return to her friends and her accustomed life.

At the taxi stand, she caught a limousine. The driver was Russian or Slavic and spoke nonstop in heavily accented, broken English. She couldn't follow his words. She guessed he was speaking about his experiences as a driver, a subject that did not interest her in the least. And he gestured with both hands, regularly releasing the steering wheel as he weaved through the maze of vehicles, making her nervous. The Russian spent more time looking at her in the rear view mirror than he did watching the cars in front of them. She turned both her face and knees toward the door in an attempt to get him to pay attention to the clogged traffic. To his credit, though, when they arrived at her co-op building, he seemed impressed with the massive façade and inset courtyard entrance. She tipped him $20.

Back home now on Central Park West, she worried Jeremy might have gone off to another terminal. She knew she should go back to check, but no, she would never find him, and since he hadn't called, she wanted to believe he flew home to Seattle.

But what if he hadn't? What if he was still there waiting for her?

Rose felt the downward tug, the sense of failure that took over each time she didn't measure up. Pathetic excuse for a mother, she thought. Jackson knew it too, and yet he kept pushing them together. Why couldn't he just let her go? She was never meant to have children. She couldn't even meet her son's plane without falling apart.

Rose sighed and dragged back to her bedroom. She needed a nap, and maybe a tranquilizer. Sleep always helped. Always dispelled the darkness.

She picked up the half-empty pill bottle and turned it over in her hand, weighing it. She thought again about her son. Yes, he might be alone right now, but he made that choice. And he knew she would react this way. The fact that Jeremy hadn't called only meant he was punishing her. Damn him, she wouldn't give him the satisfaction. She would call one of her girlfriends, go out for drinks and dinner, then maybe later a movie. But she would leave her cell phone on just in case.

HARRY

By noon, we've hung around for several hours waiting for a call or a page over the loudspeaker. No sign of Jay's mother.

I hear my internal conflict as two voices out of some '50s Disney cartoon, one on each shoulder: a miniature angel telling me to take him back to the TSA cop, and a diminutive devil tempting me to pack him into a rental car and take off. The two ought to be reversed. The angel should appeal to me to care about the kid, who's stuck with the same abstracted mother I had at his age, while the devil insists I dump him and get on with my summer vacation.

As a rule, I'm not the kind who listens to angels, but I identify with his plight. Jay's called his mother three times and left messages. No answer. Also called his father but explained to me he's in Africa and only gets to check in occasionally. Doctors Without Borders, *Médecins Sans Frontières*. Frustrating. Can't even be pissed off that Dad's away saving lives. But I am pissed off. What kind of father puts starving kids in Africa over his own son? My rhetorical question and answer only furthers my irritation. One like me.

I decide Mom's not coming back today. I ask Jay his opinion.

He shrugs.

"Not good enough, champ. We have to decide what to do next. What do you say?"

Another shrug, but he's thinking. If this were still my Disney cartoon, smoke would issue from his ears. "Can we decide tomorrow?" he asks.

"Sure. Think it'll make a difference?"

One more shrug and silence.

"Okay, kid. We'll play it your way for tonight. Tomorrow's another day though."

We hoist our luggage and take the Skytrain out to the rental car area. Fortunately, Hertz hasn't released my reservation. There's a short exchange at the desk concerning my leg and the cane I'm carrying. I point out I have a valid license and will happily sue for age discrimination. The clerk considers her options but caves when Jay turns on his sad-eyed look, the same one I've seen in Save-The-Children TV ads.

Before we go, I rummage through my bag for the ratty old B&B brochure I brought, and call ahead to let them know there's been a change of plans. I ask if either the Oriole or Nuthatch rooms are available. The owner tells me she's completely booked then asks what the problem is. I explain that my grandson is with me and I need a room with twin beds.

At first she hesitates. "Could he sleep on a roll-out?" she asks.

"Absolutely. Better than the floor."

She laughs and says how charming it is that I get to spend time with him.

"I'm a lucky granddad," I offer in response, straining to keep the sarcasm out of my voice. Then I ask if I might extend my stay through Saturday night.

"Oh, dear," she says. "Uh...wait while I check."

She's back in a minute to say that she's shuffled a couple of rooms and that it will be fine.

I load the trunk and we leave JFK behind. On our way north, I ask Jay to explain again why he doesn't know where his mother's apartment is located. I'm suffering from incredulity and wonder again if 13-year-olds lie. If so, he's good at it.

"She moved last summer," he says. "Bought a co-op somewhere near Central Park West. I have the address at home. Didn't really need to know since she was picking me up."

His answer sounds practiced. "She didn't say it's three blocks from the last place, or something like that?"

"She told me it's close to both the Harlem Meer and the Reservoir."

Not enough information. Maybe on purpose. That only narrows the search to an enclave of high-rises about 30 blocks long by three blocks deep, an impossible task. Even if we found it, she might not be home, or if she were, wouldn't answer the buzz.

Calling information on his cell phone doesn't work either. No Rose Walsh listed on Central Park West. Of course, her address could be one of the side streets, or maybe she's unlisted, or maybe that's not her name. Nothing to do but wait her out. Or wait till Jay decides to tell me the truth. Either way, three days ought to be plenty. I try asking questions now and then as we plug along through the late afternoon, stop-and-go traffic, but Jay maintains his silence. Some internal quandary absorbing his attention? Or maybe he's choosing to keep me in the dark.

JEREMY

I don't like lying to Harry, but what else can I do? And it wasn't complete bullshit—Mom did move three years ago. That's when she left us. And her name was Rose Walsh, but she's gone back to her maiden name now, Zelinski. Of course I know where she lives, but she might not be there. If we showed up, the doorman would have to report her again. Can't let that happen. Can't figure out how to get Harry to just drop me off someplace either, or what I'd do if he did. Better stay with him till I figure out a plan. Glad he didn't hear Mom paging me. Guess all old people are deaf. Or maybe he forgot my name is Jeremy, not Jay.

Mom walked right by us while we were eating. Harry had his back toward her. I ducked under the table, pretending to look through my bag. I heard her before I saw her, heels clicking tap-tap-tap-tap. She didn't even look in our direction. I could have waved and I doubt she'd have noticed. Dumb grin on her face too. Like she was happy not to find me.

Harry thinks she'll call, but she won't. Mom doesn't know my phone number. Never asked and I never told her. Dad will give it to her, but the place he's going is pretty remote, so it may be a week or two before he checks in, and she might not even call him. I haven't left her any messages. Otherwise she'd have my number on her caller ID. I left them on Dad's phone. Sorry, Harry.

Besides, Mom would freak out if I told her I was going to hitchhike. Dad's the calm one. Probably has to be since he's a surgeon. He'd be pissed, but he'd bet I could do it. At least that's what he'd tell Mom.

She isn't always this way; she swings between up and down. That's what bipolar means, up and down. Mom's down more often than she's up, but the highs are fun. Might be walking in Central Park counting squirrels, a contest to see who can spot the most. I always win or maybe she lets me win. Our record is over 200. Then we'd stuff ourselves with hot dogs and pretzels from wandering vendors. Or we'd go shopping at Macy's and J&R Electronics all day, buying everything I want from games for my PSP to the latest iPod. Or a day at Coney Island, riding the roller coaster then running back to get in line again and eating nothing but popcorn and cotton candy till I want to barf.

Then there are the hours, days, and weeks alone. She's either locked in her bedroom or just gone. The food holds for a while. I stay in her apartment mostly and watch HBO. I order in or go for takeout, but I always run out of money. Sooner or later someone notices. Mostly it's the doorman. He tells me it would mean his job if he didn't report it. He understands bipolar. Says he has a sister the same way. Wish I had a sister, I tell him, an older sister I could stay with instead of Mom. He holds off as long as he can then calls social services. I'm used to what happens next and don't fight, but it sucks. And no one really cares. They couldn't and keep doing the same thing. Mom goes to court. Dad pays the lawyer. The social services lady writes up a report. And they all tell me it won't happen again, but it does. Not this time. This time I'm running.

I watch Harry as he drives and swears, "Idiot...Moron...Bitch..." He keeps up a steady conversation with himself and the drivers around us, who fly by, flipping him off for driving too slow or for cutting in front of them. I tell him he's funny.

"Happy to amuse you."

"Where are we going?"

"Pound Ridge, a quiet but sultry little burg nestled in the foothills where the deer you aren't allowed to shoot graze peacefully in flower gardens."

We have deer at my Dad's house too, I tell him. His girlfriend has a nursery business and has replaced most of our plants with ones she says are deerproof. Those are the plants the deer won't eat unless they're really hungry, which happens just about every winter.

"Where does your father live?"

"Juanita Bay. It's in Kirkland on Lake Washington."

"I know where Juanita Bay is!"

"Really? Most people don't."

"Right on the water?"

"Yeah, we've got a dock and speedboat. Do you live in Seattle?"

Harry doesn't answer. He just looks around at the traffic. We're coming up to the Whitestone Bridge so maybe he's concentrating on that. The GPS keeps saying, "Get in the right lane." We pass through the tollbooth and continue north to Route 95.

"Where do you live?" I try again.

"No place special. An inconsequential house in a neighborhood of other inconsequential houses. Not on the water, but you have to take the ferry to get there."

"Cool. Is it one of the islands like Vashon or Bainbridge? Sometimes Dad and I take a ferry to watch the seabirds."

"I go to the beach for that. Not too far. Mew Gulls, Glaucous-winged Gulls. And diving ducks: Hooded, Red-breasted, and Common Mergansers, Barrow's and Common Goldeneye, Buffleheads, Surf Scoters. Sometimes Harlequin and Oldsquaw. They call those Long-tailed Ducks now. Also Canvasback, American Widgeon and Northern Pintail, but they're mainly dabblers, not divers."

"No loons or cormorants?"

"Sure, Common Loons, and Pelagic and Double-crested Cormorants, but they're not ducks. Loons and cormorants are from different orders. So are the Red-throated and Horned Grebes I see regularly. Then there's Common Murre and Pigeon Guillemot. They're not ducks either. Auk family."

I've only seen half the birds Harry rattles off, and they're pretty common. Too much time in front of the TV playing video games, not enough exploring, Dad says. Even living on a lake, I don't see that many different birds.

"Am I boring you?"

"Nope. Dad says I need to get outside more."

"The birds won't come to you."

"Right. Just backyard birds. Nothing cool."

"So, what's the coolest bird you've seen?"

I guess seeing a bald eagle fly right at me when Dad tossed it a fish ranks right up there. We were out trolling off Orcas Island in the San Juans. There were two eagles high up in a fir tree on the bluff. Dad's buddy held up a rockfish he caught and waved it at the eagles. One took off and dived right at us. It was only fifteen feet from the boat when he pitched the fish. The eagle caught it in mid-air then flew right over us. Thought I was going to pee my pants.

I tell Harry the story, and he smiles but asks again if that's the coolest bird I've ever seen. I think about it a minute and remember, tossing off my answer, "Laysan Albatross."

HARRY

The kid's smile can't be stifled no matter how hard he tries to make the sighting sound casual. He knows this bird might not be on my life list, and he's right. Seeing any kind of albatross from shore is a rare event. After I call him on it, he admits he was 35 miles off the coast of Oregon fishing with his dad when he saw it, but it's still a rare sighting. Occasionally they follow the whales during the spring migration north along the coast, hoping to steal a tidbit brought up from the deep. They also follow ships, scavenging garbage dumped in the wake. My best hope to see one is the Hawaiian Islands. I have it on my list of places to go while I still remember I want to see them. I call it my Footloose List. That's where I keep it, taped to my prosthetic foot. Can't miss seeing it, even if my addled mind forgets. Addled is a great word—confused is one definition, rotten is another. I like that one better. My mind is rotting.

The navigation device is helpful since I've forgotten the route. The irritating female voice tells me to take I-95 toward New England then switch to the Hutchison River Parkway and onto I-684. She's not as irritating as the shoot-em-up game the kid is playing on his electronic whatever. "Fewer sound effects would be nice," I say, and he frowns. He turns the sound off, but all the clicking is almost as irritating. Finally, after I mimic the clickety-clickety-tap-taps, he gives up and stuffs the thing into his knapsack then starts a new round of clicking on his cell phone.

"Now what?" I ask.

"Texting my friends in Seattle."

"Texting? No, don't tell me." He gets the message and puts the phone away.

"So, what did you tell them, these friends of yours?"

A shrug. Then after I glance over a few times, he says, "Nothing. Just that I'm in New York."

"Not, 'I hitched a ride'?"

Another shrug and silence.

"Okay, but I'll ask again later."

By the time we get to the exit for Pound Ridge, Jay has nodded off. As I pull up in front of the B&B, he surfaces groggily, stretching and yawning.

"Where are we?"

"Welcome to the Barn Swallow Inn. More swallows in the barn than you can count, and the cats that love them. By the way, don't pet the cats. They'll rip your arm off."

"I'm hungry."

Figures. I forget that kids this age are always hungry. Did I forget? Guess not, though I can't remember where this knowledge comes from, experience or anecdote.

"There's a burger joint down the road we can try after we dump our gear in the room. Sound good?"

"Sounds great. I have to pee."

Kids and *non sequiturs*.

"I'm quite certain the inn has a bathroom you can use. No need to wait till we get to the pub," I answer in a vain attempt to make a logical connection between 'get a burger' and 'have to pee.'

JEREMY

I really have to pee, and I'm really hungry. Dad says I have a small tank; Mom says I have a bottomless pit for a stomach. They say it so often it's a joke. I ask the lady where the bathroom is as soon as we go through the front door. "Down that hall, second door on the left. Remember to wash your hands dear."

Adults are forever telling me to wash my hands. Do they look dirty? Not to me. "Wash your hands before dinner." "Wash your hands after you use the bathroom." "Wash your hands after petting the cat or dog." "Wash your hands after picking up that dead bird, for heaven sakes." Why does it matter? They're my hands. And I hate being treated like a kid. You'd think I was five, not 13.

After dinner we walk along a trail leading from the inn and following the river. Evening is the best time for bird watching. Evening and dawn. Trees arch high above us and shrubby plants overhang the edge of the river. We hear birds singing and catch a quick dart of color now and then among branches and leaves. I recognize none of the sounds except for the Great Blue Heron that squawks at us and flies off. Harry rattles off names to go with each birdsong: Wood Pewee, American Redstart, Song Sparrow, American Robin. I've seen plenty of robins and sparrows but never a pewee or redstart.

"I don't know where to look."

"Look where you expect the bird to be," he says.

"How should I know?" I ask, pissed at his know-it-all explanation.

"You have to learn by watching. And don't fuss at me. All this chatter scares the birds."

"Sorry."

"That's okay. Look, some birds roost in treetops, some in the underbrush, and some are ground feeders. For example, look for redstarts and ovenbirds in the leaf litter, kicking to uncover insects."

We walk in silence a few minutes then he stops and trains his binoculars into the high branches. We can hear a bird singing.

"Red-eyed Vireo," he says. "Listen. Hear the song? It's a male looking for some action. He's singing, 'Look up. Here I am. In the tree. At the top.' He'll be high in the branches of one of these birches or maples. Keep looking."

I do as I'm told. For a change, Mom would say. I see the vireo before Harry. He's still scanning the branches, so I tell him, "A little to the right."

"Got him. Can you see him working that song? The ladies are watching too. I seldom see the females unless they've just paired up and are building a nest. But I know they're nearby listening."

We walk out for an hour and back along the same path for an hour, scaring up my first American Redstart and Veery, and spotting both Downy and Hairy Woodpeckers hammering insects out of dead birches and pines. Dusk is falling when Harry stops short in front of me, listening.

"Hear that?"

The song repeats over and over.

"Ovenbird," he says. "He's singing, 'Teacher, teacher, teacher, teacher, teacher.' Obviously not talking to you. You're the student."

I roll my eyes at his lame joke. It's sort of funny though. The Ovenbird keeps singing, but we can't find him among the leaves in the fading light.

HARRY

Jay is animated in a way I haven't seen yet. I'll admit it's fun to have a birding companion. Never had one before, other than my oldest friend, Birds. Silly name, I know, and not my idea. Our students hung the monikers on us, Harry and Nigel, Words and Birds, each caught up in his ethereal aerie, etymology for me, ornithology for Nigel.

Words and Birds. The terms were both demeaning and endearing, and we took them as such and only smiled when so accosted. We knew intuitively what each student meant, and we cataloged this intent along with their grades. Pluses and minuses were applied subjectively. Ah, the power of the pen when wielded by a professor's hand.

I walk into our room after taking a much-needed shower, and find Jay updating his life list. "How many did you add?"

"Five! American Redstart, Downy Woodpecker, Red-eyed Vireo, Veery, and Ovenbird."

He is so pleased with himself I can hardly bring myself to tell him that hearing doesn't count. No Ovenbird. This is a new experience for me. I spent a lifetime shooting down overly enthusiastic student explanations of word derivation. Now I hesitate to disappoint? I let the internal dilemma fester for a moment then reassert my basic nature.

"Only four. Hearing the Ovenbird doesn't count. You have to see the whites of his eyes, or, in this case, the blacks."

"But you know it was an Ovenbird!"

"Yes, I do. But you don't. Over the years I've watched dozens when there was no separation between song and singer. I know the voice well, so for me it counts."

"Wait. You mean you get to count him but I don't?"

"Right. Just hearing him is enough for me. For you, though, only visual identification suffices. If you had studied the Ovenbird call and were certain you knew the song, then you could count him. Makes sense if you think about it. But mainly, it's the rule."

"I don't like rules."

"Hmmph. Me either. How about we split the difference and call it four-and-a-half? We'll go back out tomorrow morning and find the actual bird. Then you can count him. Deal?" I say, holding out my hand for Jay to shake.

"Deal," he agrees and pumps my hand till I worry it might fall off like my missing leg.

JEREMY

Harry and I are up at dawn and out on the trail. Lots of mist along the river. Makes it hard to see the birds. We can hear them singing, so we know they're all around us. I spot bits of movement here and there but not enough to identify my Ovenbird. Harry says one was a Brown Creeper. Already on my list. So are the Great Blue Heron wading along the riverbank and the Belted Kingfisher swooping and looping and chattering at us. Harry says the kingfisher is 'clicking' his unhappiness with our invasion of his territory. The other birds stay out of sight. I'm bummed. He promises we'll try again this evening.

The sun is fully up and it's getting warm when we head back. I'm starving. Pancakes for breakfast. The inn is pretty cool. The owner, Shelley, says it was built in 1810. There's the main house and an attached barn, both painted white with blue-gray trim. She calls it federal blue. There are twelve rooms and eight bathrooms, some private, some shared like ours. The ceilings are really low. If Harry stood up straight, he'd hit his head on the beams, but since he's always bent over, he doesn't. The front porch is weird; it's only a few steps from the street, so parking is on one side of the house. The backyard is huge. Almost the size of a football field. And in the middle is a garden with more flowers than I've ever seen in one place.

When we walk through the front door, the bacon and pancake smells start me drooling. The table is set, and I wander over to see if breakfast is ready.

"Good morning, gentlemen. Sleep well?"

"Like a log," Harry says then looks at me. "And how is that? How does one sleep like a log?"

There's that know-it-all smile. I shrug. "Just lying there like a log?"

"And what sort of noise does a log make when it's being sawed?"

"Snoring!"

"Precisely. Hence the idiom, 'sleeping like a log.'"

"My father always said he slept like a top," Shelley says. "Log makes more sense."

"It only seems to make more sense because the 'top' reference is archaic, perhaps 16th or 17th century. When a top is spun properly with a string, the effect is gyroscopic. The top stays motionless in one place. The sleeper does not move in his sleep if it is deep enough, hence he sleeps like a top spinning, the sleep of the dead."

"Yes, Professor," I say and laugh when Harry fakes offense.

"Hungry?" Shelley asks.

"Starving," we reply in unison.

"Excellent. I love men with hearty appetites. Coffee's on the table. Milk for you?" she asks me.

"Please."

We spend the next half hour stuffing our faces in silence, except for Harry's coffee slurping and occasional fart. He seems to like letting them go. He makes sounds that range from a slow blat-blat-blat to a rapid-fire machine-gun blurp. He also can make it sound like air shrieking out of a balloon when you pinch the opening.

I show him how to swallow air and belch in rhythm. I can hold one for a good 15 seconds. Harry tries but doesn't quite get the hang of it. He promises to practice.

As we finish breakfast, Shelley comes out to sit with us and chat.

"Where are you from?" she asks, the obvious question.

"Seattle," I tell her.

"Or thereabouts." That response from Harry sums it up for both of us. No reason to explain where our towns are located.

"What brings you east?"

"Birding," Harry answers before I can come up with a lie. "My grandson and I are spending the summer together while his father is off in Africa saving lives. I think my grandson here is secretly pleased to be out from under his parents' watchful eyes. I count myself a lucky man. Wouldn't you agree?"

"Well, I would indeed. Sorry to say I seldom get to spend time with my grandkids. No one lives near enough, the common story these days. Things certainly were different when I was a girl. My grandmother visited nearly every week, or we went to see her."

Harry nods, and Shelley looks away. I think she's sad. I know I'm sad my grandmother is dead. My granddad too. He used to take me fishing.

When she turns back to us, Shelley says, "Don't often get guests from so far away. How did you find me? On the Internet?"

"Oh, no," Harry answers, "I've been coming here for years, long as I can remember. Though it's been a while, I think. Can't say exactly when I was here last."

"Odd that I don't recognize you. I pride myself on my return guests and seldom forget a name, much less a face. I've been running The Barn Swallow for eighteen years now."

Shelley looks confused. Harry looks worried.

"Well, I suppose it could be twenty years," he answers. "They do fly by. Seems like yesterday, but I'll admit I sometimes have trouble keeping everything straight. Not a kid anymore."

"Oh, I know what that's like. I'm getting forgetful myself. Are you off again to chase down the birds?"

"Not right away. Have to go charge up my leg. It's been beeping at me. Pretty soon it'll do its vibration buzz and shut down completely. Hate to have to crawl upstairs."

Now it's Shelley who looks worried, but I know he's kidding from the way he said it.

"Just joking. I can lock the leg and do my Festus impersonation, but stairs are not easy if you can't bend your knee. Ollie here can help if I need any."

"Ollie? I thought it was Jay, or is that a nickname?"

"It's Jay. Gramps keeps getting it messed up."

"Shit. Sorry, Jay," Harry says. "When you get old, your brain turns to Swiss cheese, full of holes. Mine's more like Stilton, slowly rotting. Why don't you head out to the garden while I plug in my bionic leg? You might score a ruby-throated hummer. Can't see those out west. And check out the barn. Bet it's filled with nesting swallows."

ABBY

Oliver's voice over the phone was so certain, so self-righteous. "It's too late, Abby," he said. "You just can't bring yourself to accept it. Dad's getting worse. You know it's true. The spells are more frequent."

This was all I could expect from Oliver? A lecture? Two days with no word, and no sign of Harry. I supposed Oliver was right, but I knew I couldn't give up that easily, and I didn't believe he expected me to. I tried to sound hopeful and replied quietly, "Yes, yes, I know. I just wish it were otherwise. But I still don't think it's too late. If he were around things that reminded him, he wouldn't be failing so fast. He might even get better, or at least he might seem better if he recognized where he was."

"Oh, Abby, you need to face facts. He's not going to get better."

"Damn it, Oliver. Don't you give up on him so easily! You don't know any more about this miserable disease than I do, and you're not around him every day, so you don't realize how clear he can be. This past week he only had one confused period—"

"Two, Abby. And this time he's driven off to God knows where."

I promised myself I wouldn't cry. I hate crying. And I hated this pointless arguing, and I hated that Oliver couldn't understand how hard this is, and I hated how he made me feel, hopeless when I should be stoic. He could hear me crying and waited until I got control again. For all his certainty that he was right and I was wrong, he couldn't bring himself to take advantage. He remained silent. In the background I heard the kids playing with their dog. He must be working from home.

"Abby?" he said, after my silence must have begun to worry him.

"What do we do, Oliver? How do we find him?" I asked, deliberately softening my tone and putting back the plea for his help.

"Damned if I know," he answered, sounding resigned. "Any chance he may have gone for a drive and actually knows how to get home? Whidbey's not that big an island. Maybe he went out to one of the beaches. Could your friend drive you around to check?"

His question irritated me. What did he think, that I'd been home waiting around for Harry to magically appear?

"I'm not an idiot, Oliver. That's the first thing we did. My friend and I searched for hours through every parking lot and along every road on the south end of the island then checked at the ferry terminal to see if anyone had seen him. And it's not as if our ridiculous red car doesn't stand out."

"Okay, okay. Don't get angry. But if he was still driving, you might not have crossed paths. Try again. He has the sense to stop wherever he is when he gets confused. He may be sitting someplace waiting to be found. Just check the beach and store parking lots."

Even more irritating. Oliver couldn't be bothered to help me. Let my friend do it. Heaven forbid he should put himself out and make the time.

"Fine, I'll give her a call," I answered, "I'm sure she has nothing better to do than chauffeur me around, and besides—"

"Right," he said. "Look, Abby, this isn't my fault. I have a job and a family and no time to play detective. I'll call the sheriff's office and ask them to look. Hell, I'll call the state police while I'm at it. He'll turn up sooner or later, and while he's not an invalid, you need to face facts. He may need full-time care someplace where they know how to handle him."

That did it. We launched down a well-worn verbal path that led nowhere, both with our backs up.

"I can't do that, Oliver. I won't do that. And you're forgetting about his prosthetic. The battery will run down if he's out walking somewhere. Then he'll have to lock the knee and hobble along. He may seem indestructible to you, but he's not. He's seventy-five, and it takes a lot out of him to walk very far. What if he's someplace in the woods birding?"

"He shouldn't be. He should be home with you, taking gentle strolls, and being content with the birds in his own neighborhood. Or, if you can't control him, he should be in a supervised facility."

"You just don't get it. You refuse to understand everything he has lost: his career, his home, his leg. Now he's losing me. Every time he blanks out, the past thirty years just vanish; he either thinks he's a bachelor or, worse, still married to Olivia."

"I know, I know. We've been over all this a dozen times. But he doesn't realize any of that when he slips into the past, does he?"

"Yes, Oliver. But when he returns from the past, it terrifies him. It's not the going, it's not the getting lost that he fears; it's the coming home and knowing that each time it gets worse. That's what slowly steals every ounce of dignity he has left. It's killing me too. No one should have to go through this. And you know, Oliver, you had better start spending time with your father. He hasn't forgotten you yet, not even once. But that day will come. Trust me."

JACKSON

Dim light filtered through the sun-baked tent and washed across the stretcher on which Jackson lay drifting in and out of sleep. He rolled over. He did this without thinking about where he was. When it tipped, the stretcher landed on top of him, and he ended up lying on the dirt floor below. His change of circumstance did not go unnoticed. A tiny black nurse soon hovered above him and peeked beneath the remains of his makeshift bed.

"Doctor awright?" she asked in lilting, broken English pitched high but soft.

"Fine," he said and waved her away.

She smiled broadly, exposing pink gums and white teeth. "Bebe sleep, bebe sleep. We call later," she murmured and settled the stretcher back over his face.

Jackson considered exerting the effort to reassemble his bed, but the cool earth beneath him and the relief it brought from the stultifying heat inside the tent changed his mind. He heard the slip-slide flip-flap of sandals and swish of tent flap as the little nurse departed, followed by more distant, muffled voices and the clinking of bed and emesis pans. A field hospital is no place to sleep, he thought then laughed at his own words. To call this collection of tents and huts a hospital of any sort was a joke, albeit a cruel one. Nevertheless, lives were saved here, though many more were lost. There were too few hospitals and not enough funds for more. Often, the distance was too far or too dangerous for villagers to travel.

But every day they came: infested, infected, or injured; all incapable of escaping whatever debilitating vector, human, vermin or virus, that had taken them down. And each one came with a belief that Jackson or another doctor would cure them. Inured to pain, so prevalent as to be commonplace, they came and they came, day after day. How many days had it been? Only two, but already too many. Worse than last year, that was certain. But for all of it, he felt needed in a way he never experienced back home. There, he was just one of hundreds of capable surgeons among whom patients were free to choose. Here, patients took whoever was available, capable or not. Yet the staff was capable, and those who were not soon learned by doing.

Yes, he felt needed here, now, in this wasteland. And despite Jeremy's accusations, Jackson knew his presence served two good purposes: saving the lives and limbs of those he mended and salvaging what was left of Jeremy's love for Rose.

JEREMY

It's been three days and no word from Africa. Don't know what I'll say when Dad does call. Maybe I should turn off the phone or ditch it. Harry seems to have forgotten to bug me about calling Mom again. In fact, he seems confused about what we're doing here at all. Even asked where I was hitching to. But he likes hiking along the river path, and yesterday we heard the Ovenbird again. It was somewhere in the wild alder along the bank. "Singing his heart out, hoping to pick up a cute chick," Harry said. But we couldn't find him or the female he was singing for. Harry gave in and told me I could count it, but I said no, I want to see one first. Rules are rules.

Ovenbirds are really cool birds. I've looked at them in my *Sibley's*. They're fairly small, only six inches, a bit larger than a chickadee. They have white breasts with black spots, reddish-brown backs, large white-eye rings, and orange crowns. Harry says they build amazing domed nests on the ground that look like leaf igloos.

He was right about the garden and Ruby-throated Hummingbirds. They were everywhere, zipping from flower to flower, dive-bombing me, fighting with each other over territory. Lots of females and at least two males with dark throats. Harry says they flash red to challenge or display. One of them hovered three feet from me for a long time, turning his head from side to side. Harry says the hummer probably thought I was a giant flower, since my T-shirt was bright yellow with red lettering.

He's right about the swallows too. Lots of nests, some with babies still in them. And lots of fledglings, waiting nearby. According to Harry, they were probably from the first brood. Sometimes the kids from the spring hatching help catch insects to feed the next batch. He says he hasn't seen any other bird behave this way but thinks crows and jays may do this too. Later we saw the kids all lined up on the power lines along the road, waiting for a handout.

Tomorrow we'll drive to New Hampshire. Harry has a cabin we can stay at on Chaser's Pond, and on the south end there's a dammed up marshy area we can hike into if he can manage to drag his leg through the brush. Lots of birds, he tells me, and resident beavers patrol the shore and gnaw birch saplings. I may have to help him find a way in. We can row as far as the beach then walk the rest of the way.

At 7:00 p.m., after our evening bird watching, we head to the pub. Harry orders a beer, a burger, and fries as usual. I get barbecued chicken and a Pepsi. After two nights of burgers, I'm ready for a change.

Harry says the same thing he said yesterday, "A burger really sounds good tonight. How about you?"

"We had burgers last night and the night before. Think I'll go for the chicken."

"We did? Huh. Guess I forgot. You're supposed to watch birds not eat them."

"A chicken's not a bird."

"What do you think it is, a dinosaur? They're related, you know."

"Okay, it is a bird. But you know what I mean."

"Yeah. Too bad it won't be still kicking. You could add it to your life list. Only live birds count."

"You can't put chickens on your life list."

"Sure you can."

"Can not."

"Can too. I've got one on my list. Saw it in eastern Kansas. Godforsaken place for the most part, but Tallgrass Prairie National Preserve is protected and unspoiled. Greater Prairie Chicken is about the same size as a barnyard fryer. Not as tender though, I wouldn't think, but I don't really know. Unlike you, I don't eat birds."

HARRY

It's fun teasing the kid. He's a good sport. Reminds me of someone, but I can't remember who. Okay with me if he naps on the way north. Guess he's worn out. The cabin is a good five-hour drive from Pound Ridge. Had to backtrack a bit to pick up the Merritt Parkway. Oldest limited-access highway in the country, I told him. He wasn't impressed. This really is a nice peaceful ride though. No wonder he drifted off. Sleeps with his mouth open and drools. Kind of off-putting, but I have to admit, it's nice to have a hitchhiker for company. Where was it I picked him up? A little young to be out on the road alone, but at my age, all kids look too young to me. What did he tell me again? Oh yeah, he's hitching west to Seattle. Might visit relatives along the way. Told him we can stop anytime he'd like to call them on his cell phone. Wouldn't have one myself. Too much of a nuisance and I can't think of anyone I'd want to call. Damn rotten-cheese memory.

JACKSON

As he slipped in and out of sleep through the heat of the afternoon, Jackson dreamed of Jeremy and Rose. At first, it was quiet, calming. He saw the two of them wandering through Central Park, Jeremy's binoculars dangling from his neck, Rose dressed in tight jeans and tank top, swinging her arms playfully while singing some show tune, happy to be where she was. Then he saw Jeremy turn to her and say something, maybe a snide remark about singing in public. Rose's expression clouded over, her internal storm moments away from breaking open in deluge.

Jackson startled fully awake, sweat drenched and still jet-lagged. His dream faded but left the strong sense of impending failure. He shifted the cot off his body, righted it, and sat back down, elbows on knees. This was not going to work. Even if somehow Rose and Jeremy could make it through the next two months together, nothing would change. He had pushed for three years now to bring them closer, and each time the authorities got involved Andrew went to court and cleaned up the mess. No matter how hard he tried, Jackson could not let Rose go; he wanted his family back together. If he failed this time, they might lose Jeremy for good. No, he couldn't let himself believe that would happen. Andrew would find a way. He always found a way.

Jeremy was their link, but that link weakened with every month that passed. Too soon Jeremy would go off to college. He would spend holidays and summer vacations bouncing back and forth between them, then he would graduate and Jackson's tenuous connection to Rose would be sundered forever. Already too late, Jackson thought some days. Rose had her friends, and he knew she dated, though nothing serious, he supposed, no more serious than he was with his girlfriend. But that would not last; there were many men who would try. His only real hope was that her condition, once revealed, would frighten off any serious suitors.

Rose never stayed on her medications. There was no excuse, but he knew this was the common story; if they took them at all, the bipolar and schizophrenic only used their meds until they felt better. Then they stopped. And each time they stopped, they slid further and further into their symptoms.

But Jackson knew Rose. She liked the manic episodes, and he had to admit he had once liked them as well. She would be so effervescent, so playful, so overtly sexual. Life with Rose was a carnival ride you never wanted to get off, couldn't get off. The Rotor, where, once spinning at full speed, the floor falls away and the riders are pressed in place by centrifugal force. Then it slows; the floor comes back up. Only with Rose, the floor didn't return. You fell from whatever height you had reached into what seemed a bottomless pit. She could take you high if you followed, but the crash was always just a few spins away.

JEREMY

I stretch and yawn then look out the car window. Harry glances over at me.

"Ah, the prince awakens," he says. "We just left US-93. Start and stop traffic probably woke you. Mostly back roads now. About an hour more to the lake."

"Thought you called it a pond. Which is it? What's the difference anyway?"

"Matter of opinion as far as I can tell. If you look up pond all you find are generalizations like smaller than a lake, shallower than a lake, and similar diminutives. Chaser's Pond is about a mile long and a third wide, maybe 200 acres, and 30 to 40 feet deep. Not many speedboats so it's quiet, during the week anyway."

"Are you married?"

"Not that I remember. Do you know what a *non sequitur* is?"

"Nope."

"It's when you say something that has nothing whatsoever to do with the thing you said just before, like, 'what's a pond' followed by 'are you married.' Get it?"

"I think so. So, you're not married?"

"I was. Seems like a long time ago some days. And then some days it doesn't."

"But you're not married now?"

"Right."

"Then why are you wearing a wedding ring?"

Harry looks down at his hand then back out through the windshield at the road. He seems to forget a lot. Maybe he forgot he's married.

"Not sure," he says and looks sad, disappointed. Mom does that all the time. I ask her something simple, and she just sighs and looks unhappy. Or angry. I like unhappy better.

I'm just about ready to ask another question when Harry continues, "I think I have a girlfriend."

"Girlfriend?"

"What? You think I'm too old? Never too old for that. Never too young either, for that matter. How about you? Any nubile beauties after you?"

"What's 'new bile?'"

"Not new bile, dummy. Nubile. As in young and attractive and marriageable. It's a good word to remember. So, you chasing skirts yet?"

"No, I'm too young. Besides, all the girls in my grade are at least six inches taller than me. They think I'm puny."

"They probably think a lot of things, but if you're anything like the rest of us, you'll never really know what that is. Trust me, stick to birds they're easier to understand."

"Suppose so." Don't even understand my own mother, so what chance do I have with girls my age?

Dad used to call my grandfather an odd duck. That's Harry. Funny, a birder being an odd duck, but it fits. He flaps and quacks and only makes sense part of the time. And he's still calling me Oliver or Ollie now and then.

"Who's Oliver?"

"Another *non sequitur.*"

"You mean it doesn't follow, but maybe it does. Is he your son?"

There's that sad face again.

"I don't know," he says after a minute then pauses to think. It's kind of scary he doesn't remember this stuff. What if he forgets something important, like stopping for lights or which side of the road to drive on?

"Maybe," he says after a while.

"Maybe what?"

"Maybe Oliver is my son. I can't remember exactly. I think the last time I saw Oliver he was about your age. So, maybe he's my son, but maybe he's my nephew or grandson. I can see him tagging along after me on a hike, moping. Don't think he liked birds. No, wait. I remember a parakeet, Petey or something. Pale blue and sitting on Oliver's shoulder in our old kitchen. He died, I think."

"Oliver?"

"No, the parakeet. Oliver is alive and well and living in Seattle."

"So you do remember!"

"Not sure. Sometimes everything is so clear, sometimes not. Sometimes I can remember what happened yesterday, sometimes I can't. I don't know why, but I think Oliver lives in Seattle. His mother lives nearby, or at least she used to. We were married for about ten years. We divorced when Oliver was seven or eight, I think. So, he must be my son. He'd be, what, 50 now I guess."

Harry seems disgusted, maybe pissed off he can't remember. I'm not sure. Should I be worried? Mom told me my grandfather had Alzheimer's when he died, but that's not what he died of. Heart attack. Dad says Gramps was just a little senile. Harry reminds me of him. They even talk alike. Sort of. Gramps always said, "Can't remember squat anymore."

I miss him. Maybe it's a good thing that I'm here in case Harry forgets something important.

"Wait! I've got it!" Harry shouts. "I did have a girlfriend. Her name was Abby."

"You had a girlfriend when you were still married?"

"I think so. Not very good, huh? I'm not sure though. Maybe Abby came after I left my wife. We worked together at the university. I can't remember. Wish I could. Wonder what happened to Abby."

"You don't know?"

"No. Don't remember. Not right now anyway. Ask me again later. If I tell you something different, remind me."

"Getting old isn't much fun, is it?"

"Nope. Not when you spend much time thinking about it. But considering the alternative, I'm thankful to be on the right side of the grass. And I've been having fun the past few days. What I can remember of it, anyway."

"Me too," I say and return his smile at first, but then I think about Mom and Dad and worry what will happen next.

ABBY

I woke with the frightening sense something terrible had happened. Harry had been gone four days. Where could he be? Oliver promised to come out tomorrow afternoon to help look but couldn't resist adding, "Abby, how difficult could it be to locate one red car and one old man?" I told him the sheriff hadn't had any luck, but maybe they weren't taking this seriously enough. Just like Oliver, they probably thought Harry would suddenly pull into our driveway back from wherever he'd been. My own fault for saying he'd been thinking clearly lately. Maybe I should have acted as worried as I felt.

The deputy was so calm, almost had me convinced Harry was just lost. And he was right, the weather was warm now, so even if Harry were sleeping in the car, he'd be okay. And he had plenty of cash. He wouldn't starve. I checked his wallet every morning. It was a way of keeping tabs without him knowing I was keeping tabs. But what if he was out walking and couldn't remember where he left the car?

When I asked that question, the deputy said, "No ma'am, couldn't happen that way. We'd have found his car by now if it were parked at the beach or one of the trailheads. No, he's out there driving around. Maybe not on the island anymore, but he's still moving. He'll give up and ask directions. Be patient. State police are keeping an eye out for his car. He'll turn up. Really nothing we can do but wait and keep looking."

I knew they were right, but it didn't matter—I was still worried. Not sleeping hadn't helped either. This was all my fault. I knew better than to move here. I never really expected Oliver to be helpful. Not on a regular basis anyway. But I wanted to be near him and the kids, especially when Harry was no longer really there anymore.

It was hard doing this myself. And I got so tired of answering the same questions over and over. Harry would forget he asked what he asked just five minutes earlier.

"What's for dinner?" "Which state is this?" "Where is my jacket?"

Those were the easy ones. Hurt a little each time he asked, but only because of what the questions portended—a slow but steady fall.

"Why can't I go back to work?"

Harder to answer.

Why? Because you can't. We're 3,000 miles from Plymouth and the university.

"What happened to my leg?"

What? You had an accident. You drove into a tree, and the engine crushed your leg. You don't remember, and that's a good thing. Be thankful. God help me, I wish I didn't remember either. It scares me every time you get behind the wheel.

"Who are you?"

That was the hardest. How could he remember nothing of our 30 years together?

"Who is Oliver?"

Second hardest, since he was more my son than Harry's, and nearly as much as he was Olivia's, though I was sure Oliver would deny that. Olivia had tied him to her apron strings right from the beginning, through a name.

As a boy, Oliver had visited us every summer and tried to know his father. But Harry was unapproachable; his work and his birding adventures took precedence. Harry did love Oliver. He just didn't like him. So Oliver clung to me, and I clung to him, the only child I would ever have. Harry had always been the outsider.

I had lied to Oliver. Harry didn't always remember him. I lied not so much to spare him the pain as to spare Harry. If Oliver came to visit us more often, he'd know. By the time he realized, it would be too late.

JEREMY

Harry turns off the state highway onto a narrow, paved-but-potholed side street. A half-mile up we turn again, passing through stone pillars and up a gravel driveway then plunge downhill, the car bouncing and jerking over the rough road. Hope Harry knows where he's going. There's nowhere to turn around, just dense woods on either side.

"You sure this is the right way?" I ask.

"Of course. Been coming here for sixty years." He sounds a little pissed off, so I don't say anything else.

At the bottom of the hill, the road bends hard to the right and empties out onto a level drive littered with pine needles. Harry pulls up in front of the second cabin on the left. There are five or six small buildings, though there might be more. I can't see them all. An old woman, a few cabins down, looks up from her raking.

"We're home!" Harry says, turning to me and faking triumph. "Let's go see if the place is still in one piece."

We walk around the cabin toward the lake. The woman is still watching. Harry doesn't seem to notice her.

"Damn," he says as he rifles through his pockets. "Forgot the keys. Looks like we'll have to break in. We can smash a pane of glass and replace it tomorrow. Won't be the first time I had to do that."

He climbs the cabin steps, and shuffles across the porch to the door. I follow along behind. He's just about to bust in when a voice behind us calls out, "Harry, what the hell do ya think yah doin'?"

It's the old woman. She's standing at the bottom of the stairway, one hand on her hip, the other clutching the rake, curly gray hair sticking out in every direction. She looks scary.

"Grace?" Harry asks, confused but smiling, "Forgot my keys. Hey, hand me that rake, so I can whack this old door pane."

"Nothin' doin', Harry," she says. "Come on down from the pawch, boy. And bring that crazy old man with ya."

I look from her to Harry and back again. Don't know what to do. Don't know what's going on.

"Come on, Harry. Off the pawch before ya get yahself into somethin' ya can't get out of. You too, boy. Be quick about it."

I decide to do what I'm told and take up a position a few steps behind her. Harry just stands there looking unsure what to do next. It's like he's 'been here done this' before. Looks like a standoff for a minute then the old woman climbs the steps, takes his hand, and leads him off.

"Come with me, ya old fool," she says and walks away toward her cabin with him, tossing a sharp, "You too," over her shoulder at me.

I follow quietly behind.

HARRY

"Ya can't be breakin' into other people's property, Harry."

What does she mean by other people? This cabin has been in my family most of my life, and she knows that as well as I do. Did I sell it? No, I would never have done that, would I? I hate that I can't remember anything for certain. I remember Grace, though. We had a thing going once upon a time. Of course, that's when we were teenagers spending summers up here on the pond. Funny that I can bring all those days back so vividly and can't recall whether I sold the cabin.

She was a real beauty in a two-piece, canoeing down the lake with me, horsing around in the water then going back into the woods off the shore. Never let me go much farther than kissing though. Smart girl. Except the late-night skinny-dipping. Caught her once in a while, and I don't think she was trying very hard not to let me.

"When did I sell it?" I ask after I return from my reverie. She's giving me a look now like she's worried.

"You didn't. Abby sold it. She's got yah power of attorney."

"Oh, I didn't know."

"Don't remembah, do ya?"

"Can't remember shit these days."

"How about the kid? He yah grandson?"

I pause a second and look at him. He smiles, holds my gaze and says, "Yep. This is my Gramps. We're on a birding vacation."

Then he turns to Grace. "I'm Jay," he says and offers his hand for her to shake.

She takes it and nods. "You must be Oliver's boy. Thought he only had girls, but my memory isn't much bettah than Harry's, I expect."

"My older sisters. They're a pain in the butt. Glad to get out of Seattle. Gramps forgets things sometimes. I'm supposed to watch out for him. I've got a cell phone just in case."

Grace looks at Jay then at me, as if to gauge the kid's story. Then she sighs and nods again. "Don't have room in the cabin for both of ya. Maybe one or the othah can sleep in the campah," she says, pointing to her rusty old one-ton Chevy pickup with its huge, beetle-like attachment, grass-green paint faded and peeling off its sides.

"Why don't we both stay out in it?" Jay suggests. "That would be fun!"

Grace squints and wrinkles her brow. She's not buying his enthusiasm but can't find a reason to decline. "That would be just fine," she says, nodding her head a third time. "Hot dogs for suppah, if that's okay with you gentlemen." Then she gives us both a sincere smile and points to the camper. "Go get settled in. Might take a swim if ya have a mind to. Lake's wahm as a bahthtub."

We take Grace up on her suggestion, stowing our gear and changing into swim trunks. Jay's hang past his knees. I can't immerse my bionic leg, so after walking the few steps to the end of the dock, I remove the prosthetic and hand it to Jay, then hold on tight to the dock post for support. He runs my leg up to the cabin. Seems fascinated by the contraption and even more curious about my stump. Says the stitches make it look like you could unzip it. He also says it's too bad he can't try the leg; it looks like fun. Kids. Anything looks like fun to them. I let go the dock post and quickly execute a perfect swan dive, or as perfect as I can, pushing off with only one leg. Jay follows me with a running jump and cannonball.

The water is as warm as I can ever remember for this time of year. Feels great. I take a few strong strokes out into the lake, while Jay struggles to keep up. That feels good too. Swam the middle distances in college and haven't lost the knack, even with only one flipper left. In fact, I hardly miss it. The loss of the extra weight helps make up for the lack of kick.

Jay knows the crawl but has never had training. That's clear from his head-above-water, flailing attempt to keep up. I stop and float on my back for a while. Don't want to tire him out. Imagine swimming kids are like swimming dogs, go all out till they run out of energy and drown.

I close my eyes and take in the lake smells. Fecund from thousands of generations of rotting fish and leaves, the heady aroma rises from the surface and mixes with softer scents of pine and flowering scrub brush wafting out from the shore.

The silence is broken by a tremolo call and an answer from farther down the lake, a loon and her mate. They call to each other but it has always felt like they call to me. They have returned every year for my whole life. Oh, I know it's not really true. They might live only seven years or so, but I count it as true nonetheless. They have lulled me to sleep each night and have woken me each dawn on every day of every summer as far back as memory serves. They are my loons, the loons of my childhood, and now, the loons of my senility.

As I float, Jay splashing lazy circles around me, I remember Abby. The memory of who we are today rushes in with a force that takes my breath away, and tears swim out of my eyes. We sold the cabin and moved west.

What am I doing here with Oliver's son? Didn't even know he had a son. Jay says so, but is he telling the truth? Do 13-year-olds lie? And what about Abby? Does she know I'm at the lake? How could she? She must be worried sick. I better call her.

JEREMY

"You okay?" I ask Harry when we pull ourselves up onto the rickety wooden dock. He looks sad.

"Not sure, Jay. Let's go get changed for cocktail hour."

We head back to the camper, which stinks like my gym bag, but otherwise is pretty cool. Grace opened all the windows to air it out. I get the big bunk over the truck cab. Harry has taken one of the small bunks at the back and is sitting staring out the rear windows toward the lake. He seems lost, like the way I feel when school is just about to start. Lost and sad to have the summer end.

"Grace talks funny," I say to get his attention.

"Does she? Oh, you mean the accent. Grew up in Boston. Spent summers right here. Guess I hardly notice anymore. She'd say, 'anymoah,' stretching the word to four syllables, an-y-mo-ah."

He stops for a minute, lost in thought, shaking his head and muttering to himself. Before I can think of something to say, he turns to look at me. Still sad.

"Grace is my oldest friend, Jay. Known her since she wasn't much older than you. And don't let the crusty talk fool you; she's just a softy."

"I know. She's like my grandma."

"She'd have made a good one," he says, looking away toward the cabin. "So, getting hungry?"

"A little, but mostly I'm kinda thirsty. Do you think Grace has any soda?"

"I'm sure she does, but..."

"But what?"

"But nothing. Just ask her."

Harry's smiling again, though why asking for a soda is funny, I have no idea. We climb down from the camper and join Grace, who is sitting in one of the painted wooden chairs on her beach and watching the lake turn to glass now that the wind has completely died. She's drinking a Budweiser right from the can.

"Want a beeah, Harry?" she asks when she hears us walking up behind her.

"Is the Pope Catholic?" he answers.

"Yup, but does he shit in the woods?" she immediately replies. "How about you, Jay? Want a beeah?"

"Sure!" I say, though I know she's teasing.

She turns to look at me to see if I'm teasing back then nods and disappears into the house and returns with two Budweisers and hands them to Harry and me.

Harry pops the top on his and chugs then they watch to see what I'll do. Caught me, don't really like beer. Should I drink it anyway? Sigh. I hold the can out for Grace to take back. "I was just kidding."

The two of them burst out laughing.

"Kids today," she says after a minute. "Don't know what they want. Not like you and me, huh Harry?"

"Nope. But Jay told me he was 'kinda thirsty,' so I know he needs something to drink. What did you say you wanted, Jay?"

"A soda?"

"That a question or a statement, boy?" Grace asks.

"I would like a soda, if you have one, ma'am," I say slowly with lots of attitude.

Grace stands and puts one hand on her hip, giving me a look, then turns to Harry. "Chip off the old block, I see."

Harry throws his hands in the air. "No *mea culpa*, Grace."

She smiles. "Alright then. One soda comin' up."

As she walks away toward the cabin, I realize she didn't ask what kind of soda I like. Maybe she only has one kind. Grace returns in a minute and hands me the can. It's club soda, the disgusting stuff Mom drinks with vodka.

"What's the mattah, Jay? Thought you were thirsty."

I look up from the can to see the two of them grinning like Cheshire cats. I grin back but don't get the joke. That's obvious.

"Ask Grace for a 'tonic,'" Harry says.

I turn to her and ask, "A tonic?"

Grace ignores my confused look and replies, "Coke, Dr. Peppah, or 7Up."

"Coke!"

She walks away laughing, and Harry explains that in some states you say 'soda,' in others you say 'pop,' but in this part of New England you say 'tonic' when you want a soft drink. "And don't ask for a milk shake if you want ice cream in it. That's a frappe here."

"Frappe? As in rhymes with crap?" I say, hoping he'll drop the English lesson, but it doesn't work.

"Yep. From the French. They pronounce it 'fra-pay.' Originally a Greek drink, coffee and milk shaken with ice. Curiously, what they serve here called a milkshake is closer to the original Greek concoction, no ice cream added. So, they've got it backwards. No surprise there."

"I'll try to remember. Frappies aren't crappy."

"Good mnemonic."

Knee monic? Think I'll shut up now.

HARRY

Jay heads off to bunk in the camper about 10:00 p.m., after watching TV for three hours. Grace only gets two channels here. "No cable?" he had asked her.

"Neighbah's have it. Not me. Only watch the news," she answered.

"Got a DVD machine, though. Ya can rent movies in town. I go for the old black and white teah-jerkahs. Got some of those inside if ya want."

To his credit, Jay just said, "TV's okay," and skipped whatever snide comments he was thinking.

When he headed for the camper, I told him, "I'll be along later; Grace and I need a few hours to get caught up."

He nodded and gave us each a hug. In the dusky light, I could see Grace tear up and felt myself do the same.

I seldom lie down before midnight. Waste of time. I'd rather read. Never know how many years are left and, in my case, how many years I'll be able to read and remember anything.

Still shaking from earlier. The three beers chilled me out some, but memory suddenly clicking back in always startles me. You'd think I'd be used to it by now, but I'm not. It's like being in a dark room when suddenly the lights come on without warning. Takes a while to adjust.

It's so good to be here with Grace. There's one name I doubt I'll ever forget. We go back too far, or just far enough, maybe. Can't get used to the gray hair, though. Always colored it auburn. Pretty nice as I recall.

"Jay's a cute kid, Harry. Happy he goes for the birds. Know Oliver never did. How are ya doin' out there on the shaky side?"

"West coast is okay. Not shaking lately. Down south in California it shakes a little all the time. Up north it's building toward the big one, 9.0 or better. Doubt there'd be anything standing after that. Nothing left but houseboats riding a one hundred-foot tsunami. Make quite a picture."

"Hmmph. Thanks for the geology lesson, Harry, but ya know what I'm askin'. Don't duck it."

"I know. Should never have left, Grace. Back here I know where I am. Hell, most of the time, I even know who I am. Out there, nothing's familiar."

"What's Abby say?"

"The same, we never should have left."

"Then why not come back?"

"Oliver won't have it, and I don't think Abby wants to fight him. It's not in her."

"And you?"

"Don't get to vote. I go in and out. Sometimes I'm there, sometimes not."

"Seem good to me."

"That's a laugh. You might recall you just stopped me from breaking and entering."

"True enough, but I mean now. Right now. You seem like ya got it all togethah. What happened?"

"Don't know. Maybe the dip in the lake and the way it smells. They say scents key into long-term memory. Sounds too. I heard my loons."

"Ow-ah loons, Harry."

"Yes, Grace. Our loons."

"Will you call Abby?"

"No, don't think I will. Would just put her in the middle between me and Oliver."

"Sounds like she already is."

"I've been thinking about it the past few hours. Have to do my thinking when everything clicks now. I know she'll be worried, but maybe all that worry will help her stand up to Oliver."

"Could go the othah way."

"I suppose. Truth is, I'm not ready to go back to my cell yet. I'm enjoying the freedom. And I'm enjoying the hell out of my road trip with Jay."

"Might be Jay is too."

"Tell me what to do, Grace. You know me better than anyone, and I know you believe in taking chances. You've been doing just what you please for as long as I can remember."

"Hah! I guess that's so. I've had an interestin' life, and I nevah took no for an answer. Have to tell ya, though, I'm worried about ya travelin' all over hell's half acres with the boy, even if he does have a cell phone. What if ya get lost? What then? And what about yah bum leg? Abby wrote yah'd been in an accident. Wrote back I was sorry to hear it. Ya seem to get around okay, but what about drivin'?"

"My leg's just fine as long as it's an automatic. I may drive slower than I used to, but I always get where I'm going. If I get confused, I'll do the usual: pull over and take a nap. Then figure it out. Always comes to me in time."

"For now, Harry. For now. But what happens when it don't anymoah?"

"Think I still have time on that. And I have Jay. He's a bright kid. And he's got the GPS thing to help us steer straight."

"Maybe so. Maybe so. Tell you what, old friend, let me sleep on it. Maybe I'll have an idea or two."

ROSE

As she circled the Reservoir, taking the mile-and-a-half upper jogging track at a ten minute pace, Rose tried to imagine what Jeremy was doing. He might be skateboarding, or playing one of his annoying video games, or jumping off the end of their dock to cannonball whichever of his friends was visiting. The thought made her smile. He was where he belonged, back home in Seattle, despite his father's insistence he spend time with her. But Jackson hadn't phoned, and that was surprising. He might be too angry to speak, but she knew he would call soon and try to mend fences. Either that or he had talked his girlfriend into playing mom for two months. When was he going to Africa? Rose couldn't remember for certain. Jackson had been vague. Maybe a week or two. She could call, but that would invite the very argument she wanted to avoid, or at least postpone.

So, what was Jeremy doing right now? Not running, that's for certain. She tried on many occasions to interest him, even promising to jog along slowly, but he would have none of it. Jeremy knew she was capable of running the Reservoir Loop in under nine minutes, and he was proud of her speed, but he did not like the looks her Spandex outfits drew from the men on the track and had said as much.

"What do you want me to run in?" she had asked him. "A sweat suit? Way too hot, even in winter."

The truth was she liked being looked at, even by the fat, balding joggers she lapped once, sometimes twice. Then there were the middle-aged men who jogged desperately, trying to lose the paunch, and pushed themselves to match her pace. Rose teased them by slowing a bit to give them a good look then she would sprint ahead, leaving them to watch her buttocks pump as she pulled away. Occasionally, a much younger man would come up alongside and match her stride for stride. This was what she liked best, knowing the questions that would come: 'What are you doing later?' or 'Big Loop?'—the six-mile track through the park's North Woods. To the former she would make her excuses, but to the latter, she would say, "You're on," then laugh when she coasted to the top of Heartbreak Hill a dozen paces in the lead, only to sprint away like a gazelle down the curving slope while the muscular man fought to control his descent.

On rare occasions, if the young man was suitably impressed, and if he asked sweetly enough, she would stop with him for a cold, nonalcoholic drink and share a park bench for a while. But she could never resist a final tease when asked for more. "Dear boy," she would say, "I'm nearly old enough to be your mother." When he refused to believe it, she would produce her driver's license from her zippered armband and hold it out, concealing her address with her thumb. The look he gave then was the most delicious; a look that said it doesn't matter, I want you anyway.

But every man would spoil it by speaking. Rose would always leave then, running off to home and a cool shower. Well, almost always.

JEREMY

Next morning I'm up before the sun. Harry is still sleeping. Grace too, I guess. There's just a faint glow to light up the lake, foggy with mist. Kind of spooky not to be able to see much more than ten feet in front of me. I can hear fish jumping but can't tell where. I take a seat at the end of the dock and stick my feet in the water, ripples running out in all directions. It's warm compared to the air.

At first, there is no sound at all. So strange. Lake Washington is always noisy, even in Juanita Bay. This absolute silence is weird. Then I hear a faraway slap-slap slap-slap that keeps getting nearer. Seems to be coming from my right, but the fog messes it up. Could be coming from in front of me. The sound gets louder and louder till I see a tiny blue kayak appear ghost-like and beach a few feet away.

"Mahnin'," Grace says. "'Spected you to be up by now. Don't suppose you'd be hungry, would ya?"

"Starving. But Harry's not awake yet."

"Course not. Won't be up for hours, if I remembah correctly. We'll save some pancake battah. Nobody goes away hungry from Grace's table. You too young to drink coffee? Got some ready to brew."

"I'm not too young! But...well...I've never tried coffee."

"Ya like coffee ice cream?"

"Yes, ma'am."

"Don't call me, ma'am. I work for a livin'. You can call me Grace like everyone else. Anyways, if you like coffee ice cream, you'll like coffee. Just have to put enough cream and sugah in it. Take it black myself. Harry, though, he likes his with cream and sugah too, so you'll be in good company."

HARRY

I lie in bed listening to Grace and Jay. She's right I should still be asleep. Instead I'm worrying about what happens next. Sometime in the middle of the night all the puzzle pieces came together, and it scared the hell out of me. It's been four days since Jay and I drove away from JFK. For all intents and purposes, I'm a kidnapper, though the Alzheimer's might keep me out of jail. Not entirely sure about that, but I'm even less sure about what to do now. Drive back to JFK? What good would that do? The kid's mother isn't there, though she might have left a phone number with security. Maybe I should force Jay to cough up one of his parent's phone numbers. He might refuse but I'll bet Grace could wheedle it out of him.

That would get me arrested in New Hampshire instead of New York. Some improvement but not much. Maybe Grace could make the call and give me a head start. But what if Jay is telling the truth, his mother doesn't answer and his father in Africa can't check often? Convenient for me to think he's not lying. Too convenient, in my opinion. Suspect he's telling half-truths.

So, what's the real truth, the whole truth, so help me God? Obvious. I want our little journey to continue. Jay does too. Otherwise, he'd be calling Mom and Dad every day, or at least talking about it. But he's not. Instead, he's been using my rotting memory to suit his purpose. And he's been keeping up the gramps/grandson-off-birding tale with Grace. Ironically, I think his deception is more truthful than a full confession would be. For me as well. Never really liked kids his age, but maybe they grow on you. Think I'm growing on him too. I suppose it really is true that we're like grandfather and grandson. Enough to make me feel less guilty about deceiving Grace anyway.

What's that gambling aphorism: roll the dice and let the chips fall where they may? Think that's just what I'll do.

JEREMY

"'Bout time you were out of bed," Grace says when Harry pops into the cabin looking for a cup of coffee. "Saved some for ya. Hungry? Got plenty of battah left."

"You must have made a double batch, judging from Jay's bulging belly. Better not go swimming for a while, Kid. Grace's flapjacks will sink you like a stone."

"Insultin' my cookin' is unlikely to get you fed, old man. Bettah watch yahself."

Grace still gives Harry a smile. She seems to like sparring with him.

After we watch Harry wolf down a big stack of pancakes, we take our cups of coffee down to the beach and sit looking out at the lake. The sun has burned off most of the fog. Just a few wisps left. Grace brings a bag of peanuts with her. She whistles and two chipmunks appear out of nowhere. One has a healed cut on his forehead, and the other is missing half his tail.

"Stumpy and Scahface," she calls them then holds out a peanut between her thumb and forefinger. Scarface is first to take the nut from her hand. Stumpy hangs back. "Probably doesn't trust you. They'ah used to havin' me to themselves."

Scarface runs the peanut in and out of his mouth several times before stuffing it in his left cheek. Grace says that's because he needs to slime it up so he can get more in. She holds out a second, and he takes it, repeating the in-and-out process, and stuffing the nut in his right cheek. Then he takes one last peanut between his teeth and runs off to hide them.

Stumpy is still holding back, but when Grace bends down and holds out the nut as far from us as she can, he snatches it and runs off to one side. He comes back for another and another then takes off in the opposite direction from where Scarface disappeared into the bushes.

"You'ah turn," Grace tells me, handing me the bag of peanuts.

"Do they bite?"

"Yep. Not that hard though. Still got all ten." She holds up her hands and wiggles her fingers.

Scarface is back chattering at us. I take a peanut and hold it out low to the ground. He runs away but sits up on his hind legs and watches me.

Grace says, "Be patient. He'll come to ya."

After a moment, Scarface takes a few quick steps then stops again. His tail is twitching a mile a minute. Then he lunges for the peanut but gets my finger instead. I snatch my hand back, and he grabs the nut and scampers away.

Harry and Grace are laughing it up. "That hurt," I say, looking at my finger. No blood though.

"Just nipped ya. Do that to me all the time. Try again but don't hold the peanut so tight. And don't flinch."

I do what she says, and this time Scarface takes the peanut from me and stands his ground waiting for another. I try with Stumpy too, but he won't come that close. Have to toss the peanuts to him. After a while, the chipmunks get tired of making return trips and leave us alone.

"You boys up for a campin' trip?" Grace asks after a while.

Harry gives her a funny look. "What do you have in mind?"

"Spent the night tossin' and turnin', old friend, don't mind tellin' ya. Don't know this is a good idea, but what the hell. As long as Jay can call me if ya get into moah trouble than ya can handle, why don't the two of ya take the campah and drive west. Must be plenty of birds ya can see along the way. When ya get back to Seattle, let me know and I'll fly out and drive it back. Always wanted to camp out west. Not sure I like gettin' on a plane. Nevah have befoah. But if I don't do it pretty soon, I nevah will."

"Cool!" I say and look up at Harry's face. There are tears in his eyes.

He reaches up to wipe them away then leans over to kiss Grace on the cheek. "Thanks, old girl. I owe you."

"Give us a kiss then, a propah kiss, on the lips. Don't get that many chances anymoah. Gotta take'em when I can get'em."

I watch at first then turn my head when the kiss lasts longer than I can stand. As I look out at the lake, the pair of loons cruises by silently.

ABBY

Now is all we ever have. At least that's what I kept telling myself.

The past few years of watching Harry decline had brought me to truly understand how fleeting life is, how fragile.

"Here today, gone tomorrow," they say. We toss off these words as if they mean nothing, but they mean so much when tomorrow really is tomorrow, and not some far off object near the vanishing point of perspective.

Today, tomorrow is just a place I have to go, wake up to see what's left of Harry. Some days it's as if a miracle has happened. I hear him call out, "Abby, where the hell are my shoes?"

"My dear, wherever you left them," comes laughing out of me. I can't stop it. I don't want to stop it. I want to scream my joy for one more day of clarity.

"I found them," he calls back, and these simple words, these words that might have irritated me a few short years ago, now fill me with the surety that my prayers have been answered, at least for today.

But tomorrow always comes. I find him rummaging in the garage for something that no longer exists, some box of student papers that he simply must have, some old book containing arcane words and phrases that only he could care about. Frustration twists his face into anger at a world which no longer bends to his will, no longer cares whether he comes or goes. I care, I tell him. Let me help. And we turn the garage upside down one more time looking for his lost memory.

Oliver tells me I have to learn to care less, reason more. That Harry would be better off in a nursing home. He says they're not bad places; Harry would adjust.

He's wrong. Harry would wither and die like the plant on his desk he forgets to water. It would just happen sooner. Then I would be alone. Why hasten the inevitable? That time will come soon enough.

I will miss him, this man who has been my life for 30 years and more, this crotchety, cantankerous, sweet man; a man Oliver may never know, never meet, his memory of his father stuck at 8-years-old when Harry walked out of his life that first time. You can't blame a child for harboring anger, but Oliver is no longer a child; it is past time to set aside childish things. And I still have hope. Maybe under all the anger he does love Harry. He never says the words, "I love you, Dad," but perhaps there's more shared in their ritual handshake than Oliver would admit.

I said that "Who are you?" is the hardest question, and it is, but the pain varies with the where and how of it. There's the casual breakfast exchange, his "Good morning..." pause while he searches for my absent name brings me up short each time. Or the midday disembodied voice echoing from the garage, "Oh, uh, Honey..." That makes me smile, but wanly, for I know his endearment is an attempt to spare my feelings, my name missing once more. Then there are the moments looking into my eyes from across the dinner table. He says nothing, but I can still read it, "Who are you?"

Worst is the bedroom "who," the naked skin-to-skin "who." From that there is no escape. I turn and bury my face in the pillow. Tears come. He takes my hand and says he's sorry. Every time. Sorry. But he doesn't know why. Except that sometimes he does. Sometimes I hear, "Sorry," then a moment later, "Abby." Worst of the worst, to not know then to know suddenly, carrying both the loss and losing in tandem, compounding pain, breaking over the two of us as we hold on fiercely to what little is left. And yet, this one brief moment, recurring, is also the best of what remains. I will savor it, treasure it, for as long as it lasts.

HARRY

It's late afternoon before we get back from returning my rental car to the Manchester Airport. Tomorrow is Tuesday. On Wednesday we'll start driving west. Grace drops us off at the cabin then heads to town to do some grocery shopping, while Jay and I get ready for some bird watching. He helps me launch Grace's beat-up aluminum rowboat from the ramp and tows it 50 feet over the sandy shallows to the dock, while I walk back along the shore. Not sure how to clamber in with my bionic leg. It's a nuisance to take on and off; otherwise I'd do that. But I'd probably drop it overboard. Jay suggests sitting on the dock and swinging my legs in, both to one side of the middle seat. That works pretty well, all except for my butt, which is still on the dock.

He climbs into the boat and sits, straddling the seat with his back to me, and plants his feet firmly and says, "Grab my shoulder with your right hand then push off from the dock with your left."

"Hope I don't end up in the drink," I answer and execute the proposed maneuver. I come to rest toppled backward, my butt in the bilge and my head whacked on the rear seat. But I'm in the boat.

"You okay?"

"Peachy. Don't sit there like a dunce. Help me up!"

He laughs then stands just forward of the middle seat and leans to take my hand to haul me up. Stronger than he looks. Between Jay pulling on my left arm, and me pulling on the gunnel with my right, we manage to slide me upright again. I take a look at what we've accomplished then realize I'm looking at the bow. "Shit. Backwards."

"What?"

"Facing the wrong way. Can't row like this. The bow has to be behind me."

"So, turn around."

"Hell of a lot easier to say than do."

Jay scratches his head like some old-timer pondering what to do next. Then he scrambles back on the dock and sits, looping his legs over the gunnels, one to each side of the middle seat. "Scoot back toward me then lift your legs and swing them over. I'll keep you from falling backwards."

It works. I look up to see him grinning from ear to ear, quite pleased with himself. Me, I'm frustrated by my ineptness. "Well, don't stand there grinning like an idiot. Go get the oars."

"Aye, aye, sir!" he says and salutes.

"Wiseass," I yell toward him as he runs down the dock.

JEREMY

Harry's a pretty good rower. Keeps the boat going straight. When I ask how he does it, he says you just pick out a point on the opposite shore and row directly away from it. Guess that makes sense. He checks over his shoulder once in a while and adjusts the course, but mostly he keeps rowing.

When the boat beaches, I hop out and pull it up onto the sand as far as it will go with Harry still aboard. I sit behind him again to keep him from flopping backwards while he swings his legs out, and I run around to help pull him up and out of the boat. Walking on sand is harder than Harry thought so I steady him till we find the path inland. As we walk toward the marsh, Harry points out the trees and bushes, naming them: blueberry, swamp alder, birch, sugar maple, white oak, black oak, white pine, red pine, larch.

All around us birds are singing. I hear both vireo and ovenbird, though neither of us can spot one among all the branches and leaves. But there are so many others I don't know. "What's the bird whistling at us? Sounds like 'feeee beeee.'"

"Black-capped Chickadee. He's saying, 'yoo hoo' to let the ladies know he's here. Keep listening and he'll tell you his name, 'chickadee-dee-dee-dee-dee-dee-dee.'"

"What's the one laughing at us?"

"You don't know? White-breasted Nuthatch. You must have heard them out west."

"I've seen one, but mostly we get the smaller Red-breasted Nuthatch. They sort of quack like a duck."

"Hmmph. Sounds more like a mechanical doll crying to me. 'Wah, wah, wah.' Kind of monotonous and nasal."

Harry locked his leg, so he limps along behind me pointing the way any time the path branches. No problem with his memory today. After 100 yards or so, the ground under foot is wet and spongy. More bird calls I recognize: chickadee whistles, nuthatch laughs, and one new one, "Pe-ew, pe-ew, pe-ew."

I stop and look up into the branches but there are too many leaves. Can't see the bird.

Harry looks up too. "Not one you should recognize, mainly an east-of-the-Mississippi denizen. Tufted Titmouse. Doesn't like the smell of us. He's saying, 'Pee-you, pee-you, pee-you.'"

I roll my eyes. More of Harry's lame attempts at humor.

HARRY

Jay and I walk some distance from the beach before we begin to glimpse snatches of marsh through the trees. I point out a young family of Red-bellied Woodpeckers, mom and dad with their fiery nape plumage, and their fledglings just showing the blush of red that will ignite by late summer.

"See the teenagers?" I ask him. "They know how to fly but haven't a clue where they're going."

Jay leans in next to me and stretches up to see where I'm pointing. "I know the feeling," he says offhandedly.

It takes me a moment to make the connection. "Me too," I answer.

"Guess we're just like them, testing our wings, fledging. Making it up as we go along."

He turns to look at me, only inches from my face, and the intensity of his gaze startles. The way my granddaughter looks just before she gives me a kiss. Then he punches me in the arm playfully and scampers ahead.

Another bend in the path and we're at the edge of the marsh, the spongy ground now soggy and pockmarked here and there with shallow puddles. Jay's sneakers are half-submerged. I left my prosthetic shoe in the boat, so the mechanical foot sinks deep and makes me list to one side. Out of the corner of my eye, I see the looping flight of a Belted Kingfisher and hear his accompanying staccato clicking. Jay is looking the other way so doesn't see him. "Know that bird call?" I ask to test him.

"Kingfisher!"

"Right. Which one?"

"There's more than one?"

"Three in the U.S., Belted, Ringed, and Green. I've seen them all, but only one lives here."

"Belted?"

"Yep. Trick question. The other two are only found in South Texas along the Mexican border. And, of course, in Mexico. They sound a lot alike though. Not exactly melodic."

"Is Texas good for birding?"

"Just about all it's good for in my opinion. Oh, and the Dixie Chicks. They're really hot. But, yeah, the Desert Southwest is loaded with birds you can't see anywhere outside Mexico, especially along the Rio Grande. They stray a short distance over the border, but that's it. In Texas, Big Bend National Park, South Padre Island, and the World Birding Center are must visits if you want to add to your life list."

"Could we go back to Seattle that way?"

"Phew. Long road to nowhere and hot as hell in summer. Won't say no, though. Let me think about it."

"I'm in no rush to get home. Dad won't be back till late August."

"Know what the word 'naïve,' means?"

"Not really." He looks like he does though, just ducking my implication.

"What happens when Dad figures out you're AWOL?"

Shoulder shrug is all the answer I get. Jay wanders off along the shore, while I trudge behind trying to keep my left foot from sinking into the muck. Around the next bend, a fallen tree blocks the path. Jay has vaulted over and moved on. This is far enough for me. I settle down to sit and scan the marsh for wildlife.

"Watch out for snakes," I holler ahead after he disappears among the trees. That'll give him something to worry about. Mostly garter snakes in these woods, though I've seen a black snake occasionally, and they're pretty aggressive. Been bitten more than once over the years. But the snake population has dropped along with their prey, frogs, and newts. Not sure why, and the experts don't seem to have an answer. Can't blame acid rain for everything. How about all the mini-mansions replacing torn-down cabins with heavily fertilized, crabgrass-free lawns stretching down to the water's edge?

When I was young, the lake teemed in early summer with tadpoles that slowly grew legs and lost their tails by fall. Newts sunned themselves in the shallows, crayfish sheltered under every rock, and bullfrogs croaked me to sleep at night. All gone now from the main part of the lake. Haven't seen a single tadpole beyond the marsh for years, nor heard a bullfrog, nor startled a newt, nor had a toe nipped by a crayfish. The deep marsh is their only remaining refuge, courtesy of the beaver family, which the Department of Environmental Services keeps trying to capture. Damn fools. You'd think they'd know better.

Still worrying what to do about Jay. His dad, and even his mom, are bound to come unglued once they realize he's missing. What will they do? Go to the police? The FBI? What would they say? Our son is missing? With no place to begin a search and Jay nearly 14, would the authorities do anything at all? A few bulletins, maybe a distributed photo or the kid's face on a milk carton. Just another runaway. Doubt anyone will try looking for Jay, not seriously anyway. If we keep a low profile, we might actually make it to Seattle.

Have to use cash for purchases. Don't want to leave a plastic trail. Shit, the rental car. Put that on my VISA. Probably got charged three hours ago. Will it read JFK or Manchester Airport? No idea. I doubt

Abby or Oliver will check till tonight at least. But I bet they can trace the car to New Hampshire even if the charge reads New York. Really don't want to get Grace in any deeper than she already is. Can't come clean with her either. She'd never let us take the camper if she knew the whole story.

What is it they say about telling lies? You have to remember every detail, and sooner or later you get caught. Not as sharp as I used to be either. Probably be sooner rather than later. Maybe a bit of misdirection will work. When Abby realizes I'm in New Hampshire, she might think of Grace, but she's more likely to expect me to show up at the college. Maybe I'll hit the ATMs in Plymouth and take out a cash advance on my Visa. Then I'll stop by the school and find someone who Abby might think to call. I'll say I bought a camper and am off birding and heading north into Maine along the coast. Probably hit Acadia National Park first. That'll throw her off our trail. The park is famous for Atlantic seabirds. We've been there together and driven all the way to Newfoundland. If she looks at all, that's the road she'll take. But maybe she won't. Maybe Abby will be reassured I'm back on my own turf. Oliver is another story, but he's so tied up in himself, I doubt he'd let Abby push him into the trip east. Wish I were wrong.

JEREMY

The marsh is way cool. Frogs leap into the water as I pass, pale-green ones the size of a quarter, medium-sized, green-brown ones with big spots, and huge deep-green bullfrogs. Big splashes when they go in. Didn't see any frogs in the lake, but there are lots here.

When I notice Harry isn't behind me anymore, I backtrack and find him resting on a log. I decide to leave him be and go on exploring. The marsh is about 100 feet across and filled with dead trees. Most of them have lots of holes, small holes probably made by the Hairy Woodpeckers I see, and larger holes you could stick your fist through that must have been made by Pileated Woodpeckers. I haven't seen one but have heard them laughing and hammering deeper in the woods. One hole looks like the entrance to a nest. It's easily four inches in diameter. Don't know what would need such a large opening.

Every few feet along the marsh newts lie motionless in an inch or two of water, especially where the sun hits. On the far shore, a heron stalks fish. It takes a slow step then stands real still, head tilted to one side with an eye toward the surface. It stabs at the water with its beak and comes up with a minnow. Bet it takes a lot of those to make a meal.

I jump when I hear a loud slap on the water. A beaver swims by, eyeing me, then slaps his tail again and dives. There are lots of birds. Kingfishers swoop back and forth, sometimes diving for a fish, but mostly chattering at me. "I've got just as much right to be here as you," I say to them. But maybe that's not true. I know from school and my bird books that habitat keeps shrinking. We're the problem.

That's what Harry says too. This brings me back to wondering about his memory. Will Harry really be able to drive us across country? He seems to know where he is right now, but I'm not sure it will last. Guess I can always call Mom or Dad if I have to. Still no word from him. I'm checking voicemail once in a while but otherwise leave my phone turned off. Don't want it to ring. Harry might ask me something I'd have to lie about.

Dad must not have called Mom yet either. All hell will break loose when that happens. Hope we're on the road and a long way from here by then.

HARRY

Back at the boat, I clamber in with a bit of help from my young sidekick. But with my weight on the middle seat, he can't budge the boat off the shore. Jay looks disgusted. "Guess we should have moved the boat first," he says.

"How about if I move to the back? Give me a hand."

We successfully maneuver me by sliding my rump along the riveted gunnels and plopping it unceremoniously onto the rear seat. That's just enough ballast shift to allow Jay to finagle the boat into the water, taking turns pulling and pushing on either end.

"Your turn to row," I say. "I'm not up for any more ass-scraping today."

With the smile he gives me, you'd think I'd handed him the keys to a new Mercedes. Hell, he could have rowed down the lake too, if he'd just asked. His rowing, though, leaves a lot to be desired. Like a drunken sailor, he weaves back and forth, pulling on the oars unevenly. The return trip takes twice as long. Still, he looks pleased with himself and only a bit sheepish when he rams the dock.

"Careful, boy. That dock has to last me anothah twenty yeahs."

"Sorry, Grace," he shouts up to the cabin at her. Then he bends down to inspect the ding he's made, holding up his thumb and forefinger close together to indicate it's a small ding. I know she's just razzing him, and if Jay had ever seen Grace row her boat, he'd know it too. Amazes me the dock is still in one piece.

Getting out proves to be harder than getting in. Jay isn't strong enough to lift me and my bionic leg battery has died. Must have forgotten to charge it. Grace can't help because of her bum back.

"Pull the boat out to the end of the dock," I tell him. In the meantime, I shed my shirt and trousers, and remove my prosthetic, carefully handing it to Grace. She sets it where it can't fall in the water. I shimmy my sore butt to the far side of the seat and roll into the lake. Must make quite a picture, because when I surface, the two of them are laughing themselves silly.

"Happy to amuse you." I swim to shallow water and stand, then put my one good foot onto the middle step of the dock ladder and hoist myself up, my arms and one leg doing double duty. Planting my stump on the dock, I lift my good leg over and get a foot under me. Grace and Jay watch the show.

"Don't stand there like a couple of ninnies. Give me a hand."

"How?" Jay asks.

"Come grab my left arm and pull for all you're worth."

"How about me?" Grace asks. "Anything I can do?"

"Nope. You'd just pull your back out or end up in the lake. How about getting me a towel?"

Jay and I manage to get me upright, down to the end of the dock, and onto one of the lawn chairs.

"You okay?" he asks.

"Peachy. Go get me a beer. Sun must be over the yardarm by now."

He disappears in a flash. Good kid. I close my eyes and feel the sun's late-day warmth. Life is good. I watch as Jay scampers up the cabin steps, then chuckle when I hear Grace scold him for waiting on me. She shouts out, "Who was yah servant in the last war, Harry?"

I smile as I drift off.

JEREMY

"What's a ninny?" I ask Grace as we sit on the dock steps and talk quietly. Harry is asleep.

"A fool," Grace replies. "Don't make much sense, huh? Ya'd have to ask his highness wheah it comes from."

"Comes from 16th century England," Harry mumbles then opens his eyes. "Diminutive of the word, innocent. Something a mother or father might have called a young child. Applies to children in general, though probably not to teenagers. Might apply to ancients like Grace and me in our dotage now that I think about it."

"Speak for yahself, Harry. I'm still hittin' on all eight cylindahs."

"You are at that. Think I'm down to hitting on four like a cheap foreign import. Remember the Yugo? That would be me. Or maybe I'm just an old Buick with a blown head gasket. Sometimes the pistons fire, sometimes they don't. Pretty good lately, though. No complaints."

Harry has been good lately. Hope it lasts.

"What would make a four inch hole in a dead tree?" I ask Harry once he seems completely awake and Grace leaves us to go fix dinner. Meat loaf, baked potatoes, and cornon the cob. Actually, she said, "Cahn on the cawb." Might sound funny but makes me hungry just thinking about it.

"You and your *non sequiturs*. Or are you testing my memory?"

"Just testing. Lots of woodpecker holes in the swamp trees. Mostly small except this one."

"It's not a swamp. It's a marsh. Well actually it's a beaver pond, but it used to be a seasonal wetlands, dry in summer. And if the DES bozos ever capture the beavers, it will be seasonal once again. Then what little remains of the frogs and newts will probably be history."

"What's the difference?"

"What? Between a swamp and a marsh?"

I nod.

"A marsh is all about partially submerged vegetation. The roots and water plants provide habitat for frogs and newts and a nursery for game fish like bass, pickerel, perch, and pike if the marsh connects to a river or lake. A swamp is different. Trees that grow in and around the water are as important to the habitat as the water plants. Bogs are like marshes but the bottom is spongy with peat moss. You can sink in up to your waist or worse. And generally there's not as much water. In fact, sometimes there's no open water at all, just peat soup."

"So, what made the big hole?"

"Hard to say. Might be a Pileated Woodpecker nest, but they're usually more secretive. If I had to guess, I'd say a Pileated made the original hole then a wood duck did a bit of trimming and took up residence. Have you seen wood ducks in Washington?"

"They're the really colorful ducks, right? Lots of green, yellow, orange, and blue?"

"Yup. Lots out in Washington. Harder to find here. They keep out of sight and prefer small ponds to open water. I see them in Minnesota on quiet lakes, but they stay hidden in the reeds as much as possible. Make yourself useful, and go get me another beer."

"*Non sequitur!*"

"Right. Now go get me that beer."

HARRY

Funny kid. Reminds me of myself, a born wiseass. Useful for beer-fetching though, and as a stand-in for my missing leg. Even offered to plug it in. I'll miss him when this charade is over. Or maybe I won't. Maybe I'll forget him as soon as he goes back to Dad. We need to talk this out while I'm still clear enough to do it.

When Jay returns with my Budweiser, I launch into a speech.

"You and I need to come to an agreement." My tone is serious and the resulting look he gives me is wary, even scared, like he might bolt. Occurs to me I need to be careful what I say. Would he take off on me too? Maybe I'm not reading him correctly. Or maybe he's thought this all through and values his freedom over everything else. I can relate to that. I lighten my words and expression. "Relax. I'm not about to turn you in. We're both on the lam now. Know what that means?"

He shakes his head but is otherwise non-communicative, facial expression neutral.

"It means we're running from the law. For you, that's Mom and Dad. For me, it's Abby and Oliver. So, here's the deal. We'll drive to Seattle

ADRIAN R. MAGNUSON

following our noses and taking our time. If you want to go south, we can do that. I'd recommend a winding path, so in case someone comes looking we'll be hard to find. We've got about six weeks if you want to be back in Seattle in time for school."

Jay nods his head. Whether he's agreeing he wants to be back west before September, or agreeing to the whole plan, I can't tell. His expression hasn't changed.

"We need some ground rules, though. First, I want you to admit you haven't been telling me the complete truth. Right?"

Another nod, this time accompanied by what might be resignation.

"And you have to begin right now to correct that. No more lies. No more half-truths."

"I haven't been lying to you."

"Yes, you have."

Jay opens his mouth to answer my accusation, but I hold up my hand to cut him off and continue, "Just once or twice and not about anything important. You may remember telling me you don't know exactly where your mother lives. That was a lie, yes?"

His hung head and sheepish look answer louder than words could.

"I figured as much. I thought you'd tell me when you were ready. Guess you just needed a little prodding. Fact is, I don't give a shit."

His head comes up. His look is searching. Am I telling the truth?

"I mean it. I don't care. It's clear to me you and your mother don't get along, and your father has set the two of you up to have to deal with each other. Didn't work, did it?"

A wry smile but a smile nonetheless.

"Thought so. But here's the thing. Your dad will be highly pissed when he finds out we're traveling together. And he will find out. There is no way we can pull this off and show up in Seattle on your doorstep with no one the wiser."

The kid's back to worrying; his body language screams it, but I ignore him.

"I suspect my wife and son already know. They just don't know exactly where to look, and I have a plan or two in mind to keep them from figuring it out. But I'm going to need your help. And I'm going to need you to be completely honest from now on. Deal?"

Big sigh, followed by an emphatic nod.

"Say it."

"It's a deal. Sorry I lied to you. I didn't know what else to do."

"No apology necessary. Would have done the same thing in your position. But no more, deal?"

"Deal."

"Okay. Here's the big problem. I won't stay clear-minded for six weeks. Hell, I might not make it to tomorrow. You have to be my memory. You have to know the plan and be able to tell me. If I seem lost, give me directions. If I don't remember why we're driving west, tell me the whole story over and over again till I believe you. If I forget who you are, remind me. Tell me about Abby and Oliver too. Last, but not least, if you get scared or you can't handle me, bail out. Make sure you always have enough cash in your pocket to get home. Deal?"

He nods. There are tears in his eyes, and I can feel them welling up in mine. "One more thing. Wednesday we'll head for my *alma mater*, Plymouth State University. I'll leave you in the car and wander the hallowed halls for a while, chatting up whoever remembers me. I plan to tell them I'm heading for Maine to camp and do some birding. Then I'll go to an ATM and take out a credit card advance. That information will get back to Abby and Oliver. They'll know I was in Plymouth and begin searching there. We'll do that each time we take an unexpected turn from the obvious path. They'll think we kept going straight, when actually we headed in a completely different direction. For example, just before we turn south to Texas after traveling mainly west. That will throw off pursuit. Remind me if I forget, okay?"

"I will," Jay says, nodding ferociously and smiling to beat the band.

Fate willing, this just might work.

ABBY

I surfaced from sleep when the phone rang and knew it was Oliver. He was the only person who would call so late. Harry will be furious at having his sleep disturbed, I thought, my mind still numb and not thinking clearly. Oliver would leave a message. I turned over and jammed my head deep into the pillows and stretched out my arm to

Harry, but his absence jarred me awake. "What?" is all I could manage when I picked up.

"Abby?"

"Of course, Oliver. Who else would it be at this time of night? What time is it anyway?" Still groggy and still annoyed.

"It's 1:00 a.m. Sorry, we were out late with friends. I found Harry."

"Where?"

"New Hampshire."

As the news sunk in, I sat up in bed and brought my knees to my chin, trying to shake out the cobwebs. I hated being at this disadvantage. He knew something I didn't but was playing it out. Just tell me, damn you, I thought, but said, "New Hampshire? I don't understand. Did he call you?"

"Not exactly. He rented a car in New York and dropped it off at the Manchester Airport yesterday evening. I just checked the credit card history."

I shook my head. So you didn't find him, just where he's been, not where he is. That was a start anyway. "Can you book us flights tomorrow? I don't care what it costs."

Silence. Then he said what I should have expected.

"No, Abby. I can't go traipsing across country looking for Dad. I just thought you'd be happy knowing he's okay."

"How can he be okay? He probably thinks it's twenty years ago and he'll head for Plymouth State wondering where he left this semester's course schedule."

Was that laughter? Damn him. I wish he'd grow up. "It's not funny, Oliver."

"Okay, it's not funny to you, maybe. I get that. But it is funny to me. It's ironic. You're forgetting all those years he never spent time with me. He was too busy with his students or his current lover. You were neither the first nor the worst, but at least you stuck around. I forgave you for taking him from me, but I have not forgiven him for what he did to my mother. Not that he ever asked forgiveness. So now, when he leaves both of us to go back to his only true love, lording his knowledge over a bunch of pimply students, you'll have to understand why I think it's funny."

Clueless. Absolutely clueless. "Oliver, Oliver. How long will you nurse this hate? How many more years do you think are left? Harry's condition is progressive. You know that. There might only be a few remaining. You need to talk to him."

"No, I don't. I wouldn't give him the satisfaction."

"You just don't get it. You need to talk to Harry for your own sake, not for his. And for the sake of his grandchildren, who you haven't allowed to get to know him."

"Not going to happen, Abby. You can see Lainey and Nessa anytime you want. Harry can see them at Thanksgiving and Christmas like always. That's enough."

"Your stubbornness makes a mockery of those holidays, Oliver. Now that's irony."

"I'm stubborn! What about you? And what about Lainey and Nessa? Don't you think they'd like to see you? I thought that's why you wanted to come out to Washington in the first place, to be near us. If you put Dad in a supervised facility, you'd have the time to watch them grow up, and they'd have a grandmother again."

That stung. After Olivia died a few years ago, Harry and I were all who were left. "They need their grandfather too, Oliver." I slammed the phone down and pounded the bed with my fists, a poor substitute for pounding Oliver. Sleep would have to wait. Coffee first, then power up the computer and sign on to Expedia.

By 3:00 a.m. I had reserved a seat on a red-eye flight and a Hertz rental in Manchester. Plymouth State, here I come. Damned if I'd tell Oliver, I thought, then realized I'd need him to monitor the credit card account.

Back to bed, but sleep came fitfully, struggling with the questions that popped into my head. How would I find him? If he dropped off his rental car, he must have bought one, right? Who was helping him? Nigel? If so, Harry must be thinking clearly. For now anyway.

Ovenbird
Seiurus aurocapillus

Migration

JACKSON

Exhausted from surgery, but unable to sleep, Jackson left his tent to walk the field hospital grounds in the warm night air. The surrounding village slept quietly. As usual, his thoughts turned to Rose. He glanced at his watch, 2:00 a.m. It would be late yesterday evening in New York, if he had the time difference right, six hours during daylight savings. Rose would be up and running in the park, or maybe just back and showering off before going to dinner. Jackson missed her but feared her illness.

Years ago, he believed he could fix Rose, find that elusive combination of medications that would allow her the heights, albeit more subdued, and prevent the inevitable falls. Hubris led him to believe this. He had convinced himself and Rose as well.

Now he realized he had lacked the objectivity to help Rose. One marriage, one son, and ten years later, she left, saying he had failed her. She was right. It was a mistake, and at some point he stopped caring enough to keep fighting. Years of too-high highs and too-low lows had exhausted him. He knew that too. Now he wanted Rose back again, and he was trying to find a way to repair the breach. Not to reunite him with Rose, not yet, but to bring her and Jeremy together before it was too late.

Was this possible, he wondered? If Andrew were here, walking beside him, he would say no; it would only prolong the inevitable, a painful string of break ups and reunions that would eventually drive Jackson insane.

He knew Andrew was right, but it did nothing to squelch his desire. He had told Andrew recently, "I can't let her go. It may seem like a sickness. Hell, it may be a sickness. But I want her back. I know the future repeats the past, but I just don't care."

Jackson smiled, thinking of Andrew. He had been there for every beginning and every ending in his life. They started grade school together, attended the same prep school and university together, even dated the same girls and compared notes. And it was Andrew who introduced Jackson to Rose and stood up as best man at their wedding.

Growing up next door to each other, they were the heads and tails of the same coin all their childhood. Andrew was studious. Jackson liked getting his hands dirty. Andrew became vocal and outgoing, while Jackson grew quiet and withdrawn. Andrew became a trial lawyer, Jackson, a thoracic surgeon, his lack of social skills unnoticed by sedated patients.

Jackson wandered back to his tent, ready for sleep now, and he allowed himself another smile. Maybe Rose and Jeremy were out in the park looking for birds if the weather cooperated. Seven days had passed since his plane touched down in Johannesburg, the number he had promised himself he would let go by before he checked in. Not that he could have anyway, his cell phone was useless in the village. Later he would ride the weekly supply truck to the airstrip where there was a landline. Then he would call both Rose and Jeremy separately and compare notes. They would be just waking. Jackson wasn't expecting a miracle of motherly love, but he fervently hoped for détente.

ABBY

I arrived in Chicago at 6:00 a.m. and wandered the cavernous hallways of O'Hare Airport, my last words with Oliver still gnawing at me.

"Abby, you need to face facts," he had said.

But I couldn't. I would not accept the end of Harry's freedom without a fight.

Crossing from one concourse to another in search of my connecting gate, I passed a security checkpoint. Early travelers were beginning to trickle in, some hastily reassembling luggage overhauled by TSA agents, some slipping on shoes or sneakers, others threading belts into trousers. The effect was comical, Chaplinesque, but did little to lighten my mood. Attendants in closed storefronts lifted or pulled aside the bars part way that excluded us, we few potential shoppers ignored until whatever official opening time had been decreed.

As I made the turn onto Concourse C, I found myself alone in the hallway, save for a uniformed woman and man engaged in desultory cleaning. One swept imaginary bits of debris into a long-handled dustpan, the other emptied trashcans that appeared to be already empty. At 6:00 a.m., the airport was just waking up. I, on the other hand, had been awake for hours, worried that my sarcasm with Oliver might harden him further against his father, and possibly against me.

I shook my head to clear away remaining cobwebs and to pass judgment on Oliver's closed mind. I was glad to be alone in my quest. Oliver's presence would have been a constant irritant, and my ability to make decisions compromised by debating each one. Another advantage: he would only know what I chose to tell him. I could filter out pieces of information, the ones that would only distance him further from Harry. Was this dishonest? Perhaps, but necessary. In fact, I had already done so twice. First, when I withheld information about Harry's most recent savings account withdrawal, $4,000. Part of that was probably spent the same way I spent too much money last night, on a one-way ticket to the east coast. My extravagant airfare was the second thing Oliver would never know. He might guess, but he would not know. I would happily lie about it. He had online access to our joint credit card account, but not to our bank account. Like Harry, I had withdrawn traveling cash and used my debit card to purchase the ticket.

We had argued when Oliver suggested the three of us open a credit card account. He insisted that he had the software to help us budget and economize. Above all, he wanted to make sure we never had to pay interest on an unpaid balance. He would connect the credit card to his own bank account and pay the bill automatically. Then at the end of each month, he would send us an accounting of all our purchases laid out by category, and we would reimburse him by check.

What sounded helpful on the surface, I knew to be mere subterfuge. He wanted to keep tabs on us from his computer. "Sure," I told him. "Why not? And while we're at it, why not install webcams in our house. That way when I go out, you can check hourly to see if Harry is all right." Oliver missed the sarcasm but Harry didn't. While we watched Oliver ruminate over just where to place the cameras for maximum benefit, Harry added, "We'll be sure to install one in our bedroom so you can watch us get it on." The conversation went downhill from there, but Oliver got his way, though not in regards to the webcams. Oliver does seem to know when he's gone too far.

Deep in thought, I walked the concourse. The realization came slowly, Harry must have planned this trip for some time. It brought a smile to my lips. He was still in control, loosely, sporadically, but nevertheless, in control. Like a general marshaling his troops, Harry had soldiered his ducks into a line and marched them right under our noses. How funny. We had believed him incapable of remembering where he put his glasses, but he had executed a perfect plan, so far anyway. Just one exception, the credit card payment for a rental he was no longer using. But that left plenty of money to buy a car. He'd drive and stay at B&B's, where he could pay in cash, and hike the birding spots. Probably Maine, but unless he ran out of money, there was no way to know. My only hope was that when I located Nigel at the university, he was enlisted in Harry's plot, and I could convince him to betray Harry. But what if Nigel wasn't involved? Would Harry have gone to New Hampshire and not contacted his oldest friend and colleague? Might he have forgotten him? There was no way short of seeing Nigel face-to-face to know. He might be able to lie effectively at a distance, but in person, he would tell me the truth.

At 7:00 a.m., I phoned Oliver before boarding my flight to Manchester, one connection and ten hours distant. I chose the time on purpose, knowing he would be in the shower. There was some advantage to his precision and predictability. When his voicemail greeting ended, I left my not-so-short, but very sweet, message, "Good morning, dear. I'm calling from Chicago to ask two favors. First, since I'll be on the road soon looking for your father, I'd appreciate it if you would check every day for credit card purchases so we can trace his whereabouts and just possibly find him before something terrible happens. Second, he must have left the car at the airport, undoubtedly in short-term parking. Also undoubtedly, he has taken the parking stub with him. Have fun convincing the lot attendant it's only been a few days. That bill, dear, is yours. Ta ta for now."

HARRY

"Harry! What are you doing here in Plymouth? I thought you moved to Seattle."

Haven't a clue who this woman is. Plymouth? Must be the university. Long, empty hallway in a big building. Nothing looks familiar. Wait, I'm supposed to say I'm back to go birding with Nigel. Why is that? Can't remember.

"You're absolutely right," I say. "Couldn't stay away. I had to come back to my *alma mater*, Ms...ah, I seem to have forgotten your name. Sorry. Getting old is for the birds. Speaking of which, where might I find my old friend, Birds. Still chasing pretty coeds, I suppose."

She's looking at me as if I've lost my marbles. Better drop the hail-fellow-well-met act and tone it down a bit. "I'm just joshing you, ah..."

"It's Margaret! You don't remember? I know it's been a long time, and I'm sure I look a lot older, but still—"

"Of course! Margaret! How could I forget? And there it is right on your ID badge, Margaret from the Registrar's Office. Please forgive me. I'm getting forgetful in my old age, and I've been busy lately. Decided I needed a break, so I thought I'd come back to my old stomping grounds and do some bird watching. Even bought an old camper. Plan to head over to the Maine coast soon and wondered if Nigel might want to join me. We did a lot of hiking in our day and spotted birds many avid bird-watchers never see here in New England. Yes, indeed. You have to put in the field time if you want to see the rare ones."

There's that look again. Too professorial? But I need her to pass along this information. Why is that again? Ah, must be for Nigel, so he'll know where I am if I can't find him.

"Oh, I see. Well, you could check at the Boyd Science Center. Though I doubt Nigel is here today. He still keeps a file cabinet and has a small desk, and he comes in now and then and wanders the halls, but he spends most of his time in summer with his Canada Warblers. The bog out near Bear Pond...surely you must remember that. But...Harry, are you okay? You seem, I don't know, different."

"Of course, of course, Bear Pond. Yes, I'm fine. Never better. Thanks for asking. I'll just go over to the Boyd and see if he happens to be around today. Otherwise, I'll check the bog tomorrow."

"Well, okay. I'm sure you'll find Nigel busily counting and tagging. And don't forget your waders. Lots of rain lately. The ground will be saturated."

Still looks puzzled, maybe even worried. "Thank you, Margaret. Wonderful to see you again after all these years."

"Oh, Harry, it's wonderful to see you again as well. I've missed you."

She's smiling sweetly now, though she looks like she might cry at any minute. I haven't the faintest idea who she is, but she seems more or less satisfied. Didn't call me Professor; I must have known her socially. Useless rotten memory. Damn, now she looks like she's about to give me a hug. Instead, I take her hand and press it gently then turn to walk down the hallway.

"Uh…Harry? The science center is the other way."

"Right. Right." I turn back toward her, smiling and shaking my head. "Thank you again."

I feel her watching me depart and turn to wave. She waves back, but the confused look returns to cloud her expression. Oh, well, I passed along the information I needed to. Now if I can just figure out how to get out of the building and back to the car, I'll be all set. Left the hitchhiker to wait for me. Hope none of the campus cops have bugged him. What was his name again? Some sort of bird. Robin? No, that's not it. Goose? Wasn't that some ball player's name? How about Booby? I chuckle out loud.

Just before I reach the end of the long hallway, Margaret calls out, "Say hello to Abby for me. I hope she's well. And don't be a stranger. Come back and see me."

Abby? I push through the exit door, I turn and wave one last time. "I will." The door closes behind me. Who the hell is Abby? Just one more name I've forgotten. Frustrating, but I'm used to it.

Thirty minutes of wrong turns and dead ends lead me back where I began. Or, maybe it's someplace else, not sure. I look up as the surrounding buildings close in. I can feel panic rising. Sweat drips off my forehead, my heart races and my hands shake. Staring behind me, nothing looks familiar. I've been here, must have been. But nothing in memory matches. I'm frozen in place.

This has happened before. Lost and no idea what to do next. Better take a few deep breaths and try to calm down. Alright, genius, what do you do when you're lost? Backtrack. I walk to the closest corner and look both ways. No parking lot. I reverse. When I get to the end and look again in both directions, nothing is familiar. Wait! Is that the turnpike? Maybe. I go right, pass what looks like an apartment building then turn left, and there it is below me, the parking lot. Even though I can't see the car yet, I can at least breathe again.

Calm down, Harry. What is it the kids say? Chill? That's what I need to do.

When my heart stops pounding, I scan the rows for my car. No success, but it must be there. Good thing Plymouth State is such a dinky school. Might have been lost for days on a larger campus. I'm still pissed off; I taught classes here for more years than I can remember. I shouldn't get turned around so easily. It's funny: more years than I can remember. Right. I literally can't remember, but it was a bunch.

My meeting with Margaret comes back to me. I have an unsettled feeling I should remember her. It's clear from our conversation she thought I should. She looked familiar in a way, but why would I have known anyone in the Registrar's Office? Never was much for hobnobbing with the Administration high-muckity-mucks, though Olivia thought I was. And that's what she always told Oliver too, the bitch. I'm certain it's why he hated birds. If I liked something, he hated it. Eventually, I gave up trying. Ah, well, can't undo the past and not sure how much future is left for me. Now if I can just find the car. Where the hell is the damned thing anyway? How hard could it be to see something that ridiculously red? Maybe this isn't the right lot after all.

JEREMY

"Harry! Over here! Hey, Harry!"

Crap, he doesn't hear me. Why can't he see the camper? It's the biggest thing in the lot. I reach in and honk the horn. That gets his attention. He sees me waving, and waves back, but he looks away again. I don't get it. I honk a second time and motion for him to come. He stands for a minute looking at me then begins walking. When he gets to the camper, he looks baffled, like he doesn't know me. I remember that look. Like Granddad when he forgot my name. Sort of scared. Only Harry looks like he forgot me altogether.

"It's me, Jay."

Still looks confused, nervous.

He repeats, "Jay," a statement instead of a question but he really doesn't know who I am.

"Remember? You're giving me a lift to Seattle."

"Right, right. But where's my car? This isn't it. Mine is bright red."

Shit, what should I tell him that will make sense? I turn around and put both hands on the truck door. "This is your new old camper. She's all yours. Let's go!"

He looks almost convinced, but walks around the camper as if he's seeing it for the first time. He checks underneath then kicks the tires. Then he peers into the cab at our mess of candy wrappers and soda bottles and shakes his head.

"Old is right. Who did I buy this piece of junk from?"

"Your old friend, Grace. She gave you a great price."

"Grace, huh. Haven't seen her in...I don't know, maybe ten years. When was it I bought this heap?"

"Day before yesterday. Don't you remember?"

"Hell no. Can't remember shit anymore. You say she gave me a good price?"

"Yup."

"Damn well better have. Must have lots of cash leftover from the trade. Better check though."

Harry pulls a wad of money out of his wallet, all hundreds. He counts to himself, but it looks like $3000 or so. Then he reaches into the cab and pops the hood, and stands muttering while tugging at this or that engine part. After a few minutes, he slams down the hood and looks at me, shaking his head. "Not sure this old heap will make it to where we're going," he says. "Where are we going again?"

"Seattle. But first we're doing some bird watching."

I can see his eyes light up now. This makes sense to him, a little anyway.

"Right. Okay, I guess. You driving or am I?"

"I'm not old enough to drive so you'd better."

Harry looks at me, trying to tell if I'm joking, maybe.

He decides I'm not.

"Right then. I'd better drive. Hop in. You can be my navigator. Just point me in the right direction."

"That would be west."

"I know that, wiseass. I meant you have to tell me when to turn. Think you can handle that?"

"Yes, sir."

"And don't 'sir' me, I work for a living. Or did anyway."

"Then, yes, Harry. Take a left out of the parking lot exit and follow the signs for Route 93. The entrance is a half-mile down the road. See it off there in the distance?"

"Of course I can see it. I'm old, not blind. Wake me when we get there."

I look quickly to make sure he's messing with me and catch him smiling.

"Relax, junior. Just kidding," he says.

Relax? Not likely. But I'm not worried. I've survived years driving with Mom watching everything but where she's going, or Dad fumbling with his pager and cell phone. I just have to pay attention and we'll be fine. I lean back in my seat, putting my hands behind my neck and respond, "It's Jay, Harry."

"Well, Jay Harry, shall we boogie?"

"Definitely."

ABBY

Manchester Airport was crowded, more crowded than I would have imagined for an evening. I waited at Hertz for 30 minutes to pick up my rental car. There were a half-dozen others in front of me. When I got to the head of the line and told the agent my name, she apologized for the delay then apologized further that the only car left was a sub-compact, a Hyundai Accent.

"That's fine," I said, even though it was anything but fine. Harry hated little cars. His legs never fit, especially now with the prosthetic. We could switch, but it would have been easier not to. "I hope I only need it for a few days."

She thanked me for being so understanding then launched into chitchat. I was too tired and too annoyed to listen. Flying has always drained me, which seems strange since all I do is sit for a few hours. I signed the rental agreement and credit card slip and was about to turn to walk away, when I asked if she remembered an elderly gentleman with a limp who dropped off a car two days ago.

"No, I don't think so. Why do you ask?"

"Well...I'm meeting an old friend in Plymouth and thought Harry might be here too. He has a prosthetic leg. We're, uh, 'distantly' related."

"Sorry, I really don't remember anyone with a limp."

"He's quite tall and thin. A bit hunched over. White, thinning hair."

"Well, we have so many elderly customers. Wait. I do remember one tall fellow. He was here with his wife and grandson, I think. They stood off to one side then followed him out. It's the wife I really remember. She had wild gray hair. Stuck out in every direction as if she had just come in out of a storm. So funny—"

"Ah, then it can't be him. He doesn't have a grandson and I know his wife wouldn't be here with him. It's...a long story."

She looked at me oddly for a moment before she offered, "Sorry I couldn't be more help, ma'am."

"No worries. I'll catch up with him soon enough if he's here."

"Good luck," she called as I walked away. My back toward her, I waved and went to find my tiny car.

On the way north to Plymouth, I thought about Harry, thoughts that veered from worry to happiness. My hope was that here in his New England backyard, he would know where he was, feel safe and not so confused. I had no illusion he was actually safe, or that he would always know where he was, but the chances were good he would recognize enough to enable him to find Nigel.

Always, always, Nigel had been his touchstone, his alter ego. Birds, his opposing bookend. Words and Birds. Between them they sandwiched so much knowledge, yet they dispensed their wisdom to their students so differently. While Nigel gently led, showing students how to discover for themselves all he already knew, Harry pontificated, bullied, challenging the best to excel, scaring the weak into dropping out. The results each achieved were different as well. Nigel raised his students the way an incoming tide raises boats in a harbor, all together. Harry divided his like a riptide.

Those who could swim with him in the current gained so much from the experience. Those who could not washed up on shore or drowned.

It was this difference that drove me to choose Harry over Nigel. Each sought my attention after my marriage failed. Each was charming in his own way. But inside, Nigel was just one person, the same gentle spirit, the same self-deprecating, sweet man, whether he was teaching a class or bedding a woman.

Harry could not be so easily categorized. He was a tyrant in class, and I expected a tiger in bed, but I was mistaken. At first I was disappointed; did he really desire me or was he just going through the motions? Then it became clear. Instead of taking me where he wanted and hoping I'd go with him, he was discovering me, slowly analyzing, testing. It took a while for me to accept what eventually became obvious; we would scale that ladder together as high as we could.

Ah, Harry. Where are you? Will I find Nigel by your side? If not, what will I do? Shall I wait patiently for Oliver to call me the next time you use your credit card?

I smiled, remembering the rental agent's comments, almost laughing at the notion of Harry married to a woman with wild gray hair. He loved mine long, blonde, and straight, even if it came out of a bottle. He was always the first to notice when my roots were showing. Then later, even after he forgot everything else, Harry would go to the store unbidden to pick up my Preference 9, Natural Blonde. One morning I'd find the box on my dresser and know the time for my monthly ordeal had come. It always brought a smile to my face to have him notice.

What would I look like with wild gray hair? I suppose I'll never know. At least I hope I'll never know, because that would mean Harry was gone.

I arrived at the Federal House Inn near the university at 7:00 p.m., and settled into Sally's Room. With its queen canopy bed and shared bath, it was the only moderately priced accommodation I could find on short notice. I purchased a nice bottle of New Zealand sauvignon blanc at the grocer's, and once relaxed, began to polish it off. Having argued myself out of calling Nigel while I drove north, I reconsidered. Always a dangerous thing to do after two glasses of wine. I worried Nigel might be able to lie to me over the phone. I needed to speak to him in person. But if I didn't catch him at home, I might never find him out in his bog. How much time could I waste? None, I decided.

Nigel answered on the third ring. "Hallo."

"Nigel?" A silly question. I recognized his voice immediately, its British spice still present 40 years after landing on our shores. Through time, some of his slang had rubbed off on me. Harry teased me once that I must have picked up my brogue in Nigel's bed. More likely it was from Nigel's unflagging friendship and love of chatting up anyone he was with. But I let Harry's comment go unanswered, save for a wicked smile. He never repeated it.

"Yes?" Nigel said, the rise in his voice querulous.

"Are you questioning whether you indeed are Nigel, or asking what I want?"

"Abigail! How are you? No, where are you? How's Harry? Still enjoying his early retirement? Well, no longer early, I'd say. Must be what, eighty by now?"

"You never could admit Harry is younger, could you? He's only seventy-five, and you know it."

"Yes, well, maybe you're right. But he still looks older than me. Acts it too. Imagine retiring at such a young age."

"He was seventy when he retired. That's plenty old enough."

"I suppose, but I still don't understand it. They'll have to move my desk out in the middle of the football field in January before I hang up my cap and gown."

"Don't tempt them. They just might do it."

"Not likely. I'm a celebrity now, I'll have you know. Invited to be a guest speaker at Harvard, of all places. Damned nuisance too. Had to buy a new suit."

"Still the same old Birds."

"Right you are. And how's Words these days?"

"I was hoping you'd know. I think he might have come back east to pay you a visit just days ago now."

"That so? Haven't seen hide nor hair of him. Of course, I've been out at Bear Pond most days, but Harry knows that and could easily have found me."

"That's just what I'd hoped, Nigel. That he'd find you. So, you haven't seen him?"

"No. What's the matter? Silly old fool run out on you? Always said you should have married me."

"Stop joking, Nigel, this is important. Please tell me the truth. Have you seen Harry?"

"No, Abby, I haven't. I don't understand. What has happened to him? Why don't you know where he is?"

"I...I just don't. He left, unexpectedly. I've come to Plymouth, hoping...sometimes he just doesn't seem to—"

"Oh, no, no, Abby. Please tell me his mind isn't going."

My long pause answered for me. Nigel's refrain, "Oh no, no," echoed the loss I had felt for years and brought the pain back stronger than I could have imagined. Tears coursed unabated, and I could not find the words to go on speaking.

Nigel spoke the only words he could have, "We'll find him, Abby. Everything will come right in the end. No worries."

Dear Nigel, neither of us believes that, but thank you for saying so. "I know," is all I could muster.

His next words were just as predictable. "Could you use a shoulder to cry on, luv?"

Yes, I could, but giving in to the emotion would be a mistake. I knew that. I answered, "I'm just tired, Nigel. I'll bounce back. What other choice do I have? No, I need to get some sleep now. Can you meet me tomorrow?"

"Certainly. The coffee shop on Main Street, Café Monte Alto. I'm sure you remember. What time?"

"I'll be up early. Always am. How about eight o'clock?"

"Peachy. Um...what if I brought Margaret along? She might be able to help. After all, she's known Harry longer than either of us."

I hesitated, not certain what to answer.

Margaret, do I really want to see you? It's been so long. The last time I had to ask myself this question was just before Harry's retirement party. I feared you would notice the change in him. Nigel, oblivious as always, so typically male, noticed nothing. But you knew Harry, and even though you hadn't seen him for years, I thought you would guess. But at the last minute you canceled, and I was spared the worry. Did you feel the same way? Did you not want to face me?

Was this a good idea, Nigel? Maybe not, but I couldn't afford to say no. "Yes, Nigel, please ask her to join us."

"Right-o. Will do. And try not to worry. We'll find him. I know it."

"Good night, Nigel. Tomorrow is another day."

He wished me a good night's sleep then repeated his offer of a shoulder to cry on. I felt my longing and wondered if he might feel the same. But I knew acknowledging it would only drag us both deeper into sadness, and neither needed that. I thanked him again for his kindness but declined and rung off. Tomorrow would indeed be another day. Another day searching for Harry and his lost memory, another day wondering if the man I have loved would still be there trapped inside the shell which remained, another day asking how many 'other' days were left.

JACKSON

The supply truck lumbered along the rutted, dusty road, lurching from side to side then pitching fore and aft whenever the driver hit a pothole. If Jackson had dentures they would have fallen out and gone chomping down the road behind. The day was unusually warm and the air in the closed cab stifling. Jackson had already sweated through his cargo shirt.

The driver wore a permanent smile. Happy for employment, Jackson wondered? Maybe just amused at Jackson's discomfort with the unbearable, long, hot ride to civilization, such as it was. Two young boys rode in the open truck bed, each with a rifle slung over his shoulder, and each wearing a deadpan expression. They didn't make Jackson feel any less uncomfortable either, though that too might have accounted for the driver's smile.

The two-hour ride passed in silence with the exception of creaking leaf springs and the rattling of side boards that framed the truck bed, that and the driver's occasional launch into full-throated song. At first, Jackson was startled by the abruptness of his singing and the strange words and tone. Even though he didn't understand the meaning, the pitch of the driver's voice and his odd smile left him with an uneasy feeling the man didn't like him, an uneasiness sharpened by being at the man's mercy if he should suddenly stop and force Jackson out of the truck. He could say or do nothing, so he rode stone-faced, his only attempt at conversation coming when they arrived at the airstrip depot. "How long?" he asked.

The driver answered in perfect, unaccented English, "One hour," then shouted something at the two boys, who dropped their rifles on the truck bed and skipped away into an open field toward a group of children playing a game of soccer. The change in the boys was even more startling than the driver's outbursts of song. With their weapons, the two looked all business, mechanical, giving the impression they'd shoot first and ask questions later. Now, as they raced to join the game in progress, they pushed and muscled each other into pratfalls, then leapt up again in laughter. Jackson watched, and the longer, leaner boy outpaced his companion and ran headlong toward the ball. Only it wasn't a ball. What it was, Jackson couldn't tell. The thing was round, more or less, but it was definitely not a soccer ball.

Watching the boys play, he became aware of the driver standing by his side. In peripheral vision, Jackson could see the man's inscrutable smile had now been replaced by a look of approval, as if he too felt the game was a more fitting activity for boys than riding shotgun in the back of a supply truck.

"Elephant dung and grass," the driver said.

"Come again?"

"The ball. It is made from cowhide stitched over grass with dung added for weight."

"Doesn't bounce very well," Jackson said. "Can't they get a real ball?"

"Certainly, but it would soon be stolen. No one will steal elephant dung."

The driver turned and walked away, tossing another, "One hour," over his shoulder and holding up a single finger to leave no doubt.

Jackson watched him go, and then headed to the small concrete building that posed as the flight office, leaving the driver to continue on to a large steel Quonset building where he would find both his expected supplies and men to load them.

Jackson called Rose first, waiting through interminable clicks and buzzes for a connection. After several rings the call clicked over to the answering machine. He hung up and dialed again. This time her sleepy voice croaked, "Hello. God, what time is it?"

"If it's 1:00 p.m. here, it must be 7:00 a.m. there," Jackson replied, trying his best to keep his voice neutral. He knew very well Rose thought the day began no earlier than 11:00 a.m., leaving her just enough time to bathe and dress before meeting her girlfriends for lunch. "Sorry for the early call, but I'm in the middle of a jungle."

There was a pause. Jackson supposed she was dragging her drugged body into a sitting position to light a cigarette. She kept trying to quit, but couldn't stay off them. Like most of the bipolar, it was smoke and drink, or take her meds. He waited patiently, but before enough time passed for her to light up, she answered. "That's not possible," her voice clear and hard-edged. Even through thousands of miles of telephone cable he could hear it.

Strange, he thought, but answered lightly, "Well, it's not exactly a jungle, but it *is* Africa, and it *is* a tiny airstrip cut out of some fairly dense bush, so yes, it's quite possible. Why do you doubt me?"

"This is not funny, Jackson."

Her voice lost its edge, lulled by his mild response, he supposed, but was still a bit shaky. He smiled, amused that waking Rose so early put her off her game. Tired or not, he had expected a verbal duel. There was no way a week with Jeremy could have gone smoothly. She would soon get her feet under her though, so he decided to admit it.

"It is funny. A little anyway. You were always hard to wake before noon," he tried, joking with her.

"Stop it, Jackson. Just stop it. I know perfectly well you are home in Seattle and Jeremy is there with you. And I really don't appreciate—"

"Rose! I swear to you I'm in Africa. What's the problem, has he run off?"

"Jeremy is *not* here with me; he's with you in Seattle." Her voice rose toward hysteria, infecting him.

"No, Rose, he's not. Jeremy arrived at JFK as scheduled. He texted me. What have you done?"

"Oh, God! I assumed he talked to you and caught a flight home."

"Are you crazy? Wait, wait! This is not making sense."

"I told you this would happen. He was as surly and quarrelsome as always. Didn't want to be here in New York in the summer. Made me so mad I walked out. I left him in baggage claim to think about the way he treats me. I told him to stay where he was, but when I came back ten minutes later he was gone. I wasn't worried because I knew he would just call you and catch the next flight back. How can you possibly be in Africa? Is Jeremy home alone?"

"Damn it, Rose. How the hell would I know? I just told you. *I'm in Africa*! I have no idea where Jeremy is. I'm standing in a ten by ten cement block room baking in the heat and sweating my ass off."

"Some father you are. Always traipsing off to save the goddamned world, one stranger at a time, never mind you have a son of your own. Then you depend on me to take up the slack when you know very well I can't. This is all your fault. You do remember you promised Jeremy would have a roundtrip ticket this time, don't you? And that he could come right home if I couldn't handle him? Remember? You promised, Jackson. You promised."

"Yes, Rose, I know I did. And he had the return ticket. But I never meant ten minutes after he landed. I expected some advance notice. And you promised too. You promised to do your best."

"I did do my best. And you manipulated me. You put Jeremy on a plane then flew off to Africa, leaving us to sink or swim. So you lied when you said he could come right home, didn't you?"

A moment of silence passed before she repeated, "Well, didn't you?"

"Yes, Rose, I did. I admit it. I'm sorry, but I thought if I made you spend time with him—"

"You always push. You just can't let nature take its course, damn you."

Rose paused a moment. Jackson could hear her breathing quietly, regaining composure. He wondered what she would say next. Rose spoke then, calmer, but still angry.

"This is so unfair, Jackson. I'm no good at this. Even my damn shrink agrees. 'Avoid stressful situations,' he tells me. You know that, don't you?"

"Yes, Rose. I do."

"And Jeremy is a walking stressful situation. You know that too. But none of that matters now, does it? Surely Jeremy is home in Seattle, isn't he? He would have found the key just where any burglar would look, right under the stupid flowerpot on the front porch. Didn't you call him whenever you got to whatever godforsaken, heart-of-darkness, rat hole of a village you ended up in?"

"What would I call him on, Rose, the grapevine?" he answered in kind. "And why didn't *you* call him?"

"I didn't have his new number. Neither of you bothered to tell me. He was *supposed* to phone the moment the damn plane landed. Remember saying he would do that? So, shall we keep arguing or try to figure out what to do?"

"You're right. You're right. Arguing isn't getting us anywhere. I don't know where Jeremy is. I'm at an airstrip. I have to go back to the village soon. And they won't let me tie up the only phone for miles around trying to find out where he's gone. For the record, you do have Jeremy's number. Check the email I sent. Apparently you just didn't read it. And another thing, I seriously doubt the airline would let him reschedule his return flight. I'm certain they wouldn't let him on a plane without an adult handing him over in person. So, he's still out east somewhere; you just have to—"

"Don't you leave me with this mess, Jackson. You stay right where you are and work this out. Better yet, get on the next plane tomorrow and fly back here where you belong. Someone else can save the refugees. You're responsibility as a father—"

"Rose, shut up! There's no plane for a week and they don't take unscheduled passengers anyway. You need to handle this. Call Jeremy and find out where he is and go get him. If I had to guess, he's hitchhiking back to Seattle. It's just the sort of thing he'd do to piss us both off."

"But there are perverts out there who prey on kids like Jeremy!" Rose shrieked. "Surely you've told him that. What if he's been kidnapped? Wait! Maybe some pedophile picked him up at the airport."

"Okay, Rose. Calm down. Maybe—"

"I will not calm down. This is serious. He's thirteen, for Christ's sake!"

"Okay, okay, but you're exaggerating. He'll be fine. He has a good head on his shoulders. He'll be careful. Even if he is hitchhiking, he'll know better than to accept a ride from someone he doesn't trust. He'll look for cars with couples or families. And he has money and a MasterCard that can be tracked if he buys anything. I sent you that credit card number a week ago too. Do you still have the email?"

"Of course, I never delete anything. You know that."

"Right. Look, maybe he bought a bus ticket. I don't know if the transit companies have as stringent rules as the airlines. I would hope so, but maybe they don't. Rose, please. I can't do this from so far away. You have to pull yourself together and call him, find him, and bring him home. And call Andrew; he can help. He has lots of contacts and can apply legal pressure if needed. I promise to get the first flight I can back to New York. If you haven't located Jeremy by then, we'll go looking together. Can you do that? Can you at least try?"

More silence then a deep sigh. "Yes, Jackson. I can try. But you have to know you have done the wrong thing in leaving this to me. You do know that, don't you?"

The softer tone in her voice relaxed him somewhat, and while he was not convinced she could do this, there was no other choice, and at least she had promised to try. The flight manager had been motioning him to end the call for several minutes now so he signed off with a simple admission, "I know, Rose, and thank you. You'll see; everything will be all right. I promise."

"Stop making promises you can't keep, Jackson," she replied softly and the line went dead.

Jackson hung up and stared at the blank wall in front of him, taking deep breaths to calm his racing heart. During their conversation, Rose had wound up tight, nearly manic. But at the end, her voice contained a resignation he recognized, one that nearly always led downward.

Frustration crept in. He needed to talk to Jeremy. He turned to catch the airstrip manager's attention and pointed to the phone. The man shook his head. Momentarily, he considered offering a bribe then thought better of it. The man might misunderstand. Who knew what would happen then.

But what about the driver? What if he could talk him into finding some high ground? Maybe his cell phone would work. Walking back out into the heat, Jackson pulled off his sweat-drenched shirt and scanned the grounds for the driver. He was nowhere in sight, but his boys rested in the shade alongside the supply truck, rifles leaning a few feet away. Jackson began walking toward them, hoping to share their respite from the midday sun, but he turned aside when the older boy reached for his weapon. Instead he sat nearby on a raised mound. The younger boy elbowed his partner then both turned their attention toward Jackson. The first bite came quickly. Jackson jumped up, but before he could strip off his shorts and skivvies, the ants had swarmed up inside, followed by searing pain.

Naked and running, he clawed at himself, scraping off as many ants as possible before sliding into a puddle left over from the morning's deluge. The water washed away the ants and the mud softened the pain. Across the open space between them, the boys stood laughing and imitating Jackson's frantic flailing. The driver, now leaning near them, ignored the boys, his inscrutable smile aimed at Jackson.

After sitting a while, Jackson rose to retrieve his shorts, and using a stick to sweep them into the puddle, rinsed out the remaining ants, turning the shorts inside out to make sure they were all gone. Then he remembered his cell phone in the shorts pocket. He fished it out and attempted to power it on. The screen lit for a moment then the image sheared and went blank. He turned, hurling it against the steel Quonset hut. The cell phone exploded into pieces.

ROSE

She stubbed out her third cigarette and stared at the phone as if it were an animal that might bite her. Rose wanted nothing more than to escape into the drug-induced oblivion available to her with a few of whatever tranquilizer the doctor had prescribed this time. But she hesitated, setting the bottle back on the nightstand. She needed a clear head to think this out.

She remained furious with Jackson for putting her in this situation but knew it was also her fault for believing what she had wanted to believe. Jeremy had not returned to Seattle. That much was clear. But he might be halfway there if he was hitchhiking as Jackson suspected. Or maybe he had been abducted and was now enduring the unimaginable. She shuddered at the thought at first then calmed again. Jackson was right. Jeremy had a good head on his shoulders. He would find a safe way to return home. But there was no denying it; she had failed him again. The guilt turned anger into sadness, and sadness into self-deprecation. A deep spiral into depression would not be long in coming, and even though she knew this, there was nothing she could do to stop it from happening. Already, unfelt chemical shifts were occurring that would plunge her downward into darkness. Rose reached again for the pill bottle, popped three tablets, and washed them down with the half-drunk, watery vodka and soda left over from the previous night.

JEREMY

As soon as we get on the highway, Harry starts talking to himself. He seemed fine this morning but something happened at the college. He's been scared ever since. I try to get him to tell me what happened, but he ignores me. Same thing when I ask him to stop for gas. Finally, I point to the gauge that now reads past empty and he seems to understand.

After we pull into the Exxon station, I say, "I have to pee. Fill up the tank while I empty mine." He looks at me like he doesn't get it. When I return, the truck is gone.

I panic, running out into the road to see if there's any sign of which way he went. Nothing.

Shit, he dumped me. What the hell do I do now? I stand, kicking rocks out into the street, getting angrier and angrier. Then it hits me. He dumped me like I get dumped all the time. Mom leaves us, dumping me on Dad. Then Dad leaves for Africa, dumping me on Mom. Then Mom dumps me at the airport. My life is just one never-ending dump. This really sucks.

I start crying again. I try to stop it, but I can't. I pick up a rock and chuck it. Then I pick up another and think for a minute. Still have my cell phone and money. Should I call her? No, this is her fault. If Mom hadn't dumped me, I wouldn't be here. No, that's wrong. I guess I dumped her this time. I take a deep breath and dial her home number, but the answering machine picks up. Figures.

ROSE

She fought to surface from her drugged stupor only long enough to gauge her depression. Not good. No way could she rouse enough to answer the phone's insistent jangling. One more ring and the machine will pick up, she thought, but the phone rang twice before Jeremy's small, soft voice intoned, "Mom?"

"Oh, God, not now," Rose groaned then heard Jeremy ask again, "Mom, are you there? Wake up if you can."

Rose listened to her son's gentle breathing, heard him sniffle, and ask one more time, "Mom?"

Rose fought back both the tears that rolled down her cheeks and her overwhelming desire to pick up the phone. But she didn't reach for it. She knew she could not speak to Jeremy in her present condition. She could hear the need in his voice but her own need was greater. Only sleep could cast out her demons. She rolled toward the wall, suffered through one last, "Mom?" then heard the line go dead.

JEREMY

She was there. I know it. Either so drugged up she didn't hear the phone ring, or she heard but didn't want to talk. At least she knows I'm alive.

I chuck the rock at a road sign and the noise brings a clerk out of the station's convenience store. A young guy, and he's pissed. Scary. Wears his hair in a mullet and looks like he hasn't bathed or shaved for a month. Smells like it too.

I expect him to yell at me but he doesn't. "You okay, kid?" he asks.

Mind your own business. Why don't you go back inside with your gum-chewing, skanky girlfriend and leave me alone. "Yeah, just fine. Why?"

He's standing there looking down at me, smiling kind of creepy, like he knows something I don't. I can tell he doesn't believe me.

"You look like you just lost your best friend, and if you're so fine, what the hell are the tears about?"

He reaches down to wipe them away, but I duck quickly and rub my cheeks on my sleeves, one side then the other. "My ride ditched me and took all my stuff."

"No shit, man? That really sucks. Which way'd he go?"

I point west, though I really don't know.

"Well, let's go get the bastard," he says then puts his arm around my shoulders and starts pulling me toward the station. "Darlene can watch the register. How much of a head start does he have?"

I shrug. "Maybe ten minutes or so. I just went to the bathroom and when I came back out he was gone."

"Wait, was that the old fart in the beat-to-shit camper?"

"Yeah."

"He never pumped any gas. Just stood there with his hands jammed in his pockets. Looked like he forgot something. Were you low on fuel?"

"Almost empty."

"Don't worry, we'll catch him. Think he'll stay on the main drag?"

"How should I know? Maybe."

"Okay. Wait here," he says when we get to the station door, and gives me a one-armed hug.

He goes in and talks to Darlene, and points to where I'm standing. She gives me a quick glance before digging through a huge black purse she pulls out from under the counter. He takes the keys she hands him, turns, and comes back out. Darlene watches me. She looks worried or maybe just annoyed. Maybe she doesn't believe him. Maybe she doesn't like being left alone to watch the store.

Whatever. I follow him to the rusty green sedan parked alongside the building. He hoists a full gas can into the trunk and reties the rope that holds the lid shut, then slips into the driver's seat. The back seat is torn up; there are empty beer cans and Burger King bags all over. And magazines, like the ones my buddy's dad has stashed under his bed.

"Buck," he says and holds out his hand for me to shake then stares at me.

"Jay," I tell him. He shakes my hand slowly until I pull it back. "Thanks," I say.

"No charge, man. I needed a break anyway. You try being stuck here with that bitch six hours a day. You'd take any chance to disappear too." Then he pats me on the leg, and adds, "We'll find him. If not, we'll figure out something else."

While we drive, Buck asks how I hooked up with Harry. When I don't answer, he says, "No rush. We'll just cruise around for a while."

He's still looking at me funny, and I keep my hand on the door handle. There's something wrong with him.

After a while I say, "My grandfather."

Buck makes a snorting sound that could mean he doesn't believe me, or he doesn't think much of a grandfather who would leave his grandson behind. I can see him working his jaw, trying to piece it all together. Neither of us says anything more.

A half hour later we see the camper parked on the shoulder with the hood propped open. Harry is nowhere in sight. We pull up in front then scan the horizon. No Harry. No cars on the road. Buck lowers the hood and gives me a questioning look but doesn't say what's on his mind. I just shrug.

"Let's get some gas in the tank anyway," he says.

While he goes to get the can out of his trunk, I check the cab. Keys still in the ignition. I pocket them then hop out, walk around back, and try the camper door. It's locked. Quietly, I use the keys to open it and peek inside. Harry's lying on the bunk with his pants off and back to me, maybe sleeping. I close the door and relock it. Something tells me I shouldn't share this with Buck.

"Gramps not here?" He sets the can down and unscrews the gas cap.

I hide my relief at finding Harry and try to sound worried. "Maybe he started walking to find a station. He's pretty old. Not sure he could walk very far. You could drive a few miles down and see. Might have hitched a ride or something. Or maybe the cops stopped and took him to get some gas."

Buck flinches then nods slowly. He seems to be thinking. "Long walk to find gas but he probably don't know that," he says after a minute. "What's wrong with him anyway? Ass-heimer's or just an ass-hole?"

"Forgets stuff. All the time. First time he's forgotten me, though. Maybe thought I was in the camper."

"Maybe so. Maybe not," Buck scoffs. "Let's drive ten more minutes then we'll come back and see what you want to do."

"No, I better wait here in case he comes back. You go."

He turns to look up and down the empty road then stares at his feet. "Don't make sense to leave you here. Might not notice him, keeping my eyes on driving and all that."

"No, he limps pretty bad. Hard to miss."

"Maybe. Even so, no reason to think he'd get in the car with me. Might scare him off."

I try to laugh but can't. I'm too nervous. He might not scare Harry, but he's beginning to scare the shit out of me.

"Looks like you don't trust old Buck," he says. "Just tryin' to help out here. But maybe you're not telling me something I ought to know. Maybe Gramps is holed up in the camper. Why don't we go take another look-see, Maybe you missed him when you checked a few minutes ago...or maybe not."

Buck turns and takes a couple of steps toward the back and I bolt for the truck cab. I barely get the door closed and locked before he's hammering on the window.

He sprints around the front for the other door but I leap across and lock it and jump back when he plants his face against the glass.

"Open it," he shouts pounding the window till I worry it might shatter. I shake my head. "No way, asshole."

Buck smiles and walks off behind the camper. I hear him try the door, but it's locked. Coming around on my side again, he comes up close to the window and smiles.

"Nice move, sweetlips. But the way I figure it, maybe Gramps hit the road after all. So, what do you say? Might as well come on out and go get comfortable in the back."

I shake my head.

"No? Okay then. Looks like old Buck may have to apply a little persuasion." He winks and heads for his car.

I pull the keys out of my pocket. My hands are shaking bad. Takes a couple of tries to jam them into the ignition. The engine turns over and coughs once then dies. I try again. Nothing.

Buck sits on the edge of his open trunk and laughs. Then he turns and pulls out a tire iron. He smacks the palm of his hand a few times with it and walks over and taps the window. "Better move over," he says. "Don't want the glass to cut up that pretty face."

I slide quickly across to the passenger side and reach for the door handle then stop when I hear the camper door open and shut. Buck hears it too.

"Now we'll have some fun," he says and walks back out of sight.

At first nothing happens. I keep looking from side to side, checking the mirrors.

Then I hear Buck say, "You comin' out, Gramps? Or am I comin' in?"
Silence.

I hear Buck turn the handle slowly; Harry must have unlocked it. Buck whips the door open, then, "What the—"followed by a thud and shriek. The screaming continues as I unlock my door and run back.

There on the ground is Buck, holding his crotch in his hands and rolling in the dirt.

Harry is kneeling on the floor of the camper in his boxers holding his prosthetic leg like a shovel. The shoe is off and the hard black foot looks wicked.

"Taste of his own medicine," he says. "Nailed him good. Grab that tire iron and hand it to me then go fill the tank while I put my leg back on. I'll watch numb-nuts here."

I'm back in two minutes but still shaking. Buck remains on the ground moaning.

"Time for you to toddle off," Harry tells him. "Before I call the police."

Buck struggles to his feet and limps away with Harry right behind with the tire iron. I toss the empty can in his trunk and tie the lid down while Harry watches him get behind the wheel.

"Thanks for the gas," Harry says then slams Buck's door behind him.

We watch him drive away. Harry puts his arm around me. I can feel the tears coming but they stop when he says, "Pretty good aim for an old fart, huh?"

"What if you missed?" I ask, half smiling now.

"No chance. Misspent youth shooting pool. Besides, could have hit him just about anywhere and gotten nearly the same result."

I look up at him and laugh.

"Just one question," he says. "Who are you?"

HARRY

While we drive down the road looking for a gas station, I wonder what the hell was I doing sleeping in a camper in Vermont? And who is this kid? Says he's my grandson, but he's not. That's certain. Never had one of those. Just a son, Oliver, and two granddaughters, Lainey and Nessa. But maybe I'm wrong. What's the last time I remember?

Christmas. Not sure what year. A little snow and colder than a witch's tit. I remember warming my butt by the roaring fire I helped Oliver build. Not much of a boy scout, my Oliver, but at least he hauled in the logs and watched.

I can see Lainey opening the present we got her. We? Olivia and me?

No, that can't be right. We're divorced. But I definitely remember Olivia holding Nessa in her arms all wrapped up in a baby blanket. So tiny. And Lainey riding that bright yellow rocking horse and shouting, "Giddy up."

And dinner, set for seven with Olivia's best china, crystal, and honest-to-god, sterling silverware. And a huge turkey with those silly, frilly turkey-feet decorations. And candied yams with coconut, weird but delicious. Oh, and butterhorn rolls and that strange cranberry and horseradish chutney we brought. What did she call the concoction? Cranberries Jezebel. That's it.

We? Who was with me? My girlfriend? My wife? I can't picture her, but I can see us sitting around the table drinking wine and talking before the turkey is carved. Beaujolais nouveau, Olivia's tradition. Oliver at one end, and his wife, Evangeline, at the other. Olivia and Lainey sit across from us with Nessa in a highchair in between. I can see each of them clearly but not the woman next to me. Yet I know she is there. It's her hands I remember, small hands, milky white, with clear nail polish on long fingernails. And the way she moves them as she speaks, slowly, in counterpoint to her voice, quick, high, and laughing. But no ring. Not my wife or fiancée, then. But who is she? Who was she?

A half hour later we've stopped to fill the tank and are back on the road. I let the kid do the pumping and paying. Think I'll stick to driving for now.

Each time we need to turn he lets me know. By the time we hit Albany I'm bushed. "Another half hour to go," he says, but what seems like only a minute later, he tells me, "Turn here...where it says, 'Arrowhead Marina and RV Park, open May 15th to October 15th.'"

He's been playing with his cell phone, which he claims is giving him directions communicated through this thing stuck to the side of his head, a big hunk of plastic that reminds me of my mother's hearing aid. Except for the eerie blue light it emits. I forget what he called this contraption. Blueberry or Blacktooth or some such nonsense. He put it on when I complained about the smarmy female voice on the speaker. Said something about his earbuds being broken, whatever they are.

"You're the boss," I tell him then turn down a long, tree-lined road that leads us to the Mohawk River. I pull up in front of the campground office and point the kid toward the door. "Go sign us up."

He hesitates at first then says, "Okay. I'll try."

He talks with the teenage girl behind the counter and looks over his shoulder at me once in a while. When he comes back, he tells me it's thirty dollars a night. I whistle.

"You have to go in and sign. I'm too young."

Damn. Figures. "Fine. I'll just drag my dead leg with me."

"Sorry. We can charge it up later."

"Too bad I can't plug myself in. I could use a charge too."

The kid pokes his finger into my upper arm and says, "Zzzzzit. Okay, you're charged."

Very funny. Glad one of us is having a good time. I try on my best withering look, but that only makes the kid laugh. I swing my legs out and lock my robotic left knee. We hobble together inside, me doing the hobbling, the kid tagging along. The girl behind the counter gives us a perplexed look. Of course, that's the expression most kids her age wear all the time so maybe I'm not the target. "Like my Festus impression, young lady?"

Ah, she does have more than one expression. Looks clueless now.

"From 'Gunsmoke.'"

Still clueless.

"Never mind. Before your time. What do you have for us?"

"Full hookup?"

I turn to the kid. He nods. "Apparently we want a full hookup."

"We're pretty booked. How about number 48? Can't have a campfire but it's right near the bathrooms."

Little twit probably thinks I have to get up to go ten times a night. Little does she know my prostate is as healthy as a 20-year-old's. I can hold my water. Screw it. Just want to get settled. And less walking till I get my leg recharged sounds good. "Fine. Number 48 it is. Now, where exactly is that?"

"About two hundred feet up that road, just past the dump station," she answers, pointing over my shoulder. "It's marked."

Fee paid, we drive up and park between two shiny, bus-sized RVs. They loom above us threateningly. The owners don't seem too happy to see us either, both them and their expensive rigs looking down their noses at our shabby wreck.

Screw'em. I wave then clamber up the steps into the camper and collapse on my bunk.

ROSE

She sat in her darkened living room. Ten feet away, a pair of windows overlooked a wedge of Central Park still draped in gray. Dressed in one of Jackson's old T-shirts, head in hands and elbows on knees, Rose tried to think. But her head throbbed, and the ibuprofen she had tossed back a while ago hadn't yet cut the relentless pain. She had chain-smoked a dozen Virginia Slims, stubbing them out with a vengeance in the overflowing cut-glass ashtray.

Still furious with Jackson, Rose imagined each cigarette butt drilling into his flesh as she thrust it in the smoldering pile. She lit another. Then rising for yet another time, she paced the floor, arms crossed and held in tight, cigarette clenched between the middle fingers of her left hand. She could not calm down, chemical signals raced through her veins till Rose thought she would scream. But she didn't. Not one word. She swallowed every epithet, every moan, every self-destructive thought waiting to be voiced, as if that might make them disappear.

Across the room, the windows beckoned, faint dawn light beginning to draw their dim outlines. Rose looked away. She knew better than to tempt fate. God, she felt miserable! Should she call Andrew? Not yet, it would be 3:00 a.m. in Seattle. Should she call Jeremy? No, again too early, and she wasn't ready to hear his voice, so soft, so hurt. Rose needed to collect as much composure as she could muster before making that call. And thinking about Jackson and the window was not helping her do that.

"Test yourself," she hissed between clenched teeth then stared out the windows again. "Just keep looking through them," she said, more calmly now. But still she paced back and forth, only occasionally glancing out. Then, without warning, she walked directly toward them, stood centered on one and within reach of the glass then stared into the distance across the trees and reservoir. Rose focused on the 5th Avenue buildings on the east side of the park, but she could feel her gaze drawn to the street nine stories below. Anxiety surfaced, clawing her attention downward. She could almost feel her hands reach out, open the window, then lead her plunge to the pavement, dragging mind and body behind. Rose knew this compulsion was real, palpable. She needed to conquer it. She wanted to live. So she faced her fear, not the fear she might fall, but the fear she might jump. In facing it, testing herself against it, Rose found the courage to turn away. She walked back to the sofa and lay down. A minute later she rose again and walked barefoot into the kitchen. Something to eat. That's what she needed. And coffee. But decaf, so her nerves wouldn't be jangled? No, she needed caffeine. God, what a mess!

With the refrigerator door flung wide, Rose peered and poked through the scant provisions for something unopened or unmoldy. There were eggs but who knew how many months they had been there. There was fruit, but the bananas were black and the apples discolored a sickly, jaundiced brown. A fat cantaloupe slice bore a glaucous, glutinous sheen. Cartons of takeout food, once opened, revealed either desiccated, granular glop or slimy, gray-green goop. Nothing appealed.

Rose tried the freezer and found only cubes of ice, malformed by weeks of frost-free cycling, and a frozen loaf of organic wheat berry bread. She ripped open the plastic with her teeth and jammed her nose inside. A vague dead-freezer aroma overlay the equally vague nutty undercurrent she supposed the wheat berries must emit. Probably tasteless, but toasted and buttered, it might still be palatable. She rechecked the refrigerated section for butter. Nothing. Wait, maybe there was peanut butter left from Jeremy's visit a year ago. She rifled through cabinets and unearthed it, one small jar of Jif Extra Crunchy. If she could only remember where she put the toaster.

Then it hit her, there was no toaster. She had thrown it away when toast failed to pop up properly. Now what? Frustration mounting, Rose threw the loaf across the room. The bag burst open, spewing frozen slices onto the marble floor. Then a smile spread slowly as she remembered how Jeremy made toast last summer. She picked up a hunk of the bread, leaving the other hunks still strewn where they had landed, pulled a pair of tongs out of a drawer, and lit one of the Vulcan stove burners. The flickering blue flame caused the dark kitchen walls to dance, painting her figure in motion though she stood still.

What had Jeremy called it? "Toasting over a campfire." Each morning they shared this ritual, and each evening they ignited marshmallows, charring them nearly to cinders then blowing them cool. She saw this as clearly as if it were yesterday, Jeremy blowing and blowing then holding out the skewer and grinning while she seduced the blackened mass into her mouth with her tongue. The memory was so intimate, so sensual, it was almost obscene. Yet, she savored it and wished she had marshmallows to reenact the moment. But they were gone. They had gone out in the trash.

The dark, hot smell of overdone toast broke her reverie. She waved the singed slice to disperse smoke, which clung to it, and slathered peanut butter over the still hot bread. Then, hopping up on the narrow island countertop to sit legs crossed and swinging her foot, Rose ate her breakfast, the cool, smooth granite against her bare cheeks and thighs juxtaposed with the warm, melted crunch of peanut butter. Wisps of smoke swirled in blue light from the still-burning flame, and in memory, Jeremy's face wreathed in smoke came back to her.

She could do this, she told herself, she could do this.

An hour later, the sun had risen. Golden light diffused through the soot-streaked living room windows, washing across the Persian rug. Below in the street, traffic was snarling its way noisily, horns blaring, brakes screeching, pedestrians calling out. As she paced again, back and forth, Rose repeated her mantra, "I can do this. I can do this. Jeremy needs me. I can do this."

She remained unconvinced, though speaking these words out loud gave her courage to take the next step. But what was it? Calling Andrew? Yes, she believed he would know how to help. He had always helped, though he also always took Jackson's side against her. But Andrew was articulate and bright, and he was good at talking people into things they didn't want to do. This was what Rose feared. She knew very well Andrew's first piece of advice would be to call Jeremy. It only made sense, but she was afraid to do it. She could not bring herself to call him. Not yet. Not now.

Rose tried to rationalize her reluctance. Maybe Jeremy would call her again. Yes, that would be best. If Jeremy called first, it would be because he needed her. She would have the upper hand. He would have to plead his case, admit he was wrong to treat her the way he did, like some complete failure of a mother. Jackson had taught him this, always criticizing her, always telling her what she should do, making her feel small and unwanted.

And Jeremy had learned that lesson well. How many snide jabs had she suffered, with no remonstrance from his father? Too many.

The sad truth was Jackson did not respect her, except in bed. Oh, yes, in bed he never criticized, always made her feel needed, desired. But for anything else, she fell short of the mark.

If she called Jeremy, he would not kowtow, he would be demanding. Whatever little thing he wanted, he would expect her to provide. How many times had she been dragged out of her home to go shopping for some new gadget? She'd lost count. The latest was his Blackberry. Jeremy could make calls, send texts, listen to his horrid heavy metal music, take and send photos, even get directions, never mind that he wouldn't be driving for over two years yet. Damn thing did everything but wipe his ass. It wasn't the money that made Rose furious. It was Jeremy's sense of entitlement. Just one more thing he had learned from his father. That and his need for instant gratification.

Those two things were at the heart of this generation's problems. Kids thought they should get anything they wanted and they should get it now. She honestly believed this had been different for her. As a child, when she wanted something, her parents made her save her allowance to buy it. Or she could wait for her birthday or Christmas. And if the item were thought to be too expensive or inappropriate for any reason, her parents would simply refuse. In all events, she was expected to have patience.

Now that she thought about it, this wasn't just a generational problem...this was also what was wrong with everything in the world today. No one could wait. No one could accept there were some things they would never have.

Rose had to admit she was as much to blame for spoiling Jeremy as Jackson was. She wanted everyone to be happy, and though she knew this was not her job, that she was responsible only for her own happiness, it did nothing to relieve the burden she felt. In fact, her need to make everything right increased.

It had always been this way. The effort of trying had worn her down, sent her running from her family, and stolen what little resilience she possessed. Now, the slightest irritation wormed its way in, angering her then dragging her into despair. Jackson could not understand. He was a doctor, but he did not understand. Oh, he knew her chronic depression was a disease, but like most people, he equated it with intense sadness, the only comparable feeling he had experienced. But sadness was not comparable. Nothing could be further from the truth. When it struck, her depression debilitated, stole all her energy, made her seek oblivion, desire an end to it all.

Rose knew very well why some overdosed and some jumped. And she knew why her 10th floor window beckoned, taunting her. She gazed through it. There was the park, and beyond, the 5th Avenue high-rises, sun ablaze on rooftops, façades still dark. Rose imagined the view from 5th Avenue, sunlight oozing down the east side of her building as the sun climbed higher, erasing the shadow. If only her own darkness could be so quickly dispelled.

ABBY

I arrived at Café Monte Alto before Nigel. It was early, but the doors were already open and the tables filled with customers. Inhaling deeply, savoring the dark aroma, my eyes swept over the room. I loved the bustle of activity, coats coming off, cool morning air yielding to the warmth of the crowded space, customers sidling up to the serving counter to order then returning with steaming mugs. And the hugs, greetings, and handshakes. Such conviviality, punctuated by outbursts of surprise and sudden laughter; some conversations across open tables, available to any who wished to listen, others with bodies leaned in and faces close, *tête à tête*.

After ordering a nonfat grande latte, I found a small table as it was vacated. A short while later Nigel showed up with Margaret in tow. He chatted with her in his typical animated fashion as they came in, but Margaret seemed not to be listening. Instead, she scanned the crowd. Would she recognize me minus the 30 pounds I had lost since we last saw each other? My hair was cut shorter too...it had only begun to grow out again since last year.

Our eyes met and locked. Instant recognition. Margaret looked away first then turned to Nigel and tugged on his sleeve, pointing his attention toward me. His initial shock shifted slowly to interest as they approached.

"Abigail, you look wonderful!" he proclaimed with enough enthusiasm to evoke an equal but opposite reaction from Margaret.

"Yes, you certainly do, considering the circumstances," she offered. "A bit more tired than I'd hoped, but none of us is getting any younger, I suppose. And Nigel tells me you've been under a lot of stress."

I nodded my acceptance but basked for a moment in the glow of Nigel's rapt attention. You're not fooling anyone, Margaret, and you're carrying the weight as well as the years. I kept the catty remark to myself.

"Nigel, why don't you go get us coffee?" Margaret asked, though her words sounded more like a command. "You know how I like it."

I'll just bet he does. We both know how he likes it, don't we, Margaret. I smiled sweetly at her as this too went unvoiced.

During Nigel's absence, Margaret told me about meeting Harry in the hallway. "He looked good," she said. "But he seemed confused. Did he really have Alzheimer's as Nigel guessed?"

"Yes," I answered. "Harry still has lucid days, and even when the day isn't a good one, he still has lucid moments. And he's become good at faking it, as well."

"Faking it?"

"Yes. He covers up 'not knowing' with reasonable excuses and sudden recognition. Only the recognition is mostly parroting back what you just said. Few people realize how confused he has become. And he seldom appears to be afraid, or frozen in place the way you might expect. He generally rolls with whatever seems to be going on."

"So, he probably didn't actually know who I was."

"Quite possibly. I doubt he would have. Half the time I don't think he knows who I am."

"Oh, Abby. I'm so sorry."

Margaret's expression changed to one so completely sincere, I felt guilty for what I had been thinking. But when Nigel returned, she shifted to more of an 'I'm glad it's not me' sort of aloofness that reminded me why I had never liked her. Still, I knew she might have more information to share from her chance hallway meeting with Harry, so I asked what he had told her.

"Well, mainly," she answered, "Harry seemed to be making excuses for not remembering me. But he was really looking for Nigel. His old friend, Birds, as he put it. I pointed him to the Boyd, though I believe he didn't know where that was, since he turned the wrong way. And he was limping! Of course, he may have just forgotten which way he had come from. I do that all the time."

"Did he say why he was looking for Nigel?" I asked, ignoring her comment on Harry's unusual gait.

"Oh, yes. He hoped Nigel would join him for a birding trip to Maine. Seems he's bought a camper."

"Ah, that explains why he took so much money with him. But it is certainly odd. As far as I know, Harry hated camping. What do you think, Nigel?"

"Quite right. Harry was always one for comfort. Insisted on going the bed and breakfast route anytime we went birding. Not that I objected, really. I prefer a soft bed at the end of a long day, as well. I remember—"

"I don't agree at all," Margaret interrupted. "I distinctly remember sharing a tent with Harry years ago."

"Probably just wanted to get into your knickers," Nigel teased. Margaret's self-satisfied smile answered for her.

"Oh. Sorry, Abby. Probably shouldn't have spilled that bit."

"That's all right, Nigel. Harry told me years ago about his dalliances. It's quite a list. And all that was before me."

Margaret's smirk was now gone, and so, I suspected, was her cooperation. A minute later she confirmed this, excusing herself by way of an appointment she'd just remembered.

"Coming, Nigel?" she commanded.

"No, dear. Abby and I need to work out the next steps to find our old friend. You've been frightfully helpful, though. So glad Harry found you. Don't know what we would have done without a clue where to begin."

"But...what about my appointment? I need you to drive me or I'll be late."

"Oh. Well, take my car. You've the keys with you, I'm sure. Abby will give me a lift home. Perhaps you can drop by later?"

My turn to smile. Margaret's, "Very well then," was sweet to my ear.

Two hours later, I drove Nigel home. We had a plan. Nigel was certain Harry would head for Mount Desert Island first and stay for a few days.

He should still be there. We would leave the next day and, with luck, find him perched atop one of the many rocky promontories that project out into the Atlantic, scanning the horizon for seabirds.

As predicted, when I pulled up in front of his house, Nigel invited me in. Knowing how that would rankle Margaret, I nearly accepted. But I might yet need her help. And, besides, I had to keep Nigel focused on Harry, not me. He kissed me on the cheek then paused a moment before getting out. When I offered no invitation to go further, he said, "Right then. Tomorrow, eight o'clock sharp. Sleep well, Abigail."

A gentleman as always, dear Nigel. Thank you for that.

JEREMY

"Lost it yesterday, didn't I?" Harry says next morning, after I fetch him a free cup of coffee from the RV park office. One for myself too, but with extra milk and sugar.

I nod then shrug. "We got here, didn't we?"

"Don't remember eating. Lost the whole day probably. Did we stop for dinner?"

I shake my head. "You told me you needed to get some sleep. I raided the candy machine."

"How about we find someplace for breakfast? Maybe you can tell me what happened. Last thing I remember was Grace hugging me goodbye. It's Jay, right?"

I nod again. Not sure what to say but I'm glad Harry seems to have his memory back. Before he died, my grandfather forgot everything but my grandmother. Kept asking who we all were. But that took years...for a long time he remembered my name. Then for a while, sometimes he knew it and sometimes I had to remind him. Guess I'll have to keep telling Harry too.

We find a Dunkin' Donuts just down the road. Coffee and jelly donuts for breakfast. The store is mobbed. The two open tables are piled with plates and cups. I help Harry clear one of them, making a bigger pile on the other. The table is still covered with spilled coffee and donut crumbs. I grab a napkin and clear a spot in front of me. Harry doesn't. I take a sip from my cup. Tastes better than the free stuff at the campground.

Harry works on his donut without speaking, glancing around at the other customers. A girl finally arrives to clear the heaped table. Looks like she eats as many donuts as she sells. What a shitty job. Guess free donuts is the main attraction. Harry grunts and I turn to look at him. He gestures in the girl's direction and winks at me. I roll my eyes. He's got powdered sugar on his nose but doesn't know it. I don't tell him. After he finishes licking all the sugar off his fingers, he asks, "So, tell me, how bad was I?"

Not sure I really know. Don't even know what he remembers about me. What should I tell him first, that he forgot where the camper came from, or that he left me at the gas station, or that we got attacked by a pervert?

"Do you remember where we got the camper?"

"Grace lent it to us, didn't she? Or did I buy it from her?"

"She wants it back when we get to Seattle."

"That's where we're going? Why?"

"We live there. I'm from Juanita Bay. You live on an island."

"Doesn't ring a bell. You sure? Maybe I said that but it's wrong."

"You sounded pretty certain when you told me, and we were on the same flight from Seattle a week ago."

"Really? I figured I picked you up hitchhiking."

"Well, you did, sort of. It's a long story."

"I've got all the time in the world apparently. Give it your best shot."

"Okay. We were on the flight then we landed—"

"Obviously, kid. Get to the point."

"My mother was supposed to pick me up but she ditched me. She's bipolar."

"Ah, so I rescued you? Doesn't sound like me. I'm better at causing trouble than facing it, or so I've been told. What about your father?"

"He's in some 'godforsaken village in Africa' saving lives."

"Your flippant answer suggests you think that's a waste of time. I tend to agree."

"Just repeating what my mother always says. Not sure what I think. Maybe he really is saving lives."

"That's the spirit. Stick up for your old man. Clearly, your mother won't. So, we met on the plane, your mom doesn't show up, and your dad can't be reached because cell phones don't work in the jungle. Sound about right?"

"Yeah."

"And you want me to drive you back to Seattle?"

"Right."

"I still don't know why I'm here or why I was in Seattle in the first place. Any ideas?"

"You left your wife?"

"Abby? But we live here in New Hampshire."

"Not anymore. She sold the lake cabin. You live near your son, Oliver, now."

"I...I don't remember where Oliver lives. Seattle, you say?"

"Right."

"Jesus, you sure?"

"Definitely. You told me to remember all this stuff for you because you said your Alzheimer's makes you forget."

"Bullshit. I don't have Alzheimer's. I'm just getting forgetful in my old age. It'll happen to you too someday."

"Don't be pissed. I'm only telling you what you told me."

"I would never have told you I have Alzheimer's."

"Okay, maybe you didn't say it, but so far you've forgotten you have a camper, a wife, a son, two granddaughters, and that you and your son live near Seattle. What would you call it?"

"I haven't forgotten. I remember all those things. Well, not the part about Seattle."

"Yeah, now you remember. And even now you forgot who I am. Yesterday you couldn't remember my name or any of the other stuff I just said. And you drove off and left me at a gas station."

Harry sighs and looks out the store window at the camper. He looks sad, down, like my dad after he's been on the phone with Mom, like he just lost an argument. Better not mention the Buck thing. "Sorry," I say.

"For what? Telling me the truth even if I don't want to hear it? Don't be sorry. I'm just an angry old man who can't remember what happened yesterday. Half the time I don't know where I am or who the people talking to me are. But the worst thing is when I actually do remember. That's when it hits me. Someday I won't ever again know where I am or who I am. Scares the hell out of me."

"That really sucks."

"Hmmph. You can say that again."

"Okay. That really sucks."

"Very funny."

"I was just saying it again in case you already forgot."

"Cute. Maybe we'll go out for dinner later and I'll forget to pay. How about that?"

I pull out my credit card. "Dad'll pay!"

"Hah! Sounds good to me. Wait...now I remember. We can't use credit cards because then they'll find us. Right?"

"Right. So you'll have to buy."

He gives me a worried look, reaches for his wallet and looks inside.

"Don't worry. You've got lots of money. Shit, I was supposed to remind you to take out a cash advance while we were in Plymouth."

"Hmmph. Why was it I wanted to do that?"

"So your wife would look for you there. You said you'd find someone to tell her you were going to Maine bird watching. That way she'd go east instead of west."

"Ah, an old Indian trick. Leave a false trail. Pretty smart, huh?"

He's smiling now. I grin back and say, "Yeah. Too bad you can't remember shit."

Harry bursts into laughter and keeps it up till I'm laughing too. Maybe I should be worried, but I'm not. Mom would be. Dad too.

I kind of like being in charge. It's pretty cool being asked what we should do, instead of always being told. That's the thing that really sucks about being a kid. Parents never listen; they just talk.

When Harry stops laughing, there's one more thing I need to say. I just blurt it out, "Give me the keys."

He looks at me funny then asks why.

"So you won't leave me again."

He pulls the key ring out of his pocket, fingers the keys for a moment then hands them over. "I'd probably just lose'em," he says. "Be safer with you."

HARRY

Jay hops into the boat and motors us away from the dock and out onto the river. I sit on the middle seat, and watch where we're going. No way was he going to let me drive. I keep reminding him to pay attention where he's going.

I'm still thinking about the keys. He's right but it feels like being punched. Just one more thing I've had to give up. "Symbolism," I used to tell my literature students. Look for it in small gestures. Like this one, a trade: freedom for security. Trust too. I trust him enough to hand the keys over; he trusts me enough to ask.

"Kingfisher!" he says, interrupting my reverie to point out a small gray bird hanging in midair above the river.

"Nope. Eastern Kingbird. If we weren't so far away, you'd have known. Kingbird's smaller. Doesn't have half the beak. Eats mostly insects but it'll swoop down to take a small fish the same way kingfishers do."

"Oh."

"What do you mean, 'Oh'? You can add it to your life list."

"Hey, that's right!"

"Keep watching the shore. Might see some herons or egrets wading in the eddies."

"I've seen all those."

"And what? You never want to see one again?"

"Well, no. I mean, yes—"

"Make up your mind, kid."

"It's Jay."

"I know that. I didn't forget."

"Just checking."

"Hmmph. Steer the boat that way. Toward the island."

"Okay. See something?"

"Nope, just a hunch. Lots of thick vegetation along the bank. Makes a good nesting place. Also dinner."

"Huh?"

"That's what dabbling ducks eat. The tender shoots are underwater. It's why their butts are always up in the air."

"Thought they ate fish."

"Diving ducks eat fish. Dabblers eat water plants. Don't they teach you anything in school?"

"Not much. I took earth science instead of biology."

"Guess you'll have to take my word for it then."

"Wait! What's that?"

"What's what? Where are you looking?"

"Right over there."

Jay's pointing but I can't tell at what. He's the one with the binoculars glued to his face. Then he kills the motor and stands up, rocking the dinky rowboat we rented.

"Whoa, watch what you're doing there, kid, or we'll be swimming."

Jay leans on my shoulder to steady himself and works to focus on whatever he's seen. Probably floating debris. The river isn't the cleanest. Then he pounds on my shoulder to get my attention, as if he didn't already have it. "He's in the weeds," Jay says, "Something bright yellow on his beak."

"Lots of ducks with yellow beaks."

"It's *not* his beak. It's *on* his beak."

"Maybe there are two birds, one beak above the other."

"No! His beak is orange. This is above his beak."

"Sure it's not a flower?"

"I'm not that stupid. It's *part* of his beak."

"Horned Grebe maybe. Should be in Canada by now, though. The male has a yellow patch on its head. Near enough the beak, maybe. Beak is black but there should be some orange feathers around his red eyes. See any dark red feathers on his flanks?"

"I only see black and white. There's too many weeds."

"Here, let me have your binoculars."

"See? Told you we should have brought both pair."

"Yeah, yeah, just hand over the specs."

Jay stands behind me as I take a look. He reaches up and grabs my ears then uses them as handles to turn my head like a periscope. Feels strange. Reminds me of something, though I can't remember what. Like something someone else has done before, maybe. Who? Not Oliver, that's for sure. One of the girls? What are their names again? Damn. Can't remember shit.

I scan back and forth for a minute. "I don't see anything."

Jay nestles into my back and puts his head on my shoulder to better gauge the direction I'm looking. I can feel him breathing in my ear.

Just like Nessa!

I can see her standing in my lap, one of my ears in each small hand, wobbly legs barely holding her upright. What was she, two? No, not even. The rest comes back...her face scrunched up in concentration, the stink of dirty diaper, then the look of blissful relief on her face. Heat and wetness in my lap followed. And Abby's, "Oh, dear. Good thing we brought a change of clothes." And Nessa's smile. Happy to shit on you, Grandpa.

"Look, Harry! He's coming out of the weeds. Quick!"

"I'll be damned. That's a King Eider. What the hell are you doing so far south, fella?"

"Score! He's not on my list!"

"Not on mine either."

"You're kidding!"

"Nope. One more and I'll have three hundred. That big boy belongs in the arctic floating around in the sea. Can't believe we got so lucky."

"I saw him first!"

"That you did. Want a medal or a chest to pin it on?"

My father's curious phrase sounds as foreign to me as it probably does to Jay. But his grin says that doesn't matter. Ah, to be young again, each new bird causing such joy. Then I laugh. Jay laughs along with me, though he couldn't know why. Probably doesn't care either. Nor does he recognize it as a wry laugh. That only comes with the passage of years.

I laugh because I've just made a new discovery having nothing to do with birds. I laugh, though I might as well cry. For months now I've felt the past slipping away. So many memories gone. So much fear. What will I lose next, I wonder, when I roll out of bed and my feet hit the floor? But how do you tell what was there yesterday that is gone today?

"What's it like," Jay asks me later over dinner at McDonald's: a Big Mac each and a huge mound of fries from our combined super-sized meals, surrounded by a dozen miniature Dixie cups overflowing with catsup.

"What, losing your mind?"

He gives me a worried look, and I take it back. "You mean what's it like to forget things you know you should remember."

He nods and waits for me to answer, though he still looks sorry he asked.

"Good question, Jay," I say to cheer him up then think for a minute. What is it like? Then I recall; it's a jigsaw. That's what we tell people.

"Imagine the biggest room you can think of. Maybe your school gym. On the floor is a million-piece puzzle. The picture of your life so far. It's filled with all the people you've ever met, and all the places and things you've ever seen. It's about half filled in, many small groupings, just a few pieces each, and big sections where lots fit together, but even those have holes here and there.

"Every day you come back in to check. Maybe you add a piece or two. But you don't seem to make much progress at completing the picture. At first you don't notice anything missing, but after a while you'd swear someone was taking pieces out of the puzzle and putting them back in the box.

"Then one day you know. What's missing isn't obvious; you can't name the thing. Just that it's always stood next to other pieces and now it's not. All you can see is the empty outline.

"So you rifle through the box to see if you can find it. You try to keep the shape of the piece in your mind, and you check the other pieces around where it should fit for anything else that might help make it stand out.

"Sometimes you find it, sometimes you don't. But no matter what, when you come back the next day, there are more holes."

I look at Jay. Maybe I shouldn't have told him. I'm worried enough for both of us. Oddly, I've gotten used to the missing pieces. It's the missing words that scare me most. Words are my life.

Across the room is an inflated playhouse filled with bouncing children and plastic balls. The kids can get out, but the balls remain inside. That's what my mind used to be like. Now it's as if each kid takes a couple of balls with him when he leaves, and every ball has a word written on it.

When it began, this slow rotting, I hardly realized, or at least I have no memory of such realization. But my innocence ended quickly. How long ago was that? I can't say. Sometimes it feels like it just happened. Sometimes it seems like it's been ages. But there was pain and fear, both growing till I thought I would go mad. Or maybe I was mad; the insane have little yardstick to measure by. But as time passed, I felt the pain slowly subside, replaced by a dawning acceptance of what was to come.

That's why I laughed. Now, at this moment, I know the fear and pain have all but vanished. This discovery makes the joy of seeing a new bird seem small indeed. I laugh again and turn back to my young sidekick. I reach across the table and tousle his hair to let us both know it doesn't matter. He smiles like he understands.

My puzzle is emptying, slowly but surely. My recent memories are all but gone. My middle years fade quickly. By tomorrow, I may have forgotten that I even had this thought. Too soon, all that will be left is this day, this hour, this moment. All the pieces will be back in the box, and someone will close the lid.

JACKSON

He stalked away from the field hospital office, fuming. Damned idiotic bureaucrat wouldn't hear of letting him return to the States so soon. Jackson offered to pay his own way, but this was rejected as meaningless. He even offered a substantial contribution, showing the administrator an unsigned check made out to *Médecins Sans Frontières*. Meaningless again. They needed doctors, not money. Jackson knew this wasn't true. Money was the fuel that stoked the MSF engine. He also knew they could not spare him till a replacement could be found. A month at least, the administrator said. "Too long," Jackson answered. No response, save a Gallic shrug, half eyebrow and shoulder lift, half smirk, all disdain; the man knew he possessed the power to refuse. Without authorization, there was no way Jackson could board a plane at the local airstrip.

Or was there? He stopped and turned to look back. There, parked to one side of the office was the supply truck, and on the back, legs dangling, the two boys, rifles draped across laps and pointed in opposite directions. They watched him watching them for a moment, and one raised a hand and saluted. The other laughed when Jackson returned the salute. Jackson was about to approach when the driver came out of the office, shouted at the boys and turned to walk away. They hopped down and followed, each shouldering a rifle, one on his left side and the other on his right. The non-uniformity of it made Jackson smile, though he was certain the boys took their job seriously. Challenging them would be a mistake for anyone of a mind to steal. This thought suggested another...in a country where poverty was commonplace, perhaps his money might be put to use in a more productive way.

Back in his tent, he mulled over the idea. How would the driver react to an offer of cash? Jackson didn't know. He did know the local currency was all but worthless; the thick wad of $100 bills he carried in his wallet were more than any of the locals might see in a lifetime. But that also might mean they'd be willing to kill for it. He had no way to defend himself against the guns that were everywhere. Only the previous day, a ragtag band of men and boys passed through, weapons bristling. And there were stories about weapons hidden in the villages.

There would be more than one man to bribe. The driver was only the beginning. There were two gunslinger boys, the airstrip's flight office manager. Probably the pilot too, though the one who flew him here from South Africa sounded English. Maybe if it were the same fellow, he would help as a courtesy, one professional to another. Or maybe not, Americans weren't popular anywhere after the second Iraq war.

No, this subterfuge would take careful thought and planning to have any chance for success. The weekly supplies would arrive in four days. It would take half the time for him to think it through. Then he would test the driver first. What if the man refused? He couldn't let that happen with Jeremy's safety and Rose's sanity at stake.

Jackson took a deep breath to relax and let go of the building tension. Jeremy would be all right. He was a smart kid, and he was used to dealing with difficulties caused by his parent's separation and his mother's crippling mood swings. Yes, Jeremy would be just fine. They had put him through the wringer more than once, and each time he had bounced back. This time, alone, wherever he was now, Jeremy would be coping and taking whatever came his way in stride.

Still, Jackson feared Rose would not be able to find Jeremy without help. He only hoped she would call Andrew for support. He knew Andrew would spare time from his casework. Would she call him? There was no way to guess. But if she didn't, the wedge between her and Jeremy would grow wider. Jackson couldn't let that happen. He wanted her. Like it or not, he must be there to take control.

ABBY

I pulled up in front of Nigel's house at 7:00 am. He bustled right out, tossed his backpack into the trunk and climbed in.

"Good morning, Abigail," he said, chipper as always. Then he gave me a hard look, gauging my mood.

"I'm not falling apart, Nigel," I told him. "I'm worried, I didn't sleep well last night, but I'm not falling apart. We'll find Harry. I just don't know when or where."

He held my eyes for a moment then nodded. "Right then. How about we stop at Café Monte Alto for a triple-shot latte to go? That'll prop open your baby-blues."

We did as Nigel suggested then headed down Main Street toward US-93. But, immediately realizing I hadn't thought out a route, I shot into the gas station just west of the entrance ramps to talk it over.

"Do we take Route 93 north or south?" I asked.

"East, actually. We'll take the shortcut to Center Harbor then stay on Route 25 most of the way to 95 North."

Nigel's British accent turned my soft "route" into "rout": a flight following defeat. Pronunciation or premonition? For no reason I could articulate, I believed it was the latter; it took all my internal fortitude not to reverse directions. But on we went, passing town after town, most no larger than one intersection: Holderness, Center Harbor, Moultonborough, Tamworth, Ossipee. Nigel pointed out Heath Pond Bog Natural Area as a wonderful birding spot. I asked if he thought Harry might have stopped there.

"Doubtful," he answered. "If he has Acadia on his mind, he'll go there directly. Always loved the place. Saw his first American kestrel there. Teased him about that—"

"What if he doesn't have anything on his mind?" I interrupted, my tone betraying my concern. Nigel gave me a look but let my comment go without remark.

"Sorry. That just slipped out."

"I know. You're allowed."

"I should be more hopeful, Nigel, but I'm not. I feel like I'm going through the motions and this is all just a waste of time."

He patted my knee. "Better than sitting home stewing, Abigail. And you don't know, really. We might trip across him somewhere along the way."

I nodded a reluctant acceptance and decided to work harder at keeping my negative thoughts to myself.

By lunchtime, Bar Harbor was still an hour away but we pushed on, stopping only to pick up lobster rolls. I wanted to get to the park, where Harry would have to register for camping. Nigel warned it was unlikely a campsite could be gotten without a reservation made ages ago, but we should cruise around looking for truck campers. "Might get lucky," he offered.

Dear Nigel, how slim are those odds? And what if we don't find him today? Should we try again tomorrow? Or should we keep driving north along the coast? How many bays and promontories are there along the hundreds of miles of Maine coastline, never mind the thousands of miles north into Canada. Did Harry even have his passport with him? And if not, would that keep him from crossing the border?

As Nigel expected, the campground visitor list did not include a Harry Herndon, so we took the Park Loop Road and pulled over each time we found a likely truck camper. It would have to be something Harry could drive and not be too expensive. Harry had not withdrawn enough money to purchase most of the fancy ones we saw, but there were also many smaller, affordable rigs.

Since the park's coastline is nothing short of majestic, we found it difficult to remain focused on our search. Eventually, we stopped to rest and eat our lobster rolls. "Before the mayo turns poisonous," Nigel joked. But I was not in a joking mood. I felt the dark irony of our quixotic quest; we were jousting with windmills. Such a waste of time, but what choice was there? And Nigel continued to insist adamantly that we might find him yet.

We consumed our late lunch, sitting cross-legged on a hardscrabble cliff overlooking the Atlantic, and Nigel asked about my trip out. I regaled him with the myriad irritations of current air travel, knowing full well he would no longer consider flying, and ended my story with the irritation of the long wait in line at the Hertz counter. Nigel laughed when I told him the rental agent's story about the "tall man and his wife with wild gray hair."

ADRIAN R. MAGNUSON

"Not bloody likely," he said, since he knew only too well Harry's love of petite blondes. "But, of course there was Margaret."

"Hmmm. That's true. I've often wondered about their relationship. She's so different from the others. Different from me as well."

"Well, you know, any port in a storm and all that."

"Be serious, Nigel. There must have been something there."

"Suppose so, luv, but Harry never came clean about it. Caused quite a row back then, young professor and even younger grad student. Something got covered up and Harry wanted it left that way. Now, though, he might tell you. Probably forgotten why he's kept mum all these years. Did you ever ask?"

"Oh, no. I knew his reputation and accepted it. I knew what I was getting myself into but didn't care. He'd either change or he wouldn't."

"And change he did. Mind you, there were moments of doubt and hesitation he shared occasionally over a pint of ale, and there was the 'look' he'd give the latest batch of freshmen, but he was just reminiscing. You were the end of that road."

"And Margaret was the beginning?"

"Yes, as far as I know. Harry never spoke of any attachments from his schoolboy years."

"But he did speak about Margaret?"

"Oh, certainly," he shot back but paused a moment. "You know, she was the one to break it off. Harry might have gone on for years, even behind everyone's back. Funny, though, Harry never called her Margaret... she was always Peg to him. She hated the nickname and told me so on several occasions. But he persisted. Even refused to answer if I asked after her as Margaret. Christ...I remember once I slipped and referred to her as Peg in her presence. She nearly took my head off."

"Strange," I said. "What few times he's ever talked about her, mostly when prodded, Harry always called her Margaret. Or maybe I called her Margaret and he didn't correct me. I never heard him call her Peg, that's certain."

"Doubt anyone else has either. After the row, we all stopped talking about her, Harry included. We knew the affair was to be treated as if it had never occurred. It was not spoken of."

"And then she left?"

132

"Yes," he said then paused again, as if considering how much to tell me. "Suppose she had to get away. I think Margaret couldn't stomach being the girl who ended Harry's career. She transferred to Boston University. The provost didn't want to have to step in and may have encouraged her. Harry thought she was just setting herself up for a long distance romance. He was wrong. She was distancing herself from him. He went to Boston a few times but quickly came to understand how things stood between them. But even after he had accepted the end to their time together, he still called her Peg. Of course, that was after a few pints. Surprised you didn't know that."

"I didn't. I have wondered about Margaret from time to time. And I've wondered about Olivia, how hard it must have been for her then. You know the way people talk. Especially the college crowd, nosey, inbred gossips that they are. I couldn't stand the rehashing. The story all resurfaced when Harry and I began seeing each other. I refused to listen, but knew they were talking behind my back."

"You're quite right about that. Then Margaret resurfaced as well and the talk escalated. I feared it would not go well for Harry—"

"Yes, but by that time, Harry's forgetfulness was becoming a problem. He kept to himself more and came home every day for lunch. And he ended our socializing as well. Took me too long to realize what the problem might be. The tests confirmed it, though."

"I never even suspected. Of course I knew he seemed to forget things, but we all did. Just part of getting on in years. And those were busy times for me. My series of bird books was always in the throes of the publisher back-and-forth. Lots of editing, working on the galleys, obtaining permissions for photos, and all the consequent wrangling. Then, you and Harry were off west."

"Well, not really," I said. "Three years passed after Harry's retirement before Oliver talked us into moving. In the end, it was as much Harry's decision as mine to leave. While he had no objection to being known as a Lothario, he knew being pitied as a has-been would destroy him. He even refused to see you when he was having a bad day. And when the bad days became the norm, he decided to move rather than face you. He knew very well you would never fly across country to visit."

"Ah. That also explains those times when Harry couldn't talk on the phone."

"Yes. Sometimes he would just shake his head. Or if he looked confused when I mouthed anyone's name, I answered for him."

"I blamed myself, you know. I thought he didn't want to see me again after..."

"After what?"

"Nothing, nothing. Water under the bridge and all that. No reason to dredge it all up."

"Margaret then."

"Yes, of course. You know, I suppose I should have realized sooner. Margaret always says I'm clueless about what's going around me." Then, mocking her, he quoted, "If it doesn't have feathers, you pay no attention."

That made me laugh. I might have liked Margaret under other circumstances. What Nigel was referring to, I couldn't guess, but didn't pursue it further.

Maybe there was something in my expression, or maybe just coincidence, but Nigel echoed my thought, "Margaret's a good sort, once you get to know her. You even might have been friends if things had been different."

"Maybe so," I answered, reaching out to lay my hand gently on his arm. "And I'm glad you have her. Heaven knows you need someone to take care of you."

"Well said, luv. Well said. Margaret and I make an odd couple, but it works. So long as we don't actually live together, anyway. But what about you? Who's taking care of Abby?"

I fought back my tears but couldn't hide them. Nigel took me in his arms and held me till my sobs subsided. His "There, there, ssh now," calmed; his gentle touch comforted. Dear Nigel, what would I do without you? But there's no time for this foolish self-pity. I need to be strong, be there for Harry the way he used to be there for me, and still is, though he doesn't remember why much of the time. I pulled away. "Enough nonsense. Time to start looking again."

"That's the spirit. Off we go then."

After three circuits of the park's coastline with nothing to show for it, we went in search of a proper meal. Nigel asked if it would be all right if he checked in with Margaret, so she'd know where he was.

I nodded and laughed. So she knows there's nothing going on, right, Nigel?

He smiled back. I laughed harder when he pulled a cell phone from his jacket pocket. Previously, Nigel's sole use for what he referred to as 'technology' had been a castoff IBM Selectric typewriter. And that was only for his most recent book. His first two had been typed on an old Underwood, one key at a time.

I watched him fumble with the phone, muttering to himself as he turned it on and punched the keys. Clearly, this was Margaret's idea, an electronic leash. I was pleased to see it needed to be turned on; Nigel had deliberately excluded Margaret from our search. Once powered up, the phone beeped Margaret's annoyance at him. Nigel held it at arm's length. "Six voice mails. I'd say I'm in trouble."

"Just tell her you were out of the coverage area most of the day and just now realized she had called."

"Think she'll believe me?"

"I doubt it," I told him, still laughing. "But otherwise you have to admit leaving the phone off. My way, at least you get plausible deniability."

"You do have an evil streak, don't you?"

"Hmmm. Don't sound so surprised."

I half listened to Nigel's conversation as I looked around the restaurant at couples talking animatedly, laughing, sharing a meal, coming and going hand in hand. I thought, "There, but for the gracelessness of God, go I." It was just so unfair. What sort of a mean-spirited creator would offer up his finest work, the human brain, then twist it so unmercifully?

"God giveth and he taketh away" came back from my teenage years. Something my mother would often say. And what I would answer, "But why? Just because He can?"

Nigel droned on, and I had almost tuned out what he was saying. Then I heard, "Yes, yes. Wild gray hair. Isn't that a hoot?" As I watched Nigel listen to Margaret's answer, a perplexed look came over his face then slowly dissolved into a smile. "Of course!" he yelled, loud enough to startle the woman at the table behind him. "We should have thought of her! Thank you, dear. You just solved the puzzle!" Margaret must have said something snippy in reply, because Nigel answered, "Yes, of course we'll have separate rooms. Never fear."

I waited impatiently while Nigel and Margaret waded through a long sign-off filled with more of his assurances. Then he reached across the table and took both my hands in his. "Harry's stolen a march on us! Your lady with wild gray hair? It's Grace."

It slowly dawned on me. Grace had spent years camping all over New England. She owned a camper. "She lent it to him?"

"Most assuredly. It's just the sort of thing Grace would do."

"Why didn't we think of her first?"

We answered in unison, "Gray hair."

Then Nigel continued, "Margaret said she must have stopped dyeing it by now. Makes perfect sense."

"Wait, Nigel. Who is the boy who was with her when Harry dropped off his rental car? Harry doesn't have a grandson and Grace never had any children as far as I know."

"Quite right. Well, I suppose we'll have to ask Grace, now, won't we?"

I felt the worry drain out of me, with Margaret to thank for pulling the plug that had held it in. If Margaret was right, then maybe Harry had fooled us all, including Grace. And if so, he must have had a clear head to set Margaret up to misdirect us. If he sent us east, he must have gone west. But to where? Back home? No, that made no sense. And what about the boy? Was he along for the ride? A hitchhiker? It would be the first time in his life Harry picked one up. Despite the unanswered questions, there seemed to be method to Harry's madness, and that was a good sign.

Nigel reached out and took my hand. "Grace will know where he is."

I hope so, Nigel, nodding agreement. But could I trust this hope? With all we didn't know, hope seemed dangerous.

JACKSON

Bathed in warm morning light, Jackson felt the tension from his sleepless night slowly recede, despite the fact that he was no closer to finding a way out. The triangular stool on which he sat consisted of a teepee: three rough branches with hide stretched across and fastened to the legs with strips of bark. The seat was unexpectedly comfortable.

Soon he would have to move into the shade, but for now the sun on his bare skin felt delicious.

When he closed his eyes, he could imagine being someplace in the Caribbean, his canteen of tepid water replaced with a frozen margarita. Rose lounged by his side in a chaise, wearing that microscopic, bright-green, string bikini he bought, her mass of long auburn curls playing across her breasts in the breeze.

"Is this for me or for you?" she had teased after opening the present and modeling the swimsuit for him, turning left and right seductively, eliciting the response she expected.

"Looks good on you," he had replied.

"Good?"

"Great."

"Mmm. How great?"

Jackson had remained silent, waiting.

"Show me," she said, fixing him with that melting look, the one he could never resist.

A shuffling of feet and a voice tinged with amusement brought Jackson out of his reverie, "Doctor is happy this morning?"

Before him stood the driver, hands on hips, smiling broadly as usual. The man always seemed amused. Was this at Jackson's expense? Perhaps. Or maybe Jackson was reading too much into it. More likely it was because the man had a cushy job. Probably made money on the black market too. Supplies often went missing.

"Doctor wanted to speak with me, I think."

Jackson frowned. How did he know this? Did the arrogant administrator say something? If so, would he expect to be paid off?

More importantly, was Jackson ready to pursue his plan? It seemed he must. "I have been thinking of asking you—" Jackson began, rising to stand.

The driver cut him off. "How to find a way out, yes?"

Exactly, a way out of the jungle, a way out of the mess he and Rose had created. Jackson nodded slowly and glanced left and right to see if anyone might overhear. The driver folded his arms across his chest. He was shorter than Jackson but he seemed taller. His skin was darker than Jackson had ever seen before, and the contrast to the smile, now broadening, was stark. "It will be expensive," he said.

Ah, the man gets right to the point. "How much?"

"One hundred American dollars."

Jackson relaxed imperceptibly, but the driver caught the change in posture.

"One hundred dollars to take you to the plane, and $100 to translate for you to the man who sends the plane. Also $50 for each of the boys."

Jackson's irritated expression must have had the right effect. The driver waited, not upping the ante.

"How much for the airstrip manager?"

"Only he can say. Maybe four or five hundred."

Jackson tried to look shocked. The driver only laughed.

"Please do not insult me. I know doctor has more. And he will need it when he gets to Johannesburg. There will be other palms to fill."

Jackson felt beads of sweat forming on his forehead. The sun was hot but it was the driver's self-confidence that caused him to perspire.

"When?" Jackson asked.

"Three days. We will leave before dawn. Be ready."

Jackson watched the driver's face for any sign of betrayal. The man grinned then his smile vaporized.

"Do not worry, Doctor Walsh. I am an honest man. With others you may not be so lucky."

Jackson paused to wonder how the man knew his name. The administrator? Didn't matter. "Thank you," he said.

"It is nothing. You will get what you paid for. Here, that does not often happen."

With those parting words, the driver spun on his heel and walked away. Within twenty paces, he broke into song. Jackson watched him disappear among the tents but could still hear him singing long afterward.

ROSE

"Good Morning. Mackaman, Martin, and Webster."

A young voice, serious, but a bit silly at the same time. Is she laughing? Rose spoke firmly, "Mr. Webster, please," trying to keep her anxiety under control.

"May I ask him who's calling, ma'am? Oh, sorry. I meant tell him. May I tell him who's calling?" Now the voice sounded like a teenager's, wrong words, wrong tone. Must be someone new. Probably young and pretty. Just the sort Andrew would hire. Men never grow up.

"Tell Andrew...tell him it's Rose...Walsh."

"Certainly ma'am. I'll put you right through." The girl burst out laughing at her own seriousness.

The line clicked. Rose was on hold.

While she waited, she thought about Andrew, and how they had dated before he gave her to Jackson. Not really true, though that's what it seemed like. He had never married, would never marry if she believed Jackson. His love life was a string of casual affairs; she had been one of them.

By comparison, Jackson had proved quiet and steady. She did not miss Andrew's devil-may-care approach to life. Less than a year passed before Jackson talked her into marriage, and she had never really regretted her decision, until she became pregnant. That event was unplanned and unwanted, but though she considered termination, she could not bring herself to do it.

Rose remembered the wild mood swings that began once her hormone changes collided with her unstable body chemistry. She stopped taking medications, worried, unreasonably Jackson said, that they might cause birth defects. Then Jeremy was born. By that time both she and Jackson had grown to love the highs, and suffered the lows as payment.

Rose remembered Jeremy's first years fondly. He had been a quiet baby and her friends envied her. Jackson made an effort to help and was attentive to her need for time on her own. But then he began working longer hours, and Jeremy slowly became more demanding. Three years ago, when she realized she hardly saw Jackson during the week and half the weekend, and when Jeremy absorbed most of what little time was left, she broke.

Now, she had to find a way. She must not fail Jeremy again.

Into this self-remonstrance, the phone clicked. "Rose! Sorry it took so long; I was on another call. How are you? And what's so important? Jeremy acting up as usual?"

Rose didn't like Andrew's flippant tone, but she needed his help. She chose to speak deliberately and without intonation. "No, Andrew. He's disappeared."

"I beg your pardon?"

"My son has disappeared."

"Oh, that can't be true. Maybe he's just out for a walk."

Rose heard the anxiety bleed through her calm. She fought the rising emotion, but the effort didn't work. She blurted, "You're just like Jackson. Jeremy's disappeared. He's gone. And where's Jackson, useless father that he is? In *Africa*!"

"I know."

"You *know* Jackson is in Africa? He *told* you?"

"Yes, yes. He keeps trying to get you and Jeremy to spend time together. He thought—"

"He thought he could force us to get along. That's *not* how it works, Andrew. Surely you know that."

"Yes, Rose, I do. I keep telling him but he doesn't listen. The reason—"

"Oh, Andrew, I know the reason," Rose said, calm again. "He wants me back. I get it. I just can't do it."

"But, Rose—"

"I can't, Andrew. Jeremy makes me crazy. You must realize that."

"Can't or won't?"

"It's one and the same. For me there is no difference between can't and won't. That's what nobody understands."

"But if you took your meds—"

"I wouldn't be me. I'd be...this is pointless."

She fought against the impulse to hang up. "I can do this, I can do this," she mouthed in silence. But her words' echo came back, "No, you can't."

"Rose?"

"I'm still here, Andrew. I don't want to be, but I'm still here. Just try to accept me the way I am and help me find Jeremy."

There was a long pause on his end of the line then "Alright. Let me think a minute. Not sure what to ask first...have you talked to Jackson?

"Of course," she answered evenly. "That's how I know he's in Africa. He didn't clue me in till he got there, but you know that already, don't you?"

"Yes, sorry. What did he say?"

"Nothing useful. He just told me to call you."

"Right. How about Jeremy? Have you tried calling him?"

Rose hesitated. How could she tell Andrew the truth...that she was afraid to speak to her own son, that she had always been afraid to speak to him because he misconstrued everything she said, bending and twisting her words? No, she must lie, a convenient believable lie. "I've tried but he must have his phone off. Or doesn't want to talk to me. I could leave a message but he'll ignore it."

"Even so, you should. Tell Jeremy what you're feeling. That you're worried sick something has happened to him. You are worried, aren't you?"

"Of course I'm worried!" she shouted then reconsidered her knee-jerk response. Was she worried? Jackson hadn't been. He sounded more concerned about her than he was about Jeremy. This thought struck her at first as reasonable, measured. Rose knew herself to be emotional; accepted this. If they really loved her, both Jackson and Jeremy would be supportive. But they had not been. Or had they? Hadn't she just finished saying Jackson seemed worried about her, not Jeremy? Hadn't Jeremy's words and tone yesterday been plaintive? "Wake up if you can," he had said, his voice soft, soothing.

"I'll keep trying, Andrew. And I'll leave a message. It won't matter though. Jeremy will only call when it suits him."

"Good. Now tell me what happened exactly, step by step?"

"Why? So you can belittle me the way Jackson did?"

"No, Rose. So I can visualize. I need to reconstruct what may have gone wrong. Try to keep it short and sweet."

"Short and sweet?" Rose asked, her voice rising as she crossed the room to find her purse and cigarettes, and then subsiding as she lit up. "Fine. Where do you want me to start, Seattle? Why not."

She paced the floor, back and forth like a caged animal. "So, let's see...Jackson puts Jeremy on a nonstop, redeye flight to JFK. He arrives... Wednesday morning, a week ago. I haven't seen him since."

"A week ago! Jesus, Rose, why didn't you call me sooner?"

She stopped dead center in the middle of the room and threw her hands in the air and shouted, "Because I thought he had flown back to Seattle. Do you want this story or not?"

"Okay, okay. Keep going."

She resumed pacing. "Right. The plane lands, some woman brings him out through Security. Then we walk down to baggage claim. He bitches at me the whole way about being stuck in New York. Then while we wait for his bags to arrive, he bitches at me some more, and begins whining that his latest toy is no longer 'the latest.' There's a new...Apple-whatever. I stand it as long as I can. Then I tell him to call his father, and walk out to cool off."

"That's it? You just left him there?"

Rose stopped again and looked out at the park. She was irritated by Andrew's tone. He should know her well enough not to sound as if he couldn't believe it.

"No, of course not, Andrew. I came back ten minutes later but he was gone."

"Ten minutes?"

"More or less."

"More then. Fifteen? Twenty—"

"Maybe fifteen. Maybe twenty. Not a minute longer."

"And you went looking for him? Had him paged?"

"No, why?" Rose lied again. She was tiring of Andrew's cross-examination and his assumption that she must be an idiot.

"*Why*? Jesus, Rose, because he's thirteen."

She turned around and sat on the windowsill, tapping the fingers of her left hand on the sill, while she took a drag on her cigarette. "Yes, thirteen, going on sixteen. And I did page him. He just didn't answer. The little shit knows how to push every button. Besides, Andrew, he was *supposed* to be good. He was *supposed* to have a return ticket and be able to fly back to Seattle at the first sign it wasn't working out. That's what Jackson *told* me. And like the fool I am, I believed him."

"Okay, okay. Calm down—"

"I am calm, Andrew. I'm not the hysterical woman you and Jackson think I am."

"Alright, Rose. Sorry. I didn't mean...anyway, you spoke with Jackson. What did he say?"

"Nothing useful. He thinks Jeremy is hitchhiking back to Seattle just to piss us off."

"Actually, that sounds like the Jeremy I know. He's probably right.

So, let me get this straight, Jeremy complained to you the whole time you were together? Or are you exaggerating?"

"I am not exaggerating one bit. I was nervous as hell, but I told him I was glad to see him. He gave me one of his wiseass remarks, something like, 'Well, I'm just so pleased to see you too.' He's always picking a fight with me."

"Is that what you told him?"

"What, that he's always picking on me? Yes, that's exactly what I told him."

"And then you both marched off together to baggage claim, Jeremy needling you the whole time, right?"

"Right," she answered, dismissing Andrew's question as obvious.

He paused a moment. While Rose waited, she walked to the sideboard and poured herself a vodka and stubbed out her cigarette in an empty glass.

"Damn. Rose, he was testing you. He was pushing to see if you'd break."

"Well, then he succeeded, didn't he?"

"Yes, Rose, he did. That's why he wasn't still waiting there twenty minutes later. He pushed, you broke, he took off. Still, hard to imagine him hitchhiking. He's small for his age. Who would pick him up?"

"Who? Oh, let me think. Pedophiles? Perverts? Slave traders? Any others you can imagine?"

"Don't be so melodramatic, Rose. I just meant that most drivers wouldn't stop to pick him up because they might fear being *reported* as a 'pedophile, pervert or slave trader.' He would look too young. But he's almost fourteen. If he's hitching, he'll be smart about it."

Rose took a sip from her vodka. She hoped Andrew was right, that nothing bad would happen to Jeremy, but she knew from Jeremy's call yesterday that he was crying. Still, he didn't seem terrified, just sad, needy. And sincere, not manipulative. Was he in trouble? She should have answered his call.

Tears welled up and she fought for control. How many more times would she fail him? Would she even get another chance? Yes, Andrew seemed to be saying, just as Jackson had insisted, "You'll see; everything will be all right. I promise." Rose knew her response held equal weight, "Stop making promises you can't keep." So she sighed into the receiver. Andrew said he would make some inquiries and call back later, and he rattled on about why calling the police would be a waste of time, but she hardly heard him as she hung up. Her mind was far away on a deserted road searching for her son. She could see herself walking, calling out to him then listening for his voice. She imagined the sounds of windblown leaves and rain falling, then the long wail of a passing train. She shuddered, and deep inside her something clicked, some instinctual shift, felt but not understood.

"I promise," she whispered.

JEREMY

Late in the afternoon we pull into Red Bridge Campground on the east side of the Allegheny Reservoir. It's about nine miles northwest of the town of Kane, Pennsylvania. We choose a full hookup site close to the bathrooms again. They even have showers. Harry seems pleased. "You'll have to mind my leg while I soap up," he tells me.

"You're kidding."

"Nope. Can't get it that wet. A few raindrops won't hurt, but I think it might short out in a steady stream. I generally take a shower sitting down."

"On the floor?"

"No, moron. On a chair."

"We don't have a chair."

"I'm aware of that. Go find one."

"Where?"

"I don't know. Use your imagination."

A quick circle of the campground turns up no loose chairs, just picnic tables. I think about asking to borrow one but it's kind of embarrassing, so I don't, returning empty handed.

"No luck, huh?"

I shrug.

"Couldn't find one to borrow?"

I shake my head.

"Didn't ask, did you?"

I shake my head again. Harry nods.

"Well, you could ask around, or I suppose I could stand on one leg while you soaped me up. How would that be?"

"I'll go ask."

"There you go."

It's even more embarrassing than I thought explaining why I need one and why we don't have one. I try a couple of the neighbors, and one of them suggests asking at a huge rig down next to the reservoir. Looks the size of a Greyhound bus. I try to see if anyone's inside, but the windows are tinted too dark. I figure the owners must not be there, but when I knock, the door opens and a ramp slides out automatically from under the bus. A really old woman in a wheelchair looks back at me from the top of the ramp. "Can I help you, young man?"

"Uh, maybe. My grandfather only has one leg. Well, only one real one. His other is mechanical. And, and he wants to take a shower. But, but he can't get the leg wet because it's electric. And we don't have a chair for him to sit in—"

"Say no more. I've got just the thing. Come on up."

She spins her chair around and wheels away, yelling, "Phillip, come help this young man with my shower chair."

I can hear someone say, "Coming."

She shouts back, "Hurry up about it."

An even-older-looking man walks down the long hallway pushing a wheelchair. He looks like he needs it more than Harry does.

"Show the boy how to fold the chair up, and how to lock the wheels so it doesn't roll, Phillip."

"I will. Quit nagging."

"I'm not nagging, Phillip. You'll *know* when—"

"Why is there a hole in the seat?" I interrupt, but before she can answer, I feel my face heat up. Must fit over a toilet. That's so gross. Not sure I want to push it.

The woman laughs. "Embarrassed, huh? You may need one of these yourself someday. Your grandfather's used one before, I'm sure. Nothing to be ashamed of. Show him how to fold it, Phillip."

"Got a name, boy?" he asks, ignoring her.

"Jay, sir."

"That so? What's it short for?"

"Jeremy. That's what my parents call me. Gramps calls me Jay, though."

"Well, Jeremy Jay, this is Edna. I'm Phil. I'm ninety-five. Edna, here, is only eighty-nine, or so she tells everyone. How old are you?"

"I'll be fourteen tomorrow."

"Really. Well happy birthday, then. By the time you're our age they'll probably invent a chair that pops out of a case and assembles itself. For now, this will have to do. Say, bring your grandfather by later. Tell him I've got a good singlemalt I'd be happy to share with him. How old is he?"

"Gramps is seventy-five."

"Ah, a mere whipper-snapper. Tell him to come anyway. He's old enough to drink."

As I wheel the chair down their ramp, Phil adds, "Tell him that scotch is twice your age, Jay. That'll get his attention."

Edna adds, "And bring my wheelchair back clean and dry."

I promise I'll let Gramps know about the scotch, and that I'll take care of the wheelchair. I roll it away, passing several other campers who point and laugh, making comments I can't hear. My face heats up again.

When I get back to the campsite, Harry is gone. Shit, did he wander off? At least the camper is still here. Now what do I do?

First check is inside, no Harry. Next, the bathroom, no Harry. Then I check each of the three loops of RV campsites, no Harry. Where the hell is he? On the third loop a lady walking a dog asks me if I'm lost. No, but my grandfather is. She looks like she doesn't believe me, but points me down a walking path that leads to the boat launch and fishing dock. And there he is, watching the Canada Geese hanging around for a handout.

"Harry?" I ask, wondering whether he'll still know who I am.

"Find me a chair?"

Apparently he's okay. "Yup. It's a wheelchair for the shower. Even has a hole you can crap through."

"Hah! Don't need that yet, but the hole will come in handy. I love to pee in the shower."

"Grr-oss!"

"All goes down the same drainpipes."

"It's still gross."

We head back to the camper and Harry checks out the chair then gets his bathroom stuff. Then he makes me wheel him to the showers. He puts on a show for some people we pass, telling them how lucky he is to have a grandson to help him. "Knock it off, or I'll leave you right here," I say, once we're out of earshot.

"Then I'll wheel myself back and make you do it all over again. Just having a little fun. Lighten up."

When we get to the showers, Harry undresses while I look the other way. He sits back in the wheelchair to detach his robotic leg, hands it to me, and I reach without looking. He's naked.

While Harry's in the shower, two men come in. They give me a strange look. I'm sitting here fully clothed, holding somebody else's leg, so I can't blame them. When they start taking their clothes off, I leave. Screw Harry. He can wheel himself back.

When Harry returns a half hour later, I can see he's pissed. He's also only half-dressed. "Thanks for ditching me," he says. "Shitty thing to do."

"Just having a little fun. Lighten up," I answer.

"Wiseass."

"You started it."

"Hmmph. No wonder your mother dumped you. I should too."

"Yeah, right. You remember that?"

"Vaguely."

"Wait. Is this the first time you remembered?"

"Don't know if it is or it isn't. Just remember following behind the two of you and watching you argue. Then Mom walked out as I recall. Sound about right?"

"Yeah."

"So, wiseass, maybe next time I'll ditch you too."

"Already did."

"Did not."

"Did too."

"When?"

"Two days ago. You left me at the gas station. I already told you once. You just forgot."

He looks like someone punched him in the gut but doesn't say anything. Damn. Shouldn't have told him. "Sorry."

"For what? I'm the one who should be sorry. Just can't keep anything

ADRIAN R. MAGNUSON

in my head. Things come back, but not reliably. You're going to have to pay better attention. And start reminding me."

"Okay."

"No, not okay. Start talking. What have I missed?"

I shrug. Harry returns the shrug, giving me attitude.

"I don't know," I tell him, "What do you remember?"

"Arguing at the airport."

"What else?"

"Let's see, the college. And talking to some woman. Stopping for gas someplace. Oh, and the King Eider, I forget where."

"That's it?"

Harry shrugs. "Standing on one leg trying to get my pants on? That count?"

"Sorry."

"Forget it. I will. Probably by tomorrow. So, what's missing?"

"A lot. Borrowing the camper from Grace. Forgetting that you did. Driving to the college. Forgetting who you talked to. Forgetting my name."

"I forgot your name?"

I nod.

"What else?"

"Camping on the Mohawk River. Renting a boat. The drive to Pennsylvania."

"Pennsylvania?"

"That's where we are. Allegheny National Forest."

Harry looks around at the tree covered hills and river below us. "Beautiful place." Then he looks at the camper. "Grace lent us this piece of junk?"

"It's okay. Got us here, didn't it?"

"Good point. That was a nice thing for her to do, especially since most likely I'll run it off the road and into a tree first time I forget to turn."

"You drove six hours today. No problem."

"I did, huh? I'd feel a lot better about that if I could remember any of the trip."

"Maybe you remember then forget right away."

"What possible difference does that make?"

"Well, I guess, you know what you're doing while you're doing it. Then later you don't."

"That's one theory. What if you're right about the second part but wrong about the first?"

"Then you're right. We'll do some bushwhacking."

"And you're okay with that?"

"Sure. I'm wearing a seat belt."

"Doubt that'll help much if we end up wrapped around a tree or upside down in a ravine. Maybe I should teach you how to drive."

"You're joking!"

"Not really."

"That would be so cool! But I'm puny. I don't think I could see over the steering wheel and my feet won't reach the pedals."

"Seat's adjustable. Couple of pillows under your butt should take care of the rest."

"Maybe. You're serious?"

"Look, kid, what if I'm getting worse, forgetting more each day. How will we make it to...where are we going?"

"Seattle."

"Jesus, that must be, what, two thousand five hundred miles?"

"There's plenty of time. No rush. I can drive a little each day."

"There you go. That's the spirit. We'll need a map. Otherwise we'll get lost."

"Can't get lost. My Blackberry knows where we are most of the time."

"Blackberry?"

"My cell phone."

"How does a cell phone know where we are?"

"It's got a GPS."

"What's that? No, don't tell me. I'll take your word for it."

"Cool. You sure this isn't a dumb idea?"

"Have a little faith in yourself. You're a smart kid. You can do it. And I'm a good teacher."

"Right. A teacher who can't remember shit."

ABBY

We turned off Middlebrook Road, passed through the stone pillars, and up the hill to the fork. It felt wrong to be here without Harry, wrong and sad. A flood of memories surfaced. All those summers Harry and I spent here.

How much did he remember? Some, certainly. He had been coming here most of his life. The pond would be among the last things he forgot. But our time together, what of that?

I took the left and plunged down the steep slope, and my thoughts turned to Grace. Would she be home? Had Harry been to see her? If so, would Grace tell me the truth or would she protect Harry's plan, concealing it from me?

Nigel had been napping but jarred back to life once I hit the bumpy gravel of the rutted one-lane down to the old camp.

"Sorry, luv. Must have dozed off. Almost there I see."

"Yes, but what will we find? What if Margaret's guess is wrong?"

"What if, what if. We'll soon know."

Nigel was right, of course, but those last few yards to the bottom made me worry that the camp would be brimming with life. This was Saturday and although I hoped to get Grace alone, I knew she might have guests or be out speaking with neighbors. Most of the cabin owners were weekenders. Friday they arrived, and in the evening the camp hopped with late night revelry: wood fires burning, coolers filled with beer, old friends drifting from fire to fire. They would chat about the busy week past and their plans for the next day and a half. Then on Sunday they would repack their cars and return to civilization.

This spirit of weekend camaraderie bonded them all together; it was what Harry and Grace loved best. For me, the partying had always been a mixed blessing, the hail-fellow-well-met backslapping and beer guzzling was just not my cup of tea. I preferred to keep my circle of friends small and intimate. Yet, I had always joined in as gamely as I could, knowing how much it meant to Harry, and knowing also how sensitive his radar was to any sign I might be at all like Olivia.

As we rounded the corner, I saw my worry had been misplaced. The camp was empty. Only Grace's old truck sat perched at the end of her driveway. We walked up Grace's front steps, and heard her talking to her chipmunks. "Come get yah peanut, Scahface. Come on now. Not goin' tah hold it all day."

"Grace?" Nigel said. She jumped nearly out of her skin.

"Jesus, Joseph, and Mary. Tryin' tah give me a heart attack?"

"Sorry, old girl. Didn't mean to surprise you."

"Didn't surprise me. Just startled me. Been half expectin' to see ya."

"Harry's been here, then?" I asked.

"Yep. Lent him my campah too. Everythin' all right, I hope?"

Nigel and I exchanged glances. We didn't know.

"That bad, is it? Been worryin' 'bout them. Harry wasn't hittin' on all eight when he was heah. Said he'd be fine though, so long as Jay was watchin' out for him."

"Jay?" we blurted in unison.

"His grandson. Oliver's boy."

"We only have granddaughters, Grace," I said, shaking my head.

"Damn. Knew Harry might lie tah me. Nevah thought the boy would."

"You'd know if you ever had children—they develop that talent long before they become teenagers."

"But you never had any eithah, as I recall."

I paused a moment. "No, but I had Oliver. One was enough."

Grace didn't seem to notice the pause. She bent down to offer a peanut to Scarface.

It remained my one true regret, not having a child. At first Harry had been dead set against it, then many years later, when he changed his mind, I was too old, or maybe I just thought I was too old.

"Enough for me too," Grace said, tossing another peanut. "Or so I'd imagine. Often wondah what life would'da been like havin' a kid. My dustin'-n'-cleanin' took that away yeahs ago. Ended up bein' a spring cleanin.'"

"Dusting and cleaning?" Nigel asked, though he looked sorry he had when Grace turned and answered, "Woman problems, Nigel. Ya don't want tah know."

Behind her back I mouthed the letters, "D & C," though Grace's "spring cleaning" must have meant she had a hysterectomy.

Nigel's face turned red, no longer confused, but looking even sorrier.

By evening Nigel and I had driven back to Plymouth and were settled into a booth at one of the local pubs, Biederman's Deli, a basement entrance sports bar of sorts with a good selection of the lagers and ales he preferred. Not being much of a beer drinker, I ordered pinot grigio to go with my Basement Bomb, a roast beef sandwich with Boursin cheese. Nigel ordered his usual, Rueben and Bass ale.

Grace had no more idea than we did who the boy was, but at least we had a name, Jay. Probably short for something, but Grace didn't know what. "Called himself Jay. Nevah heard Harry say anythin' different."

When asked Jay's age, she guessed, "Moah than ten, less than fifteen, but I'm no judge."

Grace had also provided the license plate number for her camper, but I was reticent to use it. Nigel, on the other hand, was all for involving the authorities.

"What should I tell the police, Nigel? I could try, 'My husband misappropriated a truck that he's now driving across country, harboring an underage boy.'"

Nigel looked down and shook his head.

"No? How about this, then, 'My husband, who has Alzheimer's, and who may at any minute forget which side of the road to drive on, is currently steering four tons of metal through heavy traffic with no clue where he's going.' Any better?"

"Alright, alright. We'll leave the jackboots out of it. We're on the same side, Abigail. And there's no need to be so dramatic. Harry may get them lost but he's not going to forget how a motorcar works."

I lowered my head, not speaking for a moment. When I raised it and answered, my voice was filled with resignation. "He already has."

"I beg your pardon?"

"His leg, Nigel. How do you think he crushed his leg?"

"An accident, Abby. You told me. Everyone has accidents. Had a few myself, come to think of it. One while driving on the wrong side of the road."

"Yes, everyone has accidents, but hasn't it occurred to you over the past few days that Harry might be a particular danger to himself and others? Hasn't it occurred to you that there might be a connection between losing his leg and having Alzheimer's?"

"No, luv, it hasn't. But are you certain? Mightn't the accident have been like any other?"

"Yes, I'm sure. Harry told me. When the police found him he was unconscious, in shock. Lost a lot of blood, the doctor said. No one was allowed to visit till the next day. I saw him first. He was drugged up fairly well but lucid. 'Couldn't stop,' he kept repeating. 'Couldn't stop.'"

"'Why,' I asked. 'Was there something wrong with the brakes?'"

"'Brakes? What do you mean?' he answered. I presumed he was still shaken up from the accident so I asked again, 'The brakes? Did your foot slip off the pedal?'"

"'I couldn't stop. I didn't remember how to stop,' was all he said."

"But later, when the police questioned him, Harry told them his foot slipped off the pedal. They gave him a ticket, but since no one but Harry was injured, they didn't suspend his license. Oliver told me to take it and cut it up so he couldn't drive again. That wouldn't have stopped Harry, though. And I thought maybe he hadn't actually meant what he said. Maybe his foot really did slip off the pedal."

"Perhaps it did. Perhaps he misspoke when he said he forgot how to stop."

"No. I've been over this ground so many times. And I've watched as he becomes more and more confused. Each time he backs out of the driveway, I look for any sign.

"Once he tried to start the car without the keys. I told him I'd drive then saw him study what I did. He was relearning that keys turn ignitions. He's clever that way, always observing, always covering up when he forgets a name, always lying about the things he's obviously forgotten. And each time I catch him at it, I wonder how many times I didn't catch him."

"Perhaps Oliver has it right, Abby. Perhaps it's time to keep a tighter rein. I know this sounds like closing the coop door after the chickens are gone, but when we find him, and we will, we need to clip his wings, as it were."

Ah, Nigel, I know it's the responsible thing to do. It's just that I can't bring myself to accept ending Harry's freedom this way. I wonder if there's any chance this kid, Jay, will be able to keep them both safe.

I pray that it's so, but I fear that it is not.

ROSE

She walked north on Central Park West then entered the park through the Boy's Gate at 100th street, turning left toward The Pool and Cascade. Rose paused to watch the waterfall's splash and tumbledown, the current flowing through The Loch then under Glenspan Arch and into a wooded ravine. She stopped to rest beneath the willows overhanging the pool, sat on a settee bench near the water's edge, and placed her purse and hat next to her. The small grotto seemed like a forest pond in the Adirondacks far to the north, but Rose knew The Pool was manmade, its source a huge underground pipe funneling water from the reservoir down to Harlem Meer. Traffic noise from both west and east easily penetrated and dispelled the idyllic vision.

Her thoughts turned to Jeremy. He loved this place, despite all his words to the contrary. Birds abounded here. His precious life list was filled with them. It was not New York that he hated, it was her. Why did Jackson persist in throwing them together? Surely he could find another woman to take Rose's place, a younger woman who might have something in common with Jeremy. In fact, there was one, though Jeremy didn't seem to care much for her. What was her name? Rose couldn't remember.

But was that really what Rose hoped for, to be replaced? The thought saddened her. That was not what she wanted. Yet she could not imagine living together as a family again either. Choose one, she thought, there's no middle ground. Jackson needed a wife and Jeremy needed a mother. Rose wasn't sure she was capable of doing either, but she was certain she couldn't do both.

No, her job now was to help Jackson understand this and to find her son. Jeremy could not possibly hitchhike across the entire country without something terrible happening. Wherever he was, she had to find him, though she had no idea where to begin. Since speaking with Andrew, Rose had tried Jeremy's cell phone four times, each time with the same result, Jeremy's deadpan, "Can't talk. Leave a message. Or not. Whatever," ringing in her ears followed by the voicemail beep. She had recorded two messages, one calm, one pleading, but Jeremy had not returned either.

There seemed no choice but to wait for Andrew to point her in the right direction. She sat quietly, watching a lone swan plying the pool. Then she heard a flutter of wings above her and looked up into the willow. A large black and white bird sat roosting on a branch almost directly over her head, its eyes closed. Realizing she might easily be shat upon, she slid over to the edge of the bench. The far side bore testimony to recent bombardment, greenish-white and still dripping through the open slats. What sort of bird was this? Jeremy would know. He had shown her his life list with photos of each bird but of course she hadn't paid attention.

It occurred to her then she should make an effort now, because this would be something she could talk to Jeremy about, something he would be interested in hearing from her. And if the bird was new to him as well, he might even give her some credit for caring enough to make the effort.

Rose considered trying to take a photo with her cell phone but dismissed the idea. She was afraid to get too close. The bird might fly away. Nor was she certain she knew how. Jeremy regularly criticized her technical ineptitude; Jackson did too. Rose was sure the bird would leave before she ever figured it out.

It appeared to be sleeping now, hunkered down on the thick branch. She rifled through her purse and withdrew a tiny device; her electronic memory, she called it. Push its button and it would record thirty minutes of notes. Rose found it indispensable for appointments, directions, and reminding herself where she had parked her car the few times she decided to drive. Mainly, she took cabs.

She looked carefully at the bird. Its posture, all hunched up, made it difficult for Rose to guess size or even shape. "Smaller than a swan, larger than a pigeon," she spoke into the recorder nestled in her palm. "More like a seagull."

"Black on the back, gray on the sides, white and black on the head," she continued, smiling at her cleverness. She remembered Jeremy often described the beak and legs of birds he saw, noting out loud both color and length. "Black beak," she said, speaking into her hand. A young couple passing by turned to look at her. "Probably think I'm nuts," Rose mumbled then self-consciously looked down at the way she was dressed. Faded jeans, sneakers, and a sweatshirt. A bag lady, that's what I look like, but at least my bag is Louis Vuitton. Rose laughed out loud and saw the couple increase their pace.

This was fun, but how could she get the bird to stand up so she could see its legs? She tried making more noise, shouting, "Whoop, whoop, whoop," at the sleeping bird. It did not move. Then she walked to the nearest low-hanging branch and launched herself up to grab and swing it down, thinking the motion might disturb the bird. It slept on. She recalled a TV program she and Jeremy had once watched, a nature show about crows and ravens. They like shiny things. Maybe this bird was a raven. She again rifled through her purse for something to throw, and dredged up a brass lipstick tube.

Her first toss nearly ended up in the water. Her second and third bounced off smaller branches, ricocheting haphazardly. The bird took no notice. Maybe it's dead, she thought. But then her fourth try clipped a branch over the bird's head, startling it. As the lipstick fell back toward her, the bird caught the tube in its beak. Now standing, eyes open, the bird was larger than she had presumed, its yellow legs increasing its stature. Rose retrieved her recorder from where she had set it on the bench, and spoke, "Yellow legs, white underneath, red eyes."

The bird shifted its feet, flapped its wings, then settled back onto its belly and adjusted the position of the lipstick in its beak, as if weighing to gauge the tube's likely nutritive value. Having decided it was not edible the bird let the lipstick drop. "Thank you," Rose called up, playfully. The bird shook its head then let out a raucous sound, "quark...quark," as if to say, "Thanks for nothing." That's when Rose noticed the bird's long crest, a single, thin white feather rising from the back of its head to stand straight out behind at least six inches. Rose didn't think the feather belonged there but she dutifully recorded it, "Loose white feather stuck on head, like a vintage hat."

By this time, a small crowd had gathered to watch the show. Rose asked if any of them knew what sort of bird this was. No one seemed certain; guesses ranged from duck to gull to woodpecker. This last seemed possible since the bird's beak was long and pointed. Although disappointed, at least Rose felt less ignorant. She was not the only one who understood nothing about birds. Rose was about to walk back to the bench and gather up her purse and hat, when her phone rang, its distinctive aria ringtone coming from the opposite direction. She turned and saw a woman carrying the purse, walking away quickly. Rose shouted, "Stop." The woman dropped the purse and fled.

Rose considered running after her. She knew she could easily catch the woman; her daily gym rat routine had shed twenty years from her physique, but she let her go. Had the woman asked, Rose would have handed her twenty dollars, as she had done so many times before when accosted by the homeless. "Here's a Jackson," she always said, "You need him more than I do." The dual pleasure of giving and disposing of one more Jackson brought a smile to her face every time.

Before her cell phone rolled over to voicemail, she answered.

"Rose Walsh?"

"Yes?" she said curtly, irritated to be referred to by her married name.

"Please hold for Mr. Webster," the girl said, voice rising.

A moment later, Andrew picked up, his voice tentative. "Rose? How are you?"

"How do you think I am, Andrew?"

"Sorry. I only meant—"

"Forget it. I'm as well as can be expected. And this is not your fault, Andrew. I'm just frustrated. I've tried calling Jeremy several times but all I get is his voicemail."

"Did you leave a message?"

"Of course, but that's no assurance he'll call back."

"No, it isn't. Frankly, I think he's deliberately avoiding you."

"Obviously. But why?"

"Well, it's just a theory and quite possibly wrong, but I have a hunch it's right. I think one of the passengers on his flight is giving him a ride. "

"What?"

"Just...just listen and see what you think. Yesterday I called the airline to check if there was anything unusual that happened on the plane or on the concourse when Jeremy got off or when they escorted him to baggage claim. I introduced myself as a friend of his father, but I had my receptionist place the call so they would know they were speaking to an attorney. Then I suggested perhaps they had not done the job they were supposed to do. The airline representative acted appropriately shocked and unaware then promised to make a thorough investigation and get back to me, which she did an hour ago. Though she did not actually *know* anything, and though she did not admit to any error in proper procedure, she did report three interesting facts. One, apparently Jeremy spent most of the flight in first class sitting next to and talking with an elderly gentleman. The flight attendant remembered them well. Two, the woman who walked Jeremy to baggage claim said he was not happy to be in New York. Three, a security guard remembers a young boy who looked lost was met by his grandfather. Apparently, the guard had some initial doubts so the incident stood out in his memory. The guard could not verify the day or time, but his description fits."

"And you think they're traveling together?"

"That's my theory. I asked the airline representative to provide the name of the man Jeremy was speaking to, but she declined, citing airline privacy policy. Since I'd have to go to court to subpoena the passenger lists, I tried a different tack. I asked if she would be willing to call the emergency contact for the passenger in question and ask that person to get back to me. She agreed to do that if they had a record of the phone number, but couldn't guarantee any response. I gave both my number and yours in case the contact would prefer speaking with a woman."

"So we have to wait?"

"Afraid so. Unless you want me to begin the subpoena process. By the way, I'd probably lose."

"Why?"

"Because there's no proof anyone did anything wrong. He's a runaway, pure and simple."

"But if your theory is right then he was abducted."

"No. He went off willingly. But that's the good news, Rose. Jeremy must have trusted this man or he would have done something different."

"Oh, please, Andrew. That's just how pedophiles operate. They seem so nice and sweet till they get you in their cars."

"Rose, you're overreacting again. Think about it. They met on the plane by accident. Pedophiles generally stalk their prey."

"Generally? Generally! How many times do they do it *un*-generally? And why is 'runaway' assumed? Why not assume the worst and prove it isn't true?"

"Because there are millions of runaways in this country. So common it has become the default assumption."

"My son is not a default assumption."

"I know that, Rose. But there's a difference between what I believe and what I can prove."

"That's exactly what makes lawyers so useless, Andrew. All talk, no action."

"I know it may seem that way, but that's the system. There's only so much I can do."

Rose paused to regain control. Andrew was right, the odds were good Jeremy had gone willingly with this man, whoever he was. But Rose hated trusting the odds. Before, when she had believed he was hitchhiking, she had accepted that Jeremy's good sense would protect him. Now she wanted some sense of certainty. Waiting would be hellish. "How long?" she asked.

"Till what, Rose?"

"Till the family calls back."

"By tomorrow, I hope. I'll get back to you, one way or the other. Or if the wife contacts you, let me know. How late can I call?"

"The time hardly matters. I won't be in bed."

"Try, Rose. Try to get some sleep."

Rose flipped the cell lid shut. There was nothing left to say. She considered trying Jeremy again, but what would be the point? Andrew was right. Jeremy wouldn't answer. He had called her that one time, but he had been in trouble of some sort. This thought gave Rose hope. If he wasn't calling then he must be all right. Unless...no, she would not go there. She could not, would not, face her darkest fears. Andrew would call later. "The man's family will know where Jeremy is," she said to herself, "Then we'll go bring him home."

We? Home? Who was she kidding? There was no we, no home. Just two clueless parents whose pathetic efforts had never been good enough. Tears strained at the corners of her eyes. She fought unsuccessfully to cut them off. She wanted to be held, but there was no one she could turn to. Her friends here were not the sort to share secrets with. Quite the contrary, they fed on gossip, devouring the sharer along with what had been so trustingly revealed. Ironically, it was Jackson she wanted. Unreliable, unrepentant Jackson. Not forever, just to hold her right now. She would have laughed, but irony was only funny when it happened to somebody else.

ABBY

Nigel and I had just been served our dinners when my phone rang. I answered immediately, thinking it might be Harry, but Oliver spoke. His voice and what he had to say brought a rush of hope and shame.

Harry had rented a rowboat and motor, and paid cash, but left his credit card as a security deposit. On returning the boat, he had failed to refill the gas tank, hence the $8.75 charge. Two days ago they had been in Scotia, New York a few hours drive from where we now sat. This gave me hope we might find them. They were headed west and might again make a mistake signaling their location. A slim hope, but a hope nonetheless.

Offsetting that hope was the shame I felt sitting here with a good meal in front of me and another man across the table. While I had had no difficulty fending off Nigel's meek advances, my own feelings were beginning to betray me. They betrayed Harry's trust as well. That is, if he even remembered me. Can you betray someone who doesn't know who you are? Just the sort of conundrum Harry loved.

Nigel, I knew, would not. He would never betray his friend unless I gave him permission to do so. That his testing was gentle, I took as affection both for Harry and for me.

Where does trust live? In the mind of the trusting party? If so, then perhaps it no longer exists. And, if that is correct, then my answering trust in Harry is gone as well. A person who cannot remember cannot be trusted, would have no way of knowing he should be trustworthy. Perhaps trust brooks no ownership. Perhaps trust is a thing shared between two people, existing not in separate minds but in the conjoined consciousness, a thing unto itself and independent of the individuals who share it.

I have no idea how long I sat lost in convoluted thoughts, in vain attempt to justify what I had been feeling. Nigel's, "Everything all right, luv?" spoken with his mouth open and half-full, suggested he finally noticed my absence. Harry would have realized immediately and asked where my thoughts had strayed. I smiled, knowing I had just solved my riddle. The answer lay not in the conundrum's details but in what it stood for: words. Words were both Harry's passion and moniker. It was his ever curious mind I loved, a mind I believed still as sharp as ever, despite loss of memory. In that sense, little had changed.

I looked back at Nigel. "Everything's just fine, dear." Then I explained what Oliver told me, and we made plans to leave the next day to drive across New York State. If Grace was right, and if Harry held to his abhorrence of dawdling, I expected them to stick to the interstates, hopping off only long enough to find campgrounds and birding spots.

Before we left Plymouth we would pick up some camping guides. Nigel knew all the most likely birding spots along the way and would bring his own books on the subject. We would search out each one for clues and try to find them. Failing that, we might at least be close enough to intervene when their journey came to an end.

HARRY

Enjoyed our little cocktail party last night, doubt Jay did. He seemed distracted. Funny couple, Phil and Edna, always harping at each other. Their RV rig is impressive, even more impressive when Phil told me the price tag, $600k. "Home sweet home till we kick the bucket," he said.

Edna shot back, "Still think we should sell it and move into that nice retirement community near the kids."

Phil gagged on his scotch. "Over my dead body."

"As soon as you go, I'm selling it."

"And as soon as you go, I'm mounting your ashes on the dashboard."

Watching the two of them argue reminded me of Abby and of our own verbal sparring contests. Boy did we go at it. But I couldn't remember a single detail, just the clear sense we sniped at each other the way Edna and Phil did.

My useless memory, I suppose. Or maybe not. Maybe the details aren't important. Maybe all you ever remember is the fun of give and take. Have to ask Abby. Was it Abby? Maybe it was Olivia I fought with. Or both. I seem to remember that Olivia hated fighting. Wasn't good at it. Abby liked trading barb for barb, so long as the fight was in good fun and we got to make up later. Always enjoyed the making up part.

Nice of Phil and Edna to feed us, though I can't say I enjoyed the meal. Last tuna casserole I had must have been fifty years ago. Only thing Olivia knew how to cook back then. Out of desperation I bought her a hardbound *Joy of Cooking*. About the only good that did was to give her five new ways to make a meal out of canned tuna.

Jay told Edna and Phil he wasn't hungry. But he polished off four slices of buttered bread, so I don't think they were fooled. Managed to wolf down a couple of peanut butter and jelly sandwiches later as well, the only food we had in the camper. That's what we both had for breakfast today. He took off early this morning. Said something about chucking rocks into the river. Think I'll leave him alone for an hour or two to work out whatever is bugging him.

JEREMY

Not sure what to do. The idea of driving scares the shit out of me, but it would be so cool. And when I get back to Seattle in the fall I'd get to brag about it. Harry's right, I can do it. Better than depending on him anyway. So weird he remembers stuff sometimes and sometimes doesn't. Guess what worries me is that no matter who's driving we might not make it.

I'm still chucking rocks when I hear Harry walk up behind me, his fake leg making a beeping sound.

"Fill the river with rocks yet, Jay?" he says.

"No."

"It's a joke. You're supposed to laugh."

"It's not funny."

"Okay, did you hear the one about the traveling salesman, the farmer, and the talking dog?"

"No."

"Want to hear it?"

"Not really."

"So, it seems there was this traveling salesman driving down a country road. As he passes this old farm, he sees a sign by the roadside, 'Talking Dog for Sale, $20.' Got your interest yet."

"Nope." I bend down to pick up another rock.

"Well, give it time. Anyway, the salesman looks over to the house and there's the farmer and his dog sitting on the front porch. The salesman figures it's probably some idiotic thing like having the dog say, 'Roof,' when asked what's over his head, but he can't resist stopping to check it out."

"Probably knows what a tree is made of too."

"Wood?"

"Bark, bark, bark."

"That's better. Now you're getting it. So, the salesman pulls up in front of the house, hops out, and asks the farmer, 'Is this your talking dog?' But before he can answer, the dog launches into a long speech. Want to hear it?"

"What difference does it make? You're going to tell me anyway."

"Smart boy. That I am. So, the dog says, 'I began my career as a drug sniffer. I was invaluable because I could not only smell the hidden drugs but also tell my handler exactly where to look. It wasn't long before the FBI demanded my services. It turned out I was able to smell fear in a suspect and could pick out the true culprits from a lineup. Then the CIA heard about me and I became involved in listening in on secret terrorist meetings. Imagine the things I heard posing as a friendly pup, when all the while the men would speak openly of the how, where and when of their plots.'

"Well, the salesman stands there with his mouth hanging open listening to the story, then turns to the farmer and says, 'This is amazing. Why in the world would you sell this dog for only twenty dollars?' The farmer looks up at him and shakes his head and answers, 'He never did any of those things.'"

Harry's laughing at his own joke, but I don't get it.

"Think about it," he says. "It's a talking dog for $20."

"Oh, now I get it. Pretty lame."

"Sorry. Only joke I could remember."

"Okay, it's funny. I'm just not in the mood."

"Why's that?"

I shrug then skip the rock out into the river. "I'm just not."

"Not a mind reader, Jay. Spill it. Why are you so down in the dumps?"

"Driving all the way to Seattle. It's so far. I think I can do it but what if I can't?"

"Is that all?"

I nod and then shake my head but turn to face him.

"Is that a yes or a no?"

"Both. It's my birthday."

"Hmmph. Sorry about that. Well, Happy Birthday anyway. You're a year closer to driving age. Which one is it?"

"Fourteen."

"At your age I was driving my grandfather's tractor."

"Not much traffic on a farm."

"Plenty on the highway. Granddad's fields were miles apart. Drove right down the main drag, through town, up and over a two-lane bridge, and down along the farm roads."

"But you weren't puny. You're tall."

"Wasn't tall at your age. Had to stand up to reach the clutch."

"Really? But I already tried the pedals. I can just touch them."

"With the seat all the way forward?"

"The seat doesn't move. Too rusty."

"Bet we can work that out. And Grace's camper is an automatic. It'll be a snap. Have to learn someday. Why not today?"

"I guess."

"What do you mean, 'I guess'? Show a little enthusiasm."

Can't help smiling. "Okay," I say. "Race you back. I'll give you a head start."

Not expecting him to run but he does. I take off when he's half way up the hill and only catch up just before the camper. Harry's leg beeps again; don't think he hears it.

When we get to the truck, I climb up into the cab, lean back and stretch my legs out straight to show him I can only push the pedals with my toes, and can barely see over the steering wheel.

"Wait here," Harry says and disappears around the corner. I can hear him inside the camper shuffling around. He returns with three of our dinette cushions. He slides one underneath me and two behind me after I arch my back and lift my body using the steering wheel as a brace. I can see through the windshield now and my legs reach, but I still can't push the brake pedal all the way down. Harry goes back inside the camper. I can hear cabinets opening and closing and stuff dropping.

"This'll do the trick," he says when he comes back. He's holding a roll of duct tape and four ratty paperbacks. Danielle Steele, the top one reads, *Miracle*. That sounds about right. It'll be a miracle if I can do this. I watch as Harry tapes two books to each pedal then tests to make sure they won't slip.

"Give it a try," he says.

I press on the brake then the gas. I can push all the way to the floor. "Hey, it works!"

"Finally found a use for trashy fiction. Good thing Grace doesn't read the classics. Couldn't have you stomping on Hesse or Camus. Or even Hardy, for that matter."

"Who?"

"Never mind. Promise me you'll read something worth reading someday."

"I like Harry Potter."

"Of course you do. Damn sight better than this checkout line chum. But I'd have just as happily taped Rowling to those pedals."

"Have you read any of them?"

"Nope. They're for children."

"Are not."

"Are too."

"How do you know if you never read one?"

"I just do."

"My mom likes them. Says they help her escape."

"She do that a lot? Escape, I mean."

I nod and frown. I really don't want to talk about it.

"No need to explain. I get the picture. You about ready for your first driving lesson?"

"Definitely!"

"Okay then. Gentlemen, start your engines."

I turn the key. It tries to start but doesn't.

"Push down on the gas and try again. It's an old truck."

This time the engine starts right up.

"You just passed lesson one. Now move over and take the cushions with you. I'll drive us as far as the first big parking lot."

We drive south into Kane and find the high school. The lot is mostly empty. Just a few cars parked near the main entrance. Harry pulls out into the middle and turns the engine off. We swap places and I start it again.

"I don't feel so good," I say. "Like I'm going to barf."

"Just nervous. Take a deep breath. You'll be fine. Push down on the brake pedal and move the gear lever to 'D' for Drive. Then take your foot off and see what happens."

The truck rolls forward slowly. I step on the gas and it jumps. The fence across the lot is coming toward me fast.

"Brakes!" Harry shouts.

I stand on the pedal and ram my chin into the steering wheel. Harry bounces off the dash.

"Don't recall saying give it some gas."

"But I thought—"

"Yeah, well, for now try not thinking for yourself. Thinking is lesson ten or so. Just do what I say."

"Maybe this isn't a good idea."

"Nonsense. You've still got a perfect record. Haven't hit a thing yet. Can't say the same for myself. So, turn the wheel all the way to the right then let off the brake. Don't use the gas pedal. That's lesson three or four, maybe."

The truck crawls forward and begins to turn. It goes around in a complete circle twice before Harry says anything.

"Turn the wheel back straight."

I turn too fast and we end up angling toward the row of parked cars.

"Turn it some more."

I do as he says but now we're pointing right at them.

"Other way. Quick!"

I spin the wheel as far as I can and we swerve away from the cars, but when I turn the wheel back, we're heading in the opposite direction toward a road.

"Turn back left a bit."

The truck begins to come back then I straighten the wheel and we're heading the right way now.

"Stop the truck!"

I jam on the brakes. "What's wrong?" I ask.

"Not a thing. You just completed lesson two. The truck is still in one piece, and the passengers, as yet, have no need for medical attention. Congratulations!"

"Thanks a lot."

"Don't pout. You're doing fine. Now take your foot off the brake and drive back and forth a couple of times. Try to turn just the right amount to keep going straight. Aim to keep the truck in the lane between the empty parking spaces. Pretend there are cars parked there."

Ten minutes later I can do it fairly consistently. Harry says I only nicked three of the invisible cars. He tells me to stop again.

"That's lesson three. Great job, by the way."

"Thanks. It's not as hard as I thought."

"There you go. Time for lesson four: the accelerator. Punch it, Jay! But gently."

I let off the brake and touch the pedal. Nothing happens so I push harder. The truck jumps forward so I stomp on the brakes.

"Try again. Push like you'd stick your finger slowly into a piece of hot chocolate cake your mother just baked."

"She doesn't cook."

"Her imaginary cake."

"Hard to imagine."

I try what Harry says and the truck begins to pick up speed.

"Now pull that finger out just as slowly."

The truck drops back to a crawl. "Hey, it worked!"

"Told you I was a good teacher."

We spend the next two hours driving back and forth, turning, speeding up, slowing down, stopping at a made-up traffic light. I even learn how to park, lesson six, though I can't stay between the lines.

"Lines are for wimpy cars," Harry tells me, "This is a manly truck. We'll make our own lines."

Harry asks if I want to drive back, then says, "Just kidding," when I give him a look. On the way, I ask about food. We stop to pick up some donuts and milk for tomorrow morning. "Tonight we're in for a treat," he tells me, "We've been invited for dinner at the mansion on wheels. Steaks on the grill. Scotch down the hatch. The milk is for you."

Once we're parked again, I go lie down for a few minutes. Three hours later Harry shakes me. "Time for those steaks," he says.

HARRY

Jay is still glowing from his driving lesson, chatting away about how easy it was. Still seems worried but he'll get over that. We walk down to Phil and Edna's big rig and knock.

"Evening, Edna. Where's your car?" I ask as the door opens and the ramp deploys.

"Phil took it. Come on up, Harry. You too, Jay."

Jay precedes me up the ramp and Edna points him at the big screen TV in their living room. She winks as I pass. "Phil's off shopping. Cake's done. Hid it in our bedroom," she whispers.

Phil returns to find Edna and me lounging and drinking beer, while Jay watches a nature show. We look up, eyebrows raised in question. He nods. Jay isn't paying attention, so we could have come right out and asked if the local hardware store had what we were looking for, but Phil's nod is sufficient answer.

Phil grabs a beer and joins us. When Jay's show is over, Phil asks him for help starting the grill. I tag along to watch, leaving Edna to wrap presents. While he instructs Jay in the fine art of charcoal grilling, he asks, "So, what did you do on this fine day?"

"I learned to drive," Jay answers, catching me in mid-chug. I choke on my beer.

"I just let him take a couple of turns around the school parking lot. Told him I was driving myself when I was his age."

Fortunately, Jay picks up on my attempt to make little of it. "Yeah, Gramps wouldn't let me give it any gas. I could have walked faster."

Phil laughs, but it's obvious he doesn't think letting a kid Jay's age drive a truck is such a hot idea.

"We'll be on our way tomorrow morning early." I change the subject. "Probably won't go too far. Any suggestions about where we might camp? We'd like to stick to back roads."

"Hmm, north or south. Woods or water?"

"Jay, what do you think?"

"North. Water is better for birding."

"Well, Erie isn't too far. Maybe two hours or so. There's Presque Isle State Park for day use, but there are several campgrounds nearby. Hear it's a great birding spot. I have last year's Woodall's guide if you'd like. You can call from the road but everything will be booked for the weekend. This time of year you really need reservations, but there'll be last minute cancellations and no shows, and your camper's pretty small. You'll find a spot. But plan to arrive late in the day. That's when they'll start releasing the extra empty sites they're holding for late arrivals."

Dinner is a great success. Jay laughs at the half-mashed, lopsided birthday cake and blows out the fourteen candles Edna had stuck in at random, all the while berating Phil for being so careless. Apparently, the cake slid off the passenger seat when he stopped short. Jay really lights up when we hand him the presents, a jackknife from me and a fishing rod from Phil and Edna. The expression on his face surprises me. You'd have thought I'd just given him—hell, I don't know, something big.

Nice folks, Phil and Edna. Gave me a present as well, one of their old, plastic folding chairs and a portable shower. Now we can bathe even if we go to campgrounds without facilities. Good to be heading west tomorrow though. Still have to do most of the driving, but I'll find some back roads for Jay to practice on.

At 8:00 p.m. we say our goodbyes and head home. Halfway back to the camper, my leg buzzes then stops altogether. I end up in a crumpled pile on the ground. "Shit. Didn't know I was low on battery," I say, looking up at him.

"It's been beeping once in a while all afternoon."

"Thanks for telling me."

"Sorry. Thought you heard it."

"Remind me to explain later about assumptions."

I lock my bum leg at 90 degrees then bring my knees together and use Jay as leverage to get into the kneeling position and shift to put my good foot under me. He helps me stand then supports me while I unlock, straighten, and relock the leg. "See how much fun this is? Gives you something to look forward to sixty years from now."

"Thanks a lot."

"Don't mention it. Let me keep a hand on your shoulder while we walk. Not easy to go uphill this way."

"Doesn't look that hard to me."

"Is that so? Well, wiseass, let's see you do it."

"How?"

"Three-legged race."

"What's that?"

"You're kidding, right? Never been in a three-legged race at a family picnic?"

"Never been on a picnic."

I look at Jay in disbelief then remember it's not the 50s anymore and shake my head. "Okay, then. Well, we just had a high-class picnic with Phil and Edna, and now it's time for the games. Like it or not, you're my partner."

When we reach camper, I tell him to pop inside and fetch the duct tape. "Stand on the left alongside me so our legs touch." I tape his right leg to my prosthetic in four places. "Okay then. Between us, we now have three legs. And since mine is handicapped, you'll have to provide the locomotion. Put your arm around my waist. Ready?"

"No way!"

"Yes way!" I shout and step off with my right then help a little with the left since he can't budge it by himself.

Takes a while but Jay gets the hang of the rhythm and we manage not to fall. We attract a crowd cheering us on and laughing as we make the circuit around the campground. I'd forgotten how much fun this is, and Jay's shit-eating grin says he's enjoying it too. Then a couple more teams form up and we actually have a race. We don't win, of course, but that does nothing to dampen Jay's spirits.

By dark, around 10:00 p.m., we're both beat and call it a night. Jay unwraps us. The duct tape adhesive will probably never come off his jeans but it's obvious he doesn't care. He helps me up the steps into the camper and onto my bunk, then plugs in my leg once I remove it.

"Thanks, Harry," he says standing next to me.

"Hey, it's your birthday. That was the least I could do."

"No, I mean it. This was my best ever."

Nice thing to say, but couldn't be true. Then I remember birthdays for Oliver, gala events with canapés and cocktails, designed to celebrate with other professors and their wives and to display my success. Doubt Oliver enjoyed them.

I imagine what Jay's were like: party-planner events, catered, well-liquored, band playing. I can see the white tent erected on their lawn next to the water with waiters weaving through the crowd offering refills. A contemporary version of a fete Gatsby might have proudly hosted. I try out my description on Jay. He nods and sighs.

"Still, you must have gotten cooler gifts than a jackknife, huh?"

He shrugs.

"What's the last birthday present your dad gave you."

"A sailboat."

"See! That's pretty cool. Is it remote-controlled?"

He looks at me like he's embarrassed. "It's a Sun Cat. Eighteen feet long."

"Jesus! Nice present."

"Just sits in the garage. Said he'd teach me but he never has time. Anyway, he didn't buy the boat for me."

"I don't get it. Thought you just said—"

"He bought the Sun Cat so he could complain to his friends how much it cost, $30,000."

I whistle then close my eyes and nod. That would be the same reason Olivia and I bought the stately colonial uphill from Plymouth State.

"Remind me when we get to Seattle," I say. "I've been sailing small boats since I was your age. I'll teach you."

Jay looks at his feet, an odd smile on his face, like he got caught with his hand in the cookie jar, then leans down and hugs me. My eyes fill with tears.

As I return the embrace, thoughts from the past drift off to Oliver and all the hugs I can't remember ever having.

JACKSON

He slept fitfully through the night, anxiety, fear, and the deepening sense there were too many things that might go wrong caused him to wake time and time again. By 4:00 a.m., fatigue dragged him down, so Jackson was not prepared when the driver arrived. He woke with the man's hand covering his mouth and a whisper in his ear, "It is time to go. Doctor can sleep when he is home in America."

He followed the driver across the village, the man's shape fading in and out against the dim glow from the east. It was as the driver had said, the faintest blush outlining the surrounding jungle like a watermark, sometimes seen, sometimes not.

They passed right by the truck and continued toward the edge of the clearing in which the village sprawled. Then the driver turned and whispered, "Take my hand. I know the path but doctor does not. Doctor will never find the way out if we become separated."

"Where are we going?" Jackson asked, wary of the unexpected deviation from what he had expected.

"There is another truck. We must be far away from here before the sun returns. Doctor will be missed and they will remember doctor's angry words."

The driver grabbed his hand and started forward again, Jackson tripping in the darkness every minute or two. After what seemed miles, they emerged onto a narrow road. Waiting for them was the promised truck and the boys, rifles pointed directly at him. One of them climbed up into the truck bed and extended his hand. Jackson balked. "Doctor must ride in back under the tarp. He must not be seen," the driver said.

If his previous trip to the airstrip had been teeth-rattling, this one threatened to dismember him. The truck lurched wildly as it pounded along the rough road. Jackson could hear branches scraping the truck body. The tarp covering him reeked of something foul: part animal, part vegetable, part diesel. He feared he might vomit and make the smell worse.

Jackson lifted the edge of the tarp to admit some fresh air. Behind them the road twisted through jungle sinew, rising then dropping. Monkey chatter and bird shriek filled the air, rising above engine roar and truck frame creak and groan. The combined effect of smell, sound, and motion disoriented Jackson, then when he relaxed into the pain and moved with it, his senses deadened. He hardly noticed the pace slow and the road smooth out as the truck passed along the final hundred yards before rolling to a stop. The sudden silence brought Jackson back. Alert now, he heard one of the boys whisper, "Do not move."

Jackson lifted the tarp again but an unseen hand slapped it down. They had arrived at the airstrip, that was clear. He listened but heard nothing. Gone were the sounds of birds and monkeys, gone was the truck's rattle, grind, and hum. Then it came to him, faint at first, but growing. A plane engine, followed by silence, one sputter, and silence again—punctuated a moment later by the thump of wheels touching down and soft squeal of brakes.

Jackson waited, not knowing whether he should move. The tarp lifted. "Doctor can come out now," the driver said, his odd smile stretching wide. "Hurry, please."

He leapt up and scrambled off the truck, dropping at the feet of the airstrip manager, standing there, palm open, waiting for his thirty pieces of silver. Jackson pulled out the seven-hundred-dollar wad he had stuffed into his right pants pocket the night before and handed the bills over. They were folded in half and tied with a rubber band. He placed them in the outstretched hand.

The man didn't count the money. He simply pointed to the plane waiting at the far end of the strip, its bush pilot leaning against the fuselage smoking.

Accompanied by the driver and one of the boys, now toting his single piece of luggage, Jackson crossed the short distance from confinement to freedom. He felt his fear losing its grip, his anxiety ebbing.

"Doctor will not be back, I think," the driver said as they walked.

Jackson made no reply, but turned to look at him. The driver laughed. This was the first time Jackson had heard the man laugh. Always there was the smile, but never any true laughter. His laugh had been abrupt, the laugh of a man not accustomed to it. "I meant well," Jackson answered. "I tried to help."

The driver waved off his meek reply. "White men come and go. We remain. You give us Band-Aids, but we are bleeding to death."

Jackson recognized the truth of the driver's accusation. Yes, they made a difference, but for every life saved, many were lost, the aid they provided a drop in the bottomless African bucket.

He began to respond but thought better of it. Jackson would return to his wealthy lifestyle, while the driver and his boys would return to their narrow lives. Lifestyle was a term that had no meaning here. It stood out in harsh relief against the daily fight for just one more day.

Jackson took his bag from the boy and climbed into the cockpit. A minute later they were airborne.

ROSE

She startled awake, the phone jangling her overwrought nerves. She ripped the portable handset off its cradle.

"Hello," she managed, her voice sounding far away and groggy.

"Rose Walsh?"

"Yes?" she answered mechanically. The caller had used her married name. Odd.

"This is Abby Herndon. The airline asked me to call. They said you might have some information about my husband."

Outside Rose's window the sun was setting, the park cast in deep shadow. Rose shook her head to find some clarity. "Actually, I was hoping you might have information for me."

There was a pause on the other end, then, "I may have, but I'm not sure what to say exactly. There seems to be a possibility that my husband and your son are traveling together. Do you have any idea why?"

Rose thought she did know, but wasn't prepared to blurt it all out. What if she told what she and Andrew surmised, only to have the woman hang up without reciprocating? She must be careful. "No, I don't."

"Neither do I. But, nevertheless, it seems to be true."

"Do you know where they are?" Rose tried, hoping to draw the woman out.

"No, but I know where they've been. That is, if it really is your son. Could you describe him?"

Would this reveal too much? Rose decided it would not. "He's very short, about four foot, ten inches, slightly built, with brown, close-cropped hair, and an attitude. Dresses in ripped jeans and rock band T-shirts when I let him."

The woman laughed. "In other words, just like most kids his age."

"I suppose, but I think he does it just to annoy me." Rose warmed to the conversation, but reminded herself she needed more information. This call might be the only call. "What about your husband?"

The woman paused, then misunderstanding what Rose really wanted to know, continued, "Well...he's six-foot-four, lanky, gray-headed, and never wears anything but relaxed-fit blue jeans, an oxford shirt, and a ratty old tweed sports jacket."

The woman's description calmed Rose. The frumpiness of the image brought to mind made him seem like just another guy-next-door. But was he? "Well, that's not what I meant. I...I guess what I want to ask is...is he a good man?"

There was a longer, uncomfortable pause. The woman cleared her throat. "Yes, Harry's a good man. I know that might be hard to accept, but he is. And you must be worried sick. We never gave it a thought with Oliver when he went off someplace without telling us. Times were different then, I suppose. Though if Jay were my son—"

"Jay?"

"Your son's name."

"No. His name is Jeremy."

"His nickname then?"

"No. He's never been called anything but Jeremy. I detest nicknames."

"Oh. Well maybe it isn't the same boy then, though your description fits."

"You've seen him?"

"No, but I know someone who has. It's a long story and I really don't want to involve her in this, especially if the boy isn't yours."

Rose thought quickly. Had she ever heard Jeremy called anything but Jeremy? No, but all kids had nicknames. Maybe his Seattle friends called him Jay. Wait, of course. Not Jay, 'J' for Jeremy. "What if it's not Jay like in Blue Jay? What if it's the letter J?"

Another long pause, then, "Actually...that makes sense."

Well, of course it makes sense, Rose thought. Doesn't mean it's true. But maybe now the woman would say more. Rose waited for a moment then asked, "Is there anything else you can tell me?"

"Not much, I'm afraid. I do know they were both all right four days ago when my friend last saw them. And I know they are driving west, maybe heading to Seattle. Does that sound right to you?"

Yes, that sounded right, but Rose knew the woman was not telling everything she knew. It was the way she measured out her words, the way Rose often did when hiding something from Jackson. "Who knows," Rose answered in what she hoped sounded like an exasperated mother's voice, "East. West. Anywhere. As long as it's away from me. That's where Jeremy would go."

"He's a boy. I know what that's like. Look, I'm sorry I couldn't be more help, but try not to worry. I'm sure it will all come right in the end. I'll...call back if I hear anything. Take care."

The line went dead before Rose could react. The woman, what did she say her name was? Abby. She obviously knew more than she was saying, but at least Jeremy was all right. Or was he? What was the woman not telling her? Why the mystery? Maybe her husband had a police record. Maybe he was a registered sex offender. That seemed too simple. Would the woman even have called her if that were true?

An hour passed, Rose pacing her living room and berating herself for all the questions she should have asked. What would Andrew say? "Not much of a lawyer, Rose." That's what he'd say when she called. Not much of a mother either, she added.

What had Abby told her? Nothing, really. Just that Jeremy was going to be okay, what any woman in Rose's position would want to hear. And her name, first and last, and her husband's name and son's name, or were those made up? There was no way to know, but she seemed sincere. Hard to know about the surname. That was how she introduced herself, but maybe Abby had kept her maiden name or maybe she had made it up. Herndon. Common enough so not much use, though it was amazing what you could find on the Internet. Why not try?

Rose retrieved her Apple iBook from the bookshelf and powered it up. Jeremy called it a "piece of expensive junk." Too slow for any of his games. He kept insisting she buy a PC, but Rose had never owned one. Her first Mac, long gone now, was what she used to write her student papers. Then later, after she graduated and accepted an intern position in the art department of an advertising firm, Macs were all they used. All these years later, it was too difficult to make the change. Besides, wasn't it true they were more reliable? Jeremy denied this, saying all they do is secretly restart and make you think they never fail.

Rose googled both Harry and Harold Herndon, looking for a man old enough to be referred to as elderly. There were plenty of old "Harrys" but no live ones. "Harold" returned several possible hits: CEO of some company she had never heard of, a church elder, a few professors, and others too numerous to be useful. That was the problem with the Internet: too much information.

She was reaching for the phone when it rang. Must be Andrew checking to see if she heard from the wife. Rose steeled herself against the expected barrage of questions, and picked up. "Hello, Andrew—"

"It's Jackson."

"Oh! Where are you?" Rose asked the first question that came to her.

"Johannesburg. Just booked a flight to JFK. I'll be there tomorrow evening."

"Have you heard from Jeremy?" A better question, Rose knew, but she didn't expect an affirmative answer.

"I keep trying but all I get is his voicemail. How about you?"

"Same. He doesn't want to talk to either of us, apparently."

"He did leave a few messages. Mostly to say he's fine and he'll see me back in Seattle in September."

"That's all?"

"That's all."

"He's hitched a ride—"

"I'm sure you're right. But we don't really—"

"Yes we do. He's traveling with an elderly man named Harry Herndon." Rose smiled at the silence on the other end of the line. It felt good to know something Jackson didn't.

"Did Andrew—"

"No, I did. The man's wife called. Says she believes they are both just fine."

"But how?"

Damn, Rose thought. Now she would have to admit Andrew started the ball rolling and she had learned almost nothing. "Andrew called the airline. They wouldn't give him the wife's name, but said they would ask her to call me." Not exactly true but close enough.

"Rose, that doesn't make sense."

"That's only because you don't know the whole story and I'm not going to tell you. If you had been here, you would know. As it is—"

"Damn it Rose. What's going on?"

Rose hung up. That'll teach him to yell at me. He can just wait till he gets here. Then I'll tell him.

Immediately she realized her mistake, but too late to take it back. Maybe it wasn't a mistake. So what if she made Jackson worry? He would still help her, and a little dose of worry would do Jackson some good. He had left her to fend for herself, and even though Rose hadn't succeeded in getting this Abby Herndon to tell her everything she knew, she got the most important piece: Jeremy was safe. Rose believed it; even if the woman was hiding something, she wouldn't outright lie. Jeremy must be in good hands.

Thirty minutes later, the phone rang again. Rose let it roll over to voicemail and waited a few minutes before calling for her messages. It was

Andrew; he had just spoken to Jackson. "He's furious, Rose. Please call me as soon as you get this."

"No. I don't think so," she said out loud then reached for the phone and turned off the ringer.

ABBY

I ended the call to the boy's mother and turned toward Nigel. He kept his eyes on the road ahead, pretending indifference, but he was frowning. I turned back to stare out the side window. Minutes passed.

"I told her what she needed to know," I said to relieve the tension.

"You know that's not true, luv."

Yes, Nigel, I know. But did she really need to hear about Harry's disease. It would only make her worry and what was the point. My back still toward him, I answered, "Don't hate me."

"That day will never come."

Yes, Nigel, I know this too. I shouldn't be taking advantage, but I need you by my side, whatever happens.

The miles flew by rolling along I-90. Earlier we had stopped in Scotia and spoken to the campground staff, two young girls, sisters they said. There wasn't much they could tell us that we didn't already know, except that Harry and his "grandson" were so cute together, laughing, teasing each other. Both girls said they wished they were as close to their grandparents, but they lived in Florida. Proximity is no guarantee I mused, but kept the thought to myself.

For a while I drifted off, surfacing for a moment anytime the car slowed. He must have thought I needed the rest because he didn't ask me to spell him.

I went back to what Rose had said. 'J' for Jeremy. That's probably what Harry calls him if he calls him anything. Another of his memory tricks. Easier to remember the first letter than the whole name. Easier to fake as well, but Harry didn't deserve that criticism. None of it was his fault. And it was all so unfair, the two of us suffering, and the only light at the end of our tunnel the proverbial train.

"What's it like, Abby?" Nigel asked when he saw that my eyes were open.

"You mean, what's it like living with a man who no longer knows where he is, or even who he is?"

"Yes, I suppose that's what I mean. I'm...I'm just trying to understand."

"Sorry, Nigel. It's been hard. On both of us. Sometimes he remembers, sometimes he doesn't. We say that each day is a jigsaw puzzle. We start in one corner looking for the pieces that seem like the one or two already in place, trying to build onto what's there. Some days we get quite a few to fit. But the next day most of those pieces are back in the box, unmatched. We have to begin all over again."

"But he still remembers you?"

"Most of the time. Sometimes he thinks I'm Olivia."

"Ouch. That must hurt."

"No, it really doesn't. Or maybe I'm used to it at this point. I don't know. Then there are the old girlfriends. He calls me one or the other, and reminisces about 'what we did way back when'. I just listen and say I don't remember, while he goes on and on about places we met, things we saw. Even the things we did in bed. All someone else, but I don't tell him that. Foolish to be jealous or annoyed with him for sharing a story he believes to be about the two of us. And it seems like good exercise. Might even strengthen his grasp on his memory. Makes him seem so alive and still present, even though it's a presence from the past, and not a past that we share."

I paused and looked out at the passing scene.

"One day, though, he launched into another story about one of his young women. Not the one that got him into so much trouble, he said. A later girl. Couldn't remember her name. They had been out hiking and had stopped in a quiet spot to have lunch and make love. I won't share the details, but Harry did. I listened, asking questions when he stopped, and thinking about the times Harry and I had done the same thing. I could feel the tears begin, but blinked them back. Stop crying about what you've lost, I thought.

"He didn't notice my tears. Instead he went on and on, remembering he fell asleep, and waking to see the girl twirling her long blonde hair absent-mindedly, and about how endearing he found the habit to be.

"Just then he reached across the kitchen table and took a lock of my close-cropped hair and began twirling it. I realized he was remembering me. The tears streamed down my cheeks. I was completely unable to control them. That was over a year ago, and the last time I cut my hair."

The rest of our trip passed in silence. We arrived in Erie, Pennsylvania, pulling off the interstate and continuing to the first major intersection. We turned right, cutting through the park square then past government buildings, police station, and civic center. Just north a few blocks we found a cheap place for the night. Too tired to care about propriety, and acceding to Nigel's request, I agreed to share a room with two doubles. After a quick pub dinner, we fell into our separate beds and, for me at least, a dreamless sleep.

JEREMY

"This looks like a good spot," Harry says, pulling off the road onto the shoulder.

I can feel my stomach rolling again, like I might barf up breakfast. "Not sure I'm ready," I try, hoping to get out of it

"You did fine yesterday and today you'll do better."

Easy for him to say. Yesterday we were in a parking lot. The cars were imaginary and they stood still, but I almost hit them anyway. Guess he's right though.

Harry gets out to adjust the side mirrors and I slide across into the driver's seat. He gets my cushions arranged so I can see over the wheel to the front and into the mirrors to the rear. Then he tapes the books to the pedals again and climbs back in.

"Wait till the road looks clear," he says.

I pull out, jerking forward at first, but after a minute we're cruising along at 25 miles per hour and only drifting over the centerline or too near the shoulder when the road turns and I don't.

"This is so cool!" I look over at him.

"That's the spirit. But watch the road, not me."

I smile and turn back. Route 59 is pretty wide and follows a forested ridge, lots of side roads, some places where I can see below the road on one side or the other, but few cars. Harry checks the speedometer then motions for me to go faster.

"How fast?"

"Let's try thirty for a while. We'll work our way slowly up to forty five."

I press down a little harder and concentrate on keeping the truck between the lines. It's easier than I thought.

"Might want to let up on the gas a bit," Harry suggests a minute later.

I check my speed, 40, and pull my foot off the pedal. The truck lurches. We hit the wheel and dashboard. Then, when I stomp on the gas, we bounce back. Guess it's not so easy after all.

"Know the meaning of the word, finesse?"

"No, but I'm sure you'll tell me." I finally get the truck back to a steady speed.

"Don't be a wiseass."

"You're the wiseass. Not me." I glare at him.

"Eyes on the road, champ. It's a long way down."

He's right, it is. We're just passing a steep drop-off on the left. I look back through the windshield and concentrate on staying between the lines. But when I glance at the speedometer again, it reads 45. This time I try easing off the pedal. My speed drops smoothly.

"Much better," Harry says. "That's finesse, even if you don't know what it means."

We drive along for a few miles then the road takes a big turn and drops steeply toward the reservoir. I can feel the truck speed up. I take my foot slowly off the gas, but the speed keeps increasing. I look down. I'm going 50 and the speed is still rising.

"Give it some brake. Not too much. I'd like to stay inside the cab."

I press the brake pedal gently but we keep going faster.

"A little harder, kid."

I press more but the truck doesn't slow down. Then I put all my weight on it and the front of the truck dives forward, the wheel seeming to turn by itself, pulling us toward the bank on our right. I yank the wheel back and we're across the centerline, heading for a sharp drop-off on the left. The wheel turns hard to the right again as I let go and am thrown against the door, my head bouncing off the side window. My foot slips off the brake, the right bank comes at us and I feel the truck swerve back again before I realize Harry has the wheel in his left hand and his right pushing on the windshield.

"Brakes!" he shouts.

I jam my foot down hard, arching my back against the door, as he turns back right again and we slide off the road, skidding across a wide patch of dirt and gravel, tires grinding, and slam into the bank. I do a face-plant into the wheel. Harry dives headfirst into the windshield and bounces back, the glass splitting in half with a crack that sounds like it's Harry's head breaking.

At first I'm numb, but the pain takes over and I feel blood drip down my cheek. I run my fingers across my forehead and wince. I hear my voice then, a loud moan, but it's like someone else crying. I look over at Harry. He's drooping in his seat with his head facing away from me, unconscious, but he moves when I shake him then says something but I don't catch the words. I shake him again.

"What happened?" he asks groggily, face still toward the door.

"We drove off the road."

"What's this 'we' shit? You're the one behind the wheel."

I begin to smile but wince again when the cut throbs. "Yeah, but you were the one turning it. I just stopped us."

"Brakes are for stopping, not sand banks."

I watch Harry lift his arms and turn them this way and that, then repeat with his legs. "Seem to still be in one piece," he says. "Another successful driving lesson."

"Yeah, right," I say. "Whacked myself pretty hard." This makes Harry sit up and glance over.

"Hope you feel better than you look," he says.

"Doubt it."

"Let me get some water to wash off the blood. Just sit still."

"Okay. How's your head?" I ask as he opens the truck door.

"Hurts like hell. Could use some aspirin. You too, I'd imagine. Let me check to see if we have any."

I reach up to check my forehead. It really stings and I'm still dripping blood. Not that much though.

Harry comes back with a bottle of water and a wet towel. I let him wipe off my face, pulling away each time he pushes too hard.

"Looks like that smarts. Might need a few stitches in your eyebrow.

You'll get a black eye out of the deal too. Anybody comments, just tell them, 'You should see the other guy.'"

I laugh and wince again.

"Here, slide over into the passenger seat and keep holding the towel to the cut. We'll get you to a doctor, but you'll have to take the pain for a couple of hours. Think you can do that?"

I nod.

"Atta boy."

HARRY

While we drive to Erie, Jay uses his phone to locate the hospital. The bleeding has stopped but his eye is puffing up already. He's not complaining, though. Tough kid. Suppose I could have stopped at one of the small towns along the way but they might ask more questions than I'm ready to answer. Besides, these local-yokel docs probably can't stitch straight.

I'm not hurt. Bit of a headache, big lump on the noggin, but not much else. The four aspirin I popped should take care of it. Just a little beat up and worn out. Sleepy too. Feel like taking a nap. Maybe after I get Jay to the emergency room. Grace's front bumper, on the other hand, was not so lucky. It's barely hanging on. The truck still drives but pulls to the right when I hit the brakes. Have to get it fixed.

The drive drags on. We head north back into New York, picking up US-86 at Jamestown after ninety minutes of twisting and turning along the forest highway most of the way. Jay tells me it's the fastest route to Ohio. Hard to believe, but he's the navigator. My shoulders are beginning to ache. Somewhere along the way, Jay drifts off, but I can hear him moan occasionally from the pain.

Once on the interstate, the monotony begins to wear on me. Can't fall asleep, so I concentrate on what comes next. My rotten memory seems better for some reason. I go back over the days we've been together and start worrying about Jay's parents. Why hasn't his mother called back? Is Dad still in Africa? I'd ask Jay, but it's better if he sleeps.

And what about me? Why am I driving Grace's camper across thousands of miles of road? I'm too old for this, and I know I can't trust that my mind will remain as clear as it seems right now. Should I call Abby or Oliver? Tomorrow maybe, after we get Jay's cut sewn up. Abby will know what to do. She always does. Shit, I almost killed the kid.

JEREMY

At five, Harry shakes me. He's just driving into Erie. I use my Blackberry to direct him to the hospital. While we cover the last few miles, he tells me the plan.

"I was driving, not you. If anyone asks, you hit your head on the windshield. Take that towel and smear a little blood up there where it's cracked."

"Why?"

"Look, what do you think will happen when they ask how you got cut?"

I shrug.

"Think about it. They'll want to know. Maybe they'll think I belted you one. You can't say you ran into a door or fell. They'll never believe it, so they'll report it to the police, and our little adventure will end. If I told them the truth, they'd throw me in jail."

"I get it."

"So I'll have to say I was driving and report the accident. I'll tell the police I swerved to miss a deer and lost control. Banged my head on the steering wheel and you hit the windshield. They'll take a look at the truck and see the shattered glass and your blood. They'll believe the story, and since neither of us is really hurt, we'll get off with a ticket or two maybe, and a stern warning to buckle up."

The waiting room is nearly empty, so they take me in right away. The nurse tells Harry it might be a while.

"Take your time," he says. "I'll catch a couple of winks in the waiting room."

I tell our story to the nurse and repeat it for the doctor. He shaves my eyebrow and glues the skin together. "Might have a small scar but it won't show."

"Thanks," I say.

He asks me a bunch of questions about where I am, what day it is, what year it is, who's president. Says he's making sure I don't have a concussion. I pass the test, but it makes me worry about Harry. Maybe I should tell them to check him out, but I don't want to blow our cover. When I get back to the waiting room, Harry is fast asleep.

"Oh, Gramps," I say, leaning down close to his ear, "Time to wake up and pay the kind doctor." Still no response. I shake him. Nothing.

I run to the counter. "My granddad fell asleep. I can't wake him."

The nurse stands and looks over at Harry. Then she hustles back around and across the waiting room. She gives Harry a shake. "Wake up, sir. Wake up." But he doesn't. "Wait here," she says then disappears down the hall and returns with a doctor. He shakes Harry hard and slaps his cheek then holds two fingers up along his throat.

"There's a pulse," he says to the nurse. "Concussion probably. Call an orderly."

The nurse runs off and I drop into the chair next to Harry. I can't look at him, so I look up at the doctor. "Don't worry. He'll be all right," he says.

No, he won't. I burst into tears.

ABBY

I surfaced slowly to fingers running through my long hair. I purred, lids closed. Harry must be feeling frisky. Then I startled; my eyes popped open to Nigel smiling down from where he sat on the edge of my bed. I batted away his hand. I must have looked as angry as I felt, because he jumped right up.

"Didn't mean anything by it, luv. Just to wake you. It's almost eight. We should be going soon if you want to make Chicago before dark. Loads of birding spots to check along the way."

His sheepish look made it clear he was lying, but I let him off the hook. "Apology accepted," I said, "but don't do that again."

After a quick shower and cup of coffee, we were on the road. We took a pass through Presque Isle State Park, sparkling in the morning light, then made the rounds of the local campgrounds. They were not here, but then I hadn't expected them to be. We calculated we were three days behind Harry and Jay, and even if they only drove half-days, they could be in Wisconsin by now.

We had driven for six hours when my phone rang. Oliver, I thought, as I rummaged through my purse, but I was wrong. A woman's voice answered when I said hello, and it took a moment to realize it was Grace. "They found Harry."

"Where?" I interrupted, but she didn't hear me, rattling on about an accident and the police. I kept trying to get a word in but she plowed on, oblivious. Then when she said, "Hospital," I stopped listening. Words floated through my mind, windshield, lump on the head, unconscious. That last word brought me back around.

"Wait, Grace!" I shouted, feeling cold wash across my face. She stopped talking. "Harry's unconscious? How long?"

"Police didn't say. Wouldn't have expected 'em to, though. Only called me because of the campah registration. Left a message but I was out kayakin'. Gorgeous day, only just got back—"

"Where are they?" I yelled into the phone, exasperated.

"Oh. Erie, Pennsylvania. Harry was drivin' down a long hill and—"

"Wait, Grace!" I cut her off but she kept right on jabbering. "Turn around. They're back in Erie," I tried again to interrupt her rambling, "Grace! Slow down. What happened?"

"Ran off the road into a bank. Hit the steerin' wheel pretty good. Jay cracked his noggin too. Cut his forehead but he's all stitched up now. It'll only toughen him up. He's young—"

"Stop, Grace! What about Harry?" I shouted.

"Sorry. I do go on and on, don't I? Already told ya more than I really know. Something fishy, if ya ask me. Doubt Harry would try to miss hittin' a deah. He'd just barrel into it. Might be lyin' about that. Ya know, Abby, could be Harry's gettin' worse. Time to put a leash on 'im if ya want my opinion."

I don't. I don't want anybody's opinion. But I know she's right. "Thank you, Grace. Oh, what about your camper?"

"Came through just about like the boy, a few bumps and bruises. Needs an alignment. Still thinkin' what to do about it. Might come out and drive it home. We go back a long way, that old campah and me."

The six hours back to Erie felt like six days. I could see the embankment rushing toward them, Harry's face caroming off the steering wheel. And I could see the hospital bed, rails lifted in case he rolled over, white sheet pulled up to his chin, monitor blinking with each heartbeat. I strained to listen for the beep-beep-beep that said he was still alive.

Drive faster, Nigel.

ROSE

She left the co-op building just before noon. Although Rose dreaded facing her friends, she accepted their lunch invitation. The longer she put them off, the harder they would press her for information. Already they were suspicious, and there were only so many times she could say she was too busy.

As she walked through the park toward her destination, Rose rejected one lie after another as too simple, too complicated, or too unlikely. She certainly couldn't tell them the truth; they didn't even know Jeremy was supposed to be here. Then it struck her—she could tell them Jackson was in town.

"Your ex?" they would ask. "How delicious!"

Rose could readily imagine the sly looks and dripping innuendo. But they would want details. What could she say? What could she invent that would satisfy? Something neutral at first, maybe, Jackson was attending a medical conference. Then she might admit he just happened by, and flash a shy smile.

"Ah, wink, wink, tell us more. More, more."

"Well, we went out. Drinks and dinner."

"Oooo. What about later?"

"Just a nightcap. Then he asked if he could stay."

"And you let him? What happened?"

"Nothing happened! I made him sleep on the sofa."

"Oh, no. You didn't really!"

"Oh yes, I did. But, I left my bedroom door open a little so he could watch me undress."

"You hussy! How wicked! What were you wearing?"

"Crimson silk, spaghetti straps, black lace underneath."

"And he didn't attack you?"

"Oh, he wanted to, but I closed the door and locked it. But not before giving him that look. You know, like this—"

Rose practiced lowering her eyelids, tilting her head slightly, and raising one eyebrow. A young man returned the look as he strolled by then slowly spun around till he was backing away, watching her. She glanced briefly behind, favoring him with a smile she knew could melt butter, then continued on her way to lunch, content that her story would pass muster.

JEREMY

"Wake up, Gramps," I say then shake Harry's arm again. No response. The nurse looks down at me with that stupid, oh-how-cute look on her face.

"That's right, keep talking to him. He'll wake up soon. You'll see."

That's what you said four hours ago. And what the other nurse said last night. How dumb do you think I am?

Guess she can tell what I'm thinking, because she says, "I mean it. You'll see. Sometimes it just takes time."

Right, or maybe he's in a coma and will never wake up. But I nod so she'll go away.

"I'll check back in a little while," she says and closes the door behind her, leaving me sitting next to Harry.

It's a private room. Last night they had him sharing one with some fat guy who kept moaning and thrashing around. Didn't bother Harry, of course, but it freaked me out. I left to walk the halls but the nurses didn't like that, so they moved us and put a folding bed in the room for me. Didn't sleep much. Kept dreaming about the crash.

This morning I called Mom and left messages on her home phone and her cell. Surprised she hasn't called back. Either she's got them turned off or she's not ready to talk. Didn't say anything, just that I'm fine. Had to give the cops a number when they asked who they should call. Dad's. He probably won't answer for days.

At noon, I'm still sitting where the nurse left me when she comes back carrying a food tray. She sets the meal on Harry's table-on-wheels and pushes it over in front of me. "Thought you might be hungry. Since your granddad can't eat, you might as well. No reason to let it go to waste."

"Okay, thanks." I lift the plastic cover after she leaves. Burger, fries and a soda. Looks like McDonald's. That's weird. I take a nibble. It's a Big Mac! I take a huge bite. She bought this herself. I barely choke down the mouthful of food, feeling the tears coming, then smile and blush.

"Aw, isn't that cute. He's in love."

"Harry!"

"Ssh. Let's keep that to ourselves for now. Go close my door."

"You're okay!" I drop my voice to a whisper.

"Why wouldn't I be? I'm still here aren't I? Not dead yet. Take more than a bump on the head to take this old bird out."

"But..."

"I've been faking it for hours. Now go close the damn door."

"Okay, okay."

I do as he asks, but wonder whether he's really been awake that long. More likely he's still confused, or maybe he's lying. When I get back his eyes are shut. "Harry," I whisper.

"Gotcha!" he yells and grabs my arm, scaring the crap out of me.

"That wasn't funny."

"I thought it was hilarious."

"Maybe I should pour water in the bed and tell the nurse you wet yourself. Now that would be funny."

"Hmmm. Might get a sponge bath out of the deal. Not sure I'd mind. She's pretty cute, huh?"

"I guess."

"You guess? Come on, she's hot! And probably only a few years older than you."

"Is not."

"Is too. And she's not a nurse, she's a candy striper or whatever they call them these days."

"What's that?"

"Nurse wannabe volunteers. They lurk around hoping to find a young patient to hook up with. Wouldn't be interested in an old geezer like me. You, on the other hand—"

"I'm too puny."

"Yeah, right. That's why she brought you the burger and fries, which, by the way, I expect you to share."

"No way!"

"Yes way. I get the burger. You get the striper with fries on the side."

The door opens. Harry closes his eyes.

"How's the burger?" she asks.

"Great. Thanks a lot." I look her up and down then glance away quickly. I can feel my face getting warm. No wonder they call them candy stripers. She looks like she should be hanging from a Christmas tree.

"No charge. Thought you needed a friend. Or at least an older sister."

I glance down just in time to see Harry's hand reach out fast and grab my burger. The girl screams.

"Hey! Give it back," I say.

"Nope," he mumbles while taking a bite. "Burger's mine. Thanks, sweetheart," he says to the girl. She pauses for a moment then runs out.

Harry takes another bite but hands the burger over. "Consolation prize. Good lesson too. When you lose a girl, treat yourself to a great meal. Too bad we can't get a couple of beers."

A minute later, she's back with a doctor. He checks Harry's eyes with a flashlight then asks him to sit up. Harry groans a bit but manages to sit part way over the side of the bed facing me. I've moved back to give him room. Looks like it hurts. The doctor asks if he feels light-headed or dizzy.

"Nope."

"I'd like you to try standing."

"Not gonna happen," Harry says and throws off the covers to show the doc his stump. I'm used to seeing it but the girl screams again.

"Must have fallen off," Harry says, looking at her. "Want to check under the bed, sweetheart?"

The girl looks like she's about to bolt, but the doc stops her. "Mr. Herndon has a prosthetic. Go ask at the nurses' station and bring back his leg."

"Yes, sir." She runs out.

The doctor shakes his head and sighs then turns to me. "He hit the steering wheel pretty hard, didn't he?"

I nod.

"Really?" Harry says. "No wonder my head hurts like hell."

"Are you experiencing headaches, sir?" the doctor asks.

"No, it's just the big lump that hurts. Who knows? Maybe it'll teach me something. Not that I'm likely to remember."

"Do you recall the accident?"

Harry looks up at the ceiling then back at the doc. "Nope. Nothing."

"What's the last thing you recall?"

"Hmmph. Not sure. Not much. Just my grandson, Oliver here."

"Isn't your name, Jay?" the doc asks me.

"It's both. Jay is a nickname."

"Odd nickname for Oliver." He frowns, but turns back to Harry. "Do you know where you are, sir?"

"Judging by the bedpan, I'd say I'm in a hospital."

I laugh and the doc gives me a dirty look. Don't want him to kick me out. Harry might need my help again. The girl has come back and is standing next to the doc, holding Harry's leg.

"What I meant is, do you know what city you're in?"

Harry looks down at his lap. He's thinking about it. "Millcreek?" he asks as he raises his head again. I look in his lap. There's the hospital name printed in large letters on the sheet.

"Yes, this is Millcreek Hospital. But what's the city?"

Harry shrugs.

"So, you are having memory problems, aren't you?"

"Must be."

"I think we'll keep you here a couple of days for observation. Your wife is on the way. She called and said she'd be here this evening. Till then try to get some rest. And you, young man, keep an eye on your grandfather. If he seems dizzy or confused, let one of the nurses know right away."

The doctor watches as Harry fits his leg on over the stump then locks the knee and takes a short walk around the room. Then he leaves the three of us. The girl looks at me. Not smiling anymore. "Jay for Oliver, huh? Thought I heard you say Jeremy when you were calling your mother."

Before I can answer, she turns and follows the doctor down the hall.

ROSE

Strolling uptown from the Boat House, where she lunched and regaled her friends with events that had not yet occurred, but that she was now considering, Rose tried to play out the scene in her mind. Would Jackson expect to stay with her? He would certainly ask; "Nothing ventured, nothing gained," was one of his favorite sayings.

She hiked quickly along the east side of the Reservoir and mused on the wisdom of letting Jackson sleep on the pullout sofa in her guest room. She knew it was a mistake to let him stay the night but could not find a reasonable argument that wouldn't seem petty or vindictive. With the lunch hour still in full swing, the wide jogging path overflowed with runners going in the opposite direction. She stayed on the outside edge so as not to upset their rhythm, but kept up a fast walking pace in her low heels that the slowest counter-clockwise joggers couldn't match.

When she reached the Conservatory Gardens, Rose slowed, and sat on one of the benches. The garden was alive with color and birds. Too bad Jeremy wasn't here to see them, especially the hummingbirds, with their jewel-red throats. As she began paying closer attention, she noticed that one of the birds kept swooping up and down over a nearby bed of flowers. She wouldn't have paid any attention normally, but over and over the bird dove down then flew back up, describing a nearly identical arc. Must be a male. Jeremy told her the males were almost always the colorful ones. While she watched, another hummingbird, its throat pale white instead of red, joined him. They faced off, fanning out their broad tails, and then the male resumed his yo-yoing loops, while the female hovered nearby watching him. Fascinated, and mesmerized by the repetitive motion, not unlike watching a tennis match, Rose startled when the pair flew off into a tree, one right behind the other. What had she just witnessed? Mating? It looked for all the world like a *paso doble*, each bird facing the other in a dance duel, the female standing her ground, controlled and self-confident, while the male displayed his pride and prowess. For him, a challenge to win his love. For her, a test to ascertain worthiness.

Proud of her analogy, Rose smiled, a smile that broadened as she connected the birds' behavior with hers and Jackson's. They were still locked in a *paso doble*, a mating dance, each facing the other, playing, testing the other's will, breaking apart then coming together again.

Jackson always had the upper hand. Until three years ago when she left him behind. Now, he would be on her turf. She would decide whether to invite him in or tell him to go. She would control the dance. She laughed, oblivious to the looks from others sitting nearby. She laughed because she already knew the script. She had written it, staged it, and brought the house down not one hour ago. From first hello, to striptease, to that final door closing in his face, Rose would turn imagination into reality.

Continuing uptown, Rose circled the Harlem Meer. Just before reaching Central Park West, she saw an empty bench next to the water, so she stopped to watch two small children feeding bread to the ubiquitous Canada Geese.

How many times had Jeremy beaten this into her head? Not Canadian geese, Canada Geese. She had even corrected one of her friends when she made the same mistake. Rose let her thoughts wander, knowing she was just delaying the inevitable. She had to return Andrew's call. She pulled out her cell phone and turned it on for the first time since the night before. It beeped that she had voice mail. That could wait. Most would be from Andrew and Jackson; she doubted Jeremy would deign to call.

Then she reconsidered. Andrew would ask whether she had called her son. She checked voicemail, and as expected, the first four messages were from Andrew and Jackson, alternatively berating and entreating her to phone them. The fifth was from Jeremy, cryptic as usual. "Still alive. Will call back later."

Rose frowned at his flippancy. Uninformative little shit. He did it deliberately too. Then she realized this was good, in a way; if Jeremy were really in trouble he wouldn't have left such a wiseass message. She wondered if Jeremy would answer if she called. Doubtful, pointless, as well. No, worse than pointless. If she called, Jeremy would know she had gotten his message and have less reason to call back. Fine then, she would wait. At least Rose knew he was unharmed. She felt relieved, though not completely. Still, she smiled, now looking forward to her call to Andrew.

As the phone rang and rang, she hoped he might answer so she wouldn't have to speak with whoever was his current live-in lover. But the young girl from his office picked up. "Webster residence," she giggled playfully.

It struck Rose as odd at first but then it dawned on her. Andrew had hired his latest girlfriend. Foolish thing to do. Much easier to get rid of a lover than an employee. What must his partners think? Very little, since they retired long ago from day-to-day practice. Still foolish, and irritating.

"Tell Andrew it's Rose." She let sarcasm bleed through her answer, but the girl didn't notice.

"Oh, hi! I'm afraid he's...indisposed. Can you call back?"

"No, I cannot." Rose imagined Andrew and the girl sitting up in bed naked. "Just hand him the phone."

Muffled words. Then, "Sorry, Rose."

"Will you ever grow up?"

"Not likely."

Rose sighed out loud then said, "That elderly man Jeremy is traveling with? His name is Herndon. His wife called me and I had to pry—"

"Wait! What's his first name?"

"What possible difference—"

"I have a client whose father is a Harold Herndon."

"That's his name. His wife referred to him as Harry."

"Unbelievable."

"Well...it sounds pretty common. His wife's name is Abby. End of coincidence, right?"

"That's his common-law wife."

"What? This doesn't make any sense—"

"No, it doesn't. Or...actually...it does."

"How? What do you mean?"

"I...I can't. Attorney-client confidentiality."

"Fine time to begin behaving like an adult, Andrew. This is my son we're talking about. What do you know?"

"Calm down, Rose. Let me think a minute. Umm, do you know what flight Jeremy was on?"

"Maybe. Wait, let me check." Rose opened her purse and searched furiously and unsuccessfully through all the crap she carried, before upending it and spilling its contents onto the ground in front of her. But Jeremy's itinerary wasn't there. "I must have thrown it out. All I can tell you is the flight was a week ago Wednesday, and it was a redeye. Landed about 6:00am. I remember because Jackson put him on that flight deliberately to make me get up before dawn, something he knew I would hate."

"That's the same flight Mr. Herndon was on. So it makes sense, in a way. But it's such a coincidence. Are you sure they're traveling together?"

"Yes. The wife called. Said they were driving west to Seattle. But she wouldn't tell me anything else. She definitely knew more than she told me. And so do you. Just say it!"

"Alright, alright, but you're not going to like this, and I really shouldn't be telling you. Mr. Herndon has Alzheimer's. He definitely shouldn't be driving. He's already had one accident..."

Rose stopped listening and looked into the distance while Andrew droned on.

The children and geese were gone. All that remained was a lone heron on the far shore, standing in the murky water. She snapped the cell phone closed and bent down, going through the motions of restoring the contents of her purse. For a long time Rose sat in silence, emotion draining, then she rose woodenly and walked away, not much caring which direction she took.

Black-Crowned Night Heron
Nycticorax nycticorax

Establishing Territory

JACKSON

He rolled down the cab window, allowing in the evening's hot city breath. Oddly, it had been cooler in Africa and more fragrant as well, despite the squalid poverty of the village from which Jackson had made his escape. Still, it felt good to be back in the States. And the guilt he felt from deserting his post was far less than the guilt he harbored for the mess he had caused. And for what, another feeble attempt to bring Rose back into his life? That's what it was, he knew. He might succeed in fooling everyone else, but he could not fool himself.

Jackson tried to imagine a future with his family reunited, but all he could see was the three of them standing apart in an open space, pieces of a triangle. This was how it had been, and this is how it would be again if they came back together. Ashamed of what he was thinking, Jackson told himself it was his son that mattered, not Rose, not him, but he could not erase the thought: alone, he and Rose might stand a chance.

As the cab coursed across the park on the 97th Street Transverse, Jackson steeled himself for whatever he might find. From Johannesburg, he had called and retrieved voicemail, then checked again on arriving at JFK. Jeremy's curt messages had been less than encouraging, though Jackson had put the best face on them to spare Rose, omitting anything questionable, and elaborating on what he hoped lay behind Jeremy's words.

This was the first time Jackson would see Rose's co-op. There was much to discuss, both about Jeremy, and about his failed attempt to force them together. Somehow he must convince her without admitting it was Rose he wanted back. The next few hours would be stressful.

When the cab pulled up in front of the co-op building, Jackson whistled. Not only did Rose have an incredible view, she had chosen what must be one of the classiest residences on the park. She had described the building as Italian renaissance palazzo style, which meant nothing to Jackson, but the arched entrance and deeply recessed courtyard were impressive, all the more so for the wasted square footage on Central Park West. Rose's oversized apartment had set him back millions, most of that in a mortgage. He had hoped he would only have to pay until Rose came back to him, but after three years, the monthly outlays were painful.

Jackson paid the driver, who scowled at the tip. Jackson ignored him; New York taxi drivers always scowl. Then he dragged his wheeled bag behind him into the lobby. The security guard informed him that Ms. Zelinski was out at the moment, but he was welcome to wait. Jackson cringed at the mention of her maiden name. Every time he heard it, which wasn't often, it felt like a slap in the face.

There was little choice but to wait. At least the chairs were comfortable. Jackson settled into one with a good view of the comings and goings of residents and began composing what he might say. Two hours later he was still sitting there; shadow had overtaken the park and the lobby lights were brought up. This was just like Rose, making him wait. He was tired and hungry. He could go find a café but then he might miss Rose completely. Surely she would be home soon.

ROSE

From a white wrought iron chair, with a chilled glass of Chardonnay set on the companion table beside her, Rose watched the sunlight begin to disappear from the park. She couldn't move; it would be an admission she had failed. And it didn't really matter anyway. Jeremy had not been abducted, that much was clear, but traveling across country with an old, deranged man could not lead to anything good. Nevertheless, she felt at peace with her part in this. This was Jackson's mess, not hers. Little comfort, but she took it. She could do nothing until some word from or about Jeremy filtered through the wall of silence, so she lifted her glass to her lips and drank, and watched the other patrons at Tavern on the Green. They laughed and talked in groups of three or four or huddled together in twosomes. And like her, they drank.

How many glasses had it been? More than enough to sedate her fears. Soon she would have to return to her hollow home. Jackson would be waiting, that she knew, but the knowledge did nothing to disturb her inner peace. What would happen would happen.

She thought of her earlier plan, teasing Jackson into believing she was the seductress then slamming her bedroom door in his face. Now, the plan seemed empty of purpose, something a child might do. And, loath though she was to admit it, being held again by Jackson had a certain sense of rightness, a certain draw. It was not so much desire that Rose felt, though she could not deny having at least a little. Maybe more than a little. Instead, it was the feeling of coming home to a place she had yet to live in, a place both new and old. She held this feeling close, treasuring it but afraid of it at the same time.

With this new sense of the future, Rose walked uptown on Central Park West and into Jackson's open, yet surprised, arms.

ABBY

As we entered the hospital's main lobby, I tried to find the words to tell Nigel I wanted to see Harry alone, words that would carry both my gratitude for his support and my need to do this on my own. But I could not find the right thing to say, so I just blurted, "Nigel, please wait for me here. For now, I want to be there when Harry wakes up. Just me. Try to understand."

"I understand perfectly well, Abby. Never fear."

I could see the lie written on his face. His stiff-upper-lip reserve didn't fool me. "Thank you, Nigel," I said, touching his arm for a long moment before leaving him and continuing to the elevator up to Harry's room.

I rode up to the third floor and wondered what I would find. Would Harry be awake? Over the phone the doctor had told me he had been drifting in and out of consciousness all day, though mostly out. I asked at the nurse's station and found that Harry had a private room at the end of a long corridor. The door was closed, so I knocked softly and went in. The boy sat by Harry's side, talking to him, but Harry slept on.

"You must be Jeremy," I said, smiling my bravest smile, and trying not to react to his swollen eye, already deep purple and ghastly.

He gave me a surprised look, but turned back to Harry and continued talking about a bird they saw together, a King Eider.

"Would you mind if I asked you to leave me alone with my husband?"

"Why?" he answered, without turning to acknowledge me. But he stopped talking. Instead, he leaned in and took Harry's left hand, the one closest to where he sat, turned it palm up and inserted his own, then closed Harry's fingers around his. The gesture was so touching it brought tears to my eyes. Then he said the strangest thing, "You can stay if you want."

I hardly knew what to say, so I didn't. I pulled a chair over to sit opposite the boy and took Harry's right hand. We sat, not speaking for nearly two hours before the doctor finally came in and broke the spell.

JEREMY

What does Abby want from me? At least I think this is Abby. Who else? She's a lot younger than Harry. Sort of like Mom is younger than Dad. Not as pretty, though, but okay, I guess. I don't care what she says; I'm not leaving her alone with Harry. I'm the one who crashed the camper, so it's my job to wake him up. She can help if she wants, but it sucks that she wasn't with him in the first place. In a way, it's her fault too.

"I see you two are keeping company," the doctor says when he comes in.

Duh! Why do adults say such stupid things?

"Yes," Abby tells him. "And my friend, Nigel, is waiting downstairs. I thought I should see Harry first. You know, to see...well, just to see." Then she asks how Harry is doing. The doctor hasn't said much to me, so I'm interested to hear what he'll tell her, but he asks me to wait outside. I'm about to say, "No," when Abby speaks first.

"Let him stay. It's only fair."

Not sure what she means, but I stay put.

"Very well," the doc says then walks over, lifts Harry's eyelids, and flashes a light across. Harry doesn't move.

"He's unconscious again. Hit his head hard according to the boy; probably has a severe concussion. He may not bounce back quickly, but it's really too early to know. He's not in a coma; he just needs to sleep."

"I thought you were supposed to keep a person with a concussion awake?"

"Old wives' tale, I'm afraid. His brain needs to repair itself. Sleep is the best medicine, I assure you. But it's fine to keep talking to him. He may hear some of what you say or he may not. Only he'll be able to tell you. We'll wake him from time to time to check his vital signs. Then you can ask."

"But he has Alzheimer's. Will the concussion make his memory problems worse?"

"I didn't know that. Perhaps, but not necessarily. As I said, it's too soon to tell."

Tears fill my eyes and run down my cheeks. I can't believe our accident will make Harry worse than he already is.

The doctor puts his hand on my shoulder, and I shrug it off. I don't want his pity.

"This isn't your fault," Abby tells me.

"Whose fault is it then? Yours?" She lowers her head and nods.

"This is why I suggested the boy wait outside while we spoke," the doctor says.

I shout, "You wait outside. If you can't help him, go away!"

He begins to say something, but Abby cuts him off. "Please. It will be all right. I'll come find you if my husband awakens."

The doctor nods and leaves without saying anything more.

"Thanks," I tell her.

She reaches across the bed and places her hand over Harry's and mine. "He's a tough old bird," she says. "He'll be all right. Don't worry."

I nod and wipe my eyes on my sleeves.

"Do you want to talk about it?"

I shake my head.

"Might help."

"How? I drove us off the road. I almost drove over a cliff. It's my fault."

She slowly brings her hand to her mouth and stares at me. "You were driving? I thought Harry—"

I look down. "That's just what we told the hospital. And it's what I told the police."

"But...but Harry let you."

"So what? I was still the one driving."

"But he shouldn't have. You're not old enough. You know that."

"No, I don't." I look up again and raise my voice. "I wanted to drive. I wanted to do something none of the kids in my class have done. I should have said no. Then he'd still be okay."

"It was Harry who made the bad decision, not you. You did the best you could, didn't you?"

"You're wrong. I'm not stupid. I knew it was a bad idea, but I went ahead and did it anyway. Doesn't that make it my fault?"

She bows her head again. She's crying. "He'll be all right," she says, but I don't think she believes it. I don't believe it either. I think she won't say anything more, but she does, softly, so I can barely hear, "You're too young to take this on your shoulders, Jeremy. Please stop blaming yourself."

"It's Jay. Call me Jay."

JACKSON

He stood in silence, holding Rose tentatively, not knowing what to say or do. In contrast, she clung to him, arms clasped tightly around his neck, face buried alongside, her warm breath playing across his open collar. She murmured, but not loud enough for Jackson to understand what she was saying.

"Are you okay?" he tried.

"Ssh. Don't spoil it. There doesn't have to be a reason."

Jackson resumed his silence. It struck him as romantic nonsense. Surely there was always a reason for anything anyone did. Silly to think otherwise. Yet, he could not fathom the change in her. Just short days ago, Rose was screaming at him over the phone and hanging up abruptly. Now she nuzzled into him. It brought back good memories.

As if she sensed his thoughts, she answered, "It's going to be all right, Jackson."

But what did she mean? Was she talking about Jeremy or about the two of them? And if the latter, was he ready to let her back into his life in that way? He longed for this, but now that it seemed imminent, he feared to make a move. He was standing in a minefield.

"Have you heard from Jeremy?" he asked, hoping not to break her hopeful mood, but needing to know.

She sighed deeply and loosened her hold just a little. "You're hopeless," she said, but he could hear amusement as well as criticism in her voice. "What am I to do with you?"

She's teasing me, he thought, and considered teasing back, but the hint of sadness in her voice stopped him. He stroked her back instead, and she nestled close again.

A minute later, Rose said, "I called Jeremy. Left a message. I think he'll call back when he gets it."

"What makes you believe that? He hasn't returned one of our calls."

She pulled away and shrugged. "I'll explain, but let's go up first. Maybe it's just wishful thinking."

They rode the elevator to her floor and went in. She offered Jackson a drink and started walking toward the sideboard where she kept her liquor, while he took a seat on the sofa and looked around. "All I have is vodka, I'm afraid."

"I know. It doesn't matter. I'll pass, though."

Rose turned and looked at him, putting one hand on her hip and shaking her head. "Do you ever think about what you're going to say before you say it?"

He had crossed some line, that was obvious. But he didn't know what line. "Sorry," he replied.

"Sorry for what?"

She was smiling now, though he thought it looked like the smile of a lioness just before leaping. "Sorry for upsetting you?"

"Is that a question? Do I look upset?"

No, she didn't. She looked amused, or maybe bemused. Jackson decided to say exactly what he thought. "You look like you're about to pounce on me and sink your teeth into my neck."

"Hah! You wish!" Rose slinked forward and straddled him like a lap dancer. She pulled her hair to one side and leaned in slowly to bite, playfully, one side of his neck and the other. Then she bit hard, breaking the skin, and leapt up, dancing away and swaying her hips. "Bet you changed your mind about that drink, didn't you?"

Not waiting for an answer, she poured two tumblers full of vodka, skipping the ice. She brought them back, handed one to Jackson, and sat on the coffee table facing him and crossed her legs. Her tight skirt rode up.

Jackson kept his eyes on hers. "What do you want from me, Rose?"

All she gave was a shrug. "What do you want from me?"

His first reaction was irritation at her sarcastic reply, but when he looked into Rose's eyes, something made him pause. It struck him, this was a watershed moment. To reply in kind would end all possibility. He wasn't sure what he wanted from Rose, but he was sure it wasn't 'nothing.'

"I want to keep talking," he said.

Rose looked down at her drink and took a sip. "What is there to say?"

"I don't know. I'm just not ready to stop."

"And I'm not sure I'm ready to start. So where does that leave us?"

"In your living room, apparently."

Rose stood and looked down at Jackson for a moment and walked over to the window. The park lay in shadow, now but it was still early. Traffic below coursed uptown, horns blaring. She looked across at the 5th Avenue high-rises, its facades still glowing faint pink, bright windows like eyes staring back at them. Then she set her drink on the sill and turned suddenly to face him. "Maybe we should try the bedroom."

ABBY

"Have you talked to your mother or father yet?"

Jay looked at me in the way Oliver used to at this age when I asked something he thought was none of my business. He shook his head. I'm sure he didn't suspect why I asked. I was afraid of what would happen when his parents learned the truth, and I needed to know how much time I had left. Left for what, I couldn't say. Left to think about what comes next, I supposed.

"Is your cell phone turned on?"

Another head shake.

"Maybe you should check to see if they've called."

He nodded and said, "Okay."

Jay attached a device to his right ear and listened, stone-faced, for a long time. That could only mean they had been calling regularly. I hoped they weren't frantic. I would be if our roles were reversed. I couldn't hear any of the words, just a muddled murmur.

Then suddenly, he rolled his eyes and smiled. "What's so funny?" I asked, but he just waved off my interest and kept listening. After taking time to delete each message except the last, he pulled off the earpiece and set his phone on speaker. He played the message and held it close to Harry's left ear.

I heard a woman's voice speaking excitedly. "I know you're not ready to call me yet. That's okay. But please do call. I'm not angry. Your father may be, but I can handle him. I saw a huge beautiful bird in the park yesterday roosting on a tree branch by The Pool. I remembered what you told me about identifying and recorded everything I could. I even scared the bird into standing so I could get a better look. Listen. Then call me and tell me what sort of bird it is." There was a pause then her voice continued.

"Smaller than a swan, larger than a pigeon, more like a seagull."

Jay rolled his eyes again at the inept description but smiled anyway.

"Black on the back, gray on the sides, white and black on the head, black beak."

His expression turned thoughtful. Trying to work it out, identify the bird. I had no idea.

"Whoop, whoop, whoop."

We both laughed out loud at his mom's scare tactics then startled when the bird squawked back, "Quark, quark."

"Yellow legs, white underneath, red eyes."

Now Jay looked puzzled.

"Loose white feather stuck on head, like a vintage hat."

He frowned and pushed a few buttons on his phone and the message repeated. Again he held it next to Harry's ear. When the message ended, he shook his head. He was just as clueless as I was.

"What kind of bird do you think it is?" I asked him. "It's clearly not a gull."

"I don't know. I could look it up, but I left my *Sibley's* in the camper. Maybe an egret?"

"It's a heron, dummy."

"Harry!" we shouted in unison.

Then Jay added, "Who ever heard of a black and white heron?"

"Me, obviously. Never seen one, though. I'm afraid of the dark."

"*Non sequitur!*"

"Nope." Harry stretched and yawned. "Like their name says, Black-crowned Night Herons hunt at night. Seldom seen during the day, unless you happen to catch them roosting. Your girlfriend just aced us out. That was your girlfriend, wasn't it? Bet she's hot."

"It was my mom."

"Bet she's hot, too."

Jay's groan and look of distaste suggested Harry was right. I leaned back and listened to their banter about the heron and Jay's hot mother, relieved that Harry seemed his old self.

"So, what did I have removed this time?" Harry asked after the bird and hot mom talk fizzled out.

Jay looked confused, but I recognized the behavior; he was trying to put the pieces together. I'd been living with it for a long time. Harry knew he was in a hospital, and he knew there must be a reason. He was trying an open-ended quip to gain both time and information.

"You had another accident. Smacked your head pretty good this time."

"Another?"

I drew back his covers to show him his missing leg. Maybe that was cruel, but I had to know how bad he was. He reached down to touch his stump, the same way he did the first time and every time since when he forgot. I glanced over at Jay, who took it all in.

"You don't remember the crash?" Jay asked.

"No. I..."

"He doesn't remember you either, Jay. Or me, most likely."

"Sure I do. Jay is my son and you're his aunt."

"I'm your wife, Abby. Jay is...I don't actually know who Jay is."

"Then why is he here?"

"Because you were together when you ran off the road."

Harry looks at Jay. "That right?" He nods then hangs his head.

"Damn. Don't remember a thing. Not surprising, huh?"

I smiled warmly at him. Yes, it was not surprising Harry didn't remember the accident. But it was surprising he knew that neither Jay nor I would be surprised he didn't remember. Then I laughed at my convoluted thought, because it meant the accident hadn't made Harry's memory worse, and, more importantly, his ability to reason was as sharp as it had been. I wasn't certain yet, but I hoped he would get back to normal, whatever that was, and soon.

I looked over at Jay to explain my smile, but he had already figured it out. "It's good Harry remembers that he can't remember, isn't it?" he asked.

I nodded then reached across the bed and took Jay's hand.

ROSE

Jackson drifted off to sleep, and Rose got up and pulled on the shirt he'd tossed off earlier. It smelled strongly of sweat and thousands of miles of travel. She went to the kitchen to see if anything edible remained, but there was nothing. She considered ordering in, but all the effort and the waiting seemed more trouble than it was worth.

In the living room, she took the remains of her vodka to the sideboard and fished around in the cabinet for something nutritive to add. From the depths, she pulled out an open bottle of Bloody Mary mix. She glanced at the expiration date, six months ago, but it should probably still be good, and the alcohol would kill whatever was swimming around in the mix anyway.

At first, she sat on the edge of her coffee table, staring across the room and out into the night. Then, abruptly, she rose and went to the window and sat on the sill. The anxiety and vertigo she normally felt when looking down at the busy street below didn't materialize. No, she was calm, drained of emotion the way she always was after sex. But she was also unsure of her feelings for Jackson. She had expected sex to mean nothing more than a pleasant interlude after a long dry spell, but she felt more than that. She couldn't say just what, but something, there was definitely something.

Get a grip, Rose, you're imagining things that aren't there. She lit a cigarette and stared through the window out into space, not focusing on the treetops, the 5th avenue buildings, or the darkening sky beyond. If there were stars, she wouldn't have seen them. The lights of the city never dimmed enough to see any but the brightest, unless you dared venture into the park and looked straight up.

The moon was another matter. By fall, it rose large and opalescent when it waxed full, bathing her living room in ghostly pale light, and casting multilayered, shadowed gradations against her walls. She would fling her windows open wide to let in the smells of ripening autumn leaves and roasting chestnuts, and turn up the stereo volume, playing either a fugue, or nocturne, or even a modern dance piece. She would twirl and dip to the music, the moon her partner until high overhead and small. She would strip off her clothes and lie naked beneath the windowsill, letting the pale light wash her body and the chill night air caress her skin, taking her where they willed.

Sometimes she thought of this as the ending of her life, her pallid body gray as death. But more often she felt renewed, incubated in the pale glow. She became Diana, goddess of hunt and moon, a new beginning. A strong beginning.

That's what she felt now. Rose looked up, searching the sky. At first, she couldn't find the moon and wondered whether it had already set or not yet risen. Then she saw faint light limn the high-rises across the park. In contrast to the city's yellow vaporous light, the edge of the building was tinted ice blue. She had never noticed this before. As she watched, the moon emerged over the hard border of 5th Avenue like a moth from its pupa, growing until the near-full disc flew free above the concrete. She understood then. Like the moth moon, she was breaking free from her three-year cocoon.

ABBY

I needed to call Oliver, and I knew I should call Jay's mother, but I couldn't bring myself to call either. And what did it matter, really? Oliver would be busy with his latest deal, whatever it was, and Jay's parents would only have to worry a little longer. In the meantime, the hiatus from inevitable conflict could very well suggest a better plan than just spilling what I knew and hoping for the best.

But what about the future, the days after we went home? What would be best for Harry? Should we remain in Washington close to Oliver, or should I insist we return to New Hampshire? And what about Jay, would he want to see Harry again? Would his parents let him? Too many questions, too many possibilities, and I had little control over most of them.

At 9:00 p.m. I went back to the lobby and gave Nigel the news that Harry was awake, and though he didn't recognize either Jay or me, he was coherent. "Do you want to come up and say hello?"

"If you think it might help."

"I do, and it certainly can't hurt."

"Right then. Let's go see the old bugger."

"But Nigel, after that, I want you to leave. Go find a hotel room. I'll stay here. Then come get me in the morning so I can take a shower." I laid my hand on his arm gently. "You understand, don't you?"

"Yes, luv. But don't you want to get something to eat? We could both do with a good meal."

"No, you go. I'm really not hungry. I can get something from the vending machines later if I want."

"How about the boy?"

"I doubt you could pry him away from Harry's side, but you're welcome to try," I answered without considering what lay behind Nigel's simple question. He might mean several things, and whether Jay was hungry the least of them. What Nigel really wanted to know is why I would let Jay remain and chase him away.

I doubted that Nigel understood the false choice. He knew I wanted to spend the night at the hospital. He would rather be by my side than sleeping alone in a hotel, but that was the problem. He would stay mainly for me, not Harry. Jay was here for only one reason, the same reason I was here, because he knew Harry needed him. Because he loved Harry. It was in every look and every gesture and every word. I do not know how it happened, and the irony of it hit me hard. How could this boy bond so quickly to a man most people found prickly and irascible, when his own son could not?

Nigel and I returned to the room to find Jay holding Harry's hand. He had drifted off again. Jay made no move and barely acknowledged our presence. When asked if he was hungry, he just shook his head.

"How long has Harry been asleep?" I asked.

"He's not. He's just resting his eyes. It's too bright in here."

"It's okay to turn the lights off."

"I did, but the nurse came in and turned them back on. I don't want them to throw me out."

I walked up behind Jay and rested my hands on his shoulders. "They won't do that, and I won't let them. You can stay as long as you want." I felt the tension drain away. He even smiled a little, though there was more worry in his face than any real calm.

Harry opened his eyes then, looking at each of us in turn. He had no idea who we were, but there was no fear in his eyes, nor wariness, not even confusion. Just a waiting patience, as if he knew it didn't matter, that we were here for our own reasons, but they were not reasons to cause him concern. A moment later, when the doctor walked in, Harry's expression changed, his fear apparent.

"Good evening, Mr. Herndon," the doctor said. "It's good to find you awake. Do you know who I am?"

"My doctor." A mild response that belied what he must have been feeling.

"That's right. And who are these people?"

Harry looked at me. I smiled wickedly, hoping he would get the hint that I was his wife or at least his lover. Then he looked at Jay.

"This young man is my grandson. That beautiful lady is my wife, and the gentleman next to her is my oldest friend."

The doctor turned to Nigel, his eyebrows raised in question.

"Quite right. I've known Harry longer than anyone here."

The doctor turned back to look down at Harry. "Very good, sir," he said. "And what are their names?"

Harry looked deflated. I knew he had simply guessed our relationships to him. But there was no chance he would remember our names. He glanced down then back up, suddenly smiling. "This is Jay," he said, nodding at him. "My friend there next to you is Nigel, and my lovely wife is Abby. Haven't lost my marbles yet, Doc."

The doctor looked surprised but turned to me and said, "We'll keep him another night. You can take him home tomorrow or the day after if his lucidity continues."

The doctor had barely closed the door behind him when Harry and Jay broke into laughter.

"What's so funny?"

Harry lifted Jay's hand, the one he held, and opened the palm. There written in rows were, 'Jay, Nigel, Abby.'

JACKSON

Walking along Central Park West, Jackson looked for an open convenience store. He wanted both a New York Times and a disposable cell phone. He'd been in too big a hurry to buy one after he landed and grabbed a cab yesterday. Away for two weeks, he needed to find out what was happening in the world, and especially in the stock market. Lately, his expenses had been far exceeding his income.

What worried him more was last night in Rose's bed. What did it mean? Was it as she had said, "There doesn't always have to be a reason?" Or was she reconsidering their impending divorce? Nothing had been signed; Rose had been stalling for months. Until now, Jackson had been certain she was holding out for a larger settlement. She probably thought he would be anxious to remarry. Jeremy had repeated many of her questions, most in reference to Jackson's girlfriend. But Jackson's intentions toward the young woman were not serious. How serious could he be with a woman less than half his age? He would appear pathetic paired with a woman who would be immediately referred to as his 'trophy wife,' or worse, his daughter. Besides, he knew she could never stand up to Jeremy. And Jeremy could be cruel when the mood struck him. It would take a self-confident woman to help Jackson shepherd Jeremy through the rest of his adolescence.

This thought brought Jackson full circle and right back where he started. Self-confidence wasn't Rose's strong suit either. With her, Jeremy had elevated manipulation to an art form. No, Rose was not the mother Jeremy needed, but was she even what Jackson needed? There was no way to be certain, but the fact that he would even consider the possibility left Jackson wondering. All this wondering was predicated on the shakiest of ground—what Rose might be thinking and feeling. Jackson simply didn't know.

He returned with his paper and disposable cell phone and took the elevator back to Rose's floor. Reaching for the doorknob, he found it wouldn't turn. Locked out, and by Rose. He remembered, clearly, testing to make sure he could get back in. He knocked. No answer. He put his right ear against the heavy door but heard nothing. He rapped harder. Still nothing. He pulled his new cell phone from his jacket pocket and punched in Rose's mobile number, then listened through the door again. And there it was, Rose's distinctive ringtone, some short operatic piece he couldn't name. She was inside but pretending not to be. Now what?

Jackson's hopes fell. Last night had been for no reason after all. He laughed at himself. What a fool you are, Jackson. But his self-deprecation didn't work. It didn't lift his spirits the way it usually did. The truth was he wanted Rose back. He still loved her, but it seemed he was alone in this love. That she could use him then close the door so easily, hurt more deeply than he could have imagined.

He rode the elevator back down and walked south on Central Park West a mile and a half to the Trump Towers Hotel.

ROSE

Like Mercury, she flew through the park on winged feet. Rose took the mile-and-a-half Lower Reservoir Track and burned it up, timing herself at eight minutes and fifty seconds, her third fastest time ever. She knew her manic chemistry drove her, but she didn't care. She was happy and felt more alive than she had in months. And it was not just last night with Jackson that made her feel this way. No, it was the sense everything would be right among them as a family again. She did not know how it could come about or why she was so certain, but she was.

She knew how to find Jeremy. Having copied the caller ID, she had only to ring Abby back. The possibility that Abby's husband was still missing, or that Jeremy wasn't with him, counted for nothing. She just knew. It was kismet or karma, maybe intuition. It inspired Rose to keep up the furious pace back to her apartment.

She unlocked her door and ran down the long hall. Jackson wasn't in the bathroom. Nor the bedroom. In the living room, she noticed his bag missing from where he had left it leaning against the wall. Then it struck her, he had gone. Last night was about nothing. Her high spirits fell. She could feel the downward spiral, like a vortex dragging her in.

Wait! That can't be. Maybe he went for a walk. But he never walked for no reason. He only walked with purpose—to get away from her. But just as she knew she could call Abby to find Jeremy, she knew the number to find Jackson, the Trump Towers. The Astor on the Park would have been closer but did not have the prestige and glitz Jackson preferred. No, he would have gone to the Trump.

The hotel operator rang his room, confirming her suspicion. She hung up before Jackson could answer. Then she rode the elevator to the lobby, picked up the electronic key she had left for Jackson, and returned to her empty rooms.

HARRY

Here's a switch. I'm the one awake while my companions sleep. Just beginning to get light outside the dirty hospital window with its dismal view. You'd think they'd wash them once a decade at least. My head is killing me, but I don't want to call the nurse. Afraid it might wake Sleeping Beauty and her dopey dwarf. Or was it Snow White who had the dwarf? Doesn't matter. The kid will tell me later, and I'll forget again.

Just remembered what I called Oliver when he was five: Ollie. Ollie J. Sometimes just J. Olivia hated it. Foolish name for an even more foolish TV hand puppet: Oliver J. Dragon.

Never liked the name Oliver. Olivia's father's name. He always hated me, not that I blamed him. Said I jilted his daughter. Not quite true, but true enough. Strange memory. Wish I could remember something useful.

You'd think a hospital would be quiet at dawn, but with my door open, I can hear more than I want. What is it the kids say? TMI: too much information. I haven't forgotten everything yet.

First, there's the guy in the next room who keeps puking his guts out. Then there's the enormous woman who walks up and down the hall, flip-flapping her slippers and dragging her squeaky-wheeled IV drip. The guy across the hall who must have left his bathroom door open while he took a crap. Sounded like a stuck pig in a thunderstorm. Last, there's the old lady across the hall who's been moaning non stop for an hour at least, though I can't time her, there's no clock in my room. I could turn on the TV to check, but that would wake them. Rather lie here quietly and wonder what will happen next. Snow White probably told me, but I forgot. Reminds me of what my mother used to say, "Harold, you never listen. It's in one ear and out the other."

Good analogy for senility: in one ear, out the other. No room to store anything anymore. No reason to either, if you think about it. Hardly matters whether I listen or not. Here today, gone tomorrow. Another of my mother's old saws but a good one. Describes most of what anyone tells me today and quite a bit of what I've been told over my lifetime. How many years is that again? I'll have to ask. Or maybe I can get the doc to cut another hunk off my leg and count the rings.

JEREMY

I can hear Harry talking to himself. That's a good sign, isn't it? Abby isn't awake yet. Maybe I should have given her my bed. That chair doesn't look comfortable, even with the pillows she's got jammed all around her.

I'm starving. Think I'll try talking a nurse or candy striper into an extra breakfast.

Still no word from Mom or Dad. If I can make it through one more day, maybe I can fly back to Seattle with Abby and Harry. I can leave Dad a message when I get home.

I think there's something screwy about Abby. She asked if I had called them but didn't actually seem to care. More like she just wanted to know one way or the other. Maybe she doesn't want to see them either. Guess that makes sense. They'll be pissed at me but angry at Harry. Maybe angry at Abby too, unless I tell them she didn't know who to call, and I wouldn't tell her. I'm definitely not telling them I was driving the camper.

What if Abby won't let me fly with Harry and her? Back to hitchhiking? Nope, I'll just threaten to hitchhike. She won't let me. They would get in more trouble with Mom and Dad than if she just let me come along on the flight. And I can pay, so it won't cost them anything. That'll work.

"What are you smiling at?"

I turn over to see the candy striper from yesterday standing in the doorway. "Happy to see you!"

"Yeah. Sure you are."

"No, really. I'm starving. Hoped you'd show up so I could get you to score me some breakfast." I smile so wide my cheeks hurt.

"I'm not supposed to do that."

"Pleeaase!"

She rolls her eyes. "Oh, alright. There's always an extra meal or two anyway. They never seem to know when patients are checking out."

"Thaaank yooou!"

She shakes her head and leaves.

"What a load of crap," Harry says, laughing. "Obviously you can turn it on when you want to."

I stand and take a bow, making him laugh harder.

ROSE

After her run, Rose spent thirty minutes under the shower, hot, full-force needles of water stinging her, echoing the pain of loss and reminding her why she had decided to leave Jackson in the first place. He was never there, not when she needed him—only when he needed her. She could not believe she had let this happen again.

Tearing a fresh towel from the rack, she ripped the bar off the wall, leaving it dangling at an odd angle like a crippled appendage. "Shit," Rose said, angry with Jackson, but angrier with herself. She dried off and flung the sodden towel over the shower door and stalked naked to her bedroom. There, where she had left it, was the note to Jackson, "Off to run. Back soon. Key in lobby." The scrap of paper taunted her, drawing her toward it. She ripped the paper to bits then stomped back to the bathroom, flushing the bits down the toilet.

As she passed the guest room, Rose noticed the door, which she always left closed, was ajar. Odd. She pushed it open with her foot. There on the bed was Jackson's unzipped suitcase. Alongside, were his trousers and shaving kit. Slowly her mistake dawned, he had not left. Except that he had. He was checked in at the hotel. What was going on?

She went back over her actions of the morning. She awakened to find Jackson missing, the pillow where he slept still warm and musty with his scent. She heard the door to the guest bathroom close and presumed he would take a shower as he always did on rising. She had pulled on a running suit, scribbled the message she left on his pillow, locked the co-op door behind her, and dropped off the extra key with lobby security in case he went out.

But she had found the key still in security's possession when she returned. Could Jackson have left without seeing her note? Yes, yes he could have. Especially if he had dressed in the guest room!

So it wasn't the bathroom door she heard close—it was the front door. But why would he have gone out? Rose sighed and answered her own question out loud, "The goddamned newspapers." Heaven forbid he should pass up his morning *New York Times* and *Wall Street Journal*, even now that most of it could be read online. In Seattle, he had them delivered to their damned door. So he would have walked one direction or the other until he found a newsstand. When he came back, probably while she was off running, he found the door locked.

Jesus, Jackson, you'd think you'd have the sense to check with security. Then she made the final connection. He must have believed she deliberately locked him out. It was, she had to admit, the sort of thing she'd do. Had done, if she was completely honest.

Rose laughed. Five years ago it had been so easy. She removed the front door key from Jackson's key ring in the morning, armed their home security system, and took the hidden key from its hiding place under the plant by the front door. Then she dropped off Jeremy at a friend's house and spent the weekend with a girlfriend. Jackson slept the first night at the Four Seasons downtown. He was furious, but left a conciliatory message on her voicemail, knowing there was little he could do. And since his original sin was saying the wrong thing at the wrong moment, Rose took pity and did not make him stay out the whole weekend. She returned home the next day and replaced the hidden key. But she left again.

As she thought about it now, Rose realized it was not entirely Jackson's fault that he often said the wrong thing. In a way, the fault lay with his profession. Doctors were lauded and lionized, raised onto pedestals. No wonder they treated both their patients and spouses with condescension. And Jackson was one of the kings of kings, a skilled surgeon. Like his colleagues, he had no need to measure his words.

Rose also knew she was hypersensitive to Jackson's criticism whether direct or implied. Since she was quick-witted and sharp-tongued, he suffered worse than he gave. Now, she had ruined the small tentative start they made last night. Or had she? They had both jumped to wrong conclusions. Surely he would realize this once she explained. She would call, tell him the story, and they would laugh together. Then he would come back, and they would make love again.

She walked to her bedroom and dialed his mobile number. His cell phone rang a few times then rolled to voicemail. Disheartened, Rose left the shortest of messages, "Call me."

JACKSON

He sat in his room channel surfing. Hundreds of channels and nothing on. There was always pay-per-view, but Jackson couldn't bring himself to spend one more dime when he shouldn't be here at all. It made him want to spit. Worse, his head was killing him. Between the jet lag and last night's vodka, the pain was bad. He ordered a pot of coffee from room service and a bottle of ibuprofen. He downed four capsules and chased them with 12 ounces of coffee.

He had to call Rose and ask if he could at least retrieve his luggage. And they really needed to talk about Jeremy and what they would do next. He also knew if he called too soon, it might make her even angrier than she already was. That, Jackson could not afford, so he sat drinking more coffee and punching the channel button on the remote over and over, completing pass after pass and not really looking as he did.

By late morning, Jackson was wired. Too much coffee, not enough food. He pored over the room service menu but found nothing appealing, mainly because he would have to eat alone. He sighed. There seemed to be nothing to do but call Rose and ask if he could come back. Since that was what he wanted anyway, he easily convinced himself it was for the best. That said, he didn't relish the long explanation he must offer. What would she think? What would she say? He would have to admit he needed her. Would she laugh at him?

Unusually jittery, Jackson struggled to press the phone keys in the right sequence, his shaking forefinger stabbing like a chicken pecking at insects. On the second try he managed to get it right. He listened as the phone rang five times and rolled to voicemail. He hung up and tried again. The connection clicked in his ear then signaled busy. He slammed down the handset, missing the cradle, and it ended up on the floor. He left it there and walked across the room to look out the window at the park.

While Jackson stood fuming at himself and at Rose, it occurred to him that the busy signal might mean she was calling him back. He hurried to reassemble the phone and sat on the bed to wait. It rang almost immediately.

"Jackson?" she asked, hesitation in her voice.

He heard in his head, "Who else?" but stopped himself from saying it out loud. They needed to break the habits of sniping and sarcasm. "Can I come back? I need you."

He could hear her breathing and sounds of the street in the background, but she said nothing.

"Could we talk?" he ventured.

"I...I'm sorry. Yes, please come back. Are you all right? You sound...strange."

Jackson smiled wearily, not looking forward to admitting that he had pushed Jeremy at her for no other reason than to make her feel guilty enough to come back to him. His only hope was that she would forgive his manipulation and be drawn to his need. Was this a false hope? Perhaps, but it was the only hope he was willing to entertain.

ABBY

The sounds of Jay sweet-talking the candy striper followed by Harry and Jay's laughter after the girl left, brought tears to my eyes. I was happy for them but sad for Oliver. This should have been his moment with his father, his reconciliation. But he was not here. He hadn't even called back. I woke before midnight and phoned. "He's out schmoozing with some of his business acquaintances," his wife told me. I let her know that Harry had been in another accident but was fine, just a few bumps and bruises. Not really true, but perhaps enough to satisfy. She turned strangely quiet, as if she had something she wanted to say but was afraid to say it. "I'll tell him," she answered finally. "Give Harry a hug for me."

I supposed she worried what Oliver's reaction would be. I was certain I already knew, and just as certain I didn't care, but it bothered me she had said so little. Normally, she was bright and cheerful, except when complaining about Lainey. They had one fight after the other, apparently, though Lainey was always sweet as sugar to me. Something about mothers and daughters. Fathers and sons as well, if Oliver and Harry were any measure.

Oddly, our quiet conversation had made up my mind. Harry and I would return to Seattle, put our house on the market and move back to New Hampshire as soon as possible. I planned to tell Nigel this morning. He had heard from Grace and would meet her at the airport today then follow her back to her cabin in my rental car, trailing behind the camper in case it broke down. Then he would drop the rental at Manchester Airport and tell them to leave the charges on my credit card. Harry, Jay, and I would fly out on the flight I had arranged last night. We would leave at 1:30 p.m. but not arrive in Seattle until 9:30 p.m., my insistence on the cheapest flights available resulting in connections in Cleveland and Boston. Strange to head so far east only to turn around and fly west.

I did worry I might be fueling the eventual fire with Jay's mother and father, but the fact they hadn't called made me think they were either unconcerned or just bad parents. I imagined Jay's father was like Oliver, there symbolically but too tied up in himself to make the effort.

That was Lainey's complaint. Oliver made rules for the girls that could not be broken but left Evangeline to enforce them. This set mother and daughters against each other and made Lainey run to her friends anytime things got too hot at home. What it did to Lainey's younger sister Nessa, I don't know. From the few fights I had observed, Nessa simply withdrew, either going to her room or to the loft above their garage, where she buried her face in one of her fantasy books.

JEREMY

The candy striper comes back quickly with my breakfast tray. Abby and I have taken seats on either side of Harry's bed. I smile at her and say thanks.

She smiles back and nods.

"Where's mine?" Harry asks.

"Are you hungry, sir? You should be since you didn't eat last night."

"I didn't?"

"No. The nurse said you needed to sleep."

"No wonder I'm so hungry. How about steak and eggs?"

The striper laughs and goes to get Harry his breakfast. He tries to snag a piece of bacon off my plate, but I'm too fast for him.

She's back in a couple of minutes with a tray. There's a container of juice, a bowl of green Jell-O, and a small, covered plate. When he lifts the lid we can see it's clear broth.

"What the hell is this?"

"The nurse said liquids only, sir. Sorry."

"You ought to be sorry. How about running to McDonald's and sneaking me back a McWhatever? Something with egg and cheese and sausage, maybe."

"I can't do that, sir. You can only have hospital food."

"Didn't have any trouble running out yesterday for my grandson here. You hot for him?"

"Harry!" Abby scolds. The striper hurries out.

"I was just teasing the girl. Didn't mean to run her off."

Abby pats him on the hand. "That's all right. At least you remembered she brought Jay something to eat." Then she looks across at me and says, "That's true, isn't it?"

I nod and smile.

"Nice to get something right for a change," Harry says and tries again to steal a bacon strip, but I whip my tray out of reach. "Thanks for nothing, kid."

"I'll go get your breakfast when I'm finished with mine," I say. "See if you can wait that long. Eat your Jell-O."

"Hmmph. Some loving grandson you turned out to be."

"Okay, okay. Here." I shove my tray onto his lap. "I'll go get my own."

As I leave, he adds, "Whatever you're getting, get me one too."

On my way out, I see the candy striper wheeling some old lady down the hall. "Sorry about Gramps," I say. "He's a little…" I spin my finger around my ear.

"That's okay. Thanks for telling me, anyway."

I start down the hall toward the elevator, and she calls after me, "McDonald's is about a half-mile south on Peach Street in the Mill Creek Mall."

"Thanks," I yell back and wave.

I eat my breakfast at McDonald's and order duplicates for Harry and Abby. When I return, Nigel is there too. I hand one bag to Abby and the other to Harry. "Hope you like fish," I tell him then add, "Got you a chocolate milk shake to go with it."

Harry gives me a dirty look. Then he grins and pats his stomach. "No thanks. My first breakfast was just enough."

I shrug. "Suit yourself." I hand the bag to Nigel.

He and Abby open their bags at the same time and peek in. Guess they don't like McFish either.

Abby smiles first and begins eating. Nigel gives me a funny look then takes a bite. "Best fish and chips I've had in years," he says. "Tastes more like bangers, though."

"You little shit," Harry says then cracks up laughing. "That'll teach me."

"Doubt it," I tell him. "By tomorrow, you'll forget."

ROSE

She hung up the phone and waited for Jackson, curious, hopeful, but wary. He sounded as nervous as she felt. Rose had never heard him speak this way before. Endearing in a way, but odd. Surely she was imagining things. He was fine last night. No, more than fine. He had been attentive both to her needs and her feelings. But even that seemed out of character.

Rose cautioned herself. Jackson might take the better part of an hour to check out and walk back uptown. She must remain calm. She considered taking a tranquilizer then thought better of it and poured herself a stiff Bloody Mary instead. "Breakfast of champions," she uttered out loud. "Breakfast of the damned," she chided herself. But she drank it down anyway, feeling calmer even before the alcohol could possibly have hit her bloodstream.

Then she remembered Abby. Rose should call her now and have something to share with Jackson. Or should she wait so they could call together? On the one hand, Abby might be more willing to talk to her, woman to woman. Rose knew from Abby's earlier call that she was concealing things, but it was probably only the Alzheimer's. Yet, Abby had not called back. She was keeping Rose in the dark, deliberately. Jackson might be able to get Abby to open up. He could be both persuasive and coercive. Rose had firsthand experience.

Jeremy had not called back either, except to say he was 'alive.' What if the reason neither Abby nor Jeremy had called again was the same? What if they were acting in concert? If so, it would be the first time Jeremy did anything he was told. All right, maybe that was an exaggeration, but there would have to be a good reason, one Jeremy agreed with.

Rose stared into her empty glass and considered refilling it. "Don't be stupid, Rose," she said out loud. "Call the woman and find out what happened." The self-counseling gave renewed courage. She could do this.

ABBY

We queued in the security line, inching along, when my phone rang. I had expected a call from Nigel to tell me Grace's flight was in and all was well, so I answered immediately, "Hello?"

"Abby?"

The airport paging system made it hard to hear. A woman's voice, though. "Grace?"

"No, this is Rose. Is my son with you?"

I hesitated.

"What's wrong?"

"Nothing. Jay is fine. Well, he has a bruise or two. And—"

"*Stop*! What happened?"

"There was an accident. Nothing major but they were shaken up, and my husband has been in the hospital for the past two days."

"*What*? Why?"

I shouldn't have told her that, but it had to come out sometime. Maybe it's better if she hears all this long distance. Still, I can't tell her Jay was driving. "Concussion. He hit the steering wheel."

"Jesus! No airbags?"

"It was an old truck. Just seatbelts."

"Oh, my god! What about my son?"

"He's fine. The doctor checked him over. Just a few bumps...and a black eye. "

"I can't believe this. Did he hit the dashboard?"

I felt the passengers around me listening now. Jay was listening as well but pretending not to. We were approaching the checkpoint and I would have to hang up soon. "The windshield," I told her, hoping my hesitation as I lied didn't show.

There was a long pause before she spoke again. "Can I talk to him?"

By that time, we were removing our shoes and coats and putting them in bins to pass through the security scanners. I told her I had to hang up and promised Jay would call back as soon as we got to our gate.

"Wait!" I could hear the fear in her voice. "Where are you going?"

"Back to Seattle. Jay says he can stay with his father's friend, Andrew. Or he can stay with us until his father comes home from Africa. Sorry, I have to go now. I'll call back soon."

I flipped my cell phone closed, Rose's "No, wait!" echoing in my ear. I felt the passengers around me pressing in, stealing glances at me then Jay then Harry and back to me again. I could only imagine what they were thinking and was ashamed. I knew I was not the proximate cause of the accident, but I bore the responsibility for setting the whole story in motion. The end had been inevitable from the start. I was thankful it had not been worse, but I knew the story was really just beginning. How it would end was unknowable.

ROSE

By the time Jackson knocked on her door, she had packed his small bag and a larger one for herself. She had arranged flights for them to Seattle using the credit card number Jackson had emailed her for Jeremy and was able to secure side-by-side seating.

"First class all the way, nonstop," she told Jackson, as he stood inside her door with his hands jammed in his pockets. She explained where Jeremy was headed. "I told the travel agent I wanted whatever flights got us to Seattle earliest. We're flying Alaska, leaving JFK at 4:30 p.m. and arriving in Seattle at 8:12 p.m." Then she smiled. "I put it on Jeremy's credit card."

"You mean my credit card," he replied, smiling right along with her, happy to see her take the initiative. "How much did this set me back?"

"Just about $3,000," Rose answered, her smile changing to the impish grin she knew he loved. It always meant she had something good for him.

"$1,500 per seat sounds pretty good for last minute reservations," he said, returning her grin, but she saw the unspoken question in his eyes, 'What's so funny about that?'

"Not $3,000 total, silly, $3,000 per seat."

Jackson looked at her in disbelief then burst out laughing. He always laughed at her extravagance. For some reason, she had never been able to fully understand, Jackson loved both the idea and reality of having a wife who never thought about the cost of things. "That's what money's for," he was fond of saying. He hadn't even complained after she left him and bought the co-op apartment where they now stood toe-to-toe, laughing together. "Good investment," he had said. "Too bad I won't end up with it after the divorce."

"Knew you'd think it was funny, but it's practical as well. I'm not sure which flight they're on, but we'll arrive at least an hour before they will. I checked. Our nonstop will be in long before any of the others."

"Smart girl."

"And, we don't have to leave to go to the airport for two more hours."

"Ahh," Jackson answered, brows raised.

Rose took his hand and led him back to her bedroom.

JEREMY

I sit behind Abby and Harry for the first flight to Cleveland, only a hundred miles. We'll be there in less than an hour. Almost screwed up and left the jackknife Harry gave me in my backpack; it would have belonged to some security guard's kid if I hadn't checked it in my duffle. It would suck to lose the knife. It's the only gift I've ever gotten I didn't have to beg for or be bribed with. That's the way it seems anyway.

Never been on a plane with propellers. It's pretty dinky, only two seats on either side of the aisle. That's why I'm not sitting next to them. Kind of noisy too, but I can still hear them talking. Abby is trying to explain to Harry why they need to rent a car. He says he remembers leaving theirs at the airport. That's just about all he remembers, but he's certain. She tells him he's right, but Oliver has probably picked up their car by now. They go back and forth till I get tired of listening.

We have to wait about an hour in Cleveland before we fly to Boston then we have to wait about an hour in Boston before we leave for Seattle. I like nonstop flights better. At least we can get something to eat in Boston. My stomach is already growling.

I'm nervous about what will happen once we get to Seattle. I told Abby I could go to Andrew's. Dad could pick me up when he gets back from Africa. She looked like she didn't believe me but didn't push the way Mom or Dad would have. I think she wants to believe it will be okay. Andrew will be home. Probably won't get there till after 11:00 p.m., but he always stays up late, so it doesn't matter.

I'll bet Dad shows up tomorrow. Maybe Mom too. She left me a message saying he'd be back from Africa by now, and since she called Abby, she knows where we're going. I'm in big trouble, I know it, but at least Harry will be safe. I'm not going to let Dad do anything to him. He can ground me for life if he wants, but he has to leave Harry alone. I don't care what Abby thinks; I know the accident was my fault. Or maybe it's Dad's fault. He's the one who dumped me.

JACKSON

On the way to the airport, Jackson loudly dictated a message onto Andrew's voicemail, "Find out what you can about this Abby and Harry Herndon. I want him committed. And maybe we should sue." His head throbbed with anger. He needed a drink.

Jackson could not believe the man's wife was innocent in all this. She hadn't exercised reasonable control over her husband, and she misled Rose into thinking all was well when it was anything but, deliberately keeping them in the dark. Now she had kidnapped Jeremy and was flying him back across country. He could almost hear her lie sweetly to the ticketing agent, "This is my grandson. We're taking him home to Seattle."

While Jackson and Rose waited for their flight, they sat drinking wine at one of the airport bars. Andrew called back.

"Jackson! How are you?" he asked, his voice irritatingly chipper.

"Angry as hell. And how are you today?"

"Give it a rest, will you," Andrew said, laughing at him. "I've got things under control as usual. How's Rose?"

Jackson doubted Andrew had anything under control, but his light-hearted attempt to cheer him up worked.

"Rose is Rose." He smiled across the table at her. "What else?"

She raised her eyebrows but winked. Jackson listened for a moment, laughed at what Andrew said next then gave in. "Alright, alright. You talk, I'll listen."

"That's the spirit, old buddy. So, here's the deal..."

Jackson remained quiet while Andrew related the long story. As he put the pieces together, his temper built at first, sometimes causing him to lash out at his friend. But his anger dissipated quickly, and his tight frown turned to a smile when Andrew gave him the punch line.

"Don't you get it? They're not married. Mr. Herndon's son, Oliver, has retained me to file papers with the court. He will become his father's legal guardian and put him in a nursing home."

Now, settled into his seat in first class, Jackson leaned back and looked out at the land passing 38,000 feet below. His tumbler of scotch rested on the table, Rose's vodka and soda keeping it company. Her glass overflowed with ice. Jackson took his scotch neat. The drinks were symbolic of their life together, opposite in many ways.

Could they remain united in purpose? Thanks to Rose, they would arrive at Andrew's before the Herndons and be waiting for them when they dropped Jeremy off. Rose seemed pleased to have set up the unpleasant surprise but balked at confrontation.

"I just want to take Jeremy home," she said. "Don't make more of this than it already is, Jackson. You always go too far."

Jackson tried to imagine the scene: Andrew's office? No, not big enough. They would wait just inside the front door in his living room. He relished the idea, but knew he must be careful not to upset Rose. He turned to look at her, this beautiful woman, once his wife and maybe now his wife again. He knew it was too soon to say, but she seemed so steady, so focused on the next few hours and days.

His revelation earlier did not anger her the way he thought it would. Instead, it worked in his favor. Rose knew full well he had manipulated her, and she knew why. She reacted in a tender way, holding him as they talked about Jeremy, the accident, and what they wanted to do next. She agreed they had been deceived and that Jeremy had been endangered through these people's negligence.

"We can do this, Jackson," she said, and he felt sure she meant more than just what they planned for the next few hours. "But I don't want a big scene. Let Andrew and the man's son handle it."

Yet now, her "we" still echoed in his mind, and he worried what might happen once they were alone again, just the three of them. He feared to broach the question but knew he must, so he leaned in his seat toward Rose and asked her softly, "Can we really?"

"What?" She turned to smile at him and rested her hand on his forearm. "Pick up our son and take him home? Don't be silly."

"Home" had a nice ring to it, so Jackson smiled back at her. "No," he said. "I mean, will you stay with us?"

Rose looked down and whispered, "I don't know." Then a bit louder, "I want to, but...I don't know. Nothing has really changed, has it?"

He paused. Had anything changed? Jeremy was three years older, but that hadn't helped, quite the contrary. "What if I cut back my practice? I would have more time."

"Oh, Jackson, don't you see that it's responsibility I'm no good with? I can barely take care of myself."

He watched her face fall. She sighed and patted his arm. "It's not easy for me, Jackson. Not the way it is for you. I'm like a half-deflated ball; I don't bounce. The first time Jeremy yells at me I'll collapse. You know that. It's what I've been trying to tell you all along. I'm no good as a mother. I was never meant to be."

Jackson began to answer, but Rose held up her hand to put him off. "I'll stay a week, and we'll see. I won't promise anything, but we'll see."

"I love you," he said.

"I know. I love you too. I just...can't..."

Jackson leaned back and closed his eyes, so close to putting his marriage together again, but close didn't count; it wouldn't be enough. Should he suggest boarding school again? Rose hated the idea of what she called, "those private preps," and had, in fact, refused only a year before to even consider O'Dea, one of the finest Seattle had to offer.

"I will not subject our son to the same Catholic crap my mother put me through."

He made other suggestions, but Rose had dismissed each the same way, "There is nothing wrong with public schools, Jackson. You just want to stick the foolish school decal on your car. Grow up."

But it wasn't true. Jackson's parents had sent him to Exeter back east in New Hampshire from grade nine on. At first he hated it, but Andrew went with him, and they soon made other friends, some of which remained in touch to this day. Maybe what Jeremy needed was to get away from his parents, to grow up under the care of professionals. But even if Jackson could convince Rose, would Jeremy agree?

He ran that idea through the arguments from both sides, considering the pressure Jeremy might apply, playing one parent against the other. He realized Jeremy would win, and in the process further alienate Rose. There seemed to be no solution.

ABBY

Our plane landed in Seattle on time, a blessing of sorts. Jay grabbed our carry-on bags, while I helped Harry shuffle up the jetway. He seemed calm, subdued. I worried he might not be clear-headed, but when I asked if he knew where he was, he teased, "Just where I don't want to be. Is Lincoln still president?"

I smiled but worried what would come next. I knew I should have called Rose but still couldn't bring myself to do it. I could excuse the lapse with the long run through security, especially after they made Harry prove his leg wasn't a weapon. Or maybe I could claim my phone battery went dead. The truth was I didn't want to discuss the accident again in front of anyone, even Harry and Jay. I could imagine Jay's parents becoming angrier than they already were, but there was nothing I could do about it. And the worst they could do was sue me.

After the long walk from our gate, we exited through security. Waiting on the other side was Oliver. His unexpected presence made my heart sink. There could be only one explanation: Jay's parents had somehow found him.

"How—?"

"My lawyer, Andrew Webster. He's expecting the boy. His mother passed along that you'd probably be arriving late this evening. I've been checking the inbound flights. Thought I'd save you the price of a rental car."

For one instant, I considered getting a car anyway. I dreaded the idea of being at Oliver's mercy and knew the coincidence was not a coincidence. I began to explain the circumstances of our hasty departure, but Oliver cut me off, "I know all about it. The jig is up, I'm afraid."

As the four of us trudged through the parking garage hauling our bags, I worried about Oliver's flippant remark. "What exactly did you mean?"

Oliver shrugged. "They know everything."

"And?"

"And they intend to work with me to make sure Dad is put in a nursing home before he kills somebody."

"You can't do that, Oliver."

"Can't I?" He stopped to look at me. "I think I can. In fact, I know I can. I'll sue for guardianship, and the boy's parents will testify on my behalf. We have a strong case, and according to my lawyer, you have no legal standing. Despite the rings you wear for show, you and Dad aren't married. You're just the last lover in a long line of conquests."

Oliver turned away and continued walking.

Jay glanced behind, as if considering whether to run, then back at us with an unspoken question. He could read the worry on my face, I'm certain, but not on Harry's.

Harry smiled. "Time to face the music," he said, then wrapped his arm around my shoulder and looked into my eyes. "Let's go get'em, tiger."

Oliver knew the way. We headed north from Sea-Tac Airport toward Magnolia and on to Andrew's house up on the bluff. Harry and Jay rode in the backseat, and I sat up front. Oliver's Jaguar was in the shop, as usual, so he had picked us up in Evangeline's new Toyota Prius. Jay seemed interested in the car, watching Oliver open the doors with the remote control then toss the device into the center console. The car started by pushing a button on the dash, his foot on the brake pedal. "Cool car," Jay said. His casual words seemed odd, out of place.

Oliver glanced in the rearview mirror at him. "Glad you like it," he replied in a tone drenched with sarcasm. "My wife's irritating attempt to offset my gas-guzzler."

The sky was still bright when we landed, but now, at 10:30 p.m., only the faint outline of the Olympic crest was visible. As we drove along Magnolia Boulevard, I turned to look at my best friend and husband. He stared out at the water lit by lights from ships and shore, as if he had never seen this before, though we had lived in the area for two years now and often strolled the beach watching ships, even at night.

What must it feel like to see something for the first time when you know it's not the first time? The opposite of *déjà vu*, the wonder of first looks tainted by the knowledge that you just don't remember when you should? Or is it worse? Perhaps each new occurrence is a kick in the gut. It would be for me. Yet, Harry's expression showed no pain, only the pleasure of seeing the water below us stretch out toward the distant peaks. Was this a blessing? Or was it a sign he had forgotten that he should remember, a sign portending the end of sanity?

Stop it, you'll make yourself crazy worrying about things you can't change. And you need to concentrate on the things ahead that you can. Good advice, I thought, but felt my anxiety increase as we neared Andrew's home. Oliver turned off the boulevard onto side streets and eventually pulled into the driveway of a sprawling Northwest contemporary. It sat high up on the bluff with commanding views of the shipping lanes and

Olympic Mountains looming beyond. He parked next to the only other car present, a large black Mercedes. Andrew's?

Jay answered my unspoken question, "That's Dad's car."

I could feel panic rising then realized Jay's father might have dropped it off when he went to Africa. I suggested this to Jay, but he shook his head.

"Dad left it at home. They beat us here."

I turned to Oliver. "Is this all part of your plan?"

He ignored me and got out of the car. I jumped out to confront him.

"This is beneath you, Oliver," I began, but before he could respond, the car door locks thumped into place, and the engine started. We turned in unison to see Jay seated behind the wheel and the car beginning to roll backward.

Oliver gave chase but was too late. The car jetted down the driveway in reverse, sideswiping the Mercedes and knocking over the neighbor's mailbox across the street, before turning and rocketing up the hill toward the boulevard. We stood silently and watched the taillights disappear.

I turned to Oliver. "Nicely done. Now what?"

"Damned if I know. Call the police, I guess."

"Brilliant."

"Right. This isn't my fault, Abby; it's yours. It's past time Dad was in a nursing home. I'd think you'd want that too, even though you keep fighting me about it. But I intend to do it with or without your support."

I shook my head. "I knew that when we moved out here, Oliver. That's why the first thing we did was join a church and have our 'show rings,' as you call them, turned into the real thing. We *are* married, and there's nothing you can do without my approval. Harry will remain free. But you needn't worry. We'll be back east before you know it."

With that, I turned and walked toward the house.

HARRY

The car jerks as Jay makes turn after turn till I'm afraid we'll get lost.

"Where are we going, Jay?"

"Someplace safe."

"Slow down and pull over up there in front of that pickup truck. That's safe enough. They won't find us."

"Why not?"

"Trust me, they'll think we headed back to the highway, but you drove us deeper into this maze of side streets. Just pull over before either you hit something else or we end up back where we started."

Once off the roadway, Jay kills the ignition. "What now?" he says.

"Now we talk. Know what I meant about facing the music?"

A shrug.

"It's an odd saying. Most experts think it derives from the ancient habit of drumming soldiers out of the military after a court-martial. You face the drummers and take your punishment. Think you can do that?"

Another shrug and a headshake.

"Okay, let's chat a while then. What do you think is going on back at the house?"

"Mom is freaking out. Dad is pissed."

"Oliver too, I suspect. What about Abby?"

He pauses a minute then says, "It's four against one."

"Think that's fair?"

A headshake.

"Right. But I'll let you in on a secret; she can take 'em."

That nets me a smile.

"There you go. That's more like it. Tell you what; let me ask you a question I'd guess your parents never ask. Ready?"

Jay gives me that woebegone look I've seen before, a look that says he's never been able to trust anyone important in his life, like he's waiting for the next punch.

"What do you want?" I ask. "If you could write the script for the next few years, what would it say? Where would you be?"

I look into his eyes and know I'm right; no one has ever asked him this before. Never asked Oliver, that's a fact. But then, I never had the opportunity either. Still, I can't fault Oliver. He's become his father.

Jay turns to look into the side-view mirror. Is he watching for pursuers, or like me, just looking behind him to see how far he's come? That's the thing about looking back. Once you start, you never know where it will take you. Doesn't take me very far anymore. There's too much I've forgotten. At least I still remember that.

When Jay answers, I'm not prepared for it.

"I want to live with you and Abby on Chaser's Pond."

"Heard us talking on the plane, didn't you? Abby wants to go back. Me too."

"Could I?"

"Can't imagine your parents going for that, can you?"

He shakes his head.

We sit a while in the silent car on the silent, dark street. No cars pass. In the distance, a dog barks.

"There's a prep in town," I say, thinking out loud. "Brewster Academy. Wouldn't be three miles from the lake. Short bike ride. Think your parents would go for a boarding school?"

There's that smile again.

ABBY

We walked toward the house, and the front door flew open. Out rushed a woman my height, lean and curvy with dark-red, shoulder-length hair. And behind her a stout man with dark hair streaked gray, who must be Jay's father, Jackson. Another man, Andrew I presumed, remained in the doorway.

I extended my hand to the woman. "It's Rose, isn't it?"

"Where is my son?" she demanded, ignoring both my hand and my question.

"Miles from here probably. They drove off."

"What?" she screamed.

I reached out to reassure her, though I had little assurance to offer. She ripped her arm out of my grasp and stalked toward Jackson, who was just now surveying the damage to his Mercedes.

"Stop looking at your stupid car and go find them," she continued at full volume.

He glared at me. "You'll pay for this, Abby."

I didn't know whether he meant the car repair or the entire episode, so I answered the former. "Your son was driving."

"What?" Rose screamed again. "He can't drive!"

Obviously. The path of destruction was proof enough, and I had no intention of telling her about Harry's driving lessons.

"Jackson! Do something!" she shouted.

"What should I do, Rose?" he spat back but quickly lowered his voice. "Do you want me to call the police?"

"Yes! No! Jesus, what a mess."

We all stood in silence, waiting for Rose to tell us what she wanted us to do. It occurred to me then that Jackson had probably spent his entire marriage like this, waiting for Rose to make up her mind. This may have been what poisoned their relationship and placed Jay squarely between them. Just like Harry, Olivia, and Oliver.

When Rose spoke, her voice was soft but threatening. "No, Jackson," she said. "If the stupid police found them, they'd chase till Jeremy hit a telephone pole or rolled the car. We have to wait. At least for now. Either they'll come back or they won't. I knew this was a mistake. I told you not to do it, but would you listen? No! I let you talk me into it, but that stops now. I don't want to hear another word out of your mouth, or so help me God, I'll be in a taxi back to the airport faster than you can imagine."

She paced down the driveway to the road and back again, holding her head in her hands and repeating, "I can't believe this, I won't believe this," then she stopped in front of Jackson.

She said, "I can't fail again. I just can't. It's too much." Then she walked alone back up the driveway and into the house.

JEREMY

Harry and I leave the car parked beside the road and start walking back to Andrew's house. He's right; I have to face the music. I tell him I could threaten to go to court to be emancipated two years from now, the way the brother of a friend did. You have to be sixteen.

"That so?" he asks.

I nod.

"Not sure that's the way to go. Here's another of my tired old axioms, 'You can catch more flies with honey than with vinegar.' Get it?"

"I guess."

"Good. Here's the plan. When we get there, you do your best to look sorry for ditching Abby and Oliver and for wrecking two cars. Think you can handle that?"

I nod again.

"And try keeping your mouth shut for a change. You do know how to do that, right?"

"Right."

"Then I'll apologize too and ask them if they know what their son wants. Not what they want; what you want. Wait till they ask. Then tell them you just want them to be happy, and you want to be happy too."

"But what about living with you and Abby?"

"One step at a time. Let's see if we can get them to agree to the idea of boarding school first. But don't push. That has to be their idea."

"But—"

"No 'buts.' Have patience. That's something teenagers suck at. And no sniping. You're trying to get your parents to see things your way."

"That's not fair—"

"Oh, yes it is. I watched that performance at the airport. You sniped at mom till she bolted, didn't you? I'd bet you make at habit of it. So just shut your mouth, hug your mother, and keep saying, 'I love you, mommy,' or whatever you call her."

"She'll think I've lost my mind."

"Nah, mothers are suckers for hugs."

"Not Mom."

"Even Mom. Trust me on this. So, if they bite on the boarding school bait, I'll tell them there are lots of great schools back east. Pricey, but their precious son will get a good education. Then I'll tell them about Brewster. Excellent academics and a very traditional, no-nonsense approach to discipline. That'll get'em. I won't say it's just three miles away."

"Mom'll never go for it. She hates private schools."

"Odd. Why? She went to one?"

"Saint Whatever. Catholic girl's school."

"Hmmph. No wonder. Think I can work around that. Brewster is prep for the monyed crowd, not the religious. Anyway, what have you got to lose?"

ABBY

The three men and I sat in Andrew's living room waiting. Rose paced back and forth. Occasionally, someone would begin to speak, but she cut him off quickly. Oliver was not used to this, a woman taking charge. He tried only once to argue back. Rose turned on him like a she-bear, "You're the idiot who left the keys in the car. Why should I listen to an idiot?"

I could see the words form in Oliver's mind: there is no key; it's electronic. But for a change, he kept his mouth shut.

Rose glared at him for a minute, daring Oliver to speak again, then she resumed pacing. Once in a while, she paused at the front window to peer down the driveway, as if willing Harry and Jay to appear.

A half hour later, she ordered Andrew to fix us all drinks, then marched across the room to where she had set her purse and pulled out her cigarettes. As she lit one, I could see her hands shake. Clearly on edge. It would take little to ignite her.

The spark came from Andrew, who brought Rose her drink. "I don't allow smoking in my house," he said. "You know that."

She took a long drag and blew the smoke back in his face, then dropped the lit cigarette into the glass he held.

"How's that? Better?" she said.

"It's Jackson you're pissed at. Don't take it out on me."

"Oh, really! Let's see if I have this right. Jackson's the one who came up with this harebrained idea to corner these people in your living room? No, that would be you, wouldn't it? And it would also be you who convinced Jackson and baldy over there to chuck the old man into some nursing hellhole, right? So, isn't it you I should blame for my son driving off? Isn't it you I'll blame when he drives baldy's car off a cliff?"

"No, Rose! It's not my fault. Nor is it Jackson's. Neither of us is the proximate cause of this situation. It's Mr. Herndon and that woman sitting right there. Why don't you aim all that venom at her?"

"Proximate? The proximate cause is baldy leaving the damn keys in the car. But this whole setup was your idea. Jackson isn't smart enough to think this up on his own. And besides, as he has told me over and over for the past two weeks, he couldn't do anything. *He was in Africa*!"

"Fine, have it your way."

"Yes, thank you, I will. Now go get me another drink."

As Andrew turned and walked away, Rose called after him but stared at me, "You're right about one thing. She *is* to blame for most of this mess."

"I'm sorry—" I offered, but she cut me off.

"Sorry? About what? Kidnapping my son or almost killing him?"

"Don't overreact."

"Overreact? Overreact!" she spat back. "My son has been missing for over two weeks, not a word from him, and next to no information from you either. When it's clear you knew much more than you were telling. Then you had the nerve to hang up on me after admitting Jeremy was involved in an accident! Did you think you could escape to Seattle without a word and get away with it?"

"We were held up in the security line—"

"Bullshit!" she interrupted. "I know bullshit when I hear it. You're talking to the master of weak excuses. I've made a million of them."

Rose loomed above me close enough to smell the vodka on her breath. What could I possibly say to calm her?

"Well? Anything you'd like to add?" Rose asked.

I could think of nothing that would help, so I said what I felt, "My husband may be ill, but I love him. And just as you now want to protect your son, I want to protect Harry. And for what it's worth, both Harry and I have come to love your son."

HARRY

We walk for another ten minutes along the road and up the driveway. I look at the damage to the Mercedes and whistle. "There goes your allowance for the next century."

Jay shrugs and looks back to the house. His mother stands in the window looking at him for a moment then disappears.

"This is your show, kid. Don't blow it."

He begins walking toward the house, and his mother opens the front door. He turns to see if I'm following.

"Go on. I'm right behind you. This is between you and your parents."

Jay nods and resumes walking. She watches his every step as he approaches and stops in front of her. I trail and take a place to the side.

"Well?" she asks.

Jay wraps his arms around her and stands there quietly repeating, "I'm sorry, Mom. I love you."

I wait and am not disappointed. Tears stream down her cheeks.

From the room behind her, I hear Jay's father, "What have you got to say for yourself—"

Rose lets Jay go and turns around. "I thought I told you not to speak. Do you want me to leave right now?"

His dad's just like me. Never knows when to shut up.

"As for you," she said, turning back to stare me down, I'd like *you* to answer that question. What have you got to say?"

"Fair enough. Fair enough." I hold up my hands up in surrender. "Let's start with an apology. I'm sorry I got Jay into this. I should have known better. And I should have known you wouldn't leave him at the airport alone."

Rose flinches as if she's been struck. Good, got her attention.

"And I should have known Jay would be angry with you and use me to get his way. I was once the father of a teenage boy too. Not a very good father, Oliver will tell you, but I still remember how manipulative kids can be when they set their minds to it."

Hint of a smile, but it vanishes quickly.

"Another thing I want to say is how great a kid you've raised. Can't have been easy doing that mostly by yourself. I'm right about that, aren't I? Surgeons get called away at all hours."

Looks suspicious. Careful, she may think you're trying to soften her up. Clearly not in the mood.

"The last thing is a question. Don't take this personally, but have you ever asked your son what he wants? He may surprise you."

I see emotions play across her face but can't read them. She pauses a long while before responding, as if searching for just the right words.

"Mr. Herndon, you have some nerve asking me that. But let me turn your question around. Do you know what Jeremy wants? Has he told you what he has never told me?"

Ah, that's the question I'm waiting for. "It's one of life's mysteries, I'm afraid. But things we will say to a total stranger are often more intimate than what we are willing to divulge to those who love us best. Trust me, I have a lot of experience."

Rose looks deep into my eyes, nods, and turns to Jay. He immediately blurts, "I want you and Dad to be happy."

"Since when?" She shoots back then holds up her hand. "Sorry."

"That's okay," he says. "You're right. I screwed up. I was mad at both of you, but that's no excuse. I know I'm hard to live with. I know I am."

Rose closes her eyes for a moment. She's thinking, maybe trying to find the right words. "Sometimes," she agrees. "I am too, though. You and your father both know that."

Jay nods then looks down and shuffles his feet. Rose reaches her hand out and lifts his chin. "But what do you want for yourself?" she asks.

Jay glances at me then back at his mother. "Not the way it's been."

"How then?"

"Boarding school. But not Dad's. I want to choose."

"Of course. I'm sure your father will agree. Won't you, Jackson?"

Rose waited only a moment before continuing, "But are you sure?"

Jay's eyes fill with tears. Then he nods, all the answer his mother needs.

Common Loon
Gavia immer

Mating

JAY

Over the next few days, I often heard Mom and Dad talking in soft voices long after they went to bed. I took to creeping down the hall and listening to the ebb and flow of their ongoing argument.

I'd hear him say, "But, Rose, it's just boarding school."

And she'd answer, "You know it's much more than that."

"But isn't this what we both want?"

"Yes."

"And don't we have to let Jeremy go someday?"

"Yes, Jackson, we do. It just doesn't feel right this way. How can we send him away now? We've only barely come together again."

"You have to stop thinking of it like that."

"But I do."

"Jeremy says it's what he wants."

"What he wants is for us to call him Jay. But I suppose you're right."

Their discussion continued for several days then stopped abruptly. I never heard them speak of it again. Whatever doubts remained must have been set aside, the decision made or let stand, no longer challenged.

By mid-August, Dad had enrolled me at Brewster Academy in Wolfeboro, three miles from Chaser's Pond. I would miss my friends and hoped I'd make new ones. Dad said in boarding school everyone started at zero. There would be kids from all over the country. "Just be yourself. It will work out." I wasn't sure he was right, but he went to prep school, so maybe.

This began my time living with Harry. The plan was that I'd spend most weeknights in the dorm, only staying at the cabin from Friday afternoon till Monday morning. Instead, I just moved in with them. My mother probably knew this would happen, but we didn't speak of it. I imagined it gave her the pretense of parental control. But maybe I'm just being pissy. Maybe my mother's support was sincere. She had stayed with us in Seattle for two weeks before returning to New York but had promised my father she would return. I didn't believe she would follow through, but I accepted what Harry told me. Without my sniping, they might stand a chance.

The day Mom left, she hugged me and asked that I spend a week with her in New York before classes started in September. I agreed. Later that day, our doorbell rang. I'd been sorting through which things I'd take and which I'd leave behind. I figured our visitor was Andrew. He stopped by often. But the voice at the door was not Andrew's. I listened, trying to pick up the words. Most were muffled, but I heard my dad say clearly, "He's down the hall, second door on the right."

When Oliver walked in, it surprised me. What now?

He stood looking from side to side for a place to sit. My messy room was even worse than usual. I had piles of unsorted stuff everywhere. He sat beside me on the only open space, my bed.

"I wanted to talk to you," he said, "About my father."

I nodded, though I didn't really care what he had to say. I turned to look out my window.

"He won't live long, but I'm afraid he'll be around long enough to mess you up. You shouldn't live with him. I just...wanted to warn you."

I sat quiet. Outside the window, distant boats sailed by in the stiff breeze that blew from the south. I turned back to Oliver. "Why do you still hate him?"

"I don't. I just don't like him. And I don't trust him. He'll turn on you."

"You couldn't be more wrong." I shook my head. "I know Harry won't live long. Doesn't matter. I want to be there to help as long as I can. Why don't you?"

He leaned forward and looked down at his feet. "He was never there for me when I needed him. Why should I care now? I only worry for Abby. She's strong but not strong enough."

"You're wrong about that too," I said, standing, hoping Oliver would take the hint, but he remained staring at his feet.

"Maybe so," he answered. "But I don't think you realize how hard it will be when he begins to fail. That's why I wanted to put him in a nursing home. To save Abby."

He stood then and held his hand out for me to shake. "Please help her," he said. "I can't. She'll need your support."

As my cab rolls along the eastern shore of Chaser's Pond, the scent of bone-dry pine flows thickly through the open windows. Behind the sharp pine, lurks the soft, earthy smell of rotting leaves. And behind those, the lake itself, a watery perfume that hints of fish.

September has arrived. Soon student orientation will begin, then classes. The morning is warm and humid, promising to turn hot later in the day, but that will only make swimming more of a relief. Through the trees, glimpses of blue water open then close again between overhanging pine boughs and wild blueberry. It's good to be here.

The road dips and turns, changing from asphalt, to gravel, to dirt as I near Abby and Harry's new, old cottage that Grace had helped them find. It rests several feet below the road and upper parking spaces and mere inches from the water's edge. The porch, covered and screened, gives way to wide steps down to a short dock. The cottage's dark-green shutters and trim and burnt-brown clapboard siding make it nearly invisible from the lake. Only the dock can be seen unless you pass close by. At the end of the dock sits a huge clay pot overflowing with flowers, bright red, deep pink, and white. A sign protrudes above, "The Herndon's," placed there not to welcome but to help Harry find his way back from his daily adventures, their beat-up aluminum rowboat the only vehicle he is still allowed to drive.

The cab drops me off. I take the steep steps down from the road two at a time and plunge through the front door. Harry sits in the ratty lounge chair he won't let Abby replace.

"About time you got here. I've been waiting for you all morning."

"It's only 10:00 a.m., and you're still in your pj's."

"Am not!"

"Are too! You're wearing them under your regular shirt and pants."

He looks down, ready to argue, then pauses. "Hmmph. Guess I'm cold. It was chilly before the sun hit the windows."

From the kitchen comes Abby's laughter and retort, "I've been trying to get him out of those all morning. He keeps telling me he's going back to bed soon to take a nap so why bother."

"Right. I did say that," he yells back. "Meant it too."

"You tired?" I ask.

"Not really."

"How about a swim then? Sun's on the dock."

"Already?"

"Yup. Bet it's eighty. Go change."

Abby walks in, drying a bowl she's just washed. "Need help?" she asks, walking over to him.

"Nah. I can do it. The kid can help if I need him."

"The kid?" she says, half statement, half question.

Behind her back I hold up my right hand, palm toward me, only my thumb and forefinger raised and spread wide, forming a 'J', and mouth my name silently.

"Yeah, the kid, Jay."

That earns Harry a kiss on the cheek and me a smile and headshake after Abby turns and repeats my gesture. That's when I notice the mirror behind Harry. I shrug and grin in mock sheepishness.

While Harry changes, I stow my bag in the guest room, now my room. I look around the small space, less than half the size of my bedroom back in Seattle. I smile, but in my mind, the sense of something new fights with the sense of continuity. Living with Harry will not be the same as our road trip. I know this, and it makes me anxious. What if I can't handle it? What if Harry can't handle it?

"Ready?" I hear him call from the bedroom doorway, breaking my thoughts. I look up. He's wearing red plaid boxer shorts.

"Trendy look, Harry, but they won't stay on when you dive."

"What?" he replies then looks down. "Oh, hell. Help me find a bathing suit, will you."

The rest of the morning goes without incident. We swim; we take turns rowing. We check out the marsh for birds and spot one wood duck pair, the male's eye glowing red but most of his bright colors gone now that mating season is over. Then we return for lunch, tuna salad sandwiches and iced tea.

Before Abby calls us in, we relax on the dock soaking up the rays, me at the end with my feet dangling in the water, occasionally getting a nip from the bluegills nesting below, Harry stretched out facing the cabin, eyes closed.

"Think I owe you an apology," he says after a while.

"For what?"

"The accident."

"That was my fault, not yours. I—"

"Let me finish before I forget what I want to say. This is not about you; it's about me. I'm making amends. Never was good at taking advice, but that doesn't mean I never listen. I heard you and Abby talking at the hospital. I don't forget everything. At least not yet."

He pauses a minute. I lie down, my head alongside his and wait for him to continue.

After a while, he says, "Sometimes what seems like a little thing at the time, a simple choice, ends up changing your entire life...like hopping a plane. I'm sorry for what it cost you. It will never be the same, what you had with your parents. Trust me, I know. But don't give up on them like I did with Oliver. Not gonna get all gooey about it, but I wanted you to know. I'm sorry."

I think about what he's said for a while before I answer, "You couldn't have done anything else."

"We're not birds. We can always do something else," he immediately answers then pauses a moment. "Know what an internal compass is?"

"How birds find the way while migrating?"

"Right. They orient themselves, adjusting to the position of the sun, stars, and the earth's magnetic field. Their world is simple, physical. Ours is more complicated, but each of us has an internal compass. Problem is, we make a habit of not following it."

He pauses again and turns his head toward me. "I should never have gotten on that plane, Jay, but I'm glad I did."

"Yeah, me too."

After lunch, we head back out to the dock. The sun is strong, and the morning's gentle breeze is replaced by a steady wind off the top of Copple Crown Mountain to the south.

Harry looks up and down the lake. A few small sailboats are out slicing back and forth across.

"Got a welcome home present for you," he says. "Stored it under the cabin. Want to give me a hand?"

I'm thinking canoe, but I'm surprised when he pulls aside the latticework and reveals a small sailboat I recognize as a Sunfish. The fiberglass deck is badly faded, and its sail nearly threadbare, but it looks like all the pieces are there.

"So, what do you think? Know she doesn't look like much, but I ordered a new sail. This one will do for starters."

"Very cool, Harry." I drag the Sunfish out to get a better look.

"I remember promising to teach you. Like to keep my promises. Good thing Grace hung onto her for me instead of taking her to the dump like I asked her to. You ready for your first lesson?"

I smile and nod. I don't have the heart to tell him I spent several days over the past month out on Lake Washington with an instructor my father hired.

"Well, it won't put itself into the water. Get going."

"Aye, aye, skipper."

Once launched, we work together to rig it. Harry tells me what to do. It's mostly obvious, but I wait till he gives me each instruction. Then, satisfied the rigging all looks assembled correctly, he removes his prosthetic and slides off onto the Sunfish's flat surface. The boat heels quickly, so I grab the handrail to keep it from tipping over.

"Smooth move, Harry. Maybe you're the one who needs lessons."

"Thanks, wiseass. Maybe I should duct tape your lower leg to your thigh and see how you do."

"Good point. I take it all back," I say, but not like I really mean it.

"Fine then. Let's see how you perform out on the lake. You'll get no help from me unless you beg for it."

"You're on."

I pull us away from the dock, trimming the sail. The Sunfish powers forward in a close reach, heeling over and driving into the half-foot, wind-driven waves, while we lean way out to keep it from going over.

Harry shouts above the wind, "Guess you've been studying."

"Nah, I'm a natural," I shout back.

"Natural wiseass maybe. Let's see how you handle this," he says and leans forward dumping us both overboard.

As the mast smacks the water, and I pitch forward into the sail, my first thoughts are for Harry. He slid beneath the sail and I can't see him.

"Harry," I yell. No answer. "Harry!"

"Need help?" drifts over from the opposite side of the overturned boat.

I duck underwater and surface next to him. He's floating peacefully with one hand on the centerboard.

"Think you can right her, wiseass?" He lets go and floats backward a few feet away.

I give him a dirty look. Meanwhile the boat begins to tip farther over.

"Might want to get on that before she turns turtle on you," he says.

I reach up and grab the centerboard, but the boat keeps tipping, so I pull myself up on top of the centerboard. The boat seems to stop for a moment but continues it's slow roll.

"Want some help?" Harry asks.

There's no way he can do this himself. I float back alongside him and call his bluff. "Show me, wise master."

"Are you begging?"

"No."

"I can wait."

"Alright, I'm begging," I say, though he can tell I'm not.

"You need begging practice."

"Fine. Pleeaase."

I expect him to cave, but Harry just smiles and paddles over to the now upside-down boat. He reaches up to grab the very tip of the centerboard, kneels on the edge of the boat bottom, one knee and one stump, and leans all the way back.

At first, nothing happens. Then slowly, painfully slowly, the Sunfish begins to come over. When it's part of the way back, Harry reaches up for the handrail and pulls his knee up onto the centerboard and leans again. The sunfish pops upright, and he easily pulls himself onboard.

Shit, I think, as I swim over to join him, I'll never hear the end of this. Might as well face it. "How did you know that would work?"

"How did you know how to sail?"

"Dad bought me lessons," I admit.

"Figured that. Didn't handle her like a beginner. I still might teach you a thing or two. Takes a lot more than a few lessons to master small lake wind patterns. I've been sailing this old girl on Chaser's since 1960. Now she's yours."

Before dinner, and after Harry lies down for his nap, Abby joins me on the dock. She's wearing a teal-green bikini that makes me vaguely uncomfortable. Not as uncomfortable as my mother's microscopic string bikinis make me, but still. When I avert my eyes, she laughs.

"I'm too old to embarrass you, don't you think?"

"I'm not embarrassed."

My denial just makes her laugh harder. Then she closes her eyes, and I keep my face turned toward the water.

"I hear you're the proud owner of Harry's childhood relic. I also hear you know how to sail it," she says after a few minutes of silence.

"I guess. I can't right it if it goes over, though."

"So he told me. The trick is to get up on the centerboard as fast as possible. Once the sail ships water, you need height and weight to bring it back up."

"You know how?"

"Harry pulled the same crap on me thirty years ago. Dumped the boat and made me plead with him to turn it back over. Either beg or swim a mile back to the dock."

We laugh together as Abby tells me more of Harry's tricks. Then it's quiet again for a while before she says, "It's going to be all right, Jay."

I knew what she meant. We had already talked about it. Harry would be "all right," and we would be there to be "all right" with him. He would forget how to dress himself, and we would tease him into changing. He would forget our names, and we would think up ways to remind him. He would ask the same questions over and over, even though we had just answered, and we would pretend otherwise. He would wander off, and we would follow, saying what a great idea he had to go for this walk on such a nice day. In short, we would shield him from what lay ahead as long as we were able.

Autumn came early. By mid-October, birch and ash glowed golden and maples turned red, washing the surrounding hills and mountains in color. Then the winds and rain arrived, driving us inside and shaking windowpanes. By November, faded leaves covered the ground. December brought the first snows, wet and slushy at first, then crusting over so hard you could walk on top. We watched the lake skim with ice overnight then thaw by the next evening, leaving only the shaded shore white.

By January, the sun had long given up, Chaser's Pond froze hard and thick, then settled along fault lines, leaving wide cracks. We could hear the ice booming in the night, breaking and resetting. By morning, the night's upheavals crisscrossed the lake like the veins on Harry's arms. A day later a nor'easter dumped a foot of snow and our world went white and soundless.

Harry withdraws. Is it the silence? Is it the thin sun? Is it the cold? He begins to claim fatigue and need for sleep, often heading for bed right after dinner. But later I hear the two of them talking.

Sometimes in the middle of the night, I hear the soft crunch of Harry's leather lounge chair as he settles into it. He never turns on a light, never moves enough to disturb me, but by morning, when I wake to the sounds and smells of breakfast, and rise to dress for school, I peek in their bedroom and there he lies, head on a pillow, sound asleep.

At first, Abby joins him in bed as soon as we finish the dinner dishes; she washes, I dry. Then I turn to my homework, watching TV at the same time. I keep the volume down, and neither Harry nor Abby complains. Sometimes she resurfaces after Harry has drifted off, but increasingly she disappears for only a short while, "Just for a quick kiss and cuddle," she says. She sits next to me on the sofa, her bare feet tucked beneath her. We watch whatever stupid show is on, arguing with the writers, calling them names when they trot out some lame joke or over-the-top scene. We talk about my schoolwork or the weather or what she's planning for dinner tomorrow. We do not talk about Harry. There is really nothing to say. At 10:00 p.m., we retreat to our separate places and our separate thoughts.

Why did it take so long to understand what should have been obvious? We wasted a winter, one of the few Harry had left. We knew he wasn't sleepy, but we let him go off early to bed anyway. Why didn't we realize the

TV shows we watched didn't make sense to him, especially the ones that carried a plot forward from the previous week? I remember the moment we figured it out. It came after Abby asked if Harry might like to join us for a change and watch a show. "It's the one you used to love," she said.

"Nah," Harry answered. "Can't tell one blonde from the other."

Abby and I turned as one to face each other, both finally knowing.

For a while we coaxed Harry back to his lounge chair in the evening with nature shows or sporting events, but even these seemed too difficult for him to follow, so we turned off the TV, stowed away the remote control, and talked. By trial and error, we picked our way through the maze of dead ends that were becoming Harry's mind. Sometimes we found a way in. More often, ways that had been open now closed.

Winter's back breaks in mid-April. We watch each day as the snow disappears and exposed ice creaks and groans and pulls away from the shore. Then it is gone, seemingly overnight. Within weeks the loons return, their voices lonely. Most hang out in groups of four or more. "Teenagers," Harry calls them. "Not ready to hook up yet." Sometimes we see a mated pair, but they don't stay long. Chaser's Pond has no good nesting sites.

All winter we feed the birds, hanging suet feeders with beef fat and making sure our seed feeders are filled daily with black-oil sunflower, thistle, and millet. The birds make their rounds in all but the worst weather. Black-capped Chickadee, Tufted Titmouse, Dark-eyed Junco, Hairy and Downy Doodpecker, and Nuthatch, both white- and red-breasted.

On warm days, once spring seems just around the corner, waking chipmunks and red squirrels invade. Harry goes after them with a broom, and Abby scolds, "Better not. I'll tell Grace." He stops in his tracks and looks around quickly.

"It's too early. She won't be here till the snow's gone," he says.

"Don't be so sure. Could be any day now."

That day arrives May first. I watch her blue kayak cut across the mirrored lake, heading directly from her cabin one-third a mile away. She put in at the boat ramp. I can see that her dock is still raised, tied to an ancient pine by steel cable and a winch. We dropped ours as soon as the ice went out.

"How's the crazy old man doin'?" she asks as soon as she paddles up alongside the dock.

"'Bout the same, I reckon, ma'am," I tease.

"I'm from Back Bay, boy. Not Texas. Think he'll still recognize me?"

"Who knows?" I shrug. "He calls me 'kid' most of the time and only calls Abby by her name when she's wearing the apron I bought her with 'Abby' printed all over it. She wears it a lot."

"Well, damn. I hoped for bettah. I s'pose I'll take what I get."

I trail behind Grace up the steps and into the house, where Harry sits in his lounge chair, as usual, poring over a roadmap.

"How're ya doin', old man?" she says.

"Grace! Is that you?"

"Always has been. Probably still is."

She leans over to kiss Harry on the cheek, but he pulls her onto his lap and kisses her on the lips.

Abby watches from the kitchen doorway, leaning against the frame. Harry turns toward her.

"Look! It's Grace!" He pauses for an extra second and glances at her apron, before adding, "Abby."

"It certainly is. You can let her up now."

As Grace hoists herself out of Harry's lap, I see him reach around and pat her on the ass. I hope Abby hasn't seen but know she must have. Grace seems at a loss for words, looking back and forth between Harry and Abby.

"Lots of unpackin' to do. Sweepin' too. Dead bugs everywheah. Bettah get to it. Just wanted to stop and say I'm back for the summah."

She waves and heads outside. I follow and hold the kayak steady as she clambers in. Don't want to have to fish her out of the 50-degree water. Once settled and pushed off the dock, Grace says, "Didn't know what to say—"

"It's all right. That's what we say now. He's all right, we're all right, it's all right."

"You believe that?"

"Actually? Yeah, I do."

Grace stops by most days, as spring warms the lake and new leaves appear in the treetops. She and Harry sit on the porch or dock gabbing about nothing or about their childhood summers together. Abby and I leave them alone for the most part, but we can hear their words drift through, now that it's often mild enough to leave windows open. Harry begins to wait for her on any sunny morning. He helps her pull the kayak up on the beach and boosts her onto the dock, his help always accompanied by a pat on the ass. Grace seems to accept it as a simple sign of affection. I don't know what Abby thinks.

With May come the black flies. "Mothah's Day to Fathah's Day," Grace says, and it proves true. At first, you can't go outside without being attacked. I have bite welts anywhere my skin isn't covered. If that's not bad enough, they fly into eyes, nose, ears, and mouth. Then one day they're gone. Grace reports she spent the morning raking off leaf and pine needle accumulation from winter and hasn't been bitten.

Grace is not our only visitor. All winter Nigel showed up like clockwork, and he continues this pattern into spring, every Monday and Thursday afternoon, from two to four. He and Harry reminisce about the old days, the only days Harry now seems to recall. They talk about birding mostly. Harry has Nigel fetch his life list from the bookshelf. Unlike mine, hardbound and filled with photos and printed descriptions of each bird, Harry's is plain, handwritten, with thirty lines to a page and vertical bars separating each page into three columns: bird name, both common and Latin, date observed, and where spotted. The first entry is, *"Robin, American Turdus migratorius 5/8/1944 Nashua, N.H. - my backyard."*

One cool night in mid-May, Nigel and Grace join us for dinner and manage to keep Harry up long past his usual bedtime. Whether it's their company or just good luck, Harry is pretty clear-headed for a change, though he's still having trouble with names. We can always tell because he calls me "kid" and calls Abby "dear" or "honey."

When Nigel and Grace hit the road at 9:00 p.m., I wave from the door and say goodnight to Abby and Harry. My days start early, and I'm beat. By the time my head hits the pillow, I'm asleep, but an hour later I startle to the sound of their bedroom door closing. I lie in the dark, half-awake, and hear Harry remove his prosthetic and let it drop. If the door hadn't woken me, that would have. "Ssh," I hear her whisper. "You'll wake Jay."

"Who?" Harry asks, his voice loud.

"Never mind. Just be quiet."

Their bedsprings creak as they climb in and settle. A moment later, Abby says softly, "Had a letter from Oliver."

That brings me alert. Ever since our conversation in my room months ago, I've been hoping he might change his mind about Harry. Often I've heard Abby talking with her grandkids and asking about their father.

"Who?" Harry asks.

"Your son, Oliver."

"Oh. A letter, huh. Sounds serious...what's up?"

"Nothing, I'm afraid. I wrote him a long email a few weeks ago asking if the kids could come out to visit while..."

"While I'm still kicking, right?"

"No, while you still remember them. But Oliver—"

"He said, 'No dice,' huh?"

"Yes. I'm sorry. I really miss them, especially Nessa."

"I'm sorry too. Thanks for trying anyway."

They are quiet for a while. I can hear them turn over in bed. Then Abby says, "It's just not fair."

"All's fair in love and war, dear. Anyway, it's my fault."

"Even so, it's not fair."

I hear her sigh, and he coughs a few times then asks, "You still mad at me for skipping out on you?"

"I never was. Just angry with myself for moving us west when I should have known better. I was afraid to do it alone."

"Take care of me, you mean?"

"Yes. Scares me a little."

"Helps to have the kid here, doesn't it. Think he'll stick it out?"

"I'm certain of it. I don't know why, but I am."

More silence, but then Abby makes an odd noise and says, "Have you lost your mind?"

Harry laughs out loud. That makes me smile. It's funny, really, to ask him if he's lost his mind.

Then Abby says, "Not unless you can tell me my name."

I frown. Don't get it.

"Hmmph," he says after a moment. "Hildegaard? Or maybe...Muriel? No, wait! Rapunzel. That's it."

She laughs softly then says, "Not even close."

"Okay. How about running out to the kitchen and bringing back your apron? You know, the one with 'Abby' written all over it. You can put it on and we'll play 'What's for supper.'"

Now I get it. I grab my blanket and creep out quietly to the dock, where I spend the next hour sitting in the cold night air wrapped tightly. When I return, snoring is the only sound I hear.

On graduation day from ninth grade, a month before my fifteenth birthday, my parents show up together. It's the beginning of the Memorial Day weekend, and they've decided we should take a family vacation. I hide my attitude but worry it might poison the trip anyway. Since neither has spent a day in New England, with the exception of connecting through Logan Airport on the way to Europe, they are determined to see it all. That means visiting every tourist trap they can think of. We will begin by driving the Kancamagus Highway through the White Mountains then head for the Maine coast where we will, "See some birds," as they put it.

Then we will drive south to Gloucester, where they think we'll learn about whaling. Then to Provincetown on Cape Cod, where we'll learn more about whaling. Then back to Boston where we'll pick up the real Revolutionary Road, the Old Post Road from Boston to New York, and along the way we will stop at Mystic Seaport, where we'll learn more about whaling than anyone could possibly want to know.

I'm not looking forward to the trip. I try a modest proposal: a weekend in Boston. "You'll love Cambridge. It's your kind of place." By that I mean loaded with money, the closer to Harvard the pricier. Harry's words but I'm happy to repeat them. Their expressions say it all. Nothing doing.

"We're not interested in that. We've changed," Mom says.

"We've started over," Dad adds.

That's when I notice their rings. They're wearing them again. Great, another round of bedded bliss followed closely by boredom and backstabbing. But I'm wrong. The next two weeks show me something I have never witnessed before, friendship. They actually enjoy being together.

Instead of one trying to outdo the other, they act relaxed. Only it isn't an act. It's real. Somehow they have become comfortable with each other.

I have no clue how this new relationship has come about, but I don't trust it. The whole thing makes me nervous. I'm not sure how to relate, but I realize it doesn't matter anymore. I am free to live my own life, and they are free to live theirs. If those separate paths converge a bit, okay. If not, no problem. "No worries," as Nigel often says.

So we make the journey together, ending our trip at JFK, where they put me on a plane to Manchester Airport, and they fly back to Seattle.

Gone is the Central Park West condo. Gone is the Juanita Bay lakefront mansion. Home is now a twenty-fourth floor high-rise apartment, their lives a mix of sunsets over Puget Sound, short trips to Portland or Vancouver, shopping at the Pike Place Market, and frequent dinners out. My father has cut back his surgical practice to two days a week. It seems impossible, but it's true.

On the flight north, I realize I am happy for them but sad for myself. No, not sad, I think, lonely. I kissed my mother goodbye and shook my father's hand. They were proud of me and said so. Their affection shone in their eyes. But it was not the same look they offered each other, not the look I had seen time and again over the past two weeks.

All my life I had been their center, the point around which their lives revolved. It had not been fun. Often they pulled at me or pushed me away. Always they circled, looking through me, part of their game of cat and mouse. I believed I was the one thing that held them together. Now I could see I was wrong; I had held them near, but my presence prevented them from closing the gap between them. My recent departure from their day-to-day lives had healed a long-opened wound. Yes, they looked at me with affection, but they looked at each other with love.

That summer something happens that I thought would never happen. I grow. After seeming stuck forever below five-feet tall, suddenly I'm five foot, eight inches. I don't actually grow that much in three months, but it must have been at least half that. On entering tenth grade, I now stand eye-to-eye with the girls in my class. I notice. They notice. I notice they notice. But maybe they have always paid attention, and I've been oblivious. Never mind, I don't care.

So I fall in love. Who doesn't at this age? The problem is I don't know which one of several girls I am most in love with. That proves unacceptable to half the girls I like and a challenge to the rest. One, a petite, blue-eyed, butch-cut blonde named Bryn, whom Harry refers to as "the cute chick," is my first choice. But it becomes obvious she has mainly been interested in winning the contest.

The second, Evie, also blonde and blue-eyed, but with long hair and longer legs, Harry dubs, "the hot chick." Turns out he likes her better than I do, and after seeing her sit on his knee one afternoon, she's history. The last thing I need is for Harry to forget how old he is and embarrass us all.

The third sticks. If I were honest, I'd admit height is the main attraction. I tower over her. Hyla may be five feet tall, but I'd bet against it. Her long chestnut-brown hair falls straight down the middle of her back and ends at her knees. Harry calls her Peg. She finds the name funny. Thinks he's teasing her; that he means peg legged, since she's so short. I know better but don't try to explain. Hell, I'm not sure I can explain, and I don't want to go there. What little I've overheard, I haven't followed. I'm just happy he doesn't call her Margaret. Abby seems amused too. Maybe it gives her another way to see whatever Margaret/Peg means in Harry's failing memory.

Fortunately, Hyla steers clear of Harry, as if she knows the light in his rheumy eyes implies more than just a friendly, fatherly interest. Or maybe I'm imagining a danger that doesn't exist. Certainly, they delight in teasing each other, Harry's "Good to see you, Peg," matched by Hyla's "Good to see you, pops," followed quickly by Harry's "Don't call me pops, you midget." And her "The name's Hyla; you're the one with the peg leg."

That summer Hyla and I do all the usual things 15-year-olds do, stopping short of actual sex. Mainly, we become best friends. She shows me the way it can be between boy and girl.

A year later, we graduate 11th grade, and Hyla leaves for home and never returns. She'd been at Brewster on a scholarship. She lost it by spending too much time with me and too little on homework. We write at first, and I promise I'll get my parents to make up the difference in what her folks can afford, but she refuses. Soon, we stop writing. She sends one last letter. "It's better this way," she concludes then signs off, "Fondly, Hyla."

Fondly?

Why did it hurt so much when it ended, and only a month later seem unimportant? I had given her nearly two years of my life. Why didn't it matter?

One thing only is certain. While I was looking the other way, Harry had changed. By the time I realize, snow covers us again. Christmas approaches.

The first thing I notice is a scattering of crumbs in Harry's lap, leftover from a sandwich he had eaten hours before. Such a small, insignificant thing, yet it signifies all that will follow. It is so unlike him. Abby reacts the same way but quickly sweeps up the evidence.

The next day, he hasn't combed his hair before breakfast, and when he sits at the kitchen table, he almost misses. If I hadn't grabbed his chair he would have toppled.

Abby sets two bowls on the table, pours both cereal and milk, and hands Harry a spoon. And I watch him watch her, mimicking her moves, spoon to bowl, spoon to mouth.

When had this happened? Where had I been? With Hyla was the simple answer. Living my life was the more truthful.

My sense of failure returns. I should have been there for Abby, not pursuing my own desires. I promise myself I will do better. Later, I make the same promise to Abby. Her answer is a hug I cannot escape and tears on my neck. Then she pushes me away.

"It's time for you to go," she says.

I stand staring at her in disbelief. How can she tell me to leave, now, when she needs me most?

"I don't need your help," she answers my unspoken question. "I need your love, and I need you to remember. What remains of Harry is nearly gone. What comes now will be hard, but I can face it. Your love for Harry is newer, more tenuous. It is too precious to lose, so you must not. Save it for me. I will need it back when this is over."

Reluctantly, I sign up for student housing to fill out the remainder of my senior year at Brewster but put off packing till after the holidays. There's no rush and Abby has relented in part. We agree that I will visit often and help out where I can. Somehow I've convinced her Harry's progressing illness will not alter the way I feel. Perhaps she believes me, or maybe her need for relief is more pressing than she will admit, even to herself. Regardless, over the next five months, I visit Harry most weeks. When classes end in May, I move in with Grace to be nearby whenever Abby calls.

On one such occasion, Abby's voice over the phone is particularly strained, as if the weight of caring for Harry has finally broken her indomitable spirit. We trade places, passing in mid-lake, Abby crossing to my side and I to hers.

"You'll have to feed him," she says as she rows by. "Just keep company. Don't worry about anything else. He's diapered."

I nod and continue paddling. I'm used to the routine but worry that maybe this time something is different. I could see the pain written on Abby's face. But when I walk up from the dock nothing seems unusual.

"Hey, old man," I say. "How're you doing today?"

Harry doesn't answer as he usually does. He just lifts his hand and shakes it. Must not be up for conversation.

"Hungry?" I try.

He nods.

I go check what Abby has made for his dinner. Pea soup. Can't stand this stuff myself, but I know Harry's been having difficulty swallowing lately, and Abby has begun making only soups, and cereals, and other meals that go down easily.

The spoon-feeding works okay, though quite a bit dribbles down onto the bib I put on him before beginning the process: spoonful of soup, sip of milk, spoonful of soup, sip of milk. Repeat till bowl and glass are empty.

Tonight he seems to have more trouble swallowing than I remember. About halfway through the meal he closes his mouth and shakes his head.

"No more?" I ask.

Another head shake.

"Okay." I set the bowl down. "What would you like me to read tonight?" This too is part of the process. Sometimes it's Robert Frost. Sometimes, Dylan Thomas. Lately I've been reading Kafka. *The Trial.* Harry had said it reminded him that what happens to you doesn't always have a reason.

He opens his mouth to speak, but nothing comes out, just an incoherent gurgle.

"Try again," I say, and feel both panic and tears begin to take over. He's choking. I jump up and run to get a glass of water, but when I return, he shakes his head.

"You all right?" I ask.

He nods.

Then I understand. He has lost the ability to speak. His words are gone.

I lose it, tears welling until he lifts his hand and points toward the bookcase.

"What?" I ask, wiping my eyes on my T-shirt.

Harry brings his hands together, locking thumbs, and flaps them like a bird in flight.

"Bird book?"

He shakes his head and moves his hand as if writing.

"Life list!"

He nods and something vaguely resembling a smile creases his face. Under other circumstances the smile would be frightening, a grimace. But on his face at this moment, it just makes me grin. He's still there.

I locate the ratty, old spiral notebook easily. It stands out. While I watch over his shoulder, Harry leafs through the pages, though slowly, then starts over when he doesn't find what he's looking for. He runs his finger down the first column on each page. In search of some particular bird, I suppose. He finds it on page five and taps on the entry:

Ovenbird Seiuris aurocapillus 7/18/1953 Wolfeboro, N.H. Chaser's Pond

I laugh. He's teasing me. I still haven't seen one. "That's nice, Harry. Go ahead and rub it in."

He shakes his head and taps on the entry again then points to me.

"Nope. Still haven't seen one."

This time he nods and again taps and points.

I frown. Not sure what he means. Then I think back to that first time when he told me it didn't count. It was against the rules. Can it possibly be that he remembers? I ask and he nods.

"So, you want me to count it?"

He nods again.

What the hell, why not? "Okay," I say. "But if we're going to break the rules, then you have to count the night heron. Deal?"

Harry pauses for a minute then reaches out his wobbly hand, and we shake on it. There's that smile again.

"Congratulations. That makes three hundred" I say, still shaking his hand. He presses mine harder and closes his eyes.

I return to the bookshelf and pull out the *Sibley's* to look up the Latin name, then take the life list from his hand and turn to the last page. At the bottom, just under the entry for our king eider, is one more blank line. Guessing at the date Harry heard it squawk, I write:

Heron, Black-crowned Night Nycticorax nycticorax 7/10/2006 Central Park, NYC

I glance up at Harry, his eyes still closed, and add a postscript:
Hearing is believing.

Epilogue

Canda Geese
Branta canadensis

Epilogue

Canda Geese
Branta canadensis

JAY

It's late June, nearly four years to the day that Harry and I took our flight together. I'm back in Seattle for a visit and sitting at the breakfast table. Across the kitchen, the phone rings. My mother stands in the kitchen doorway, face in profile. She answers and listens for a moment. Then her arm stretches toward me, handset held tight, as if to ward off a curse. "For you, Jay."

It's the call I've feared. Harry is gone.

By noon, my bag, unpacked a week ago, is repacked. I've called my father to let him know I'm leaving, and I've haggled with the airline over the exorbitant price of my replacement ticket.

"It doesn't matter," my mother says, dismissing my complaint. "Jackson will pay for it."

Yes, I think, my father would pay, but not without some comment that would only irritate me.

My short visit had been punctuated with such comments. At first, I thought it was only my presence that caused them, but then I realized my parents' basic natures had reasserted their differences. It made me wonder if they would remain together after all. Then I remembered something Harry had once told me, "You can't make someone else happy." I could see the truth of this; my visit had simply brought their conflict to the surface. My father could not do what my mother needed; he could not make her happy.

I should never have come, and I wouldn't have if Abby hadn't sent me away. Her voice, when I took the phone from my mother's hand, begged forgiveness without ever asking for it.

"I'll be there tomorrow," I told her.

"I know," she said.

On the way east, we pass Mount Rainier, dominating the skyline, still snow-covered and glowing red. The flight from Seattle is long but uneventful, just one plane change in Detroit. I sleep through much of it, arriving in Manchester at 9:00 p.m., having left Seattle just after sunrise.

As I wait curbside with the other arriving passengers expecting rides, I think again about what Abby told me. There was no pain. Rising early, as usual, she waited till breakfast to wake him, but found Harry dead. The coroner judged it a massive stroke.

"A stroke of luck," Abby said.

That's the way it seemed to me as well. When I left last week, Harry was already so weak he could no longer respond, eating little if anything, and barely able to sit upright. But I missed him and wished he were still here with us.

As I continue to go over the past few weeks in memory, my phone chimes. It's Abby.

"I'm running late. Sorry," she says. "I'll be there in fifteen minutes or so. Look around. Do you see a girl your age waiting? She's fairly short, maybe a bit over five feet. Pale-blonde hair. She'll be reading a book. That's our granddaughter, Nessa."

I glance around quickly, easily locating her, then walk up and hand over my cell phone. "For you," I say.

Nessa looks up from her book, a question in her eyes. Then she smiles.

The next day we scatter half of Harry's ashes on Chaser's Pond, a little here, a little there. We row the shoreline together, Abby in the bow, Nigel and Grace at the stern, Nessa and I side by side, each wielding an oar. Then we row to the center of the lake opposite the dock and slowly release what remains. The afternoon breeze rises and veers as it always does before settling its direction. A rivulet of light ash clings to the surface and meanders away till it stretches out far behind us. As we watch, a loon surfaces nearby and paddles through the ash, cutting the stream in two. My first reaction is sadness, both for loon's interference and the unfortunate symbolism. Then I smile. It is as if Harry has orchestrated this moment, leaving us a visible sign: there was a part of him we would be allowed to keep and a part we must let go.

That evening we prepare a meal together and sit long into the night telling stories. Nigel describes the birding trips they had taken, Grace complains about how hard it was when they were teenagers to get Harry to pay attention to her instead of the damned birds, and Abby embarrasses Nessa by going over in great detail the time long ago when she had "crapped in his lap." When it was my turn, now that it no longer mattered, I admitted I was the one driving when we crashed Grace's truck.

"Already knew that," Grace says.

"How?" I ask.

"Sticky pedals. Still had glue on'em from the duct tape. B'sides, didn't make sense ya could cut yahself that way on smooth glass."

We all laugh, even Nigel, but he gives Grace an evil look.

"Sorry, old boy," she says. "You'd have blabbed to Abby."

"I knew anyway," Abby admits. "Jay confessed at the hospital."

Nigel looks at Nessa, who shrugs. Maybe Abby has told her.

"So, I was the only one in the dark," he complains. "Always the last to know. Story of my life, I fear."

There's a moment in every conversation when an awkward silence falls, and someone must speak first. Grace breaks it.

"Bettah be goin'," she says but offers to help with the dishes. Abby dismisses her with a wave. Since Nigel had brought Grace, they depart together, farewell endearments and promises to come whenever called trailing in their wake.

I need to say my final goodbyes, so I leave Nessa and Abby to talk privately, and walk down to the lake where we have spread Harry's ashes. It feels like he is out there, eyes closed, lying deep.

With shoes and socks removed and pant legs rolled, I sit at the end of the dock and trail my feet in the water. The warm night air, nearly still, clings to the surface in tendrils of fog. Harry's last breath. I chuckle when I imagine his response, "Sentimental nonsense."

I sit for quite some time before I hear Nessa's soft footsteps. She stands for a minute, honoring the silence, then sits close beside me, bare feet dangling but not reaching the water. She leans against me and takes my hand.

"I wish I had known him better," she whispers. "You'll miss Harry, won't you?"

There are no words adequate to answer her question. I let my tears speak for me.

Harold Herndon's Life List

	Species	Date	Field Notes
1	Chickadee, Black-capped *Poecile atricapilla*	5/8/1941	*Nashua, N.H. - pecking sunflower seeds from our feeder*
2	Crow, American *Corvus brachyrhynchos*	5/8/1941	*Nashua, N.H. - eating a dead squirrel some car hit*
3	Dove, Mourning *Zenaida macroura*	5/8/1941	*Nashua, N.H. - pair of them sitting side-by-side in our dogwood*
4	Flicker, Northern *Colaptes auratus*	5/8/1941	*Nashua, N.H. - pounding on our porch roof with its beak*
5	Goldfinch, American *Carduelis tristis*	5/8/1941	*Nashua, N.H. - bright male and dull female eating our thistle seed*
6	Grackle, Common *Quiscalus quiscula*	5/8/1941	*Nashua, N.H. - big yellow eyes, mom says he looks evil*
7	Jay, Blue *Cyanocitta cristata*	5/8/1941	*Nashua, N.H. - our noisy thief*
8	Robin, American *Turdus migratorius*	5/8/1941	*Nashua, N.H. - five of them pulling fat worms out of the wet grass*
9	Woodpecker, Downy *Picoides pubescens*	5/8/1941	*Nashua, N.H. - holds onto the feeder by his toes*
10	Starling, Eurasian *Sturnus vulgaris*	5/9/1941	*Nashua, N.H. - over a hundred flying in a cloud*

Harold Herndon's Life List

	Species	Date	Field Notes
291	Wren, Bewick's *Thryomanes bewickii*	6/7/2005	Whidbey Island, WA - on a red cedar branch flicking his tail
292	Oriole, Bullock's *Icterus bullockii*	6/17/2005	Whidbey Island, WA - hunting insects among the blackberry vines
293	Quail, California *Callipepla californica*	6/17/2005	Whidbey Island, WA - on our back fence, must be a dozen or so right in a row
294	Thrush, Swainson's *Catharus ustulatus*	6/17/2005	Whidbey Island, WA - singing up high in a madrone, gorgeous trilling song
295	Sandpiper, Western *Calidris mauri*	7/17/2005	Olympic NP, WA - working the shoreline, dodging waves
296	Sapsucker, Red-breasted *Sphyrapicus ruber*	7/19/2005	Olympic NP, WA - hammering small holes in a Douglas fir
297	Vireo, Hutton's *Vireo huttoni*	8/8/2005	North Cascades - whistling from the high branches of an oak
298	Swan, Tundra *Cygnus columbianus*	3/17/2006	Skagit Valley, WA - thousands of them scattetred across the flooded fields
299	Eider, King *Somateria spectabilis*	7/6/2006	Mohawk River, Schnectady, NY - Jay scores an accidental!!
300	Heron, Black-crowned Night *Nycticorax nycticorax*	7/10/2006	Central Park, NYC - Hearing is believing

Acknowledgements

Where should I begin? There are so many to thank for so much that it is hard to find the right starting point. Do I first credit the largest contributors of advice or those who told me not to quit when I so easily could have? All are important and without each I might have never found what it takes to put this book in your hands.

What if my critique group had hated those first 16 pages? But they didn't; they loved them. So, thanks to Cindy Arnold, Juanita Busot-Morgan and Teresa McIlhinney. They were there from page one until the end. And to Brett Rebischke-Smith who was there for most of the work. And to Glenn Jolley, who joined our group late, but read and critiqued the entire novel. A special thanks to David Hollies, no longer with us, but living on in his poem, "Lost and Found." His words helped me to see Alzheimer's disease in a more balanced way, and to find the heart and spirit of Harry, oft-confused but never really lost.

And what if I hadn't joined a workshop with other writers and agent/editor Andrea Hurst? It wasn't a hard decision to make. The eight-week class would cover the first 50 pages of our novels. Any aspiring author would jump at the chance to have an agent read so much. Thanks, then, to my class members, Sarah Martinez, Rowena Williamson, Gordon Labuhn, Doloris Ament, Mary Moeller, and Bill Grimm. And a huge thank you to Andrea, who loved *Taking Flight* well enough to invest so many hours in expert editing. And to her interns, Sarah Martinez and Vickie Motter, who helped Andrea edit after edit until we were all pleased with the result. Thanks also to my readers, Susannah Folcik, Calla Papademas, Julie Mackaman, Cindy Hurn and Katie Flanagan.

And a special thanks to Frances Wood, author of *Brushed by Feathers: A Year of Birdwatching in the West*, whose expert advice helped correct my amateur birding errors, and whose generous endorsement of *Taking Flight* is much appreciated.

Then came the search for a publisher, with its inherent ups and downs in this time of flux when indie publishing is on the rise. Enter Pink Fish Press and its captain, Renda Belle Dodge, without whom you wouldn't be holding this book now, and along with her, my editor, Brandon LaFave. They guided me so well through the detailed re-vision of *Taking Flight*, that even when I felt beleaguered by their suggestions, I understood the merit.

I would be remiss if I didn't also thank my mother, Jeanne Magnuson, who, at 89, suggested I better get something published soon if I expected her to be around to read it, and a long-time family friend, Sally Frederickson, who my character Grace is in many ways based upon.

Writing is an all-absorbing process, one that demands understanding from those whom you sometimes neglect. So, thank you, Sarah Mackaman, for all your love and support, and even your gentle editing advice. You have been there for me always.

Adrian Magnuson graduated from the University of Washington with a focus on creative writing. He is a full time writer, participating in three ongoing critique groups, and as an active member of the Whidbey Island Writer's Association and Pacific Northwest Writer's Association.

AdrianMagnuson.com